DEATH BENEATH THE CATALINAS

A Sonoran Desert Thriller Novel

BY

JACQUELINE COHEN

A Sonoran Desert Thriller Novel by Jacqueline Cohen

- *Death Beneath The Catalinas*

Photograph By: Jacqueline Cohen

DEATH BENEATH THE CATALINAS

A Sonoran Desert Thriller Novel

Book Cover Design by Ethan Kaplan

Photographs by Jacqueline Cohen

ISBN: 979-8-9928478-0-2

For my beloved husband, David,
And my darlings Andrew, Eryn, Jennie, Katie, Adira, Ronen
Thank you for going on life's journey with me.

CONTENTS

CONTENTS *(cont)*

Preface

Hollywood's depiction of America's deserts, regardless of where that desert exists, is usually bleak, barren, and full of unsuspecting dangers. Of hot, dry winds and tumbleweeds blowing across gritty terrains as far as the eye can see; and, needle-sharp thorny bushes and cacti, riverbeds and waterholes turns to dust under the blazing sun. Where poisonous snakes and scorpions, crafty roadrunners, circling vultures, scurrying lizards and javelinas hunt for food and water with shy bobcats and brazen hawks, owls, coyotes, and mountain lions. Each creature doing its best to escape the day's deadly heat in the shade of sparse vegetation, inside crevasses, or the underside of rocks. Where conserving energy is a must, and waiting until the sun gives way to cooler nighttime temperatures to venture out could mean the difference between life or death.

The imagery makes for great cinematic impact. Is it an accurate depiction of the Sonoran Desert? Well yes, and no. The Sonoran Desert is this, and so much more.

Covering approximately 100,000 square miles (260,000 sq. km.), the Sonoran Desert is mostly found in Baja California and the state of Sonora Mexico. Approximately a third of the desert exists within the United States' southern third of Arizona and a small area in southeastern California that borders Arizona. A subtropical desert, the Sonoran is the most complex and lush of the four deserts in North America. With its bi-seasonal rainfall during the winter months and frequent, violent thunderstorms from July through August, it means plants do not have to wait long between drinks. Because of this, it also means the Sonoran Desert is rich in wildlife and habitats.

And unlike Hollywood's inaccurate representations, the Sonoran Desert is the only place on earth where the majestic giant Saguaro cactus grows naturally; mostly in southern Arizona and western Sonora, Mexico from sea level to about 4000 feet in elevation. Protected in the U.S., Saguaros, a symbol of our American West, provide food and shelter for many desert species. It also plays an important role in the culture of the area's Tohono O'odham people.

This is where I have lived most of my life.

It is a place I learned early to both love its phenomenal treasures and respect its true dangers. A place where daytime summer temperatures can reach 118 degrees Fahrenheit (48 degrees Celsius), and where winter nights can drastically drop below freezing.

Where outdoor tasks are performed in the morning under a wide-brimmed hat and staying hydrated is a must; as is keeping small pets on leash, walking in the open, staying on trails, and checking around and under trash cans. Remembering, rattlesnakes do not always rattle before striking.

Where you do not place an ungloved hand where you cannot see what is around or underneath, or lean against a doorframe without first glancing to see if a scorpion is present. And, where you never enter a flooded wash or street, but go around the long way. (Hence the Arizona stupid motorist law.)

In return, the Sonoran Desert will bless you with spectacular skies, vast untouched landscapes, unparallel flora and fauna, and yes diverse, and sometimes dangerous, wildlife; deservedly living free from human harm.

Chapter 1
Tashia

The old sighthound sprang forward fixed on her target. Her long limbs catapulting her strong streamline body faster, still faster, into the deep, dark vastness of the immense backyard.

Moments earlier she had just barely spied the desert cottontail's movements as she drowsily waited by the sliding glass doors inside her home. Yet, that slight movement was all it took.

Howling inconsolably.

Foam spewing from her jowls.

The hound's impatient paws repeatedly pounded the transparent barrier causing the tempered clear glass to uncharacteristically vibrate against its metal tracks. Still, the door held fast. Hindering the excited dog from pouncing on the small creature meekly nibbling sweet blades of winter rye grass under the Tucson dark sky. Its false sense of security making it oblivious to the deadly threat nearby.

The door latch clicked.

The cottontail froze.

Sliding the glass panel open mere inches before opening it all the way, the old woman shouted at the top of her lungs; giving the rabbit fair warning.

"Run bunny. Run!"

Shattering the winter night's crystalized air.

Eyes wide. Ears pricked.

The rabbit's survival instincts kicked in.

At the same time the borzoi bolted through the open doorway with the relentless power, speed, and intent for which she was bred – to give chase. Steadfast, her old legs mimicked her prey's evasive maneuvers. Gracefully pivoting right, then left, in a spirited pursuit reminiscent of her youth.

The rabbit, making the most of its slight head start.

Darting towards the rosemary hedge at the farthest edge of the yard, the cottontail barely eluded its single-minded pursuer; lunging into the dense thicket.

Confounded by the rabbit's sudden disappearance, the borzoi methodically circled the area. Nose to the ground, her prey's alluring scent enticing her to extend her search beyond the aromatic shrubbery.

"Tashia. Come!" commanded the old woman in a loud, firm voice.

No response.

Straining to see into the darkness, 64-year-old Esther Chana Liebowitz Hausman could no longer see her old sighthound's silhouette from the doorway of her cozy, adobe-styled home.

"Really," she uttered.

Said more as a resigned declaration. Then, glancing at the clock on her stove the very next words out of her mouth would have made a sailor blush.

Three a.m.

The last thing she wanted to do was traverse her enormous backyard to retrieve her uncooperative furry companion.

"Well. That didn't go as planned," she huffed.

Chiding herself. Questioning her sanity for opening the door in the first place.

"What was I thinking?"

It was not the first time she had asked herself this question when it came to the elusive Tashia.

The first time was shortly after her beloved old collie, Jake, had died.

Resolved not to compound her immense heartache with feelings of guilt and betrayal by replacing Jake with another enthusiastic "what-can-I-do-for-you," herding dog. Esther had giddily delved into the unknown with renewed excitement.

That was when Tashia entered her life.

Finding out very soon after her new, gangly black and white borzoi's "what's-in-it-for-Me" sensitive nature and strong-willed mindset required a vast new treasure trove of training skills and activities.

Quickly Esther learned not to mistake Tashia's refusal to comply for stupidity. If anything, the borzoi's high intelligence and independence proved she was often too smart for her own good. Proving too, molding the sighthound's behavior would, at best, be achieved with a lot of patience, consistency, and a good sense of humor.

And laugh she did.

For Tashia's high-prey drive inevitably took precedence over human directives almost any time a small creature came anywhere in proximity to the borzoi's keen sight. Lizards, rabbits, round-tailed ground squirrels, bees and flying insects of every shape and size were all fair game. Making the construction of the backyard six-foot high wrought iron fence an absolute must.

Over the countless hours and many the years spent together the woman and sighthound's bond had greatly deepened. These days Tashia rarely left her side.

Esther had been confident the cold night air would bother the old hound's aging, arthritic legs. Certain Tashia would give the rabbit a quick chase, pee, and then trot back to the house and her warm, plush dog bed.

Figuring too she could then return to the comfort of her own covers where she would blissfully swaddle herself among her many thick blankets, content to sleep until morning.

Evidently, she thought wrong.

With an exaggerated groan of resignation, Esther removed an oversized, well-padded man's jacket from a peg on the wall by the backdoor. Slipping it on over her flannel, violet-flowered nightgown that hung loosely on her five-foot, three-inch frame, the old woman grabbed the flashlight off the windowsill and braced herself for the desert's frigid night air.

Once outside, bitter winds from an unexpected late February cold front assaulted her eyes. Salty wet tears streaked down her cheeks, stinging her freezing flesh. While at the same time, moist nose hairs stiffened inside her nostrils, burning, biting the membrane lining.

"Tashia!" bellowed Esther.

"Easy... Stay calm," she cautioned herself. "No dog is going to come willingly to a crazed lunatic."

Suddenly, strong gusts of wind lashed mercilessly at her exposed raw flesh.

Teeth chattering.

Desperately yearning to be back in her own bed.

Esther quickened her pace to where she last saw the sighthound.

"Tashia, where are you?" she moaned loudly; both worried and irritated.

Moving further away from her home within the dark of night's haze the rosemary hedge was becoming more visible. So too, the tall wrought iron fence beyond the prolific aromatic evergreen which separated the backyard from the rest of her acreage.

"Tashia, you inside the yard?"

But the borzoi was nowhere in sight.

Relying only on the beam from her flashlight to slice through the night Esther pushed on; wielding the torch back and forth, back and forth. Searching the vast grounds; praying for a glimpse of white fur, black fur, any fur.

Miserable, chilled to the bone, she refused to give up.

Doggedly walking into the darkness until suddenly caught off-guard by several damp, slimy, indiscernible blades of grass coiled tightly around her exposed chapped ankles.

"Yew! What the hell is that?" she cried. Wildly swiping at the tickling annoyance prickling her legs.

"Esther... Get a grip," she demanded of herself.

Fighting her overactive imagination. Trying whole-heartedly to regain her composure, Esther said with a lack of conviction.

"Probably too cold for rattlers to be slithering this time of night... Right?"

She professed giving her best impression of a gutsy frontier woman.

However as poisonous snakes were one of Esther's greatest fears, it was not long before her fragile courage waned. All too aware these particular southwest vipers did not always rattle before they struck.

The breezes grew stronger.

Shivering, Esther's attention changed to the deep, throbbing pain within her ears as the bitter night air penetrated her sensitive eardrum canals. Turning her jacket collar up to help block the unforgiving winds nipping at her neck, the frigid gusts attacked her exposed arthritic fingers. Stabbing her agonizing joints with a knife-like precision until the pain became almost too debilitating for her to grasp the heavy, wide barrel flashlight.

Rubbing her hands briskly up and down her coat sleeves in an attempt to generate much-needed heat. Instead, all Esther could successfully kindle was a sharp, burning desire for the coat's owner, her late husband, Max.

Max and she had bought the place in the late 1990's, when bank foreclosures were high and real estate values had tanked. Every free moment, every dime saved went into planning and building this, their retirement utopia.

Then one day Max kissed her goodbye after breakfast, went to work, and never came home.

Flashing back to that heartbreaking day; the images of those cold gray and white congested hospital corridors. Standing there, watching the doctor's mouth move, hearing his gut-wrenching words, yet comprehending very little.

"Husband… Massive heart attack. We did all we could. So very sorry."

Afterward, resolved to make their dream home a reality, Esther worked relentlessly for the both of them. Ignoring numerous protests from badgering, well-meaning friends to sell the place and take life easier.

"They called me nuts… Remember Max? Ach… Maybe I am. Who else but a nut would chase after dog on a night like this?" speaking to him in spirit.

But it had been Tashia who had saved her. Tashia, her constant companion since Max's death. Once Shiva was over. Once family and friends resumed their own lives. It was Tashia who comforted her during those lonely days and nights when she cried for her husband's smile, yearned for his touch.

The gentle giant had consoled her in ways no human could, in ways only an animal lover understood. And, for as much as Esther had adored all her dogs and various pets over the years, it was this sweet, quirky, old borzoi that had

14

captured her heart eleven years ago and never let go; even at three o'clock in the morning.

"Stop being such a cry baby," she ordered.

Wiping her eyes with the back of her hand as she quickened her pace.

Snap!

"That didn't come from the rosemary… Did you get out?" she yelled.

Searching for signs of her dog beyond the fence.

Crack!

"Tashia?" shouting again; taking a step towards the sound.

Her foot suddenly catching an uneven patch of turf.

Stumbling uncontrollably, Esther began to fall; hurling the flashlight into the dark abyss as she faltered. With her arms flailing wildly, she unsuccessfully grasped at the air as if it held ropes on which she could grab and regain her balance.

Then, staggering forward, her right toe caught the edge of a divot. As her footing gave way, Esther's ankle twisted abnormally and buckled. Down she went, hard. Scraping her knee on the turf as she fell and jamming her hip into the solid ground with great force.

Stunned. Esther lay prone for several moments facedown atop the stiff sod, all too ready to give up.

"Shit!" she screamed, adding a sore throat to her injuries.

Ears ringing.

Pulse racing.

Esther rolled onto her back very slowly; then gently eased herself into a sitting position. Voicing colorful original obscenities, she examined the extent of the damage. Praying nothing was broken.

Although her scraped knees and chin stung badly, she opted instead to pay particular attention to her throbbing hip, which still seemed intact. Her right ankle, however, was another matter. Upon moving it, the unbearable pain told her she had surely suffered a severe sprain, possibly even a break.

Exasperated, on the verge of tears, Esther exhaled long visible puffs of the night's icy vapors. Trying to figure a way out of her present predicament she gazed upward.

Noticing for the first time the night's dazzling celestial bodies, stars, and nebulas populating the sky above her. Life in a dark zone beneath the Santa Catalina State Park Mountains did have it perks. One most notably was the high mountain range close by which blocked Tucson's light pollution from obstructing the awe-inspiring neighboring objects within the Milky Way.

Under different circumstances Esther would have enjoyed laying on her back contemplating the brilliant mysteries of the galaxy above her.

"Could've used a little more moonlight down here," she shouted to the heavens.

Then, spotting the flashlight she had flung somehow managed not to break and was shining skyward like a beacon. Esther gingerly stretched her sore body towards the light source so to retrieved it and continue her search.

"Tashia… 'Wanna cookie?" forcing the calm plea in her voice.

Finally overcome with complete frustration at once again seeing no response, Esther lost patience and let her temper fly.

"Oh come on Tashia!" she wailed angrily, pounding her fist on the ground.

To make matters worse, not far off in the distance frantic yips of several coyotes stalking their soon-to-be meal broke through the night. Their fever-pitched yelps and squeals growing menacingly louder by the moment.

Given her isolated desert home had been built as sanctuary for an assortment of domestic animals and wildlife alike. It made perfect sense that Tashia and she were not the only creatures awake and on the move at the ungodly hour.

Now a hungry pack was heading her way.

Time had run out.

Wincing, Esther pushed herself up onto her protesting knees. Slowly positioning her feet underneath her, she walked her hands up her legs until eventually she reached her pained thighs. Straightening up as best she could. Once standing, she tested her weakened ankle by cautiously leaning her weight onto the ball of her foot; finding although badly injured, the ankle held.

The coyotes' yelps grew ever louder, soon they would appear.

She needed to find her dog, now.

Limping badly, eager to return inside her home, Esther doggedly resumed her search. Her heightened adrenaline driving her to this, the farthest edge of her fenced-in yard and the overgrown shrubbery. The last place inside the massive yard where Tashia could hide. Praying Tashia was there. That she had not escaped the confines of the yard, escaped wrought iron barrier.

Snap!

"Tashia?" she called tentatively.

Not certain what caused the unexpected sound or from where it came, Esther strained to see within the darkened orchard. Not seeing anything move she gave up and continued her trek to the rosemary with renewed purpose. Once there, she pushed apart some sparse branches and peered through the opening to the other side of the hedge where she unexpectedly caught a glimpse of illusive white fur.

"Thank God," she shouted; then barked at her dog. "Enough Tashia. Come."

This time the sighthound immediately responded to her command.

Stretching her long, graceful neck above the bushes the borzoi's alert eyes connected with her human's. Tears of joy poured down Esther's frosty cheeks; thrilled to have at long-last found her beloved companion. Even more elated to find her unharmed.

It was then she took a good hard look at where the borzoi was standing. Estimating the distance between Tashia's head and where she had just spotted the dog's white fur was a good nine feet, Esther became completely baffled.

Nervously biting her lower lip, her insatiable curiosity getting the better of her, Esther slowly hobbled behind the rosemary hedge to where the flattened ground met the fencing.

Eyes wide.

Freezing where she stood.

Uncontrollable fear took hold of the older woman as a stranger's stark figure appeared before her next to the black wrought iron.

Trembling, Esther came to the sudden realization.

She had not been talking to Tashia.

Chapter 2

"Either he's dead or my watch has stopped."

~ Groucho Marx

It was nearly 6:30 a.m. when the Pinal County Medical Examiner arrived on the scene. Dawn was fully underway. By then a small kettle of Turkey Vultures interested in the activity below them were lazily hanging around. Floating on early morning warm rising air, the imposing birds circled endlessly under the Arizona soft powder blue and pastel pink sky as dazzling sunrays escaped from behind the Santa Catalina State Park Mountains. The glistening ribbons of gold randomly attaching to edges of billowy dingy-gray clouds transforming from dust balls into white cotton puffs.

Even the vultures with their impressive red heads and immense black and white wings, soaring on thermal lifts above, were breathtaking. The birds, however, took no notice of the splendor surrounding them. All they really cared about was the carrion hanging off the carcass below them.

As Esther Hausman's gaze lethargically shifted from the circling birds to the rotting dead body in her backyard, it struck her as being quite peculiar how daybreak could unveil such beauty and such horror all at the same time.

Earlier that morning, she had managed to slide the backdoor screen closed behind her while awkwardly juggling several distinct souvenir mugs and a large pot of hot coffee for grateful investigators to share. All the while, trying not to put too much weight on her extremely swollen, right ankle.

Tashia, now caught and incarcerated indoors, watched with intense interest as menacing strangers trespassed upon her domain. Investigators loudly ordered assignments to subordinates who busily photographed areas, gathered samples, and placed plastic numbers near various evidence items around the property.

Eventually, the sighthound's senses overloaded. A watchdog a borzoi is not. Soon, Tashia chose a more desirable activity. That of returning to the bedroom she shared with Esther and circling her plush, oversized burgundy dog bed several times before settling down into peaceful slumber.

Being deterred from their delectable meal, the vultures too grew tired. Eventually giving up and moving on in search of a more, accessible, restaurant.

Had it been only a few hours since Tashia chased that silly rabbit?

"Guttenyu!" she said under her breath with a shiver.

For as much as Esther wanted to forget last night's ghastly discovery, she could not stop her mind from revisiting the unsettling events. The pack of coyotes' threatening yelps. Searching for Taisha in utter darkness. The terror she felt for both the borzoi and for herself as the howls grew louder, closer.

A single coyote, usually, was not a threat to a large animal. And, generally they avoided the more dangerous, human, species. However a hungry pack could prove deadly, especially for the old hound.

Then, searching aimlessly in the dark. Desperate to find her companion as quickly as possible and return to the safety of their home.

That was until she had found, him.

Fixated.

Unable to move.

Finding herself utterly incapable of holding the flashlight steady. Its jerky beams dancing like fireflies over the severely mutilated body.

The coyotes' cries heard again; only this time softer, becoming more distant. With the threat no longer immediate, curiosity won out. Warily she had limped closer. Trying to make sense of her unexpected guest.

What had first caught her attention was how the man's torso bizarrely bent at the waist. Much like a dancer stretched forward onto a ballet barre, one leg was lifted high above his head thrust through a railing opening. His other leg clumsily crumpled beneath him like a string-less marionette in a heap.

"How the hell did you end up in such a mess?" she had asked the dead man, not really expecting a response.

Suspecting whoever this was, or rather had been, had obviously tried and failed to scale the six-foot wrought iron fence; and, had gotten his foot wedged between the rungs for his efforts. Remembering too, her own shock at finding the corpse entangled there; especially in the dead of the night.

"You know… If you wanted in here so badly you could've just used the gate."

She exclaimed, using sarcasm to help suppress her fears and regain some semblance of self-control. At the same time checking the gates of the yard's wrought iron fencing which provided easy passage from the backyard to other areas within her property. Feeling an odd sense of comfort in visually validating each metal gate handle was latched closed.

Then, turning back to the corpse, Esther pointed out the obvious.

"What a putz… Could've saved yourself a lot of trouble if only you'd waited a couple of hours 'til sunup."

Mocking the dead man's unfortunate circumstance. Meanwhile rubbing the recently healed blister she had received after absent-mindedly grabbing a scorching metal handle without wearing work gloves, she added.

"Well, maybe that's a good thing."

Still trying to make sense of the corpse's appearance.

"What if your death was no accident? What if… something, someone, chased you here… killed you… and, is still hanging around… Hiding. Watching."

The very idea chilling her to the bone.

Then came the noises from inside the orchard followed by an unusually loud.

Snap!

Whipping her head towards the grove, vivid possibilities came to mind; each more menacing than the last. Curtly, she reprimanded her uninvited guest.

"Now what's all this farkakteh…? It's bad enough you're… well, you know."

The orchard disturbances unnerving Esther more than she cared to admit, even now hours later. Then, torn between her fears and insatiable curiosity, she had carefully turned her aching body to the trees. The intense pain in her weakened right ankle, a souvenir from her earlier fall, significantly impairing her movement.

Up until that moment Esther had loved every branch, every bud, every leaf of her lush orchard. It had taken years of fastidious planting and nurturing to coax each fertile sapling to produce the delicious fruit she now ate and sold. The trees shaded and cooled her home during Tucson's hot summers; and, except for the evergreens, shed autumn leaves to allow the desert sun to warm and light her home in the winter.

Yet, last night her orchard had felt threatening. As if the trees were harboring something deadly. Something which did not need a gate handle to enter the yard to get to… her.

Recalling too, mustering all the bravery her small frame could gather while hollering.

"Who's out there?"

Demanding with unabashed conviction; yet met with dead silence.

"You better not come closer. My dog will attack on command," she warned.

"My dog will attack… Are you nuts?" she had said to herself. "You can't even get her to come for a damn cookie. If there's an axe murderer out there… he's gonna die from laughter."

Her threat having sounded ridiculous to her, even now hours later.

Letting out a loud snort, Esther startled a technician approaching the patio. The timid man, already apprehensive, had not wanted to disturb the older woman who at first seemed to be dozing on her lounger.

"Mrs. Hausman… Could I possibly?" he asked tentatively, nodding to the coffee pot and mugs on the patio table.

Welcoming the distraction from her obsessing Esther sweetly announced.

"Everyone… Please. Help yourself," she offered graciously pointing to the fresh pot of coffee.

Then later, when again left to her solitude, her thoughts returned to the unsettling orchard. So incredibly dark was it, she had stood staring into the grove for what seemed forever until feeling immensely foolish.

"Stop yelling at the trees."

She remembered scolding herself before shifting her neuroses to the barn.

"The horses. They're so quiet," she had noticed with concern. Then added, "Of course they're quiet… They're sleeping, idiot. Like you should be."

Crack!

"There!" she exclaimed; then held her breath.

Her injured ankle painfully protesting her quick turn towards the noise.

Still, the motion had not been her imagination; yet she was clueless as to what caused it.

"Kyle… Kyle, wake up. I need you!" She had cried.

In reality her words escaping her lips as little more than whispers.

Her anxious pleas unheard by Kyle Lucas, Esther's part-time ranch hand full-time University of Arizona (UA) veterinarian student, who lived in her barn's studio apartment. However, that night he had stayed on campus.

"Another bad decision," she had joked nervously.

Recalling it was she who had insisted Kyle stay there and finish a paper.

Standing frozen, afraid to confront the unknown threat before her, afraid to turn her back and be at its mercy; she remembered whispering.

"Tashia."

Staunchly refusing to leave Tashia in the slightest risk of danger. Waiting till no further movement was seen; no further sound was heard.

No snaps.

No cracks.

By then the night's cold blustery winds had diminished into pre-dawn gentle breezes; bringing with it a light scent of citrus off premature spring blossoms. Even now she regretted her momentarily lapse of deeply inhaling the sweet therapeutic aroma tickling her cold nose. The smell causing her to sneeze and her sinuses to clog.

As the sun began peeking above the Catalinas, some of her pluck returned.

"Maybe I saw a deer… An owl. Rat. Okay… too big for a rat," she admitted.

Unwisely returning her attention to the corpse.

"Still here?" she asked the deceased flippantly; shivering with disgust.

The dawn's light revealing a more grotesque image entangled in the fence. Here, a gaping bloodied mouth; its lips badly torn. There, the right cheek missing. Gone too, the right ear lobe, portions of wispy hair and balding scalp. Where once a right eye existed, now a deep bloody gouge.

Even now, hours later, the image was crystal clear in her mind. Feeling sickened Esther took a hard gulp of coffee to keep the sour bile in her throat from rising any further. Forcing her memory to move on to less gruesome areas of the mutilated carcass. His ripped dusty khakis. The bloodstained white shirt she had seen through a sparse area among the rosemary's needle-like leaves. Mistaking the man's shirt for Tashia's beautiful silky white coat.

"Not so white now," she had recalled saying dryly to the dead man.

No longer feeling like joking; yet unable to look away from the ghastly sight.

Maybe it was because the carcass no longer looked human, or real; but rather like a badly created science fiction character.

Maybe it was the way his raised right leg was thrust through a railing opening. Where his shoe should have been, the entire foot was gone; ripped off clean.

Remembering quickly diverting her eyes to avoid another gut-retching episode. That her gaze, unfortunately, had landed on the man's wrist; his missing right hand. The arm, similarly thrust through a different opening, angled toward the missing foot. Its tattered shirtsleeve flapping in the wind, exposing shredded flesh and bone clean-up to the shoulder socket.

"Where the hell are all your missing parts?" she had asked, looking around.

It was then Esther remembered exactly what had upset her most about last night's grisly scene. Strangely enough it was not the missing hand, or foot, or bloody flesh. Rather it had been the partial tattoo on the inside bicep of his missing right arm.

Fragmented and dirty; red, white and blue inked flesh bordered partially by a thin, black line hung loosely in tattered strips of flesh. Like a jigsaw puzzle with pieces missing, Esther had been unable to imagine what the original tattoo might have been. All she could make out were two stylized red letters, KA, and a white number one centered below them.

"Enough… enough," she had protested.

Annoyed with herself for gawking at the body as long as she had, Esther turned her back on the corpse and limped to her house; Tashia sleepily trotting behind her. Then, once the hound had been placed inside and the horses checked, Esther called 911 from the barn.

"You don't mind waiting, do you?" she had asked the lifeless body. "After all… It's not like you're going anywhere."

Adding simply.

"Besides."

Frowning as she stared at the half-eaten arm; having never liked tattoos.

Suddenly a loud crash yanked Esther from her memories to the here and now.

With her heart wildly pounding, she searched for the clatter's source. Then, realizing the cause had been metal tools falling off a collapsible table, Esther decided it was high time she ended her unsettling trip down memory lane.

Realizing too, while she was reliving the horrors of last night the police investigation had moved into high gear. Wondering if anyone had come across those missing body parts; sincerely hoping it would not be her who stumbled upon them later.

Out of the corner of her eye Esther noticed the medical examiner's staff preparing the body for removal. As she watched their efforts with great interest, off in the distance she heard the chilling squeals and yips of coyotes celebrating a successful early morning hunt.

If she had to guess, it was that pack that had visited her backyard and snacked on her trespasser hours before she and Tashia went outside.

That rabbit had been lucky twice last night.

***

The police investigation dragged into late afternoon, their search expanding to the remainder of Esther Hausman's 68 acres and well beyond. Resigned she could do nothing about the investigators' intrusion, Esther gingerly lowered her bruised, aching body onto an over-stuffed, rust-colored lounge chair. Then, after taking a deep breath, she relaxed; enjoying the serenity of her backyard patio. A cool breeze off the mountains swirled around her; a sign the prior night's frigid 39 degrees temperature would warm to the new day's more pleasant 78 degrees.

"And that's why we live in Arizona," she proclaimed proudly.

Propping her enormously swollen foot onto the ample seat cushion of the nearest patio chair. Esther gently enveloped her several shades of purple, magenta, and ochre sprained ankle with as many ice packs and frozen peas packages she could find in her freezer. Its soothing benefits immediately penetrating the puffy discolored tissue by somewhat dulling its throbbing.

Throwing a lightly woven colorful Mexican blanket over her lap and legs. Esther contently settled back in her lounger drinking a fresh cup of coffee as she listened to her kitchen radio broadcasting her favorite shows through the sliding screen door.

As the investigators performed their duties, Esther became especially amused watching the Pima County Medical Examiner, Dr. Warren Lee Singh, whom she met earlier, examine the corpse and enter data into his electronic note pad.

Not particularly tall, Dr. Singh appeared as many men his age, a bit pudgy around the edges. His kind expression seeming a bit exaggerated by a receding hairline which looked to be entering into its final stages.

As Esther watched Dr. Singh from her lounger, each time the good doctor would bend over the deceased behind the dense rosemary the hedge seemed to gobble him up. Then as he straightened, it looked like the bushes were spitting him out in a comical up and down bobbing motion.

This particular activity had kept Esther happily entertained for nearly forty minutes. When it finally lost appeal, she searched for something different to distract her. Finding it all along in her unobstructed, memorizing view of the Santa Catalina Mountain range.

Spectacular on any day, today the landscape's deep troughs were cloaked with wide patches of clinging dark shadows caused by swollen low-hanging clouds. Yet, the real eye-candy was the Catalina's crown jewel, Mount Lemmon's breathtaking 9,157 feet zenith covered in white, glistening snow.

Squinting, Esther could barely tell the sparkling snowflakes from the frequent flaring off the UA's Steward Observatory facilities atop the summit. Its Catalina Sky Survey (CSS) telescopes and the Schmidt telescope on Mount Bigelow a main reason why her property and the entire district were designated a dark zone.

As she lowered her vision to the foothills, Esther smiled at the docile cattle and deer grazing together on the newly sprouted spring grasslands. The cows, owned by her dear neighbor, Joseph Tadai, a welcome sight of normalcy. The green fields a happy indication that soon thousands of brilliant wildflowers would be blooming; bright orange California poppies, deep violet lupines, gigantic cacti and succulents blossoms. The flowers enticing hordes of hummingbirds, bees, butterflies, and moths to savor their sweet nectar.

Likewise not looking forward to the day they would disappear due to the brutal summer heat. When wildlife rarely moved during daylight and waterholes and mountain runoffs became sandy gorges. When lush vegetation turned into combustible dry tinder; perfect fuel for the wildfires caused by lightning strikes, careless campers, and smokers tossing smoldering butts. The thousands of acres of scorched earth taking decades to recover.

Eventually though, the rains would return and begin the cycle once more. Debunking the depiction in western movies that the Sonoran Desert is a lackluster, sterile wasteland. When in actuality, the Desert is quite alive; full of fascinating diverse creatures, flora, and if not careful, real hidden dangers.

Then, compulsively returning her gaze to the corpse, Esther was glad to see the dead man finally being placed inside the heavy plastic, human remains pouch (HRP). She was even happier when the body bag zipped closed and the cadaver finally disappeared.

"Okay, so nothing's perfect," she exclaimed dryly; turning her gaze to the barn.

About a half hour earlier Kyle Lucas had returned home from campus looking both dog-tired and perplexed. His curly hair badly in need of combing. His rumpled clothing the same he had worn yesterday. His eyes half-closed, he leaned his slim frame against his old pale-red Honda Civic parked alongside the paddock.

Speaking with a uniform officer who was taking notes, Kyle's wandering gaze clearly exhibited his earnest desire to sit or lay down.

"Must've been a late night for him too," noted Esther compassionately.

Her sympathetic mood suddenly changing to self-pity.

"Tough... Today he can pull double-duty... And, fix that damn hole in the grass I fell in. God forbid Tashia breaks a leg." she sulked.

Snuggling deep into the lounger's plush pillows; closing her eyes as she huffed.

"Me, I'm taking the day off."

***

Because Esther Hausman's property overlapped both Pima and Pinal counties, chaos had understandably resulted after she placed the 911 emergency call. Before long, representatives from both provinces converged on her property, where heated arguments ensued about who had jurisdiction.

In due course Tucson Violent Crimes Homicide Detective, Michael Flores, arrived on the scene. Emerging confidently from a spotless black, unmarked police SUV, Detective Flores assertively sauntered into the middle of the passionate discussions and took charge.

"Kid's got balls," chuckled Esther.

Watching the handsome detective establish himself as lead investigator. Closely studying the young man's demeanor, Esther would have bet her social security check he was late twenties to mid-thirties. The age when ambitious over-achievers worked their butts off to advance their careers and make a name for themselves.

Clean-shaven, not a black hair out of place, the policeman's athletic square-shoulders hugged his crisp, tailor-made midnight blue suit. From head to toe, Homicide Detective Michael Flores shone like a newly minted silver dollar.

"You gonna that good when it's 100-degrees?" she thought, suppressing a giggle. Then wondering. "What about brains? Got any to go with that handsome head of yours?"

Watching the detective search the grounds and delegate assignments. Particularly curious in the way he regarded the deceased. Paying close attention if he treated the dead man as refuse, or showed some respect.

She had been thoroughly impressed with the young man, at first. That was until she overheard him publicly dress down a field worker over some trivial issue like an egotistical bully. Whatever respect she had for him previously completely vanished; and in its place, undeniable growing contempt.

"Need to work on your people skills, asshole," she huffed.

Deciding her time from then on would be better spent focused elsewhere.

Unfortunately for Esther, the same could not be said for Michael Flores.

Soon after the detective established himself as lead in the investigation, Esther Hausman had been pointed out to him as the only possible witness.

Gazing over his shoulder at the old gal dressed neatly in a light blue work shirt and stone-washed jeans, something about her set his teeth on edge.

And then it hit him.

His only witness in what he hoped would be a highly publicized, career-advancing case, was a frail old woman with the dulled look of someone experiencing the onset of dementia. Appearing neither traumatized, nor scared after witnessing a violent death right outside her home; she was smiling as if she was watching her favorite show on television and entertaining guests.

"All she needs is buttered popcorn," he thought irritated as hell.

Observing his only lead lounging on her comfy sofa with her feet casually propped up on a matching, equally-plush patio chair; grinning like the Queen of Sheba.

"All tucked in nice and cozy under a blanket you probably bought on your last seniors' bus tour to México," he scoffed under his breath.

Certain talking to the old woman was about to be a colossal waste of time, Flores tended to other responsibilities until he could no longer put off the inevitable.

Sipping a fresh brew from her favorite mug, Esther's tranquility faded away as she watched the detective bullishly approached her.

Arrogantly flashing his badge without introductions or niceties, Detective Michael Flores demanded immediate answers to his questions.

"Okay Mrs. Hausman… What'd you see?" he commanded curtly.

"Blowhard," muttered Esther under her breath softly, smiling at him sweetly.

"What was that?" he asked, not sure he heard her correctly.

Deciding one of them should act like an adult, Esther forced herself to be civil.

She was about to speak when from her kitchen radio the recognizable voices of her favorite sports talk show hosts, Ron Wolfley and Luke Lapinski, distracted her. Both shouting, neither paying attention to the other; Esther was having a great time listening to them heatedly debate the Arizona Cactus League spring training prospects for this season's 25-man roster for her favorite baseball team, the Arizona Diamondbacks.

"Cold and nasty it may be for most the country," she thought giddily. "February in the Desert means the boys of summer are back to play ball."

"Mrs. Hausman… Mrs. Hausman!" yelled Detective Flores.

Each time a little louder than the previous; as if Esther were hearing impaired as well as mentally challenged. The detective's deep mahogany eyes widening with frustration with his failure to gain the old woman's attention; switching to a more intimidating tactic.

"You know Mrs. Hausman… If you can't focus here, we can always continue our conversation at the station. Where… it might be easier for you to concentrate," Flores threatened condescendingly.

"Look kid… Don't get tough with me," retorted Esther.

Returning his glare, not bothering to hide her distain.

He was about to put his threat into action when Dr. Singh trudged passed the two of them in pensive thought. The interruption was enough to, momentarily, diffuse the escalating confrontation.

"Well, Doc?" demanded Flores, just as rudely to the respected pathologist.

"Look… Michael," began Dr. Singh with his ever-calm, professional decorum.

"With so much damage to the body… it's anybody's guess as to what killed this poor man. You're just going to have to wait until I'm finished with my autopsy," declared the doctor with indisputable finality.

Before Michael Flores could say anything further, Dr. Singh slowly shook his head no. Waving off the detective as he continued walking toward the ambulance parked in Esther Hausman's driveway.

Clearly talking to himself, the preoccupied doctor climbed into the passenger seat and started reviewing his notes. Patiently waiting for his associates to remove the body and ready it in the medical vehicle for transport.

Between Dr. Singh's rebuff and the old woman's lack of cooperation, Michael Flores' stamina began to wane.

"Mrs. Hausman. Please! Think I could get a little cooperation?" he pleaded.

The veins in his neck beginning to bulge.

"Listen schmuck… I care more about what my chickens think. And that's before they hatch," said the defiant voice in Esther's head.

Then, something changed.

The witty voice of Ron Wolfley had once again reached her ears quelling her anger. She no longer needed, no longer wanted, to fight.

Several Cactus League Spring Training games were just moments away from opening pitch. And in just a few minutes, a special pre-game show was about to begin from the Salt River Fields at Talking Stick on the Salt River Pima-Maricopa Indian Community near Scottsdale. The first Major League Baseball Spring Training facility built on Indian land in the nation; and home to both the Arizona Diamondbacks and the Colorado Rockies baseball teams. Now she had reason to give Detective Pompous-ass her full cooperation. Not because she felt sorry for him; but, because the game was about to start.

It was then a few impatient squeals resonated from horses inside the barn.

It had been early morning and still dark when Esther placed Tashia inside the house and limped to the barn to check the horses. At that time she had pounded on Kyle Lucas' door inside the barn, hoping he had returned home from campus while she was otherwise occupied.

Clearly he had not.

Most times that would have been fine. She and Max had planned it that way from the conception of their dream.

Each year they would obtain the free services of a veterinarian student focusing on large animals to help run the place; and in exchange, the student was given, gratis, a stylishly furnished studio apartment inside the barn complete with up-to-date smart home amenities, including Wi-Fi. Furthermore, students were given whatever time they needed for classes, studies, and just as important, a social life.

If there was a drawback, it was only one.

"So, it's a barn. So… it gets a little aromatic from time to time. It's still a win-win." Max would say with an endearing chuckle and twinkle in his eyes.

It was last spring when Esther hired Kyle Lucas. A likeable enough kid originally from Anderson, Indiana. Pleasant. Quiet. Very knowledgeable about horses; however, she had felt he was not especially comfortable around them. Thought him better suited for smaller creatures, like perhaps a Pekingese.

But Tashia had quickly warmed to him, so she gave him a try.

As time went on, she was glad he had proven her wrong.

Another burst of protesting neighs and whinnies emanated from the barn. Although Esther had fed and watered the horses before returning to the house, the police had distracted her from letting her charges to pasture; interfering with their daily routine.

"It's like I told your guy," Esther said annoyed; pointing to the policeman standing beside Kyle Lucas.

Kyle having finally returned home only within the last hour.

The officer being Alvin Pawlak, a valued member of Michael Flores' Homicide department. A seasoned lawman whose slightly ample belly hung over his trousers and jiggled a bit as he wrote Kyle's statement.

"I was sleeping… I didn't hear a thing… I didn't see a thing… Tashia woke me to go outside. I let her out… Then, I had to chase her down to get her back inside," she explained succinctly.

Still glaring at Kyle and the officer standing beside the paddock as she again told of how she discovered the corpse. Happily noticing Kyle, too, looking concern for his protesting four-legged roommates.

A loud bang came from a hoof slamming into a stall door startling the investigating team. Some froze where they stood, others took a more duck and cover approach. Each stopping work to see if they, themselves, were in danger.

Kyle's eyes locked onto Esther's; seeing she had reached her breaking point. He knew if he did not do something soon, she would probably get arrested.

"Officer Pawlak. How about I give you a tour while I let the horses out?" Kyle offered amiably.

Not waiting for a reply, the young vet student started walking toward the barn. Doing his best to cajole the police officer who accompanied him.

"Thirsty? I just happen to have a cold…" continued Kyle.

Pawlak, nodding cheerfully to Kyle's offer. The young man's words becoming inaudible as the barn door closed behind them.

"Not bad, kid," said Esther aloud with renewed admiration.

"And… what time was that?" asked Detective Flores, digging for more useful information from the older woman.

"Around 3:00 a.m.…. Geez, don't you guys talk to each other? That's when I found… him," she snapped.

Nodding towards the corpse inside the body bag being wheeled passed them on the gurney to the ambulance.

"That's all I know," she exclaimed losing her cool. "I didn't see anything!"

Then, taking a moment to regain her composure, Esther watched the techs wheel the body pass them on the gurney and asked pensively.

"Don't you think it's strange?" she started to ask quietly.

As if she changing the subject to something completely unrelated.

"What… You don't think finding a dead guy in your backyard is strange?" retorted Flores rudely.

Thinking the older woman might have lost her grip on reality.

"Listen kid… Do you have to be such a schmuck?" pointing out to Flores they had both had a very long day.

It was the first time they agreed on anything.

Apologetically Michael Flores asked Esther to continue her thought.

"I mean, the guy… Outside of… you know… being chewed up and all. So many things just don't add up."

Turning her head towards the rosemary hedge where she found the body.

"Really Mrs. Hausman? Like what?" prompted Flores smirking, humoring her.

Ignoring Flores' impertinence, Esther pointed out certain observations.

"Like why here? Robbery? Why enter from the backyard? There's no roads behind our property. The back pastures merge with open range and my closest neighbor, Joseph Tadai's land. Their house is way the hell over there. Did the guy come down Catalina's backside… That's miles away. Too far to walk. Driving it can break an axle, even in daytime. Did 'ya find an abandoned car on the old road in front of my house? My driveway gate was locked. Did he climb over it, or the brick wall? So, Mr. Detective… Where the hell did this guy come from?"

Michael Flores took a good hard look at Esther Hausman as if he was seeing her for the first time. Realizing he misjudged the older woman; that perhaps she was not the addled senior citizen he first believed. Because if she was, what did that say about him? He had been asking himself the same questions all day.

Then Esther said.

"My gut tells me this guy wasn't here to hurt me, or rob me… What little clothes he wore were clearly high-end. So, he didn't need money… Maybe he was stranded looking for help and his death was an accident… Maybe someone was after him… Killed him," she speculated.

Realizing she was finally being taken seriously, Esther added with conviction.

"And, if he was murdered… Should I expect another visit from his killer?" she asked solemnly.

Before Flores could reply the sound of a car speeding past the open front gate and up the driveway caught everybody's attention. So too, the racket caused by thousands of stones being hurled in all directions as a car sped pass the bordering rows of majestic, yellow-budding Blue Palo Verde trees.

Soon, a faded army-green vintage Jeep came to a screeching halt behind the ambulance. As dust rose around both vehicles, the dented driver's door burst open with tremendous force.

That was when Matilda Rose Kaplan emerged from the Wrangler.

Fists clenched, determined to enter the Hausman backyard, Matilda stormed up to the officer stationed at the police barricade.

The officer, with a look of alarm on his face, held his palms high in a defensive posture in an effort to stop the young woman from going any further.

"Hold on there, missy. This is an active…" he began saying.

"Listen bud. That's my aunt," she interrupted; gritting her teeth.

Her firm voice spoken with uncharacteristic restraint as she pointed to Esther.

Standing his ground, the policeman remained steadfast.

"Either you let me pass, or you'll have a hell of a lot more to deal with than some dead guy," promised Mattie with a conviction.

"It's okay, kid," said Esther waving off the officer. "She's my niece."

Then turning to Flores she added with a broad smile, "Such a sweet girl."

Michael Flores gave Esther a look of trepidation before nodding to his colleague to let the young woman pass. Surmising, and rightly so, that Esther's sweet niece had no intention on waiting for his permission.

"Wise choice detective," Esther said, confirming his decision.

As the woman advanced, Esther's loving eyes twinkled as she opened her arms for a welcomed embrace.

Noting with mild amusement the young woman's single-minded resolve as she approached. Flores allowed himself a brief moment to appreciate her undeniable, feminine silhouette hidden underneath baggy jeans and an oversized work shirt.

Without so much as a glance in his direction, Esther's niece pushed pass the detective and pulled a chair next to the lounger; giving her aunt a hug and her full attention. Her graceful neck tilted downward ever so slightly causing the thick auburn bangs of her pixie haircut to part slightly; revealing a pair of hypnotic stormy-gray eyes that flashed with brilliant golden flecks. The likes of which Detective Michael Flores had never seen.

With a worried look on her angelic face, Esther's beautiful niece parted her full rosy lips and ardently demanded.

"Tante… What the f…?"

"Mattie darling…. How 'bout some nice hot coffee?"

Chapter 3

"There is a remedy for everything; it is called death."

~ Portuguese Proverb

He sat motionless.

His strong hands, bruised and bloodied, clenched the RAM® steering wheel so tightly his knuckles were now ashen-white. Keeping his icy pale-blue eyes riveted upon the small angled rearview mirror, he searched relentlessly for early-rising busybodies who might have taken notice of him.

He sat there, motionless.

All the while the noisy garage door slid slowly downward, closing behind him. Each irritating squeak, each grinding gear clank further eroding his wounded pride and self-control.

He sat there.

Finally, the thick 24-gauge steel door butted tightly against the concrete slab with a resigned groan.

He sat quietly, no more.

"Damn… Damn!" he screamed; his pent-up fury now safe to unleash.

Pounding a bruised fist against the Rebel steering wheel, he let out a primal scream that began deep within his gut and escaped through his parted chapped lips in one, long, agonizing wail. The repugnant rhapsody concealed from the outside world, courtesy of his pickup truck's well-insulated cab.

"Moron!" he roared with contempt regarding the entire fiasco.

That his near-perfect scheme might have had a flaw which caused a downward spiral of incriminating events after the fact was, unthinkable. What had caused it, or who was responsible was irrelevant. It happened.

Now it was up to him to clean up the mess.

"Thinnnkkk!" he yelled in a long, drawn-out wail.

Unable to clear his clouded mind as to what to do next.

Highly regarded for his painstakingly devised plans and meticulous methods for executing operations that sometimes bordered on obsessive-compulsive. A trait which, although irritated others, had never failed him. This time he had to take the chance and deviate from his normal practices.

He should have known better. Seeing now he had overreacted to the morning's incident with a kneejerk solution.

Now, there would be consequences.

"This is all your fault Pac Man," he spat.

Accusing the invisible recipient of his ire for his current predicament. The recipient? A recently disfigured corpse he had left against a black wrought-iron fence only a few hours earlier at a rural home in Tucson, Arizona.

Continuing to hurl allegations at the empty passenger seat beside him, his tirade escalated.

"I told you what would happen if you broke the rules... You thought they wouldn't apply to you. Why? Because we have history? Well buddy... You thought wrong," he exploded.

Bellowing the many infractions his imaginary adversary had committed against him which had necessitated the man's permanent termination.

"It's bad enough you broke rule number two. No public fraternization… You caused a public scene. Drew attention to us… Put the entire business in jeopardy… But then… you broke rule number one… You quit," he seethed.

"What'd 'ya think would happen Pac Man?" threatening his imaginary sidekick.

"Aaawwwww!" he screamed with clenched teeth.

His eyes glaring like a cornered animal. He squeezed the steering wheel with a vise-like grip; pretending he was wringing his former associate's neck. Strangling the life out of him again and again.

Looking back, he had been aware of the man's discontent for some time. He thought he had appeased him, had him under control. That was until yesterday morning when the irate man confronted him in the crowded True Brew coffee shop close to his work.

Unlike others in the room he had not noticed the man's arrival, at first.

But then, there really never had been anything truly eye-catching about his associate. Even though the man had been regarded as brilliant in his field by all who knew him. His reclusive demeanor, ordinary features, and unpretentious attire often resulted in him disappearing into the background, even at intimate gatherings. An attribute which had proven most useful to both, since their shared endeavors were not as legit as their professed professions.

Be that as it may, yesterday had proved to be anything but clandestine.

Clearly peeved. The pale-skinned middle-aged man, whose most distinctive physical features were his partially balding head and thick-rimmed, black glasses, brazenly marched into the coffee shop. Not bothering to stop its door from slamming shut behind him.

The forceful bang startling several patrons savoring their last moments of freedom and quiet before beginning their hectic day. Many of whom scowled at the man creating all the fuss. Others purposely turning a blind eye as he stomped across the room to confront the object of his annoyance.

Surprised, he had caught sight of the incensed man approaching him out of the corner of his eye: much too quickly, much too aggressively, and much too close for comfort. Dressed in a white cotton, button-down, crisply pressed business shirt and perfectly creased, gabardine khakis. The man's attire exemplified most in his profession who lived in this arid climate. In fact on that morning, more than half of the male and female café customers had dressed exactly like him.

"I want out!" bellowed his adversary hotly in a voice too loud to be ignored, even amidst the noisy café.

"Lower your voice," he hissed softly.

Squaring his broad shoulders, he had straightened his six-foot plus stature to its fullest height to loom over the man and intimidate him into submission. His enraged nemesis, several inches shorter and slight of built, did not back down.

"Not until I get absolute assurances… Or, maybe you want everyone in here to hear." he threatened, standing firm.

Conscious of already attracting several onlookers, each man canvassed the room for different reasons.

"Okay wait… Look, I understand your position," he had quickly interjected.

Holding his hands up in an acquiescent gesture.

To which the disgruntled man heaved a heavy sigh and nervously stared at the floor; not really knowing what to expect next.

Taking advantage of his adversary's obvious indecisiveness, he successfully led the man to a newly vacated booth toward the back of the café. Hoping once seated, bystanders would no longer find them interesting.

Presenting an upbeat front, he had continued lavishly cajoling the man as they sat across from each other. Completely unaware that when he had slid onto his bench cushion his shirt cuff had caught the edge of the table and pulled the button from its hole. An untidy wardrobe malfunction which, under any other circumstance, would have irked him to no end.

Then, making every effort to diffuse the volatile situation, he purposely leaned back in a non-threatening pose and rested his hands on his lap under the table.

"Pac Man... Can't we work this out?" he had asked in a soft, friendly voice.

His ploy cut short by the man vehemently reiterating his demands.

Suddenly a waitress appeared taking them both by surprise. Donned in all black, her fitted short-sleeve T-shirt with a stylish True Brew logo on the back gave the perky pony-tailed brunette a certain Parisian mystique.

Breaking eye contact with one another, the two men quickly looked down at their stained paper menus and stared at their options.

Casually standing there with pen and pad in hand. The twenty-something young woman smiled at her new customers waiting a moment for them to acknowledge her before saying.

"Morning guys... I'm Zoe... I'll be taking your order. Our specials today are warmed cranberry scones, apple-crumb muffins, and iced caramel macchiato. What'll it be?" she asked with a practiced lift to her voice.

Her intention to sound friendly, but not so friendly she grated on her customers nerves at that early hour.

"Coffee... Two. Black," he commanded curtly. "Okay. You can go sweetie."

Decisively dismissing the amiable young woman with his thumb signifying she should take a hike. He was determined to continue his conversation with the man across the table before the situation once again escalated.

The brunette, regarded by True Brew coworkers as hard-working and conscientious, was usually thick-skinned. Blowing off jerks like him as easily as blowing powdered sugar off her fingertips. However, that morning had been particularly tedious and this guy… this guy made her skin crawl.

Miffed, Zoe shoved her order pad into her apron pocket and turned on her heels. Her bouncing ponytail violently swishing behind her from side to side just one indication of her ire.

"Damn… What's got her panties in a twist?" he thought.

Seeing the server's smile change to a pout, completely clueless.

Certain he was not the cause of the little girl's soured mood; he did not want to take the chance she would remember him if things between him and his old pal went wonky. Deciding he would put the charm on when she returned.

"Humanity at its finest," grumbled Zoe; entering the coffee station.

"Tell me about it," agreed a coworker; passing her with a large tray of pastries balanced on his shoulder.

Still bothered by the man's rudeness, Zoe exacted a little harmless revenge by selecting the oldest pot of coffee. With a strained smile she returned to the men; filling their black and gold mugs to the brim with hot, stale, bitter liquid.

"Thanks sweetheart. You're the best," he had said; his grin a little too cheesy.

Then, taking out his cellphone he gestured he had to make a call so she would not hang around any longer than necessary.

The physical action of his pantomime causing his unbuttoned shirtsleeve to slide down his arm and gather haphazardly around his elbow. Still unaware of any fashion mishap until the server cocked her head and stared at his now bare arm a little too long; making him feel as if his fly was gaping open.

Fumbling to button his cuff while keeping up his pretense, he desperately wished the bitch would just go away and do her damn job.

His disgruntled companion, on the other hand, did not have to fake coyness.

He too felt uneasy about the perky young woman lingering. A true introvert by nature, the shy man usually did avoid direct eye contact. One exception being his dealings with the man seated across from him.

"Anything else?" the server asked dryly.

Not buying the customer's act, or waiting for further requests before adding.

"No... You all have a nice day."

Then, without further ado the pretty brunette placed their bill on the table and disappeared. Having absolutely no intention of returning. Figuring the tip, if any, would not be worth her effort.

Relieved they were finally alone; he remembered making one last attempt to persuade his inconsolable companion to reconsider his decision.

"Can't we work something out? Something we can both live with? After all... it's us, Pac Man," appealing to the man's sense of loyalty.

Trying too, not to sound phony as he offered his regrets for any misunderstandings; choosing his words carefully.

"Look... I want to make you happy," he had said with sincerity.

Although seething underneath; he had hidden his contempt for the double-crossing dweeb. Nodding, agreeing to each stipulation the moron demanded. Allowing the man to believe he had won. That he was safe. Untouchable. Meanwhile, he was cooking up the perfect plan to end the bastard's life.

But that was this morning.

Now, several hours later, sitting alone in his pickup truck inside his empty garage, the full extent of the preposterous position the double-crossing traitor had placed him in fueled the poison deep within him.

"Well, you wanted out?… I gave you out," he giggled nastily.

His mood becoming darker recalling how his perfect plan had crumbled into utter chaos. Now hoping the solution to his current situation would miraculously spring forth from his brain.

Twisting a tuft of fashionably styled wind-blown hair around his index finger, he grabbed the locks and pulled hard. Each strand straining to remain seeded in his gritty scalp as he yanked.

"Shit!" he wailed, frustrated; unable to think clearly.

Then, staring at his reflection in the rearview mirror he gave pause.

"Had his story been too convoluted? Had Pac Man seen through his guile from the start?… Impossible," he said aloud.

Drained.

"Okay… Work the problem," he ordered himself.

Tapping his forehead firmly with his index finger.

Grasping for some vestiges of clarity.

Exhausted, he pushed opened the pickup's door and stepped down slightly off balance. As his shoe slipped off the RAM running board he staggered backward against the truck's filthy body.

"Problems?… We have no problems. Just opportunities," giggling once more in that same malevolent way.

With detached objectivity he looked down at himself, then at his truck.

The RAM's windshield was coated with the recent bug impacts. New scratches marred its granite-colored exterior; hidden temporarily under thick layers of coarse sand and mud. The once sparkling tires bulging with compacted earth. Its previously pristine, black interior smudged with grimy scuffs and traces of blood. Particularly, a distinct shoeprint across the glove compartment; its door unable to completely close tightly due to noticeably damaged hinges.

Any one of these things could have linked him to last night's debacle, he admitted. Making him at the very least, a person of interest. Yet before the cops could suspect him, they had to know he existed. They had to know the two had a connection.

And except for the unfortunate public display in the café yesterday, only a few people in his inner circle knew. And they would never talk, if they knew what was good for them.

Looking around the truck cab he took mental stock of what he needed to do; confident he could accomplish most by himself. It was then, the empty center console tray between the bucket seats caught his eye.

"Damn. Where is it?... Where the hell is it?" he cried on the verge of hysteria.

Panicking, he dug into the folds around the seats; frantically searching between cracks, under floor mats and inside each door well. Grabbing everything loose and tossing them carelessly out of the truck. Scattering them willy-nilly around the garage floor.

"It's gone. Gone! Okay... Okay. I've got this... I mean, how bad could it be? It's a worthless piece of shit. Who's going find it way out there?... Doesn't matter... Means nothing."

Trying to reassure himself.

Then, a voice of reason kicked in. First, calculating the probability of the item being discovered by a person who actually understood its importance. He factored its exposure to the harsh desert and hot sun and figured it had already been rendered a worthless piece of inoperable junk, if indeed found at all.

"What are the odds?" he asked himself yawning as fatigue took over.

It had been a long twenty-four hours and an exhausting trip back home. Still, there was no time for sleep. Determined not to arouse suspicion that something was amiss; plus, he needed time to identify and correct any issues which might tie him to last night's deadly act. Even if that meant going to work today, and making the trip again tonight.

Disrobing, he closely examined his blood-spattered torn apparel. No doubt the deep ruby stains saturating the fabrics belonged to both men. Standing naked in his garage he considered his options.

"Burn?" he pondered aloud.

Thinking he could throw the tell-tale clothes in his fireplace or his backyard fire pit. But that would probably draw unwanted attention from his neighbors, and more than likely, a visit from the police.

"No... Burning's out."

For years now Phoenix and its surrounding communities, or as it is affectionately called, the Valley of the Sun, had grown into one of the nation's most heavily populated areas. Unfortunately as government officials pushed for this rapid urban sprawl, they did so without considering, or caring about environmental impacts.

Zealous developers bulldozed farms, orchards, and open desert and replaced them with an overabundance of concrete, housing developments, strip malls, and countless freeways.

The Valley, now one giant grid surrounded by several mountain ranges soon began drowning on its car exhaust and other air pollutants which could not escape into the atmosphere. Trapped too close to the ground, the Valley's once clean, blue skies turned into a year-long dirty Brown Cloud negatively impacting the air quality and its climate.

Daytime temperatures are now higher and last longer. Nighttime temperatures no longer significantly cool down, resulting in morning heat that is already too warm. Pollution warnings to those with respiratory illnesses are cautioned to stay indoors, more and more common.

This week had been especially unhealthy. Official no-burn days were in effect until further notice.

"Maybe it's as simple as taking out the trash," he reconsidered.

"Or, construction dumpsters... Yay... People chuck stuff in those things all the time... Scatter the shit all over town so there's no way to pin down a location," he exclaimed with elated.

Even so, there was the matter of the blood-soaked fabric from which blood types could be identified.

"But first, vinegar and bleach... Tons of vinegar and bleach. No reason to make it easy," he said to himself cheerfully.

Happily humming a nonsensical tune, he entered the laundry room from the garage and loaded the washing machine with ample suds, cold water, vinegar and bleach. Washing away any obvious evidence that could tie him to his former associate and the previous night's activity.

Noticing three overly large bloodstains had penetrated fibers in his shirt, he aggressively rubbed dishwashing liquid into the spots.

The stains, although lessened, remained.

Somewhere in the back of his mind he remembered a supermarket butcher telling him powdered meat tenderizer breaks down blood proteins. Grabbing the tenderizer from the kitchen, he spooned some into a small bowl and gradually stirred in water until it became a thick paste. Heavily smearing it onto the stains, he let the chemicals penetrate the threads before rinsing away the pesky blood residue.

Next, shoving his clothes and shoes into the washer he watched with a smile as the machine's drum filled with water. Feeling more in control, he strolled back into the kitchen and grabbed an old-style glass bottle of freshly squeezed, ruby red grapefruit juice from the refrigerator. Taking a generous swallow of the cold, sweet citrus he ambled down the hallway to his main bathroom. The thirst-quenching nectar suppressing the scratchiness in his throat; a souvenir from last night's desert chase.

The brass mantle clock on his office desk chimed.

Less than three and a half hours until he needed to be at work.

Determined not to be late, he quickened his pace.

Turning on the shower he immediately stepped inside, not waiting for the water to warm. His raw knuckles, cuts and bruises stinging as the frigid liquid pelted the sensitive skin. Ignoring the pain he scrubbed the blood and filth from his body, feeling purified by the soap's creamy lather.

Eventually the water turned steamy.

Shifting his weight under the rain showerhead he blissfully groaned as the hot liquid engulfed his entire being. Enjoying the water massage on his strained muscles he lingered; reflecting on how beautifully his plan began, and, how badly it unraveled.

"You know what your problem is Pac Man?" he asked his absent cohort, as if the man was beside him.

"Was?"

Letting out another of his peculiar giggles.

"Trust... Trusted me way too many times."

Rationalizing the man's demise was his own fault.

"Or at least… you did," he acknowledged, giggling again.

Flashing back to where he left off reminiscing, yesterday morning at the café.

"Come with me… One last time," he recalled saying; imploring the man sitting across from him in the booth.

"What part of out, don't you understand?" his adversarial companion replied.

"I do get it… Really… But c'mon you're the only one Vaxq trusts. Without you there's no deal," he had pleaded earnestly.

His story was not too far from the truth. The man opposite from him had been an integral part of his organization. Without him, the entire operation would need to be revamped. However, that was a problem for later. The more pressing problem was sitting right there, across from him.

"Look, it's your money too, pal. But, if that's what you want… I'm more than happy to keep your share," he had offered, playing to the man's greed.

Detecting a small glimmer of softening. He had known the man well enough to recognize he was now struggling to maintain his hard stance. That was when he knew he had him.

Money is a powerful persuader.

It was time to reel in the fish.

"Great. We'll deliver the goods. Get our cash. Maybe grab a beer for old-time's sake… And, you'll back in your wife's loving arms before she gets her nose out of joint," he proposed with a congenial smile.

"Look, I'm not kidding… After tonight, we're done… I'm taking my cut and that's the last you'll see of me. Understood?" The man stated emphatically.

"You're out… Understood… I promise."

***

In the beginning his plan had worked perfectly, he reflected.

He had successfully hidden his excessive cellphone use from his coworkers and discreetly found the perfect, secluded, spot to execute his plan. Then during lunchtime, he slipped away from the facility. As very few employees ever went offsite for lunch, this was the trickiest feat to navigate. Next, at a hardware store several miles away, he paid cash for the materials needed to construct a simple, but lethal, garrote.

Parked under the shade of an ample mesquite tree, he spread the items onto the empty bucket seat beside him. It had taken him only a few minutes to create the weapon by securing a wooden-peg handle at each end of the four-foot wire.

Now tucked deep down inside the RAM pickup's driver side door well. The silent killer rested safely in place, ready for easy access.

Much earlier in life he had been taught to use a similar one and had become notably proficient. After finding himself rusty, he was pleased it had taken few practice maneuvers before the garrote felt like a long, lost friend.

Bullets could be traced. But a common, everyday wire… impossible.

"Piece of cake," he said, admiring the shiny wire and his handiwork.

Confident in his plan, still he went over it one more time looking for flaws.

He had the weight advantage. He had the element of surprise.

"Just two old friends taking a ride. A little small talk while we wait at the predetermined spot for Vaxq. Who won't be coming… Cause he was never invited," he giggled.

"And when the opportunity presents itself discreetly pull out the wire and… strangle the bastard. Then… leave his sorry carcass in the middle of nowhere for the critters to finish off," he crowed enthusiastically.

The time had come.

The day's blue skies were rapidly giving way to sunset's panoramic array of blazing yellows, oranges, and grays.

Sunset would quickly follow.

The two men met at their usual secluded spot in the Casino Arizona parking lot. Strangers coming and going barely glanced their way; as it was the habit of casino clientele to beeline in and out of the building. It was also common for vehicles to be left in the lot for hours, even days; and rarely caused the casino's security to consider them abandoned.

He had watched with heightened anticipation as his former associate took his regular shotgun seat beside him inside his pickup. Settling in for the long ride south, the man had looked around expecting a package to be waiting for him.

"Where is it?" The man demanded, still a bit on edge.

"Under your seat," he had answered in a spirit of camaraderie.

Annoyed at the inconvenience, the overanxious man blindly thrust his arm into the open void beneath his seat. Thrashing about until his fingers eventually touched the elusive object.

Upon retrieving a silver case, he placed it carefully on his lap. Next he removed a pair of white fiber, electrostatic discharge (ESD) gloves from his front pocket and carefully inserted his hands into them.

Cautiously. Expertly. He removed a small, green printed circuit board (PCB) by its thin edges from a polyethylene terephthalate antistatic pouch and inspected both sides of the assembly. Once satisfied, just as carefully, he inserted the board back inside the protective pouch and then secured it back inside the case. Placing the object in the center console between them before launching another search.

"Schematics?… Memory stick's in my pocket. Wanna see?" he had chuckled.

Egging on the soon-to-be dead man as he patted his breast pocket and smiled.

Shaking his head no, the man removed his gloves and replaced them back inside his front pocket.

"Where're we meeting Vaxq?" The man asked, maintaining a business attitude.

In an effort to lighten the mood, he remembered purposely tossing a folded Arizona state map onto his passenger's lap and replying coolly.

"Remember these… Open it."

Turning the pickup onto Highway 87 to Florence.

"This is really off the grid." the unsuspecting man exclaimed in utter disbelief.

His brow furrowing as he warily examined the circled coordinates on the map.

"Don't look at me… It's Vaxq's idea," he had uttered, feigning ignorance.

Rolling his eyes, he light-heartedly shrugged his shoulders to give the impression that he had no say in the matter.

"You navigate." he had ordered the man. "I'm not taking a chance the route can be recovered from the truck's GPS system if something goes wrong."

Then, with a smile he added.

"Like I always say. Careful's ma' middle name."

Attempting to convince the man the precautions were necessary.

Giving his passenger the job of ushering them to the very spot he was going to kill him had proved exhilarating. So much so, that he had to keep biting the inside of his cheek to remind himself to keep a cool head.

He had chosen familiar backroads to get to the isolated location knowing there were only a couple traffic lights, no cameras, and few streetlights along the way. He also knew those roads were basically deserted that time of night.

Now, feeling he better get his ass moving, he turned off the glorious hot water and stepped from the shower.

Steaming hot water beads trickled down his legs forming a small puddle on the tile floor around his feet as he paused to study his reflection in the full-length mirror. Gently he toweled his battered, aching body. Upon closer inspection of his cuts and bruises he wondered how the hell he was going to hide them from his alternative world.

"I should've stayed closer to home," once again thinking about last night.

"Two hours to get there… too long. No… Vaxq was the bait… Vaxq never travels further north than Tucson. Pac Man knows… knew this. Maybe someplace familiar? No… Had to desolate… Somewhere I could dump his sorry ass," he revaluated.

"The tale was solid… I told was totally believable," he declared.

Convinced he had devised a perfect plan.

"It all went the way it was supposed to. Right up until…," he said aloud, truly perplexed. "What, or who tipped him off?"

Finding no fault on his part whatsoever, he was absolutely stumped as to why his plan had not worked.

"Watch… It'll come in three quick bursts of light. That's the signal," he had ordered his companion; taking the truck offroad into the desert.

"What? Here? This is crazy," yelled his passenger.

With frayed nerves on the brink, the man had searched the darkness for Vaxq's signal hoping his suspicions were wrong.

"What can I tell you… Vaxq's squirrely. Thinks the Feds are watching his every move… Maybe they are… Anyway, he insisted we meet, here. Guess you're not the only one getting cold feet," he remembered joking.

Mockingly calling both men paranoids; hoping to put his rider at ease.

Regrettably, it had served only to validate the agitated man's suspicions of an ambush, or a double-cross. Because without any warning, his passenger had grabbed the parking brake lever on the center console and pulled up hard.

Probably thinking the truck would abruptly stop and cause enough confusion that he might be able to get away; however instead, all hell broke loose.

Immediately, the truck's front tires locked, causing the pickup to go into a severe skid. Bouncing off the desert floor the pickup's grill gouged out deep ruts of dirt as well as any rock or thorny shrub that got in its way. With its rear raised off the ground, the RAM was in serious risk of flipping end-over-end.

While all that was going on outside, he remembered inside both men were being tossed around the cab like rag dolls.

Hitting the side of his head hard against the driver window, he had blacked out for several seconds. Only to regain consciousness and find himself defenselessly being hurled forward; his chin colliding with an unyielding steering wheel while his hands slammed into the dashboard.

Leaning in, he wiped away a large circle of water beads on the steamed bathroom mirror. Carefully, he touched the smarting gashes on his chin and lower lip with a couple of bruised fingers; then cocking his head, he gently probed a larger, swollen bruise already discoloring under his jaw.

Staring into his reflection's icy pale-blue eyes, he found himself reliving his futile attempt to both brace himself from the impacts, and retake control of the truck. Remembering too how he had firmly grabbed the steering wheel with one hand while trying to release the emergency brake with the other.

Meanwhile, the pickup's rear had crashed back down to earth and lunged forward in a serpentine motion; ultimately ramming head-on into a massive earth mound where it stalled in a cloud of gritty sand.

Shaking off his disorientation as quickly as possible, he had been shocked to find it was Pac Man who had recovered first. Propped against the passenger door, his adversary had pulled a hidden NAA Black Widow .22 revolver from his pocket and was now pointing it directly at him.

"How stupid do you think I am?" Screamed the man.

"Are you crazy. Vaxq will be here any…," he had started protesting.

Stopping his pretense in mid-sentence, he smiled broadly and rubbed his smarting forehead. Wishing he had padded the man down before they had left the Scottsdale casino.

"What the hell… Ya' got me… Did you really think?… Look Pac Man… you're the one who wrote the damn rules in the first place," he stated matter-of-factly.

Wondering how he was going to get the upper hand.

The man holding the gun hesitated, realizing the gravity of his situation. Realizing he would have to kill, or be killed.

Seeing that flicker of doubt cross his associate's paled face was all the hesitation he had needed. Lunging, he grabbed his adversary's wrist, slamming it against the dashboard. Hoping to force the man to release his weapon.

Instead, the firearm discharged with a deafening bang. The bullet whizzing passed his ear and lodging deep into the driver seat headrest.

Flinching, he had counterattacked. Driving the man's hand into the rigid steering wheel as hard as he could in an effort to dislodge the revolver from the man's grip.

Screaming in excruciating pain the man had dropped the gun. As the revolver fell to the floormat, the two fought for its possession. The struggle causing the firearm to slide far out of reach underneath the driver's seat.

With the gun lost, the terrified man knew his death was imminent. He had to get away. Kicking his door open, he launched himself out of the pickup. His thick glasses flying off his face, landing somewhere in the dark.

His escape, however, cut short as his right ankle was snatched in mid-air.

Shocked. Fighting for his life. The man had indiscriminately violently kicked with his other foot, but could not break free. Feeling himself being jerked back inside the cab he gave one last solid thrust; his heel successfully making solid contact with his attacker's right cheek, sending him flying backwards.

"You got lucky, Pac Man," he remarked looking at himself in the mirror.

Wincing as fingered the swollen souvenir in the mirror. Remembering the kick which had caused him to release his grip on the man.

His struggling passenger, having tumbled out of the RAM onto the ground, had scrambled to his feet with surprising agility and bolted into the desert. Trampling everything in his path which had fallen out of the pickup with him; and leaving him, holding only the man's brown loafer.

Wasting no time, first he retrieved the revolver; firing three shots into the night's void in the direction of his fleeing prey. Knowing if a bullet struck his adversary in any capacity it would be by sheer dumb luck.

Having no choice, he tucked the .22 into his pants and gave chase. Determined to put an end to this ridiculous game once and for all.

The darkness had made pursuing his quarry almost impossible; yet, he persevered. The desert's treacherous terrain and sharp vegetation ripping his clothes, skewering his skin.

Whether by instinct or chance, twice he had caught up with the man; both times underestimating his opponent's former combat abilities. The smaller man out-maneuvering him, leaving him flat on his back.

The man fleeing, wide-eyed; knowing all too well what was in store for him if he was caught. Blindly running for his life. Not knowing or caring where the hell he was going. His only thought, to save himself. Unaware his bloodied, bare foot was leaving a trail.

Smiling at himself in his bathroom mirror, goosebumps tickled his flesh as he recalled the night's exciting finale.

Those final moments had been like old times. Tracking his prey in a black void, discovering clues as he hunted; the traces of blood, disturbed terrain. Then, the feeling of alarm seeing the man's silhouette run across an open field toward a dark, isolated farmhouse.

"Shit. He's going for help," he had screamed.

Picking up the pace he pushed himself harder, still harder. Knowing he had to catch the fleeing man before the residents were awakened and the situation became more complicated.

And then it happened.

Pulling up to catch his breath, his heart pounding in his chest, he became overcome with laughter.

His frantic prey, in his valiant attempt to climb over the backyard fence and get to the house, had lost his footing. And, no matter how hard the exhausted fool thrashed and clawed, it was apparent his bare foot had gotten firmly stuck between the wrought iron rungs.

Regaling in his adversary's misfortune he covertly advanced upon him. Delighting as his foe, like a fly, became entangled in the iron web. And him, the deadly spider, closing in.

Meanwhile, the trapped man mustered what little resolve he had left. Jackknifing his flexible torso toward his raised leg, he had maneuvered his right arm through a fence railing opening so it was on the opposite side. Stretching both arms forward as far as they could go toward his entrapped foot; his fingertips barely touching his Achilles.

Then, gathering his last vestiges of strength he was finally able to grab his ankle. With renewed hope, he struggled to free his swollen appendage; too afraid to call out to the house for help in fear his pursuer would hear him. Unaware, that might have been his only chance.

After he had caught up to his prey, he briefly hid alongside the barn to assess both the ensnared man's condition and the activity inside the house. Even now, hours later, he was so pleased with himself at the way he had carried out the kill his body shivered with delight.

First he pulled the .22 from his pocket thinking it would be fun to shoot Pac Man with his own gun; basically adding insult to injury. Then, deciding the gunshot would wake everyone in the house, he changed his mind.

Not that he minded killing everyone there. But the more he thought about it, the more he was inclined to believe the residents probably had an arsenal of their own.

After all, this was Arizona.

Putting the revolver back in his pocket, he decided to use the .22 only as a last resort. Regretting having left his handy garrote back in the truck, he searched for something he could use as a silent weapon.

Noticing a utility knife atop a nearby bale of hay, he picked it up and pushed the blade out of its sheath; sliding the razor-sharp tip gently across his pinky. Taking pleasure in the sensation as he watched a small trickle of glistening ruby-red blood ooze from the cut.

Next, making his move, he approached his target's blind side.

"Idiot!" he had heard the man declare, struggling with his foot.

Deciding to chance it, the ensnared man was about to yell to the house for help. Yet, before he could utter a sound, a large hand appeared from behind him; muting the cry no one would ever hear.

Wielding the razor-sharp blade, he quickly, silently, finished off his old pal.

And, although still high on the kill, he desperately needed to rest before trekking back to his truck. Even more so, he was extremely anxious about people inside the house; concerned they had witnessed his carnage.

Securing a perfect spot inside the orchard he watched the house.

There was no movement.

No shutters closing. No sounds. No lights. No sirens.

Feeling a bit more at ease, he had settled back against a large tree trunk and closed his eyes. Yet not long after he began his catnap, threatening noises inside the yard jolted him awake.

Fighting a yawn, he watched with fascination as a pack of hungry coyotes of various sizes, ages, gender, cautiously made their way to the wrought iron fence. The pack, having caught the scent of the blood, carefully approaching the recently deceased.

Adhering to their position in the hierarchy; each coyote tool its turn nibbling and ripping flesh off the body. Then suddenly, a food frenzy started. Some fought over scraps of his would-be friend, while others tore off bones and ran away with their prize; making sure they were not followed.

"Bon appétit boys," he had joyfully whispered.

Pleased the coyotes were helping dispose of his handywork.

Then he had settled back against the stout trunk once again for a short catnap with plans to leave much before first light. His rest abruptly ending for good when an old woman dressed in a nightgown and oversized man's jacket found the remains, and let out a blood-curdling scream. Then, she looked straight in his direction.

***

Rifling through his extensive wardrobe inside his large walk-in closet, today of all days he could not afford to be late to work. Although painstakingly well-organized by color and functionality, what was proving difficult was finding clothing that was both appropriate and hid the numerous injuries he incurred last night. Ultimately pairing a long-sleeved cotton shirt and sharply creased pants, both quite suitable for the warm day ahead.

Studying various angles of himself in the full-length mirror, he looked closely for the slightest tell-tale signs of anything physically noteworthy. Confident, for the most part, that his coworkers would be too deeply absorbed in their own world to notice his many abrasions.

"Keep it simple, stupid," he affirmed, should he need to invent a story.

Hoping to get through the day without attracting attention to himself. His pickup truck, however, was another story.

The RAM's once perfect chassis was now full of scratches, caked mud, and stuck debris not to mention the scuffed, bloodied interior; all dead giveaways of yesterday's misadventure. Immediately driving to the nearest automatic carwash, he figured he would deal with the superficial now and attend to the rest later. More specifically, the disposal of the bullet lodged in the driver's headrest from his late associate's gun.

As the pickup yanked forward onto the carwash conveyor track, he found himself again behind the steering wheel dealing with the same vexing problem. How to get rid of the annoying little man once and for all.

Lost in the hypnotic spray of water and thick suds covering the mud-caked exterior, he identified his most pressing issues. Having the beginnings of a working plan by the time the powerful cleansing water and hot wax jets had washed away the vehicle's participation in his transgression.

"Who else knew about our little trip Pac Man? Wife? Kiddies? Maybe I should pay them a visit," he declared; whining. "Another mess I have to clean up."

Feeling nothing for the man he had known for decades. A man he just killed.

The truck jerked to an abrupt stop.

Suddenly a flashing green light came on as six high-powered dryers began loudly oscillating, blowing gale-force currents of air onto the clean vehicle. As the dryers steadily moved over the pickup droplets danced and bounced off the hood and windows putting him, momentarily, in a better mood.

Except for some touchup paint for the scratches, the chassis sparkled like new. The interior, however, would require a bit more effort.

Arriving at his facility with ten minutes to spare, he casually smiled as he greeted the familiar security guards manning the doors and strolled inside. Had he been one minute late the guards, or timecard police as he called them, would have written him up for the infraction and put it in his personnel file. As ludicrous as that rule was, today was not the day to draw attention to himself by testing its enforcement.

Arriving at his cubby, his confidence had swelled to the point that he felt comfortable coolly nodding hellos to his coworkers as he slipped on his work jacket. Certain that so far he had gotten away with murder. He was going to make sure nothing, or no one, prevented him from keeping it that way.

"First, get rid of any evidence," he mused; solidifying his next steps.

"Then, disassociate myself from every aspect of you, old pal."

"Finally…"

"Eliminate any witnesses."

Chapter 4

"This is no time for making new enemies."
~ Voltaire

Shy of 8:45 a.m., 125 miles northwest of Esther Hausman's Tucson estate, Antonio Luis Silva stood facing his locker deep in thought. He took little notice of the unruly people moving around him. He was, however, having difficulty ignoring the obnoxious stench emanating from the room's freshly painted Kelly-green walls and newly lacquered seats. Blaming the irritating chemical fumes for his enormous headache, clogged sinuses, and ringing ears.

Gingerly, he removed his light-weight windbreaker and folded it into a neat rectangle. Then, after carefully placing the jacket atop the natural oak slatted bench before him, he returned to the task of getting ready for work. That was until an involuntarily muscle twitch seized his right shoulder, catching him completely off guard. The intense pain accompanying the severe spasm forcing him to take immediate, discreet action to relieve his great discomfort.

Using swollen, bruised knuckles, Silva applied pressure directly to the center of the hard mass; forcefully pushing down on the knot until it eventually gave way. Quietly bushing off the incident as just one of the many maladies annoying him that day in lieu of sharing his problems with the world.

With the muscle spasm now relaxed, Silva stealthily glanced around the room to see if any of the wise guys he worked with noticed his discomfort. Satisfied no one saw, or if they had they were smart enough to keep it to themselves, Silva returned to his duties unaware he was being watched.

His observer, a handsome strong-featured young man in his late twenties, had been mentally dissecting each coworker since his first day on the job. Looking for any hint of activity or behavior he could exploit for his own gains; thereby making it his business to poke around into theirs. Determined to discover which of his coworkers' outside interests might provide him a lucrative opportunity, Antonio Silva was one such person who had caught the young man's attention. Now from behind an opened locker door at the farthest corner of the room he watched as Silva fumbled; reminding himself exactly why the older man had peaked his interest.

Certainly his suspicions were not based on Silva's physical appearance, far from it. Fairly run-of-the-mill, he guessed the man to be in his late fifties.

True Silva was a bit taller than average, and he carried his frame upright where others his age tended to begin stooping. He did sport a slight, middle-aged paunch which overshadowed what once must have been a remarkably fit, agile physique. That, plus entrenched crow's feet around his dark-brown eyes which deepened whenever he furrowed his brow, made Silva look much older than his actual years.

Then there was his overly tanned, olive complexion; due, no doubt, to a lifetime spent under the harsh sun. Figuring in his day the guy had probably attracted loads of women; however now, he just looked like one big age spot.

"Well, there's no accounting for taste," he snickered.

Trying to picture a much younger Silva.

However, there was one physical trait that Antonio Luis Silva possessed which the observer found very impressive. Marveling how a man his age still managed to keep such a thick, healthy head of hair and equally notable Chevron mustache. More salt than pepper, the younger onlooker was not at all surprised the older man chose to keep his mane cropped short and neat; further adding to his prosaic appearance.

"What's your secret, Jefe?" he chuckled, suspecting Silva was not one to indulge in high-end hair products.

Also resolved that if he had even half the hair gene pool Antonio Silva did, he would flaunt his luscious silver locks until hell froze over.

But mostly there was Silva's many conflicting sides; making him more and more a paradox, and causing the younger man not to buy his act. On one hand, the older man projected a rather odd, unassuming image of someone who did his job well and then went straight home. Yet, the observer had seen too many slipups where Antonio Silva's hidden temper or quick reaction had given him away. Showing he was not the man he pretended.

Furthermore, whereas most everyone in the group tended to share every aspect of their lives from what they ate for morning to who they slept with last night. The older man rarely shared anything other the time; and almost always with a crisp, no-nonsense air of authority.

"Give it up Tony... What are you hiding?" grumbled the observer. "Not buy 'n your humble-pie, laid-back shit, old man."

Staring through his locker door slates with the determined persistence of a jackal stalking its prey, the observer maintained his single focus. Blocking out the noisy distractions around him until an unexpected display of testosterone erupted nearby resulting in pushing and shoving, and ending with several metal doors being loudly slammed shut. One such deafening bang coming so close it took the observer completely off guard, causing him to duck for cover behind his own door.

Wide-eyed and breathless, the young man searched the room for the cause of the chaos. His reddening face returning to normal after discovering the clatter came from a small group of men playfully teasing one another. Their pleasant conversation, which began as quiet murmurs, now an elevated debate.

Feeling rather foolish, he was glad the others were too caught up in their own world to notice his overreaction. Then, almost as one, each person grabbed their gear and gathered on the other side the room, waiting.

The exception being the observer who held back, focusing on Antonio Silva.

Remembering his first day on the job getting the lay of the land. It was not long before the older man came on his radar. How whenever he tried to get information about the old guy everyone clammed up; unable to determine if their silence was because of loyalty or out of fear. How even Clarence, the group's most ill-tempered, contrary member kept his mouth shut.

"I get it, Silva… You're the man," he griped, frustrated. "But why?"

Remembering too, his first glimpse of the real Antonio Silva; a complex man with a keen logical mind who acted decisively and kept cool under pressure.

"So, what're you hiding, boss? What don't you want the world to see?"

Yet this was not the Silva he saw today. Today the man seemed, broken.

"Have 'n a bad day, Jefe?" chuckled the observer, noting Silva's grimace.

Usually Antonio Silva methodically went about his day with unflappable purpose. Today, however, an undeniable malady was causing a wince here, a twitch there; the simplest of tasks seemingly a great burden. Whatever war was being waged against the old man's body; the war was winning.

Looking around the room, none of his coworkers apparently noticed any of this about their fearless leader. Even if they had, the observer was pretty sure they had learned not to comment on Silva's business a long time ago.

This was also true about Silva's eccentric, almost obsessive compulsion for maintaining a disciplined routine; including his laughable pre-work regimen.

To begin, regardless of how old Silva's clothes, he was fastidious about his appearance. Clean, crisply pressed from head to toe, never a button missing, or a shoe scuffed, the old man was meticulous. So much so, the observer would often mimic the man's predictable behavior under his breath in a kind of National Aeronautics and Space Administration (NASA) countdown.

Today was no different.

"Nine… Silva removes his windbreaker. Now, neatly fold it and set it on the bench right in front of you."

"Eight… Take a clean, freshly pressed red and white stripped jacket from your cubby and put it on with the care of a full-dress uniform."

"Seven… Straighten up. Then, starting at the top, snap each shiny silver jacket button closed."

"Six… Perfectly align your shirtsleeve cuffs with your jacket's."

"Damn! Those must really hurt," he noticed.

Wondering if Silva received those badly bruised knuckles via a not so legal enterprise, or maybe someone just did not like the old man's face.

"Five… Ah, the shoe brush in your cubby. That's right. Get every speck of dust daring to cling to those ultra-white Nikes."

"Have'n trouble with those puppies?"

Noticing Silva's difficulty tying his shoes laces.

Then taking a moment, the observer marveled once again that he seemed to be the only one in the room witnessing the boss's distress.

"Four… Check yourself in that full-length mirror. Khakis perfectly creased? Long-sleeved shirt well-starched? Puckering… That's right. Tuck it in nice and tight," he snickered.

"Guy's a perfect poster child for obsessive-compulsive disorder," he declared under his breath.

"Three… Here we go. Clip on the official identification badge. Make sure you center that sucker on your jacket's breast pocket… That a way," he mocked.

Suddenly realizing the old guy had almost finished changing, the observer began changing while resuming his count down.

"Two… Okay, secure your equipment… What In The Hell," he said a little too loudly; causing others to look his way.

The agony on Silva's face unmistakable.

Pondering the kind of trouble the old guy must be in to receive those kinds of injuries, the observer glanced away just as Silva's eyes shot a look in his direction.

"One… Time to check that wall clock, Jefe. The minute hand touches the twelve… And, blast off!" he whispered.

Watching Silva through his own locker door's metal slates.

Yet the older man stood there, silent. A minute passed, then another. The voices in the room falling silent as all eyes fixed on their stone-faced leader standing in front of the wall clock.

"Well, this is new," thought the observer; sensing Silva's irritation.

Then, unbuttoning his shirtsleeve cuff, Silva pushed up both shirt and jacket sleeves revealing an ultra-sophisticated black MTM multi-functional wristwatch.

"That's some expensive alarm clock old man," the observer noted excitedly; ogling the jewelry.

Checking his wristwatch against the wall clock, Silva removed the fixed timepiece from its lofty place and chucked it in the air. The faulty chronometer ultimately landing perfectly dead center in the trash container, a concerto of clanking metal parts. Then, without a single comment, the older man turned to his group who were silently waiting for their orders.

Readjusting his cuffs until once again perfectly aligned, Silva glanced around the room a final time. Satisfied his team was ready to start their day, he gave the go-ahead.

"All right people. It's time," he announced with undisputed authority.

With one exception, the entire group hoisted their equipment and rose as a finely tuned unit. Some still joking and teasing while others behaved in a more subdued, professional manner; each person moved in an orderly fashion out the doorway at the back of the room. This in itself told the observer the command his boss held.

That, plus the pricey MTM timepiece with its impressive high-tech operational features, confirmed his suspicions. That Silva secretly lived beyond the meager means he projected. And that if he stayed vigilant, stayed on the guy's ass, he would soon discover how and cut himself in on the action.

Lost in his own thoughts the observer stared into his locker's abyss. Suddenly, feeling a pair of steely eyes upon him, he realized he was no longer invisible. That perhaps, he never was.

"You plan'n on work'n, Terco? Or you just goanna chill back here and play with that fancy phone of yours all day?" confronted Silva sternly.

The hairs rose on the back of the younger man's neck as his boss moved in closer, encroaching on his comfort zone. Becoming increasingly uncomfortable, the observer suddenly felt like a child caught in a whopper of a lie trying to squirm out of the consequences.

"Right behind you, Jefe. Hey… need help with your gear? Just say'n… I noticed you…" he prattled on; his lame efforts backfiring.

Recognizing it was imperative he get back in Silva's good graces if he were to keep his present employment.

"Noticed what, asshole? You really want to mess with me, Terco?" retorted Silva.

The observer now clearly regretting both his words and current predicament.

"Like you said boss… Time to go," he responded acquiescently, quickly gathering his gear and following the others out the door.

Scolding himself in an inaudible whisper as he quickened his steps.

"Nice going, Terco… Well, if you weren't on the old guy's radar before you sure as hell are now."

Hurrying to his assignment, Terco considered several possible strategies to turn today's fiasco around to his advantage.

Convinced more than ever after glimpsing the luxury wristwatch and being the object of his boss's ire that Silva was involved in something sweet, something he adamantly did not want to share. Terco knew he had to regain Silva's trust if he was ever going to find out the older man's secret and worm in on his action.

"Okay, brown-nosing's doesn't work," he acknowledged. "Sooo, what will?"

He considered.

"One things for sure… No way in hell is that old man's keeping me from finding out what going on. If nothing else works, Jefe… You just might have to disappear."

***

Standing alone in the middle of the locker room, Antonio Silva admitted his confrontation with his young coworker had been building for weeks. Now suspecting the punk was targeting him, setting him up; but, for what?

"I don't have time for his bullshit," he seethed.

Inhaling as deeply as his sore ribs allowed.

Then, holding his breath just long enough, Silva properly adjusted his equipment straps. Finding it difficult to shake off both his aggravation and the physical toll on his damaged body, he decided he could do nothing about his injuries. The kid, however, was another story.

"Terco… You just better keep out of my way if you plan on stay'n healthy," he vented angrily; glaring at his reflection in the mirror.

Having no patience for the kid's tomfoolery with everything else going on.

An unexpected pain surged down his arm where the shoulder strap pressed against an enormous bruise. After readjusting its tension, Silva realigned his sleeve cuffs; pulling down each as far as it would go. Knowing there was little else he could do to hide his red, swollen hands.

Then, straightening his posture, Antonio Silva walked out of the Kelly-green room; determined the rest of his day would be free from further incident. His mood brightening even before the door shut behind him as he listened to the familiar melodies being played on an organ through a massive state-of-the-art audio system. The hot sun bathing his throbbing joints as nostalgia and mouth-watering aromas carried him back to a time when his life was simpler.

Immediately reacting to the sound of a loud crack as a hurled baseball hit the sweet spot on a wooden bat. The ball lifting high into the air, sailing deep into centerfield and over the wall; the crowd tracking its trajectory, heartily cheering their approval.

Allowing himself the brief distraction, Silva watched the Arizona Diamondbacks' celebrated first baseman round the bases in his usual unassuming manner as the ecstatic stadium announcer recapped every detail of the team's first homerun of the spring season. The D-backs dugout enthusiastically emptying to greet their teammate as he stomped onto home plate; swarming him with congratulatory pats and high-fives, their faces beaming and eyes twinkling. Leaving no doubt the professional athletes still treasured the game they fell in love with as boys.

Then, with professional decorum, Antonio Silva turned his back on the excitement and began his workday. Joining his fellow vendors up and down the stadium steps; each singing their luring Sirens' songs at the top of their lungs in their own personal bravado. Catering to ravenous fans whose hands waving high in the air beckoned the men and women in the red and white striped jackets to bring them the mouthwatering indulgences they so greatly craved.

"Peanuts… Popcorn."

"Cotton candy."

"Icy cold beer hhheeeerrrre."

"Rrrreeeeedddsss… Get yer red hots!"

Chapter 5

"Death is not the end.
There remains the litigation over the estate."
~ *Ambrose Bierce*

For more than 20 years, leading forensic pathologists have regarded Dr. Warren Lee Singh as both an exceptional Chief Medical Examiner and an exemplary professor at the University of Arizona's College of Medicine, Department of Pathology. The fact that several renowned institutions still tried to coax Singh's out of his intimate lab and could not, said more about Dr. Singh's devotion to his family and their love of Tucson than his desire for national accolades.

Gazing down at the mutilated body on the cold, stainless steel autopsy table, Dr. Singh tried to recall the last time he had had such a grueling task.

Ever the perfectionist, each postmortem Dr. Singh performed adhered strictly to The Autopsy Committee of the College of American Pathologists (CAP) Practice Guidelines for systematically establishing identity, evidence, and cause of death. Having felt these procedures were not strict enough, Warren Singh then instituted additional comprehensive practices for gathering evidence. Insisting his entire forensic team adopt the same fastidious methods for their field and lab work.

Updating even these techniques over the years to ensure his department's, analyses were precise and above reproach. This included the practice of changing latex gloves each time a new piece of evidence was handled, examined, and cataloged. Moreover, Dr. Singh mandated that each autopsy participant must wear complete protective gear per the Center of Disease Control (CDC) guidelines to protect both the evidence and the examiner from contamination.

Donning his first set of protective, double surgical gloves, face masks and shields, eye protectors, garments and booties, Singh approached the corpse.

"Rest assured my friend… You deserved no less than our best," he promised the dead man on his slab. "So… unless you have any objections, let's begin."

With Singh's first word the overhead audio, video actuated system instantly began recording the procedure which would inevitably accompany the official police medicolegal postmortem report. The video feature likewise displaying the body on a large interactive monitor alongside the examination table.

Dr. Singh needed only speak a valid command and the system's camera zoomed in or out on a specified area of the body. Eliminating any possibility of contamination by the examiner since neither the remote control nor monitor were touched.

"Now… Let's see how you ended up in this sorry state," he said to the deceased with the upmost respect. "Case PM687-34B. Caucasian male. Mid to late forties."

As always, Dr. Singh began the autopsy with a general description of the body followed by a painstaking removal of the victim's clothing. Studying each item one at a time, meticulously collecting and cataloguing any and all evidence such as blood and foreign particles, Singh succinctly documented his findings and attached the supporting photographs.

First he removed the dead man's sockless, size 9 Arezzo Italian loafer. As the pricey shoe was the only one found on the deceased and at the scene, the doctor had nothing with which to compare it. He then photographed, bagged and tagged the bloodied shoe, and created individual packets for the embedded fragments he found.

Next, he thoroughly explored the victim's beltless, size 34 khakis. Finding the trousers similarly marred and tattered, Warren Singh left no rip, crevasse, seam, or cuff overlooked. Carefully inspecting each pocket in hopes of finding a hidden treasure. All the while continuing his casual conversation with the deceased; keeping himself distracted from his tightening neck and shoulders.

"You don't happen to have your wallet or an ID stashed away, do you?" he joked lightly.

Fishing out assorted debris from one of the man's back pockets with a pair of long post-mortem tweezers.

Shifting his examination to the front pockets, Dr. Singh noticed a small, hard bulge deep inside the left. Gently inserting the metal evidence tweezers as far as they could go, Singh latched onto a spongy wad; retrieving two bloodied, white anti-static fiber gloves. The very kind used in certain industries to prevent skin oils from contaminating electronic hardware surfaces, cleanroom galvanized wafers, even photographs. As the weary doctor bagged and tagged the items, he became rejuvenated at the thought of further secrets he might soon discover.

The last article of clothing Singh removed from the victim was the now infamous white blood-stained shirt he had heard so much about. Smiling, he recounted the delightful chat he had with the lovely woman, a Mrs. Esther Hausman, who both owned the estate and found the body.

Her account of how she had shockingly found the deceased in her backyard in the dead of night was utterly spellbinding, and had captivated the others around them. Especially amusing was the part about mistaking this very shirt for her mischievous dog's white fur. He could only imagine the look of dismay on her face when she discovered its real owner.

"You know my silent friend… Had someone of lesser fortitude found you… Well, let's just say I might be performing two autopsies today," he said playfully.

Acknowledging the immense shock someone might incur finding a corpse in their backyard day or night.

And, as this person was so terribly damaged, Dr. Singh knew it was essential he conduct an extensive internal postmortem if he were to have any chance of finding how the man died. Now fully naked on the autopsy table, the deceased lay waiting for Singh to finish his fastidious inspection of the instruments he planned to use for such an in-depth examination.

Evaluating the glistening, sterile medical equipment table with its shiny scalpels, scissors, forceps, rib shears, and bone saw for opening the cranial cap; the Medical Examiner decided he had everything he needed to remove and or dissect the chest, abdomen and pelvic organs, as well as the face and limbs; and of course, the brain.

"Chief Medical Examiner Warren Lee Singh, Pima County Office of the Medical Examiner. Date," he began.

Speaking clearly, Dr. Singh systematically described both the subject and his ensuing actions as he picked up a scalpel. Proceeding with his first incision, he made two deep cuts into the flesh that ran from each shoulder joint and met at mid-chest. From there he continued the incision from the chest down the abdomen to the pubic region, thus creating a Y shape.

Afterwards, peeling back skin, muscle, and soft tissue with his scalpel, he pulled the chest flap over the deceased's face exposing the ribcage and neck muscles.

Engrossed in the body cavity, Warren Singh was none too pleased when the sliding glass doors parted and a young woman dressed in green medical scrubs nosily entered the forensic autopsy room; derailing his train of thought.

"Hey Doc. Can you believe… Oh, I am soooo sorry," she said way too loudly.

Abruptly halting her apology at seeing her boss' incensed expression.

Glee Anne Piozzi, Dr. Singh's assistant several years his junior, had shown to be an extremely gifted and inquisitive technician. Having grown up on the East

Coast the middle child of a large, boisterous Italian family, Glee learned very early a soft voice and reserved demeanor only got her ignored.

Eventually she discovered, the way to get the attention she so dearly craved was to speak louder than anyone else with an overdramatic flare.

However at work, the flamboyant Glee greatly annoyed most of her coworkers. Giving her the unfortunate reputation of being an uncontrollable chatterbox in a profession where quiet and order was preferred; and earning her the unflattering nickname of Megatron Disruptor.

Today of all days, the doctor could do without whatever drama Ms. Piozzi was intending to share. On the brink of sending her packing he only reconsidered because; one, he truly needed her help with the immense task before him, and two, in many ways his demonstrative assistant reminded him of his free-spirited youngest child, Jasmine.

So, once again making allowances for Glee's over-exuberance, Dr. Singh's heart softened; even though his head told him he should know better.

Glee, seeing her mentor's disapproving expression, silently secured her thick honey-blonde hair inside her surgical cap, then covered her medium frame with the appropriate personal protective equipment (PPE).

"Sorry... What do you want first?" she asked sheepishly, rushing to his side.

Her subdued manner lasting less than a minute after seeing the condition of the corpse on the autopsy table.

"Holy Moley! Man, he's a total mess... This is going to be so much fun!"

Her outburst typical of her inability to keep her ill-timed enthusiasm in check.

"Ms. Piozzi... You can begin by showing this poor man some respect. Glove up over there. You can help bag and catalogue. After that... We'll see," sighed Warren Singh disapprovingly.

Still not quite sure whether she was going to help or hinder if allowed to stay.

Approaching the boxes containing various sterile gloves, Glee recognized several of the photographs she had taken onsite during the warm morning now attached to the wall x-ray film illuminators. Then she had been so absorbed in taking the appropriate photos of the deceased entangled in the fencing, the body's disfigurement had not quite registered. That, plus her sweating hands necessitating frequent Latex glove changes, made carrying out the simplest investigation tasks frustrating.

Yet perhaps even more irritating than the gloves was the abundance of biting gnats, mosquitos, and horseflies clearly intent on assaulting every cavity and every inch of her miserable being. It was this part of Glee's job she hated most; the necessity at times to be outdoors. Preferring instead a clean lab, hospital, or library; actually anyplace inside equipped with closed doors, plumbing, and generous air conditioning.

But then she remembered the morning had not been a total loss.

While swatting an annoying insect insisting on biting her chin, flying into her eyes, and up her nose; she spied him. The utterly handsome Detective Michael Flores, talking to the senior citizen who owned the horrible place.

By her own admission, Glee had never had trouble speaking her mind.

However for some reason one look at the gorgeous detective and his well-defined, firm physique, and she turned into a tongue-tied dolt. Flabbergasted by her own ineptness, unable to stop any form of absurdity from pouring out of her mouth.

Slightly taken aback by his arrival Glee was bound and determined that today would be the day she got up the nerve, intelligent Homo sapiens to intelligent Homo sapiens. She would gather her courage, choose the perfect moment, and then, dazzle him with her brilliance.

Taking out her cellphone she reversed the camera lens and checked her appearance.

"Eeewwww," she uttered; disgusted with the vision.

Using the towelette she had just used to clean her camera lens; Glee rubbed her sweaty brow and dirt smudges. Hoping she could remove enough grime to make herself halfway presentable.

This was her moment.

Tidying her thick bun and wisps of hair escaping her lab cap, Glee next straightened her disheveled lab coat and joined the cadaver team.

Waiting as her fellow technicians placed the corpse inside the HRP and secured the dead man onto the gurney, Glee pretended to be one of them. Blending in as the group transported the body to the ambulance in the driveway; and knowing full-well they had to pass Detective Flores on their way to the van.

As their silent guest of honor led the procession closer to her target, Glee's palms and armpits suddenly began profusely sweating. With her anxiety rising, she decided to engage in small talk with the person next to her; thinking that way it would be easier to pick the right moment to reveal herself.

Feeling giddy, she had almost reached Michael Flores when her inner-voice suddenly screamed.

"What… am I going to say? What possible reason would warrant my interruption?"

Closing in on the patio, Glee found herself once again losing her nerve. The little resolve she had left, vanishing with each hesitant step.

"Shit!" she exclaimed a little too loudly.

"What's that?" asked Norm.

The technician with whom she had been speaking.

"Oh… Nothing," replied Glee, laughing a little too loudly.

Her mind desperately trying to invent something really clever to say to the detective before they reached the patio.

"What the hell," she grunted, deciding to just seize the moment and wing it.

That was when Glee noticed her detective's otherwise exquisite face now red and blotchy. Clearly upset, Flores' angry directed at the older woman caught Glee completely off guard. Regarding him as the epitome of professionalism, she cringed as his heated argument with the homeowner continued.

"Damn old bat… You're ruining my big chance! Tell him what he wants, and get out of my way," she cursed.

Devastated, realizing her perfect opportunity was disappearing into thin air, Glee let out a heavy sigh and chickened out.

Invisibly walking by the quarreling twosome, Glee opened the ambulance rear double doors and stepped in, shutting them behind her. Aimlessly she gazed out the square windows, feeling sorry for herself; no longer wishing to invest in the drama taking place outside.

That was until the sound of a car speeding up the driveway compelled her rush to the ambulance backdoor windows. Terrified at seeing a green jeep barreling towards her, Glee stumbled backwards; falling against the body bag as she shrieked in horror. Certain she was about to be crushed to death.

However, at the last moment the jeep skidded to an abrupt stop.

Coughing violently as billowing dirt clouds engulfed both vehicles. Glee hastily threw sterile blankets over the HRP; making sure the corpse was not contaminated by the lingering dust and debris floating inside the van.

Hurrying back to the rear windows just in time to see a woman approximately her own age, march across the driveway and push past the officer standing in front of the barrier without the slightest reservation.

And, although the policeman clearly tried to stop her, the young woman completely ignored his orders. Not stopping until she was sitting next to the older woman and focusing solely on her; never once acknowledging Detective Flores' presence.

"Who does she think… Treating him like that," snarled Glee protectively.

Finding herself both hating and admiring her competition's audacity.

"And he's grinning… at her. Not grinning… Beaming!" she shouted, crushed by the detective's response.

"Ms. Piozzi… Glee," called the doctor kindly.

Seeing his lab assistant solemnly absorbed in the photographs.

"Boy… Something really didn't like this guy," she commented.

Returning Singh's gaze; forcing herself to behave more demurely.

"Something… or somebody," added Dr. Singh; measuring the body.

Then, joining forces, the doctor and his lab assistant melded into a fierce cohesive team. Hour after hour, barely taking a break, the two performed extensive surface and internal examinations of the tragically mutilated body.

Dispassionately describing each item as if nothing more than a nut or bolt instead of human remains, Dr. Singh adeptly documented his findings while Glee bagged and labeled the specimens. Likewise, documenting the precise location of each discovery on the deceased as well as marking a large aerial photograph; showing the body's relationship to the evidence found.

"Eyes, light brown… Interesting… He's wearing a contact. But skin indentations on both sides of the nose, and this scratch from his bridge extending into his eyebrow, suggests he was also wearing glasses." somewhat surprised by his discovery.

Skillfully removing the contact from the one remaining, lifeless eye, Dr. Singh handed the lens to Glee who then placed it into a labeled container; and added TBD for further investigation.

"Is that common? Wearing contacts and glasses together?" asked Glee.

"Well, let's see… Our friend is, was, around 40 years old. If he suffered from presbyopia, a refractive error in vision which affects older people's ability to see close up… His contact lens could have been used to correct his nearsightedness… but, he still would need both, contacts and glasses, to maintain or improve his close-up vision. It's an uncommon condition which may help identify him," expressed Singh with optimism.

"Let's continue… Thinning medium brown and gray hair. Thirty-seven percent of hair follicles and scalp absent from skull due to… Cause? TBD… However angled gouges on the skull suggest possible predator incisors," stated Dr. Singh pointing to specific areas on the skull.

"You mean his scalp was chewed off?" asked Glee in horror.

"Mmm… Glee, please swab these indentions and analyze them. Also, please fingerprint and scrape all ten fingernails," he requested with a slight grin.

"Really?" replied Glee, looking at him dismayed. "You do realize he's missing his right hand and foot? Not to mention most of his right forearm."

Aware of his impossible request; grinning Warren Singh had intentionally phrased his request thusly to lighten the mood rather than to be taken literally.

Realizing the doctor's attempt at levity was for her benefit, a weary Glee appreciatively nodded and smiled.

"Speaking of forearms. See if you can identify that partial tattoo," he requested seriously, returning to his examination. "I believe there's enough of the remains to discover what it looked like intact. We just need to dig a little harder to find it."

And with that, the good doctor resumed his comprehensive body examination.

"We, Dr. Singh?" asked Glee good-naturedly.

Knowing full well Singh had already blocked out the world around him, and was once again fully absorbed in his investigation.

Redirecting her energy to the tattered tattoo on what was left of the deceased's right bicep, Glee enlarged the photograph she had taken earlier and closely scrutinized its red, white and blue remnants.

"Is this thin black line part of these red and white shapes? K. A… What the heck does K, A, stand for? And this numeral… Is it a single digit, or part of a larger series of numbers? Rats!" she yelled, completely frustrated.

Tossing her pen onto the table Glee removed her glasses. Rubbing her eyes she vented.

"How the hell am I going to…?"

"Tattoo parlors… law enforcement, the military. Anyone of these would maintain tattoo design databases… Well… some might," she said aloud.

Thinking with any luck she might find a match through one of them. However, before she could act, Dr. Singh exclaimed.

"Glee… Come here!"

The doctor, after placing bloody hairs stuck around the missing earlobe into an evidence container, had gently exposed an area on the back of the skull where the scalp was missing. Magnifying the section on the video monitor, Singh noticed tiny particles embedded in the cranial bone protecting the occipital lobe; glistening like glitter under the lab's ultraviolet light.

"See… The occipital bone… Bits of a pulverized metallic compound which I believe he must have been living with for a long time. Computer, increase magnification x5. Photograph… I'm going to extract some of them, then remove the skull cap," he informed Glee, requesting she analyze both.

"Interestingly, this particular area of the brain is primarily responsible for vision." he added, wondering if the original injury contributed to his guest's poor eyesight.

Then, reaching across the dead man's throat, a laceration caught his eye. Quite different from the other wounds he had encountered, Singh's eyebrows lifted as he commanded.

"Computer magnify D22, times 5."

Keying on the area surrounding the larynx.

"I can't believe I missed this… Look Glee, the laceration of the epidermis is so clean it fits together almost perfectly… Just now, when my hand brushed the neck, the skin parted. Measuring precisely .635 centimeters in length, the cut looks like it was caused by a sharp blade of moderate length. See how the larynx's arytenoid cartilages, vocal folds and ligament are not completely severed," he proclaimed zealously.

Using the important discovery as a teaching opportunity.

"Is this what killed him?" asked Glee, equally fascinated.

"Maybe… At the very least, the cut rendered our dearly departed incapable of shouting… even whispering for help," he declared.

Then added solemnly.

"I'm not ruling it out… But I believe our friend has a lot more to say before making our assessment definitive," returning to his examination energized.

"Hey… I'm going to send the fingerprints and dental impressions to the Tucson Central Investigations Division. After, I have a few avenues to check out concerning that tattoo. You okay without me for a while?" she asked her mentor, waiting patiently for his reply.

"Doc… You listening?" she grinned, knowing better than to expect a response.

As the automatic autopsy doors parted with a swoosh, Glee Piozzi walked into the hallway; glancing back momentarily. Smiling sweetly at the older man she held in high regard, Glee wondered how long it would be before he realized she had gone.

Completing his examination of the internal cavity and extremities four grueling hours later, Warren Singh sat back and smiled.

He had found cause of death.

Chapter 6

"Nobody owns life, but anyone
who can pick up a frying pan owns death."
~ *William S. Burroughs*

Scowling at the dusty vinyl floor beneath his desk, Homicide Detective Michael Flores took great pleasure in kicking off his equally filthy shoes. As each black oxford hit the floor with a loud thud, Flores at long last felt a small degree of satisfaction he had not experienced the entire day. Frustrated at the lack of evidence found at the scene where an unidentified man had brutally died the night before, the detective leaned his exhausted body back against his lumpy, old leather office chair and closed his eyes. Then after plopping his feet atop his desktop, he repeatedly crossed and uncrossed his ankles in an unsuccessful attempt to get comfortable.

Keenly conscious that his badly wrinkled dark-blue suit was now sorely in need of a good dry cleaning. Flores noticed too his clothes were not half as bad as his expensive, once immaculately shined shoes; which were now caked with clotted dirt, embedded pebbles, and unidentifiable animal waste. Reeking of sweet grasses and pungent manure, the combination of aromas fueled his foul mood and completely soured his appetite.

Long abandoned, the detective's half-eaten sub sandwich and withered pickle slice laid drying out and ignored atop a badly crinkled wax paper wrapper next to his desk phone. Alongside the pathetic meal, a cup of cold acidic coffee had created a miserable brown ring above the undrinkable brew; staining the untouched generic white mug.

Deciding to get back to work, Flores repositioned himself in his squeaky chair and began pouring over the skimpy preliminary documents Officer Alvin

Pawlak had brought earlier. The lack of information in the files fueling his surly disposition.

Priding himself on his ability to quickly and accurately interpret and resolve difficult cases, the curious circumstances surrounding the man's death at a home in rural Tucson had him both stumped and vexed. Furthermore, the reports in front of him contained little else than he had already assessed on his own at the scene. Adding to his irritation the valuable investigation time he was losing waiting for more in-depth reports to materialize. Until such time remaining in the dark regarding his most basic questions, like: was the grisly death an accident, or was it murder?

Antsy, Flores pulled out the existing photos showing the gruesome scene from different angles. Searching for any clue he might have previously missed; he brought the images of the mangled dead man entangled in a black wrought-iron fence up close to his face.

"Well, what's left of you looks like a typical white-collar working stiff," he surmised.

His gut telling him the dead man was not some druggy or member of lunatic fringe or cult. Not seeming like someone intent on randomly going onto a property with the intention to sadistically harm the inhabitants or their animals.

"Who knows? Normal looking people do all kinds of weird things these days," he mused, brooding over possible motives.

"So what… Robbery? A victim of unfortunate circumstances? You got lost in the boonies and went looking for help… Found the Hausman place… No… This is ridiculous," he admitted.

His investigation needed facts, not speculations. Because if he followed his gut, it would tell him someone dangerously sinister had caused the man's death.

"If you were lost, why the hell did you try and climb the backyard fence? Why not just ring the front doorbell? Unless... unless you were in a hurry. Unless you were running for your life," he contemplated.

Conceding all this guessing was counterproductive, he sat at an impasse staring at the photos; eager to receive Dr. Warren Singh's autopsy findings.

Drumming his fingertips on his desktop the detective frequently stared out his department's open doorway mentally willing the reports to arrive. Then, as if tired of waiting for a bus to round the corner, for a lack of anything better to do Flores reread the files again and again; until he almost had them memorized.

***

It had been slightly more than four years since a younger and more impertinent Officer Michael Flores joined the Arizona, Central Investigations Division's Tucson Violent Crimes Section Homicide Unit. From his very first day on the job, Flores had consistently achieved a high crimes cleared rate on every case he was assigned. In other words, the number of crime investigations assigned to him had resulted in a high number of accurate arrests.

Needless to say this achievement, among others, duly impressed the top brass.

The kid was intelligent, effective, articulate, and good-looking. A perfect public relations poster-boy for them to parade in front of city legislators and community action groups when seeking law enforcement funding.

With his career rocketing, the elevated Homicide Detective Michael Flores had proved time and again he was worth the hype. However, where many in his department performed their job without fanfare, Flores sought the spotlight to promote himself. Leading some to hold the young detective in less esteem than their bosses; thereby dubbing him, *His-Royal-Pain-In-The-Ass*.

This of course, was not to his face.

Yet what had fueled his colleagues' ire most about Flores was his condescending habit of delegating assignments to coworkers at or above his own grade. Especially the department's female officers whenever, with an underlying chauvinistic tone, he tried assigning his clerical tasks.

For their part, the policewomen would have none of Flores' Neanderthal nonsense.

Not waiting for management or Human Resources to resolve the issue, the women took it upon themselves to admonish his caveman stupidity. Sternly schooling him in the ways of the twenty-first century anytime he was out of line; and sometimes, even when he was not. All proving a rude awakening to the overly-confident young detective from San Diego who was hell bent on quickly moving up the ranks.

If anything a quick learner, after some heavy-duty educating from every women in his unit, Michael Flores saw the light and abandoned his antiquated androcentric notions without sacrificing his masculinity, confidence, and drive.

That was, until he met Mrs. Esther Hausman earlier that morning.

Something about seeing the older woman lounging on her couch all snuggled under that cozy blanket had set him off. At the very least he had expected someone to be alert, even agitated, after making such a gruesome discovery. Instead, here was a senior citizen smiling ear-to-ear, calmly staring at the world around her. As if the horrific death and ensuing investigation were a television episode of Law & Order she was enjoying over a freshly brewed cappuccino.

That image, plus the surge of testosterone after assuming command of the investigation, had prompted Michael Flores to lapse into his old self with a vengeance. Abandoning professionalism and good manners, he once again became his parents' overly-indulged Miguelito.

Believing he had evolved into a better person than that, Flores now cringed at the thought of his despicable behavior. He had been unnecessarily rude to Esther Hausman for idiotic reasons; yet did so simply because he could.

Had the detective taken the time to learn underneath Esther's blanket was a swollen ankle the size of a grapefruit and the color of a ripened eggplant, he might have felt ashamed.

Had he also found out she had just sat down after tending to her many animals, and dragging her injured limb around her backyard to provide coffee and ice water to his investigators after not having slept for almost 24 hours, Michael Flores would have been… mortified.

***

Born in California, Michael Alejandro Eduardo Flores had always taken full advantage of being the baby of five children. While his doting father, mother, and brothers worked in their family-owned auto repair shop, his equally devoted sisters cleaned posh homes in several areas of the city.

Honest, hard-working people, Flores' ancestors had arrived in the Spanish Empire territory of what was to become San Diego long before Juan Rodríguez Cabrillo stepped foot on its soil in the year, 1542. An unimportant detail to those who made young Michael feel white skin was better than brown;

93

unless a car needed fixing, or a house needed cleaning. Fueling his anger year-after-year for those who treated him as a lesser person because his name was Flores and not Flowers.

Ironically, this did not stop him from treating the women in his family much the same. Following his father and brothers' beliefs that males should dominate females simply because they had a penis.

Living in such toxic confusion Michael decided to break away; joining the California Air National Guard while attending the San Diego Regional Law Enforcement Academy at Miramar College right after high school. Then, while working an entry-level law enforcement position in Newport Beach, he learned about an opportunity in the Tucson, Arizona Police Department.

Barely checking his rearview mirror, Officer Michael Flores kissed his family goodbye and headed east on Interstate Highway 8. Excited about his new life in the Sonoran Desert in a city rich in Hispanic heritage and possibilities.

***

It was days like today when Michael Flores wished he was back on a San Diego beach surfing. He would have even settled for quietly soaking in his two-bedroom apartment's bathtub with the latest issue of Sports Illustrated™ in one hand and a cold beer in the other. Unfortunately, neither was happening any time soon.

"Crazy," he uttered.

Thinking about the turbulent day while still waiting for the updated reports on the dead man. Recalling too, how his morning had begun so well with him masterfully resolving the Pima and Pinal counties jurisdiction mess. Then, his maneuver to place himself in charge of what his gut told him might be a high-profile investigation.

"Hell… You never know," he mused.

Making a notation to document his management skills in his next status report, and to make a copy for his personnel file. Still fuming at how he had allowed a senior citizen to get under his skin.

"That… old lady," he grumbled; shaking his head. "Guess she won't be providing any glowing testimonials."

Then, reevaluating his part in their prickly encounter, he asked himself.

"C'mon Flores… Was she really that terrible?"

Recalling his own brash manner while speaking to her. Knowing she had every right to be upset with him. Knowing too, he would have behaved much worse had someone browbeaten his mother, or his abuela.

"Got to hand it to you… You held your own," admiring the old gal's grit. "It's just… You were so obstinate… Every response… like pulling teeth."

Acknowledging he needed to be more tolerant of someone her age.

"I mean… How many old people would still be sharp after finding a half-eaten guy in their yard… in the middle of the night? By morning I'd be acting pretty senile too," he admitted with remorse.

"I am such an idiot," he said aloud.

"You got that right."

Shouted a female detective from across the room working at her desk.

Instead of zinging back a retort, Michael Flores ignored her comment and allowed his thoughts to turn to the arrival of the homeowner's attractive niece.

"Damn gutsy… Pushing passed the barrier. Protecting her tía loca," he smiled. Recalling the young woman's determination to aid her aunt.

Noticing the unmistakable grin on Flores' face was likened to the Cheshire Cat, the same female officer briefly stopped her work; wondering what the hell his Lordship was up to.

"Those full lips… Those hypnotic eyes… Don't put that in your report Flores," he thought, pursing his lips to avoid any further comments.

Trying to refocus on both the case and possible career advancements afterwards, the detective struggled in vain to divert his mind away from the lovely young woman's image. That was until Officer Pawlak dropped three new folders onto his desktop; right in front of him with a solid thud.

"Okay Flores… Here you go," said Pawlak matter-of-factly.

Michael Flores' charming smile quickly turned into his familiar scowl as he submerged himself into the updated information. Absent-mindedly grunting a thanks to the officer who had vacated the room long before the detective attempted his lackadaisical acknowledgement.

The fact was, veteran Officer Alvin Pawlak was just as eager for the new reports to arrive as was the detective so he could finally go home to his wife's special pot roast. That, along with some much-needed family time and his comfy La-Z-Boy® recliner, had occupied his mind and sore feet for the last two hours.

Flores, on the other hand, was recharged. Finally getting his mitts on tangible data he jumpstarted his investigation.

Upon opening the first file, he was elated to find the field investigators' extensive findings also contained impeccably organized evidence photographs. Within each photograph was an identifying plastic number cross-referenced to details about a specific object.

Also included was a large topography map of the Hausman property and beyond, pinpointing where each piece of evidence had been discovered in relationship to the deceased. Comparing the findings against the witness's transcript, Flores highlighted pertinent facts in yellow marker and jotted questions and comments in the margins. All which seemed to verify his earlier suspicions about the circumstances leading up to, and ultimately causing, the unidentified man's demise.

"Oval-shaped, Canis latrans… Coyote pawprints on the property and near the deceased… Explains the body mutilation," he assumed.

Deferring to Dr. Singh's autopsy findings for official confirmation.

"Also rounder, less symmetrical pawprints… Canis familiaris, domestic dog… That's a given," he conceded.

Having gotten a glimpse of the homeowner's large dog watching the activity through the patio sliding glass doors from inside the house. Yet, it was the information on the next page that began to excite Flores.

"Two distinct men's shoe imprints, 9-inch and 10 1/2-inch, found near the barn and beside the fence behind the body. The left 9-inch shoe tread matched the deceased's loafer; similarly his 9-inch footprints. None of the prints matched those belonging to Esther Hausman, Matilda Kaplan, Kyle Lucas, or Joseph Tadai," read Flores; highlighting data and adding notes.

"Well, buddy… Looks like your death was no accident," he declared.

Gratified the science had confirmed his theory.

"Mm this is new… Identical 33-inch Toyo tire tracks were found at three separate locations in a 3-mile radius of the Hausman property. Treads do not match vehicles belonging to residents or nearby neighbors."

"What does that prove? Tracks could've been there for days for any number of reasons," questioning the relevance.

Then he read the notes detailing the changing weather conditions during the 72-hour window before, during, and after the body was found.

"So, 72 hours before the body's discovered a cold front moves in bringing 2.4 inches of precipitation to the valley and snowfall on mountaintops down to 6,000-feet in elevation," he read with the tread impressions in mind. "About 12 hours prior to body discovery winds gust up to 11.5 miles per hour, subsiding around 2:00 a.m."

Deducing the tracks could only be made after it rained and the gusts lessened or else they would have muddied or blown away beyond identification. The detective figured since the impressions were well-defined, they most likely were created around the man's time of death and when the homeowner found him.

"So, the Toyo tire tracks were found on an Ocotillo Lane soft shoulder here, and another set off-road four miles into the brush. Ending abruptly here... A third further north, back onto Ocotillo."

Careful not to jump to conclusions since there was no definitive proof linking the occurrences.

Slowly stretching his aching muscles, Flores lazily considered the information through a long, drawn-out yawn.

"Circumstantial... Could've been hunters. A late-night hookup."

Closely examining the map and enlarged photograph showing the section of uprooted earth; the importance of what Flores read next solidified his theory.

"Type A positive and AB negative human blood were identified near the tire impressions and at locations in the brush; see map. Furthermore 10 1/2-inch, 9-inch left shoe and right foot, imprints matched those around the desert tread marks and the victim."

"Well, that settles it," he declared.

Taking a hard gulp of his abandoned cold coffee, with a look of disgust Flores quickly spit the vile black liquid back into his mug and rose from his well-worn squeaking chair. Intending on retrieving a fresh cup, he no sooner stood than Officer Pawlak's nightshift replacement handed him Dr. Warren Singh's long-awaited autopsy report. Absent-mindedly placing the cup back on his desk the homicide detective immediately sat back down; eagerly opening the fingerprint and dental files.

There it was. The man's identity, driver license photo, and miscellaneous public records. Distracted by his good fortune, Flores took another gulp of the foul coffee and grimaced; his desire for a fresh cup no longer taking precedence.

"Well, hello Peter… You're looking a sight better than you did the last time I saw you," he said sarcastically, then continued reading.

"Peter Anderson Cavenaugh, 45 years old. Married to Taylor Morris Cavenaugh, age 42. Resides Gilbert, Arizona… Retired Army… Says you work for Carpstra LLC… Who doesn't up there?" he commented, absorbing the information.

Studying the dead man's Arizona driver license photo, Flores looked closely into the man's eyes; somehow hoping they would tell him what happened.

"So Peter Anderson Cavenaugh, what the hell were you doing last night over 100 miles from home in middle of nowhere?" he asked the photograph.

Then, tossing the license onto his desk, Detective Flores turned to Dr. Singh's autopsy conclusions; anxious to get to the bottom of the doctor's findings. Tentatively leaning forward so as to not aggravate his stiffening lower back, Michael Flores spoke the three words in bold caps he had been waiting for, Cause of Death.

At the same time Flores was devouring the autopsy report, from other side of the room a tall, thin man in his early forties was studying the detective with great interest. Unable to hold back a mischievous chuckled, Detective Vernon Levi Rub quietly strolled across the room and sat on the edge the Michael Flores' desk.

With his concentration broken, Flores looked up and smiled as Rub took a substantial swallow from his cherished mug that sported the image of a man, a guitar, and the words, Bruce Springsteen and the E Street Band.

"Hey Mikey... What's so interesting?" asked Detective Rub candidly.

Flores hated being called Mikey. Even so, he let the irritating nickname slide because Vernon Rub was one of the few people he genuinely considered a good friend.

"Who'd you piss off to pull graveyard, Vern?" ribbed Flores.

"Well, you should know about pissing people off Mikey... Why are you keep'n me company?" retorted Rub light-heartedly.

Pulling a chair close to his desk, Flores gestured to his friend.

"Mind if I bounce a few things off of you?" he asked; genuinely interested.

"Shoot," joked Rub.

"Okay... Here's what I think so far," smirked Flores reacting to his friend's familiar dryness.

Then, turning the conversation serious, Michael Flores repositioned the large aerial photograph and map so they both could view it.

"There's evidence a medium SUV, or pickup drove off-road and stopped at this isolated spot late last night. I have reason to believe that this vehicle and my investigation involving a man's suspicious death are related. See these terrain gouges... To me, it looks like the vehicle went out of control here," explained Flores, showing Rub the terrain photo.

"It's here I believe two men exited the vehicle… My dead guy, Peter Cavenaugh… and an unknown. There's no indication more individuals were involved but, it's still speculative," said the exhausted Flores. Pausing to let his scenario sink in.

Studying the topography map and photos Rub nodded; urging his friend to continue.

"Okay… I believe Cavenaugh's struggles with, uh… let's call him X for now… outside the vehicle… Cavenaugh gets free and runs in this direction. X catches him here, and probably here," he stated; pointing to the map. "Each time he gets loose."

"And you know this how?" probed Rub, enjoying watching Flores' keen analytical mind at work.

"The field guys found traces of human blood and broken vegetation beside the vehicle and at these other two sites… Also, Dr. Singh found abrasions on Cavenaugh's knuckles, and types A positive and AB negative human blood on his clothing. Oh, A positive… it's Cavenaugh's," affirmed Flores, pointing to the autopsy paragraph.

"So, you're thinking," encouraging Flores to elaborate.

"I'm thinking, it's dark… Visibility's shitty… Cavenaugh's running from X and finds the Hausman place by accident. The guy makes a beeline for the house hoping to get help, steal a car, maybe a gun… He's winging it."

Adding next.

"Right… He climbs the backyard fence, here… Maybe he thinks it's the fastest path to the house. Who knows? He loses his footing. Gets his bare foot stuck between the rungs… I imagine it's pretty cut up and swollen by now from all that jagged terrain. Anyway… His foot slips through the opening and…,"

Stopping to hand Detective Rub photographs of Cavenaugh entangled in the wrought iron fence.

"Gggeeeezzz Louise!" cried Rub, seeing the mutilated body for the first time.

His outcry so loud two sleep-deprived officers flinched simultaneously, then looked around for the cause of the disturbance.

"Yeah, I know... Look at his body, Vern... This guy's trying like hell to unwedge a stuck foot... Like... like he's fighting for his life."

Pointing to the arm and leg remains thrust between the different rail openings.

"It's here I believe X catches Cavenaugh, and kills him," he concluded.

"What about the people in the house? They didn't hear anything?" asked Rub.

"You'd think... But Singh found two distinct lethal wounds, slashes really. Both were made from the same sharp blade about 18-millimeters, like a utility or Swiss Army knife," answered Flores handing his friend the autopsy report.

"And no weapon was recovered on the premises," assumed Detective Rub.

"None."

Then Michael Flores read a paragraph aloud so they could discuss it.

"Singh specified the first cut was a .635-centimeter razor thin laceration across Cavenaugh's arytenoid cartilages and vocal folds... The second's a .859 centimeters laceration... same weapon... severing Cavenaugh's right femoral artery and deep femoral vein."

Both detectives certain that although the first wound was fatal, combining it with the second had caused the victim to bleed out that much faster.

"Poor shmuck never had a chance," added Rub.

Reading two mortal knife wounds were inflicted by a person unknown officially designating Peter Cavenaugh's cause of death, murder.

"Yeah… Pretty sure X came up behind Cavenaugh, placed his hand over the guy's mouth so he couldn't scream and cut his vocal cords. Scream… Hell… Cavenaugh could barely breath," surmised Detective Flores, adding. "X knows the guy's done, yet he goes ahead and severs the trapped leg's femoral artery for good measure."

"It's obvious X knew where to cut. Maybe he's medically trained. Maybe he's military, an experienced hitman," offered Rub, listing several possibilities.

"Agreed. But this is weird… After X kills Cavenaugh, for some strange reason there's evidence he hangs around the property. Why? A fetish for watching wild animals tear into fresh meat?" asked Flores sarcastically.

Showing Rub the page identifying coyote fur and saliva found on several areas on Peter Cavenaugh's body.

A long, low whistle escaped Vernon Rub's lips as he read the information and leafed through numerous crime scene photos showing the damage the coyotes inflicted on Peter Cavenaugh's corpse. Then, a photo caught his attention.

"What are these?" Rub asked Flores; closely examining foreign particles embedded in the back of dead man's skull.

"Those… The report states they're pieces of… shrapnel. Uh, wait… Cavenaugh's military discharge papers… Here… He was regular Army. Could be he saw some action," offered Flores.

However before Flores could divulge Cavenaugh's military file further, Vernon Rub commented.

"It's pretty obvious X's plan went south. Too bad Cavenaugh had that fence mishap. He was this close to getting away. Well, wherever you are Peter Cavenaugh, I hope you're reunited with your hand and foot," he joked; trying to lighten the mood.

"You know, this shows X premeditatedly picked an isolated spot to kill Cavenaugh… But after Cavenaugh's runs, he's forced to do so in Esther Hausman's yard; conscious he could be seen," conjectured Michael Flores.

It was then Vernon Rub offered his friend something else to consider.

"Mikey, it is possible your victim died too far from the house for the residents to hear… After all it was some time before the homeowner found the body… But what if the dog heard? What that's why the dog insisted on going out? The timeline might be closer than you think. If so, your Mrs. Hausman really dodged a bullet… Had she'd gone outside sooner, she might have… Well, I don't figure your Mr. X as the kind who leaves messes," suggested Rub.

The hairs on Michael Flores' neck rose as Vernon Rub's words sunk in.

Quickly placing the reports side-by-side on his desk, the detective opened each document to a specific page and compared the highlighted texts and margin notes with Esther Hausman's statement.

"Vern, I gotta check something," requested Michael Flores mysteriously.

With his face drained of color, Flores grabbed his coat and dashed out of the room; leaving behind an extremely puzzled Vernon Rub.

Surprised by his friend's sudden departure, Detective Rub looked down at the reports. Flipping back and forth, reading each notation out loud until the significance of one crucial detail jumped out at him.

Of the two sets of unidentified shoe imprints found that morning at the scene, the men's 9-inch shoe had since been identified as belonging to Peter Cavenaugh. The second set, 10 1/2-inch men's shoe prints, suspected belonging to the victim's killer, was found near the barn, around Cavenaugh's body, and,… inside the orchard.

Racing down the dark unfamiliar country roads, Detective Michael Flores chewed himself out for not giving credence to what Esther Hausman had told him earlier that day. Now, the older woman's words screamed in his head.

"I can't explain… but, I swear something in the grove was watching me."

"Not something… someone," he thought with dread.

"The killer had remained on the property afterwards. What for? Hid in the orchard for some time… Esther Hausman had said she heard coyotes. It's obvious they had already eaten their fill on the victim. Why stay longer? Because Esther Hausman had come outside and headed almost straight to the body. As if she knew what had happened."

Still several miles from the Hausman estate, Michael Flores took a turn a little too sharply. Cursing the fact the woman lived so far away.

"That's what he's thinking… He doesn't know her leaving her house when she did and finding Peter Cavenaugh was a coincidence. That she was just trying to retrieve her dog. That she accidently stumbled onto the murder victim," grimaced Flores; trying to get inside the killer's head.

"He believes she saw him, saw everything… Witnessed the kill… That she can identify him."

"He could still be there. Watching. Deciding his next move… That is, unless… Unless Esther Hausman's already dead."

Chapter 7

"Everybody has got to die, but I have always believed an exception would be made in my case."

~ *William S. Burroughs*

As sun set, Esther Hausman, Mattie Kaplan, and Kyle Lucas dragged themselves onto the chairs around their alder, southwest-styled kitchen table. Taking great care, Esther gradually elevated her enormously swollen ankle onto an unoccupied padded seat; then, gingerly slumped against her own chair's backrest. Clasping her hands atop her midriff, she slowly closed her heavy eyelids and gave out a sigh of relief.

Likewise in one fell swoop, Mattie sprawled her upper body onto the beautiful wooden tabletop and, using an outstretched arm as a pillow, snuggled her heavy head atop her dirt-embedded skin. Staring at nothing in particular, just grateful for the chance to rest.

Across from Mattie, a barely conscious Kyle Lucas sat with his elbows fixed atop the table and his sleepy head cradled within his cupped, callus-worn palms. Certain his heavy noggin could no longer remain upright without assistance; periodically he jerked awake only when required to participate in the conversation.

Content to sit and vegetate neither felt the need to look at the other. Each vowing that nothing short of divine intervention could, or would force them to move from their seat. At some point though, Mattie began speculating about the dead man Esther had found in their backyard less than eighteen hours earlier. The conversation centering mostly around the authorities insane reasons for not officially ruling the man's death a homicide immediately. Because from what they saw, all three wholeheartedly agreed the stranger's death was definitely no accident.

Coincidently, that seemed to be the consensus reached by traditional and social media outlets; as every few minutes stations would interrupt a regularly scheduled program with an annoying, unnecessary, Special Newsbreak banner.

News anchors glued to their studio desks along with field reporters, spewed self-serving renditions about how they exclusively uncovered the story of a gruesome dead body found at a rural Tucson home. As if their news organization alone had just exposed something of relevance which no one else knew. Playing and replaying the same, monotonous B-roll footage in slow-motion of Dr. Singh appearing in the window of the ambulance driving away from the Hausman property and down the narrow country road.

When in fact, it had been shortly after the police's arrival that morning that reporters and cameramen first appeared. Each scurrying to unload their field equipment in hopes of recording the morbid scene. Or, at the very least, obtaining an interview with the person who discovered the body. All ending up utterly disappointed and frustrated by their thwarted attempts to peek, or trespass onto the property.

One reason for their failure was due to the abnormally high, red-brick privacy wall and numerous mature trees and shrubs beyond the wall which hindered nosy intruders from glimpsing Esther's flat-roof, Pueblo-styled adobe home. Not to mention a quite large wagon-wheel solid gate which further obscured spying from the road and barred unauthorized access to the driveway.

Of course, there was nothing to stop anyone from using a drone. But, since no one appeared to have had one, the only thing of interest their cameras could capture was the coroner's ambulance departing the scene.

However if indeed they had had one, they would have seen the lovely sandy-brown stucco home accented with dark-walnut beams and shutters. Maybe too, its beautifully blended natural terrain, classic southwest copper artwork and original one-of-a-kind sculptures. Each strategically placed throughout the grounds; creating hidden treasures among reading nooks, edible gardens, aquascape ponds, and stone paths.

All of which transformed Esther Hausman's modest residence from a prosaic tract home into a tranquil refuge, or at least it had been. If only the reporters had known the corpse left the premises in the ambulance with Dr. Singh they might have gone too, instead of sticking around as long as they had.

To avoid the chaos, Esther and Mattie had fled inside their home. Locking the heavy Spanish-styled double front doors and closing their interior off-white plantation shutters. Yet, it was not until after taking the telephone receivers off the hooks of their vintage landline phones and turning off their cellphones that both woman felt they had escaped the outside world.

By late afternoon the news outlet field units had had enough and packed up their gear. They, and their high-tech mobile vans, departing as quickly as they came. Chasing yet another breaking news story across town.

After sneaking onto the property to help Kyle tend to animals and essential chores, their friend and neighbor Joseph Tadai promised to return the next day with his sons and again lend a hand. Stealthily slipping across the open fields where their properties joined, Tadai was careful not to let anyone see how he gained access to the now famous backyard.

Several hours later, Officer Harvey Nolan of field operations authorized the release of the site from police custody; announcing no further evidence had been discovered. And, since the residents refused to relocate or leave their livestock penned any longer, there seemed little point in continuing to hold the place hostage.

That, plus a new weather report had just come in about a second front now moving in bringing another round 35-miles per hour high wind gusts. Admitting it would be a miracle to sustain the integrity of the crime scene under such conditions, Officer Nolan instructed all field investigators to pack up and leave. After which, he performed one final walk through, then vacated the estate just as the hazardous bio cleanup team turned onto the driveway.

Fascinated, the two women watched from inside their home as the cleanup crew immediately got to work expertly scrubbing, sanitizing, and removing anything which did not belong. They even fixed the nasty backyard divot after Esther admitted to a bio crew member it was how she had injured her foot.

By dusk, plastic numbers, latex gloves, yellow crime scene tape, and more importantly all traces of blood, bodily fluids and body parts had been removed. Guaranteeing Esther and her dog would find no surprises anywhere on her property, including the deceased's missing foot. Then, the team returned Esther's home to her in most of its previous glory.

The exception being the rosemary hedge which had not fared well after the morning investigation efforts and recent disinfecting and scrutinization by the hazardous bio team after human blood was found on it. It would take a long time before its evergreen needlelike leaves and sturdy branches would recover, if ever; now sadly appearing completely downtrodden.

When at long last the hazardous bio team did depart, only two crime scene security officers remained. It had been their job to deter anyone from sneaking onto the property and disturbing the scene. Before they too left, one officer cautioned the three residents to stay vigilant and immediately call 911 from behind locked doors should anything unusual arise.

So there they sat, around the kitchen table; finally alone, barely able to keep their eyes open. Too tired to move, even though famished. Discussing what to make for dinner, with no one in particular interested in getting up to cook.

***

It was, in fact, their dear friend, Joseph Tadai, who talked Officer Nolan into releasing the crime scene that same day; and, who got the hazardous bio cleanup company to remove and disinfect the property before dark.

It was also Joseph Tadai, and his wife, Emily, who in the late 1990's had reluctantly sold a parcel of their land to Phoenix city folks, Max and Esther Hausman. During that time real estate and crop prices had been on a dramatic downslide. The Tadais, like many of the nation's family ranchers, farmers, and homeowners were drowning in debt, upside-down mortgages, and lost revenue. Nevertheless their taxes, as always, continued to rise.

With little choice, the Tadais decided to sell their farthest unused parcel so as not to lose their entire ancestral home. A ranch which had belonged in the Tadai family since before the American Civil War's westernmost battle was fought on Arizona's Picacho Peak on April 15, 1862 between the Confederacy and the California Union Calvary.

It was Joseph's great, great, grandfather, Simon Forbes, heir to a San Francisco fortune, who had chosen the call of the untamed west and a commission in the California Calvary over his family's business. After his deployment to the southern Arizona Territory near what would become Tucson, Forbes fell in love and married a young woman from a local Tohono O'odham Nation clan.

Purchasing close to 2,950 acres near the Santa Catalina Mountain northern foothills, Forbes vowed to his wife they would remain near her family. Soon after, he changed his surname to Tadai, which translates in English to roadrunner; because, that was the first native creature to cross his path on his new land in his new life.

Together they, and their future generations, established a thriving cattle ranch while also growing some of the nation's finest cotton and red durum wheat. Hit hard during World War II, The Great Depression, droughts, and plummeting markets, the ranch suffered greatly; acreage had to be sold to cover expenses. However, even though smaller in size, the ranch remained a solid enterprise in comparison to many other family-owned spreads which eventually collapsed.

In fact, under Joseph Tadai's stewardship real progress had been made towards returning the place into a financially-sound working ranch. Then in 1987, the stock market crash led to the 1990's economic recession. With little options the Tadais found they had to sell their northern 68 acres. Filled with remorse for having failed their ancestors, denying their children their rightful heritage, Joseph and Emily's bitterness spilled onto the new owners.

Their children, Sammy, Matthew, and Nina, took their misdirected cues from their parents; acting out whenever Esther and Max visited their new property. That was until a prank went terribly wrong and Esther ended up in the hospital, bringing all hostilities to an immediate halt. Still even then the kind, elderly new owners were merely tolerated.

Then news came of the husband's death before the couple's new place could be completed. For months after, the Tadais watched the widow's tireless efforts to fulfill her husband's dream. Their hearts softening with the knowledge of the couple's love and plans for their former land; resentment and guilt were ultimately replaced with pride, and eventually, love.

Knowing their new neighbor would never ask for help, the Tadais made a family pact to simply show up during certain times with the proper tools and equipment. Like whenever her grazing fields needed planting, or sweet grass needed baling. In turn, they often found bushels overflowing with fresh fruits, vegetables, and jars of homemade preserves on their doorstep from her orchard and gardens.

Then somewhere along the way all the silliness disappeared and in its place, a deep friendship. Esther eventually considering the Tadais mishpucha, her family; and they, lovingly calling her si:s, older sister.

***

The kitchen telephone ring seemed unusually loud, startling the comatose-like threesome from their stupor. Simultaneously groaning, the repeated "bbbrriinngg" from the antiquated phone grated on their collective last nerves as it shattered their cherished quiet.

Acknowledging the intrusive device with contempt, it was Kyle who noticed the caller ID on the ancient answering machine. Lethargically rising, he activated the phone's speaker so all could hear as the person on the other end cleared his throat.

"Hello... This is Michael Flores. Uh... Detective Michael Flores from this morning... Sorry, I know it's late. But, I really need to ask Mrs. Hausman a few questions. Is she available?" he asked politely, anticipating a cold reception.

Knowing his excuse sounded lame, he had to know if the older woman was there; still alive. And, at that particular moment, he did not care about coming up with a better reason.

A long pause of silence ensued as he waited patiently for a response.

"It's really important," he insisted; worried something had happened.

Another long pause followed.

"Uh, I'm here... At the gate. Is there some sort of code I need to enter... Sorry, I didn't hear what you said," he added, determined to gain access.

Although Esther's heart was still pounding in her chest from the abrupt rings, she comically crossed her eyes at her two companions and pursed her lips in an attempt to inject a bit of levity into the room.

Then, motioning to Kyle to hand her the telephone, Esther graciously conceded and spoke directly into the receiver.

"We're just getting ready to eat a light dinner, Detective. You hungry?"

A few minutes later, a relieved Michael Flores found himself seated at their kitchen table making small talk with Esther Hausman, Kyle Lucas, and the captivating Mattie Kaplan. Contently watching the gentle borzoi sprawled on the living room couch, happily munch one of many homemade biscuits available to her whenever she requested.

Before long, a large bowl of steaming heirloom tomato cream soup garnished with a fresh sprig of leafy-green basil was placed before him. Plated alongside the rich bisque, a decadent grilled cheese sandwich with sautéed onions, thinly sliced sweet cherry tomatoes, and ripe avocado stuffed between the layers of melted Gouda and sharp cheddar on two slices of lightly toasted, golden homemade challah.

Slowly raising a tablespoon of the steamy broth to his lips, Flores took a small sip. The delicious rich base caressed his dry throat as a rush of well-being surged throughout his body. Releasing a quiet sigh, it was the first time all day he had been allowed to relax.

As dinner carried on Flores was surprised at how easily he could talk with the three; not at all like his earlier confrontation. Meanwhile, he glanced around their cozy home decorated with stylish, comfortable furniture, family photos and religious artifacts. One particularly beautiful pair of candlesticks prominently displayed on the credenza caught his eye. When asked about them, Esther told him they were crafted by a relative who was a silversmith a couple of generations earlier in her mother's hometown of Vilnius, Lithuania. Her mother had reclaimed them after World War II and given them to her upon her wedding to her husband, Max.

"And one day… Maybe on your wedding day, Mattalah… They'll be yours," added Esther lovingly, patting her niece's arm.

Mattie's creamy cheeks tinted a pale pink as a look of shock appeared on her lovely face. Feeling vulnerable, the niece immediately avoided eye contact with the others; opting instead to pretend she had found something interesting in her soup. Grateful when her long auburn bangs fell into her eyes, partially covering her embarrassment.

Flores, noticing the young woman's adorable reaction made her even more appealing to him. Even though he was hard pressed to find Mattie Kaplan more irresistible than she had been during their first, feisty encounter.

Conscious of her uneasiness, the detective changed his broad, knowing grin into a small, pleasant smile. Wishing he could tell her he too had been put through similar awkward situations in his own family.

Instead, he gently guided the conversation away from Mattie's love life. Asking Esther about Tashia and listening to her amusing history about borzois and the sighthound mentality. Not to mention her charming stories about people mistaking the borzoi for a longhaired greyhound. Observing too, the fondness the two women had for Kyle Lucas; and unexpectantly, feeling small pangs homesickness.

Eventually though, Detective Flores found the opportunity to ask about the discovery of last night's unexpected guest.

"Mrs. Hausman," began Flores hesitantly.

"Michael… You're sitting at my table… sharing a meal. Don't you think we've gone a little beyond you calling me Mrs. Hausman? Call me Esther," she requested, encouraging him to be less formal.

Clearly worn out by the day, barely able to keep her eyes open, Esther smiled at the handsome young lawman and nodded for him to continue.

Feeling uneasy about breaking his unwritten rule of maintaining a professional distance between him and those directly involved in a case, Flores gave in and granted her request out of respect.

"Esther, I need to ask… Has anyone other than Kyle, Mattie, and Joseph Tadai been on your property this past week? Anyone… Say a friend, handyman, someone working in the barn, or maybe the orchard?" he inquired matter-of-factly.

Trying to downplay his question so as not to raise undo alarm. Knowing full-well in Esther's official statement she noted she had feelings of being watched.

"You mean outside of the dead guy?" she responded.

Her tone sounding a bit harsher than intended.

"Sorry. You haven't seen me at my best today," Esther said apologetically.

"That's okay… Me neither," he replied softly; regretting his earlier behavior.

Tashia then demandingly nudged Esther's arm with her long slender snout. After stroking the borzoi's long elegant neck, Esther rose from her chair and hobbled to a counter and a large ceramic canister decorated with dog bones. After handing Tashia one of her favorite tidbits, the bright-eyed hound gracefully trotted to the living room couch and settled down.

It was the first time Michael Flores noticed the enormous elastic bandage wrapped around Esther's swollen ankle; now twice the size of her other foot. Noticing too the unused walking stick leaning against Esther's chair, which she had intentionally forgotten to use. As Esther silently limped back to the table, Flores got the impression she wanted neither to be pitied or helped; regardless of her obvious pain.

"That happened last night?" he inquired casually, not risking another confrontation.

Understanding now what should have been obvious to him earlier.

Carefully taking her seat Esther sheepishly nodded yes; embarrassed to go into the whole story about tripping on the damn hole in the grass and falling flat on her face. Then, after a small reconciliation smile exchanged between the two, neither said another word about it.

"Fayleen Lambert... She and Dora Crewe board their horses here. They came out a couple of times this week. Probably Joseph's kids. They come over and ride whenever they want. It's fine... They come. They go. Ask Joseph, or Emily," she affirmed.

"How about the orchard. Anyone there recently?" he asked coolly.

Leaving out the fact shoe prints found there probably belonged to the man who murdered Peter Cavenaugh.

"No... No one. There's no reason. It's too early in the growing season. Say Michael, what's this all about?" she inquired suspiciously.

"I'm just clearing up a few things... for my report. Hey listen... I got what I need for now. Thanks for the great dinner. I should let you all get some much-needed rest," concluded Flores, pushing away from the table.

Placing dishes in the sink Michael Flores turned to Esther, pensively asking.

"Mrs.... Esther... I'd like a couple of my people to hang out here for a few days. Do a little more poking. That okay with you? They'll stay out of your way," he promised with that engaging smile of his.

Clearly not buying the detective's visit or his request as routine, Esther sweetly nodded her permission; allowing him to keep his secret a little while longer before calling him on it.

"Sure kid, whatever you want," she replied amiably.

Then, stifling a yawn, Esther added a request of her own. "Okay folks, I've had it... Mattie, Kyle... Be good hosts and show Michael out."

Noticing the detective's all too familiar discreet glance at her niece, Esther chuckled to herself. Wondering if she should warn him, or let him discover the bumpy ride he was headed for.

Slowly rising, Esther decided what was best for herself was to keep quiet.

"Night Michael... Careful going back. You just never know what'll jump onto the road from the brush," she called out walking toward her bedroom.

Limping badly, Esther leaned heavily upon the walking stick for balance as she made her way down the long hallway with Tashia close behind her. Then, with a final backwards wave to the three younger people, she and Tashia disappeared behind her closing bedroom door.

"Detective... Let me show you out," Mattie offered with a friendly gesture.

Having clearly recovered from her earlier humiliation.

"Actually, I'd like to speak to you both. Uh... Outside?" requested Flores.

His politeness not hiding the obvious insistence of his voice.

A few minutes later, Mattie and Kyle stood in awkward silence beside Flores' black SUV waiting for the detective to disclose the true nature of his visit.

"Look... The real reason I came out here," he began.

Trying his best not to alarm them, yet finding no easy way; Flores briefly paused before beginning again in a calm voice.

"Our field investigators found several suspicious men's shoeprints around your property," he relayed somberly. His eyes meeting Mattie's questioning gaze.

Then the detective elaborated.

"One set, 9-inch shoe and same sized foot imprints, we determined belonged to the victim. The other, men's 10 1/2-inch shoe imprints, were found similarly to the deceased's with one exception... Your orchard."

Flores' implications were not lost on the young veterinarian student as a look of dread immediately appeared on his face.

"So, he was murdered… We all thought so, didn't we Mattie?" exclaimed Kyle.

His excited voice growing a bit louder and higher as he spoke.

Now understanding Flores' implications, a look of horror appeared on Mattie's lovely face.

"The killer was… in the orchard watching her? That's why you're here… The killer believes Tante can identify him… because he also believes she saw him… What? Commit murder? I'm right, aren't I?" demanded Mattie with the same tenacity she exhibited earlier.

"My suspicion is… Probably," the homicide detective replied soberly. "I do think extra precautions are warranted for your aunt's safety."

"Are we all in danger?" inquired Kyle, alarmed.

Lowering his voice to a whisper as he searched the darkness.

"You and Mattie? No. You weren't home; so, he has no knowledge of your existence. There is proof he was in the orchard. Was he watching Esther? Does he suspect she witnessed him… killing…? I don't know for sure. In any event, it's a moot point since the guy's most likely long gone. I'm just taking precautions… In case," responded Flores, his voice trailing off before adding.

"So, tomorrow I'm placing Esther into witness protection… For a few days… Until I know more."

Finding his plan was not having the support he expected, Flores elaborated.

"Meantime, tonight I'm posting uniformed officers. We'll leave early in the morning for a Phoenix safe house where a 24-hour protection team is already in place. I've got an undercover detective who'll move in here and act as your new ranch hand… He'll feed Tashia and the other animals while helping me with the investigation. Our hope is to quickly identify the perpetrator and make a swift arrest… Until then, if anyone asks… you all took a much-needed vacation," expounded Flores.

Desiring to initiate protection protocols as soon as possible.

"Not me," adamantly protested Kyle Lucas. "I can't miss school."

"Stay on campus… I'll have a plainclothes officer assigned to you until I know it's safe," affirmed Flores offering a workable solution.

"I agree my aunt needs protection; however," interrupted Mattie, seeing the flaw in the detective's plan.

"Look… My aunt's not stupid," cautioned Mattie. "You need to be straight with her, or she won't budge."

"Right… Don't try to manipulate her, or sugar coat things," asserted Kyle.

"Agreed," Mattie seconded.

Recalling the many times in her life growing up when she unsuccessful tried to outwit her aunt.

"Wait… Esther will never leave Tashia, or the horses. Especially to some stranger who won't care for them the way she insists… You know I'm right."

Stated Kyle, looking first to Mattie then to Flores.

"Detective, your guy better be able to protect me cause… I can't believe I'm saying this… I'm staying," declared Kyle. Wishing he could immediately take it back. "Anyway, she'll never go unless… you dangle the right carrot."

As Mattie's hypnotic eyes met Flores', she offered him the perfect solution.

"I can get Tante to go to your safe house; but, you have to agree on a couple stipulations," proclaimed Mattie.

Pretty certain the detective was not going to like what he was about to hear.

"Okay… Let's have it," Flores said hesitantly.

"Tashia… Tante takes Tashia with her," asserted Mattie firmly.

Certain he did not like this first condition; Flores was positive he was going to hate the second.

"And," said the detective; waiting for the other shoe to drop.

"You let her go to a Diamondbacks spring training baseball game," timidly suggested Mattie with a sheepish grin.

"What! Are you crazy?" vented Flores a little too loudly at the bizarre proposal. "No… Absolutely not."

"Look… You said yourself the killer could come back. Since I'm not leaving my aunt and she'll refuse to leave her home, can you promise your cowboy cop can keep us safe if we stay," retorted Mattie. "I'm giving you your best chance of getting her to cooperate."

"Detective Vernon Rub… His name," interjected Flores, grasping for ideas better than this one.

Then Kyle Lucas piped in with his own endorsement for Mattie's idea.

"Rub… Really? Okay, your Detective Vernon Rub can snoop and protect to his heart's… or rather our hearts' content. But if you're really serious about getting Esther into a safe house… and, not risk her sneaking back home… You need a kick-ass incentive," swore Kyle, agreeing with Mattie.

"Guys… It's imperative Esther go into witness protection, or else I can't guarantee her safety. As for the dog coming… Sorry, she has to stay here. It opens up too many safety issues. Mattie, you have to be Esther's voice of reason. Convince her," demanded the homicide detective. "Kyle if you're staying, you stick to Detective Rub like glue. Got it."

"What about the game?" she argued. "Do we have a deal?"

"Shit! I've got two papers due next week. Tashia… the horses… You're sure that guy was murdered?" ranted Kyle. "What the hell was I thinking."

Realizing the situation he had placed himself in; not to mention the good possibility of flunking out of veterinarian school.

"I'm sure Detective Rub will be happy to help out. He loves nature… and all that outdoor stuff. Besides, helping you makes his cover more believable," said Flores; trying to calm the student's anxieties.

Discounting the big lie he just told, and knowing Rub did not know a cow from a bull, Flores figured after this case he would owe his friend big time. Then, suddenly he recalled his initial introduction to Esther that morning; and that she had been having a hard time concentrating on his questions.

"Why? Because she had been listening to a baseball game on the radio," he said to himself.

Now it made sense.

"One game… Only if the brass approves. But, and this is a big but… If they do approve it, you both must obey the officers on your security detail without hesitation, without question. Can you do that, Mattie? Can Esther?"

Demanded Flores sternly with great apprehension.

"Detective Flores… My aunt will agree to almost anything if you say the magic word." Mattie replied with confidence.

"Baseball."

Snuggled inside her bed, Esther Hausman drifted off into peaceful slumber. Not buying Detective Michael Flores' excuse of a routine nighttime visit, she was certain whatever secret plans were being concocted in her honor could wait until morning.

Meanwhile outside, the other three were unaware of the danger looming nearby. Well hidden within the dense orchard adjacent to Esther Hausman's house, a shadowy figure was perched high on a sturdy limb. From there, the observer watched the three silhouettes conversing in the front yard; disappointed the woman was not his intended target.

Studying the group it soon became apparent the man in the suit leaning against the SUV was a cop. Unable to hear what was being said, or see faces clearly in the night; the observer surmised he was a key topic in their conversation.

Anxious to know what they were talking about; he was about to move in closer when two police cars pulled into the driveway and parked in front of the house. Shortly after, four uniformed officers emerged from the vehicles and approached the suit.

"I thought so," acknowledging the suited silhouette was the cop in charge.

Straining to see the suit's face with only a dim porch light for illumination, the observer disappointedly watched as the cop got into his SUV and drove away. Leaving one police officer to escort the remaining two silhouettes into the house, and the others to return to their police cars for a night's vigilance.

Now he knew for sure.

"She saw," he uttered under his breath. "Why else the protection?"

"I could snuff you all out right now. Still, that would be messy," he considered.

Then again, he had never minded messy.

Yet, if the other night taught him anything, it taught him not to rush a plan.

"Should've taken her out last night," he lamented. "Never mind… just work the problem."

Certain no one could connect him with Pac Man, or the old woman.

"One thing's for damn sure… They can't protect her forever."

122

Hunkered down inside the orchard the onlooker made himself comfortable for the long night; confident no one was going anywhere until morning. Then, he would have the chance to familiarize himself with faces and routines. And, if the opportunity presented itself, he could take out the old woman and be done with it.

Shoving the gun in his pocket he leaned against the trunk thinking through his next move; certain of having another chance. Figuring if not tomorrow then the next day, or the next. Figuring too, it was time to return home, go about his business, and bide his time. Then, at his own choosing, squash the old woman like a pesky bug.

Chapter 8

"You Can Observe A Lot By Just Watching."

~ *Yogi Berra*

"Chill Flores… Mrs. Hausman, Mattie, and I have been joined at the hip since we arrived. We even flocked to the ladies room together like a bunch of peahens," professed Officer Mitzy Burton confidently into her cellphone.

As she spoke, the plainclothes officer narrowly avoided colliding with a frazzled looking mother ignoring her two out-of-control young children in the overcrowded ladies room. Steadfast in front of the wall-length mirror above a row of white, ceramic sinks, Burton stood her ground as she touched up her creamy mahogany makeup and reapplied her deep violet lipstick.

When Homicide Detective Michael Flores informed her that she and her security detail were going to the Salt River Fields at Talking Stick baseball stadium on the Salt River Pima-Maricopa Indian Community near Scottsdale, she had her suspicions. When she learned the real reason they were going was to protect his witness in a murder investigation and her niece who were promised the outing, she was furious.

At first she thought Flores was kidding; after all, she knew he could be an asshole. But then she learned his witness needed extra precautions because said murderer might make an attempt on her life, even in public.

"No way… That idiot's clearly out of his mind," she exploded at her boss.

Adamantly opposing the entire outing, Officer Burton was ready to turn in her badge; then turn Michael Flores into mincemeat. However now two-thirds into the game, Burton had to admit the relaxing afternoon in the sun had been a pleasant distraction for everyone concerned. And, with no incident yet to report, she was determined to keep it that way.

"You left them alone?" vehemently protested Flores, hearing the officer was not in direct eye contact with her charges.

"No Detective, I did not leave them alone. Well… not completely," Burton said nonchalantly, cutting off Flores' gripe in mid-sentence.

"I'm waiting for them beside their stalls. Look Detective Flores. It's not like we can all sashay up side-by-side to a urinal. They're fine," she reassured him.

"You guys fine in there?" directing her question to Esther and Mattie's partially exposed shoes below their doors.

"No, we're not fine," retorted Esther unhappily. "We're losing five to two in the bottom of the fifth."

Outside the bathroom, the crowd cheered as the announcer excitedly described the play action.

"Make that five to three," added Esther elated.

"Look… Game's almost over. Then it's straight back to sanctuary," confirmed Officer Burton, hoping her words would have calming effect.

"Well, watch your six Burton… Other than the fact that our killer wears a size 10 1/2 size shoe and has type AB positive blood… I've got absolutely no idea what he looks like… Or, what he's capable of. The faster the women are tucked in, the better I'll like it," responded Flores uneasily.

Still angry with himself for giving in to Mattie's cockamamie scheme of using a ballgame to get Esther to agree to witness protection. He had only done so, because it had proved the only thing that worked.

"I should've put my foot down. After all it's her neck we're trying to save; not to mention my career," he thought miffed at his decision. "I mean, it's not like I don't have a murder to solve and a cold-blooded killer to catch."

"I must've been nuts to agree to this," he muttered unintentionally.

Then, realizing he had spoken out loud, Flores cringed with embarrassment.

"Copy that Detective," laughed the officer. "Call you later Flores."

In the five years Officer Mitzy Burton had known Detective Michael Flores, she had never seen him this concerned, or, go out of his way to accommodate anyone; regardless of how brutal the case. Stone cold, aloof, and by the book, Flores detachedly solved his cases as means to further his career and nothing more; and everyone knew it.

"How'd these women pierce that armor of his?" wondered Burton, shadowing the two back to their seats.

Retaking her position on the aisle of Section 114, a few rows directly behind Esther and Mattie, Officer Burton had poised herself to better survey the crowd and, if necessary, act appropriately. Six of her plainclothes colleagues, members of her specialized protection team, too had stealthily escorted the women during their trek to and from the bathroom and were now back at their inconspicuous stations.

"Geez... Bottom of the sixth. Shit... Could this game go any slower?" she groaned into her hidden lapel microphone inside her jersey.

Squirming in her seat, Burton checked the crowd for suspicious activity; eager as hell to return the women to the safe house where she had more control of the situation.

Here... they were sitting ducks.

Scanning the rows in front of her, Mitzy smiled as determined Esther Hausman traversed the stairs back to her seat with her niece trailing behind her. Limping badly, the older woman had stuffed her thick, elastic-bandaged swollen right foot into an oversize men's work shoe. Her other foot, sporting a stylish neon green and pink athletic sneaker accented with deep purple laces.

The odd footwear combination seeming perfectly suitable for the independent Mrs. Hausman.

In the short time Officer Mitzy Burton had been assigned to Esther and her niece, Mattie, she had taken an instant liking to them both.

"One tough old gal," she uttered softly gazing at Esther.

Considering it had been less than 72-hours since Esther Hausman suffered that painful injury; right before discovering a brutal murder had occurred in her backyard while she slept. And, said dead guy's unknown murderer was still on the loose possibly believing Esther witnessed his kill and wanting her dead too. Esther Hausman insisted on carrying on, living her life her way.

"What was it her niece had said? Oh yeah… Chutzpah," said Burton, grinning.

Esther, lost in her own little world, was finally using her hiking stick. Carefully she maneuvered to her seat; her inflamed ankle still causing her great discomfort, though she would never admit it.

Instead whenever asked, her standard reply was always, "I'm on cloud nine."

Following closely behind like a mother hen, Matilda Rose Kaplan flopped her five-foot, five-inch hourglass frame into the aisle seat next to her aunt. Ready to spring into action, Mattie kept her aunt engaged in small talk so as not to give Esther the impression she was hovering; which of course, she was.

Regardless, anyone who had ever met Esther Hausman quickly found out about her insatiable curiosity. So, it was not surprising these days small talk centered around their uninvited dead guest and the circumstances surrounding his gruesome demise. Speculating who the deceased was and the events leading to his undignified end. Questioning the killer's motive; if he meant for the man's life to end in such a barbaric fashion. And why, of all places, had he chosen her place to carry out his horrific deed?

Mostly though, Esther wondered when she and Mattie could go home.

Mattie, finding it futile to change the subject when Esther was thus absorbed, supported her aunt's harmless obsession with one important exception. Until Esther was certifiably out of danger, Matti was hell-bent on keeping Esther under police protection and not becoming the killer's next victim.

For now, however, the two women blissfully basked in the warmth of the desert's afternoon sun; drowsily watching the baseball game through half-closed eyes. It was the perfect diversion for their overactive minds, even if the Arizona Diamondbacks and Colorado Rockies veteran ballplayers had been pulled the prior inning. Leaving in their place hopeful rookies and unsigned players to battle for the few open spots on the roster. Still it was baseball, so Esther happily settled in for the remaining innings.

Suddenly, a loud gravelly voice rose above the crowd grabbing Esther's full attention.

"Rrreeeddddssss… Get your red hots!" the man's voice bellowed.

The call rousting Esther from her stupor.

"He's here," she said astonished, sitting straight up in her seat.

Grinning broadly, Esther systematically searched the stadium hoping at long last to put a face to the familiar voice. Mattie, who had been busy filling out her score sheet, was only slightly aware her aunt had spoken and uttered a half-hearted reply.

"Did you say something, Tante?" she asked Esther somewhat distracted.

Then, noticing her aunt's glowing face, Mattie became far more intrigued with Esther's expression than what she had actually said.

"No, no. Go back to your program," assured Esther with restraint.

Patting Mattie's hand before returning her attention to the ballfield; hoping that Mattie would do the same.

"Rrrreeeedddsss…. Get your red hots!"

Distinctly echoed his call above the crowd; this time the orator's proclamation capturing Esther's complete attention. Her darting eyes scouring the stands for the person who was responsible for evoking sweetest of nostalgic memories.

Remembering one particular summer when Esther Chana Liebowitz first met Maxwell William Hausman at a popular University of Chicago hangout; he was studying law, she business. That day, groups of students had gathered round the pub's television to watch a ballgame between two of Major League Baseball's (MLB) biggest rivals, the Chicago White Sox and Chicago Cubs.

While sitting with friends, Esther became distracted by a gorgeous hunk who was strongly criticizing an umpire for a boneheaded call. Deciding it might be fun to antagonize the zealous young scholar, she began relentlessly teasing him for his allegiance to a bunch of has-beens. Causing him to make pacts with the baseball gods if only they would let his south-side team beat those north-side bums. She, countering, by yelling at the Cubs pitcher to knock the Sox batter on his goozle. Which apparently translated to throwing an inside pitch just close enough, the batter would lose his balance and fall on his ass.

By game's end Esther and Max were sitting side-by-side, neither really caring about the final score. After, rarely apart throughout decades of marriage, their love deepened during life's joys, and sorrows. Generously giving of themselves to their community, religion, and passions; they made time for the game which had brought them together and continued to enrich their celebrations and helped distract their heartaches. Then when an opportunity came to move to Arizona, a baseball mecca, the two jumped at the offer. Embracing all their new state offered, especially during MLB Cactus League and Minor League spring training season.

At that time, Phoenix was considered a quaint western city; not the metropolitan giant it is today. Old Town, the heart of elite Scottsdale, was thriving due to its art galleries, restaurants, and tourist shops. It was the "in" place to take out-of-town guests to acquire original Hopi pottery and DeGrazia paintings. It was also the primo spot to buy less pricey tchotchkes such as prickly pear cactus candies, scorpion paperweights, and T-shirts with skeletons touting, It's A Dry Heat.

From the end of February through March, much as today, baseball fans assembled from everywhere to watch their favorite teams play ball. However back then, the game was more homespun, good-natured, bighearted.

It was not uncommon for MLB spring training teams to use neighborhood ballfields to practice. Not caring if onlookers sat and watched for free on the four or five rows of wooden bleachers. Hot new prospects, stars of the day, even legendary ballplayers were approachable afterwards.

At least once a season, megastars such as Ernie Banks, Billy Williams, and Ferguson Jenkins would partake in a Chicago Windy City or New York Subway style old-timer's grudge match in a small stadium. Fans who called out to their heroes were rewarded with smiles, waves, even a cheerful, "Hey there."

The early Pacific Coast Minor League games were even more intimate. Frequently incorporating corny gimmicks to entertainment their fans.

Esther chuckled recalling the San Francisco Giants affiliated Triple-A Phoenix Firebirds games played at the old Scottsdale Stadium. Specifically, their iconic seventh inning stretch when the ballpark's organist played discorded music while a man dressed as The Phantom of the Opera appeared atop the announcer's wooden broadcast booth.

As the eerie music played, with great melodrama the Phantom would retrieve whatever foul baseballs had landed on the structure's rooftop. Then, one-by-one in dramatic fashion the Phantom tossed the coveted treasures down to his clamoring fans; including a much younger Mattie who was always in the middle of the action.

Then, as with the official MLB spring training, ballplayers freely scribbled their names for young and old alike; some not leaving the field after a game until the last remaining fan left with a signed souvenir. Ticket prices were so low, most people could afford seats behind home plate with money left over for a dog and a drink; unlike the MLB multiplex spring training facilities today. In fact, it was common for local businesses to buy a block and collectively treat their employees to what they called, a team building day.

That was before March of 1995, when the Arizona Diamondbacks became a National League expansion franchise; which led to the newly created D-backs' inaugural season in 1998 at their originally named Bank One Ballpark with its retractable roof and field-side pool.

Eventually, the MLB Cactus League took over Arizona's professional baseball market and pushed Minor League teams out of the valley. Sadly forcing the Phoenix Firebirds and their Phantom to leave in 1997.

And, although owners still pack the seats with loyal fans; today it seems the uniqueness, the intimacy, of baseball has gone. Gone are the older stadiums demolished, or abandoned; replaced by newer, mega training complexes. Gone too, the low ticket and concession prices. Teams' starting ballplayers still play, but only a few innings at the beginning of a game... if lucky.

Exhausted, Esther's raw emotions turned from joyous reminiscing to sorrow, then to Mattie.

***

Matilda Rose Kaplan had been nine-years old when Esther and Max Hausman's melancholy niece came to live with them for good. Six months earlier her gutless father, Bernard, had boarded the 10:45 Amtrak morning train at Chicago's Union Station bound for New York City. Unable to cope with his wife, Sara's, advance breast cancer, or take care of his energetic daughter, Mattie. As the train pulled away from the station, Bernie felt nothing but great relief leaving his unsuspecting wife at Rush University Medical Center during chemotherapy and abandoning his child.

Adamant to become the caregiver her father would not, the weight of the world came crashing down on her small shoulders. One day, walking back into her mother's bedroom with a glass of freshly squeezed orange juice, a smiling Mattie approached her mother sitting in her favorite floral-covered winged-back chair looking at the photo album, Matilda's First Birthday. It was then Mattie found herself staring into hollow eyes.

After the funeral Esther purposely sought her out. Ultimately finding her alone in the dark bedroom, curled up in that same armchair. A shattered child quietly staring at the empty bed belonging to her mother, Esther's younger sister.

A week later Max and Esther carried Mattie aboard a westbound jet headed for her new home in the hot Arizona desert. A world so different to her that animals, birds, even the trees were strange.

Esther's eyes began watering remembering the utter sadness of it all. With one concealing movement, she quickly wiped away her tears before anyone noticed. Yet, her heart remained heavy, thinking of the years that followed and the difficulty their niece had coping. Then, by sheer accident, an unconventional conduit helped fix their broken family.

Baseball.

It began as a simple backyard game; Mattie running makeshift bases with their collie, Copper, prancing at her heels. Evolving over the years with Mattie playing in coed softball leagues. The family attending various ballgames; each requiring them to dress in grandiose fan attire.

Later when the study of sports medicine proved unfulfilling, Mattie turned to the family business, Max's law firm. The threesome proving to be a dynamic legal force for the downtrodden persons and creatures they represented; becoming for Mattie her passion. One which Esther believed had taken hold on a Wednesday morning when a northbound 10:45 a.m. Amtrak train left Chicago Union Station.

***

It was during Mattie's formative years that Esther first heard the illusive hawker at a ballgame. Then, the voice had simply been a curiosity; a deep, gravelly distraction. Today, however, she was on a mission.

"Rrrreeeeeddddssss…. Get your red hots."

Roared the loud siren song delivered like a fiery preacher on Sunday morning. Lifting her from her doldrums to happier times when Max and she were young and life was filled with endless possibilities.

"All right old geezer, show yourself," she demanded, figuring they must be approximately the same age.

Squinting at every red and white striped vendor jacket, Esther scoured the stadium section by section, row by row. Her obsession pulling her away from the very game she had insisted on attending.

"Beer… Get your cold beer here!" shouted the equally strong voice.

With a startled look over her shoulder, Esther was surprised to see a strapping beer vendor amusingly peddling his merchandise. Having always prided herself on being keenly aware of her circumstances, Esther swore softly; irritated she had missed important areas behind her.

Gradually working down the stairs, the beer man eventually stopped on the very step beside the two women. Leaning against the middle iron railing, he good-naturedly interacted with those around him as he continued his attention-grabbing schtick.

"Last call folks… Refreshing cold brew… Get it while you can."

Grinned Terco, amused with himself for his double-play on words as he pointed to the aluminum beer can he was holding.

As he confidently filled his customers' requests, Terco found himself unexpectantly intrigued by an extremely wide-brimmed sunhat being held in place with a raspberry-colored scarf. With is hypermasculine hormones supercharged, unable to refrain from attempting to discover its owner's face; Terco found himself instead stealthy staring at feminine hands as they applied thick, creamy white sunscreen to firm, well-defined, bare legs.

Meanwhile, under the large brim Mattie's basic instincts told her she was being watched. Nonchalantly placing the sunscreen back in her bag, she coolly sat back in her seat all too ready to confront her voyeur. In fact, not shying away from uncomfortable situations was something she embraced very quickly in sixth grade; which coincidently was the year she began to physically mature.

Subjected to endless teasing and body shaming from male and female students alike. Mattie honed her sharp, articulate tongue into a perfect weapon to shut down uninvited comments, or advances; as well as a mean right cross.

To further downplay what she called her maternal European ancestors' curse of thick thighs, round bottom, small waist, and ample breasts Mattie typically wore clothing which minimized her well-defined figure. In fact, it only had been year or so that she had actually learned to love her curves; still, setting her own terms as to when and where to reveal them.

Emphatically deciding today was not that day, Mattie had deliberately worn an extra-large men's D-backs' jersey over a tight, plain gray sports bra to hide her well-defined breasts. Intent on focusing exclusively on Esther's needs, she was absolutely not in the mood for this type of distraction.

"What's it gonna take, Bozo? she thought, ready to bite the guy's head off.

"You look like you could use a cold one. How 'bout it?" Terco asked Mattie flirtatiously, still trying to see under that hat.

Mattie's body stiffened as she crossed her arms and turned to her aunt.

Noticing the woman's defensive posture, Terco took a couple steps back from Mattie's seat and leaned against the center railing to project a less threatening demeanor. He was having fun likening his innocent game to that of capture the flag; still, he did not want to go too far and come across as creepy.

With the exception of Kyle Lucas, Mattie's experiences with men in her age group usually ended up awkward at best and disastrous at most; rarely having to endure such discomfort a second time.

Remaining aloof, Mattie leaned toward her aunt.

"What do you say, Tante… Buy you a beer?" she asked, hiding her irritation.

Then, a tingling sensation rushed through Mattie as she felt the beer vendor's attention fix solely upon her, waiting patiently for her answer.

Esther, who was talking to Kyle on her phone, paused her conversation.

"What'd ya got kid?" she asked; unaware the vendor was flirting with her niece.

Using his most alluring smile Terco rattled off several brands while never once taking his eyes off Mattie's hat; still trying to get a glimpse.

Rolling her eyes at the kid's obvious tactics, Esther had become used to being ignored whenever she was in her niece's company. Oddly enough, Mattie never encouraged the attention; which of course, made her all that more irresistible.

Still, thinking a cold beer would taste pretty good about then, she gave Mattie her order and returned to her conversation with Kyle. Keeping one eye on the two of them, and the other on the ballgame.

"Make it two," replied Mattie indifferently.

As Mattie reached down beneath her seat for her purse, Terco suddenly became aware he was ogling the way her breasts pressed against her jersey. Quickly averting his gaze before getting caught, he turned to his other customers while waiting for payment.

Esther, however, noticed. Taking full advantage of the vendor's obvious discomfort, she took the opportunity to ask him some of questions.

"Hey kid, answer this. You guys… Do 'ya sell the same stuff every game? Or do you trade? I mean… How does it work? You always sell beer? Somebody else always sells cotton candy?" she asked innocently.

"Different rules for different places… Here, it's seniority. Those here longest pick first… Beer usually… I'm the newbie, so I go last… I got lucky today," he replied sweetly, passing a Corona Lite to another customer.

Hoping the older woman's intriguing companion would notice how utterly charming he was.

"Really?… And what about the reds?" Esther asked eagerly.

"Reds… Oh… Hot dogs. Not a favorite… The box's a real pain to haul. Although there's this one old guy, been here forever. Can pick any assignment… Every time it's dogs… Go figure," divulged Terco, starting to feel he better move on.

It was then while handing the beer man a twenty-dollar bill, Mattie tilted her head upward ever so slightly.

Finally seeing the young woman's face, Terco fought to suppress his sophomoric expression of triumph.

Then, finding Mattie quite different from the women he was usually drawn to, Terco noticed her sensual frame, the way her dark auburn pixie-cut hair framed her face, her silky rose-pedal lips. But mostly he noticed her riveting smoky-gray; completely catching him off guard.

"Do you see him now?" interrupted Esther. "The hot dog guy."

Wishing the kid would come back to earth and perhaps help her solve her mystery man puzzle before the ballgame ended. Unfortunately, his eyes remained on Mattie.

Mattie, on the other hand, had had quite enough of Terco's unwanted attention. She was about to deliver one of her tried-and-true dissuading zingers when she got a really good look at the striking man before her holding out the drinks for her to take.

Distracted during the hand off, Mattie fumbled one of the beer cans.

Catching the beverage before it spilled, Terco leaned in close; handing Mattie the cans one-by-one. Her eyes coming face-to-face with the beer man's identification badge clipped to the breast pocket of his red and white striped vendor jacket; beneath the charismatic cocky grin and twinkling deep-brown eyes a name in black, bold type.

"Renan Cardoso," she read to herself.

Wondering if people called him Ren. Picturing him on a Brazilian beach. His strong arms reaching for her.

"For you…" the masculine voice said in her head dreamily.

"… A buck seventy-five," is what he was saying in reality.

His hand extending towards her with her change.

He, wondering about the young woman's far-away gaze as his outstretched fingertips innocently brushed across her open palm ever so slightly. Dropping the coins as an undeniable spark ignited between them.

Recovering the loose change, Mattie's internal flight defense reared its ugly head. Blushing, she handed Esther the beer then curtly turned away; pretending to watch the ballgame. Wanting nothing more to do with him.

"Hey Terco… Some people down here are getting mighty thirsty," yelled a cotton candy vendor in a section closer to the field.

In seats across the aisle a couple 13-year-olds wearing D-backs jerseys watching the exchange began snickering and elbowing each other. Their loud comments at Terco's expense adding to the vendor's embarrassment.

Esther, attributing the boys' bad manners to adolescent immaturity, resisted taking them to task; not wishing to make matters any worse.

"Thanks kid," interjected Esther kindly.

Attempting to soften Mattie's incivility.

Terco, clumsily offering a few amusing parting words of his own; then, all too happily escaped down the stairs to his waiting customers.

Observing moments of Mattie's fiasco, Officer Mitzy Burton continued he surveillance of the crowd while making a mental note.

"I gotta talk to that girl about her social skills," she chuckled quietly.

It was Esther who seemed disappointed at the vendor's departure; having more questions for him about her mystery man. Then, shaking off the setback she impishly grinned at Mattie; teasing her ever so lightly.

"I thought he was kind of cu…," Esther started saying.

"Don't even go there," protested her niece; her face still a pale pink.

Accomplishing the chilly snub she thought she had desired, Mattie gently admonished her beloved aunt's matchmaking attempt as she took one last peek at the irresistible Renan Cardoso vanishing into the crowd.

Returning their attention to the ballgame, the two women lazily sipped their cold brews as the next batter stepped up to the plate.

Appearing barely out of high school, the young man raised his bat high and dug in. His determined expression conveying decades of committed long hours, hard work, and a journey from T-ball, travel leagues, school ball, and the minors. Nervously waiting to react to the baseball hurling his way; his childhood dream about to come true.

"Oye… He swings like a rusty gate," commented Esther. "Com' on kid. You got this."

Both women shouting with the crowd; encouraging the young ballplayer to blast one out of the park.

The count rose to one ball, two strikes.

With a high-leg kick and resounding grunt, the opposing pitcher hurled a split-finger fastball towards the plate.

Miscalculating the ball's trajectory, the batter wildly swung with all his might as the baseball curved inside, than sank sharply below his knees as it crossed home plate. The Homeplate umpire, raising his clenched fist high into the air in a grand gesture, yanked it downward just as dramatically proclaiming in no uncertain terms.

"Yyyeeerrrrr Out!"

"Auch… Better luck next time kid," shouted Esther; feeling badly for the young man.

In disbelief, the heartbroken rookie slammed the bat head into the dirt. Then, pausing briefly, he straightened up and composed himself. Certain his dream of making this year's roster would not be realized as he walked slowly back to the dugout; avoiding eye contact his with teammates as they hurried by him to take the field.

Chapter 9

There's More To Life Than Stars

Pulling into the parking lot on the far southeast side of Scottsdale, Homicide Detective Michael Flores found his uneasiness had persisted; even after speaking with his extremely competent head of security detail, Mitzy Burton. Then, after hearing the baseball crowd's roar on her end of their phone call; not only did his concern grow, but his envy as well. Wishing he was at the ballgame and she here, performing what probably was going to be an enormous waste of time.

Once inside the grandiose main lobby, Flores waited patiently for assistance at the security counter. Taking in the sights, he could not help notice the corporation's name plastered high near the cathedral-high ceiling; jutting from the rich, natural fieldstone wall before him. Each enormous metallic letter dramatically spotlighted with just the right amount of flaring off its top-right corner; accenting the name, Carpstra LLC.

"Seize the Stars," he said cynically.

Reading the smaller, italicized inspirational motto below the corporation's name. Having heard if you work for Carpstra, the company expected no less.

"I'm here to see Ryota Ito… Human Resources should've called," announced Michael Flores; showing his police credentials to the guard.

His gut telling him Peter Cavenaugh's department head might have just the information to help jump-start his stalled investigation.

The unimpressed security guard, looking as if he was military police in an earlier life, verified Flores' identification against his notes. Then, witnessing the detective writing his signature on the sign-in log, the steely eye sentinel compared the handwriting against that on Flores' license.

"I guess at Carpstra, even cops aren't above suspicion," Flores let slip.

Unphased by the comment, the guard methodically determined all was in order before phoning the deceased's manager. Next, he handed Flores a numbered clip-on badge and gestured to the detective to take a seat in the lobby.

Examining the badge more closely, Flores noticed there was nothing subtle about the nonexistent security designation the guard assigned him; as against its stark-white plastic background the word, VISITOR, appeared in large red bold type at the very top. Below the designation was the meticulously printed current date and time, and finally below that, Flores' name at the very bottom. Leaving absolutely no doubt in anybody's mind the person wearing it was an untrustworthy outsider with limited facility access, who must be accompanied by appropriate personnel at all times.

Settling into one of a lobby's contemporary swivel chairs closest to the elevators, Flores clipped the visitor's badge to his newly pressed midnight-blue suit jacket lapel and waited impatiently for the murder victim's boss to show.

Frustrated that Cavenaugh's killer was still at large, his investigation was growing colder by the hour, and the Hausman ballgame situation was out of his control, Michael Flores' last nerve was beyond frayed.

"Shit… They're too exposed," he lamented, fixating on Esther and Mattie.

His insides tied in a huge knot as his inner voice scolded him for allowing the women to attend the ballgame in the first place.

"Never again," he gritted, refusing to repeat his lapse in sanity.

"If that sick bastard was hiding on the property after he killed Cavenaugh; and, he followed us to Phoenix… I handed just him the opportunity to take her out. Hell! He could be sitting next to her right now. Who'd know?" imagining a worse-case scenario as he rubbed his throbbing temples.

Unaware his fears were not imaginary.

Fighting the urge to call Officer Burton and order her immediate return to the safe house, Flores instead dialed Detective Vernon Rub.

"First of all I wanna thank you pal, for this choice assignment," declared Rub with biting sarcasm.

Assuming the undercover role of ranch hand at the Hausman place, the Newark, New Jersey born and raised Vernon Rub had always felt more at home among steel beams and city lights than country wide-open spaces.

"Nuth'n I like better than muck'n stalls n stack'n bales of hay," he continued in an overly dramatic western drawl.

"My pleasure Vern," retorted Flores, needing the laugh. "Look at it this way… I'm saving you a month's gym fee."

Both quite aware Rub's assignment was not as blasé as he led on; because if Cavenaugh's killer did return, he and Kyle Lucas were pretty much on their own. Recognizing too ever since that first night, Rub would have eaten him alive if he had given the assignment to anyone else.

"Any luck finding what brought our victim to our fair city?" inquired Flores.

Confident in Detective Vernon Rub's handling of the Tucson side of the investigation. Freeing him to pursue Peter Cavenaugh's associates and activities in the Valley; as well as staying fairly close to Esther and Mattie.

"Not one iota," answered Detective Rub, trying to hide a yawn.

Neither one of them having slept much since the case began.

"I decided to expand our suspect list, Mikey… Looking into people we didn't initially consider. People who might've hid the fact they knew the victim;

including Esther Hausman, Joseph Tadai, and your lovely Matilda Kaplan," he snickered lightly.

Teasing Flores about his obvious attraction to Mattie; which in turn elicited his friend's groaning denial.

"Put a tail on the Lucas," added Rub matter-of-factly. "Kid's just as anal about his studies as he is about this place… Friends are just as boring. No wild parties. Like I said, it's been pretty dull."

"What about his friends? Maybe one of them was using Kyle, or the place without his knowledge?" wondered Flores aloud.

"Mmmm… possible. They're all vet students… Could be selling veterinary grade Ketamine, Morphine, even Buprenorphine on the human market… Great way to pay tuition. Maybe Cavenaugh was their Phoenix connection. Anyway, kid's got me ride'n the range with him on a horse no less, later today," complained Vernon. "I'll put the notion in his head then… See how he reacts."

"You go cowboy," joked Flores; then suggested. "Hey Vern… Steer Kyle over to that large damaged area in the brush. It's possible things will look different from atop that horse. Maybe you'll find something. And Vern,… thanks."

"Yeeee Haaah!" replied Rub in another western drawl.

Ending his call, Michael Flores made a silent vow to buy his friend a substantial bottle of very expensive whiskey right after they solved the case.

Checking the time once more, his good mood disappeared.

Mr. Ito had yet to appear.

Stretching his legs, the detective picked up one of Carpstra's dynamic four-color marketing brochures from a nearby chrome table. Muttering to himself he flipped through the pages quickly.

"Five minutes. That's it," he swore, feeling precious time slipping away.

Everyone in Arizona knew someone who worked for Carpstra, LLC. The innovative technology's parent company had moved its government division from the east coast to Scottsdale in the mid 1940's to support and partner with several of the State's military bases. Over time, Carpstra became unequaled in the research and development of reliable, groundbreaking communications products. Playing major roles in the United States modern warfare conflicts, space program, and security systems. As a result the Carpstra name became as synonymous with communications as Kleenex® is to tissues.

In fact, in its quest to dominate high-technology fields in diverse markets worldwide, specialized facilities popped up all around the state; making Carpstra, LLC, the State's second largest employer right behind the Arizona government itself.

Why Arizona? For one, government incentives, and two, at that time land was dirt cheap. Both enabled Carpstra to acquire hundreds of acres in Phoenix, Scottsdale, nearby cities, and unincorporated communities. The other driving factor was the strong, symbiotic relationship it developed with fledgling Arizona State University (ASU) in Tempe.

Although ASU began as a teaching college in the 1800's. With the help of corporations like Carpstra, its School of Engineering grew into one of the nation's preeminent engineering, technology, and research and development higher learning institutions in America. In turn, ASU provided Carpstra with a constant flow of top-notch interns and highly skilled future employees.

As years passed, major corporations such as Honeywell International Inc., Intel®, Microsoft®, and Motorola made Arizona their home. Rapidly growing cities annexed more and more land. Borders of municipalities soon butted, resulting in the entire region becoming one massive grid affectionately referred to as the Valley of The Sun.

Tick… tick… tick.

More time lost.

Reviewing his notes from his early appointment that morning; Flores, along with Gilbert police Officer Robert Evans, had met with Cavenaugh's grieving wife, Taylor. Inconsolable, she and her two little girls were unable to answer even the simplest of questions; such as what time they had last seen the victim.

When it came time for him to leave for his Carpstra appointment, Evans had agreed to remain with the family.

"Bob keep her talking," urged Flores. "She knows something… even if she doesn't think so."

"Hey… Think your guy will show up here? I mean pretty creepy… killing her husband like that… Like it was personal," asked the jittery officer, walking Flores to his car.

"If he thinks she can tie him to her husband… anything's possible… Bob, can we get a few of your people out here?" requested Flores.

Realizing the people who might need protection from Peter Cavenaugh's killer was not exclusive to Esther Hausman, Flores was pleased to see Evans on his phone as he drove away.

Ding… Ding.

Two delicate notes chimed as a down arrow lit above one of the elevator doors. When the stainless-steel double doors parted in the middle they revealed a slight-of-built, middle-aged man wearing wireless-rimmed glasses. Dressed in a modern, open-neck white business shirt, twill khakis, and spotless white athletic shoes, the Carpstra employee walked toward the detective with his hand extended.

As he approached, Flores noticed the Carpstra ID clipped to the man's breast pocket was quite different from his meager visitor's badge. To begin a noticeable, royal-blue rectangular border surrounded a color snapshot of man's face followed by his name and department in bold, black print. Suspecting the badge signified a much higher security clearance than his, Flores hoped his wait was over.

"Hi, I'm Ryota Ito. But please… call me Ryan. I believe you want to speak to me about Peter Cavenaugh?" he asked with a quizzical brow.

***

"Oh my God. Peter Cavenaugh's dead… I can't believe it. You're sure it's Peter? This is horrible, just horrible," repeated Ryan Ito in absolute shock.

"Yes… A body was discovered in Tucson a little over two days ago. It has since been positively identified as your Carpstra employee," apprised Michael Flores; interested the manager's reaction. "I'm… uh… Sorry for your loss."

"My God… Tucson?" Ito questioned in dismay.

"Well… what the hell was he doing in Tucson? He's got a deadline… Wait… I know that sounded really callous. I didn't mean… Tucson… Does Taylor know?" he rambled, absorbing the news of his coworker's death.

"Mr. Ito… Is there a place we can talk in private?" suggested the detective.

Not expecting the department manager's volatile reaction, prompting so many people in the room to be interested in their conversation.

With a subtle nod, the truly shaken Ryan Ito ushered Detective Flores into an open meeting room adjacent to the main lobby. Quietly closing the door behind them, Ito took a seat at the high-glossed walnut conference table across from Flores and waited quietly for the detective to speak first.

The news of Cavenaugh's death had obviously frayed what Flores suspected were Ito's already last nerves. Yet, the detective could not tell if the manager was upset because his colleague was dead, or because his colleague's death put a Carpstra project in peril. Expecting if he could see, Ryan Ito's mind would probably show a desperate man searching his group's skill sets for someone who could seamlessly step into the dead man's role.

Contrary to first impressions, Ryan Ito was not completely heartless.

He was, however, a realist.

Ito knew without a shadow of doubt that one missed deadline, regardless of the circumstance, was inexcusable in the eyes of Carpstra leadership. Knowing too the domino effect of such a travesty would definitely result in a substantial loss to both Carpstra's revenue and its brand's reputation. Having seen firsthand past fiascos of this type befall others, Ito equated missing a deadline to career suicide.

He could do nothing for Peter, but he still had a chance to save his own career. Panicking, Ito speed dialed his secretary.

"Sally... Book a conference room for 3:45 p.m. and call a mandatory department meeting. Yes... today," ordered Ito curtly; ignoring Michael Flores' attempts to catch his attention.

Grabbing the phone out of Ryan Ito's hand, Flores quickly ended the call.

"Mr. Ito... You can't tell anybody about Peter Cavenaugh death until after I speak with certain individuals. Even then... until I give you the go ahead. Hold your meeting... Make assignment changes. But if anyone asks why... Lie. Tell them Corporate reassigned Cavenaugh... Say he's on a fact-finding mission. Whatever... Understand?" insisted the homicide detective.

"But why? Why keep Peter's death a secret?" protested Ito.

Then, after careful reflection, Ryan Ito leaned forward and whispered.

"Peter's death… It wasn't an accident, was it?"

Warily nodding a confirmation, Michael Flores slowly handed the stunned Ryan Ito his phone. Then, while waiting a minute for the manager to come to terms with the situation, Flores took out his notebook and turned on a small voice activated recorder; deliberately; pushing it in front of the manager.

"If you're ready Mr. Ito… Tell me about Peter Cavenaugh's responsibilities concerning this big project of yours," insisted Flores.

However just as Ryan Ito was about to open his mouth, the conference room door abruptly opened. In marched a stern looking woman dressed in what Flores guessed was standard corporate lawyer attire; noting too, even her badge's steel-gray border screamed lawyer.

"Don't answer Ryan," ordered the woman. "Elizabeth Donovan, Carpstra Legal."

Taking a seat next to Ryan Ito, Elizabeth Donovan immediately informed Michael Flores of the limited parameters she would allow during his questionings.

"Detective Flores is it?… Well Detective Flores, as Carpstra has always supported law enforcement we certainly do not wish to impede your investigation. That's why we have so graciously allowed you onto this facility to conduct your questioning. However, you are not privy to any information Carpstra deems proprietary or inappropriate."

"Carpstra deems… or you deem," he asked, testing her.

"It's one in the same thing… I speak for Carpstra. We are willing to afford you some courtesies. But, you may not question any employee without corporate or private counsel present. Are we clear?... Yes?" demanded Ms. Donovan, as if she were a teacher taking a student to task.

"Look, Ms. Donovan... I've got the brutal murder of a Carpstra employees to solve and his killer's still at large. So, you can either let me do my job here and now, or, I can start hauling Carpstra people out of work and interrogate them in Tucson... for say a day, or two, or three. Your choice," countered Flores, just as persistently.

"Fine... But I'll be sitting in on all your interviews from this point on. Now, perhaps you'd like to ask Mr. Ito a relevant question which does not fall under Carpstra proprietary information," cautioned Donovan.

Paraphrasing so as not to be torpedoed again by the lawyer, Flores was determined to learn if there was any connection between the victim's job and his death.

"This facility caters to Government contracts... Does that mean all your work here top secret?" asked Flores.

Wondering if Cavenaugh had succumbed to domestic or foreign attack, or influence.

Ito skirted talking about Cavenaugh's specific assignments and instead regurgitated Carpstra's vanilla product descriptions; then said seriously.

"All Carpstra data is proprietary information Detective Flores. Even that which is categorized unclassified. It's fiercely protected. You experienced just a small taste when you walked through our doors. Corporate espionage threatens more than our company's stability. It threatens our nation," stressed Ryan.

"And, Cavenaugh... What role did he play in your fiercely protected projects?" pressed Flores.

"Peter is, uh… was, our most valued senior product architect. He designed unprecedented communications systems and enhancements from our simplest hand-held devices to black boxes," said Ito quietly; then, paused.

Feeling the squeamish sensation of Ms. Donovan's icy stare impaling him, the department manager realized he had probably said too much and fell quiet.

"Black boxes? Like flight recorders… or spy stuff?" pried the detective.

"Move on detective… I'll get you some approved marketing literature if you're truly interested," cut in Donovan; her stone face focused on the detective.

"Given Peter Cavenaugh's work… is it possible someone had threatened him, or tried to abduct him. Maybe forced him to steal designs?" he asked Ito.

Half expecting Donovan to object; yet, realizing Cavenaugh was in the perfect position to greatly profit off Carpstra's products, Flores went a step further.

"Mr. Ito… Was Peter Cavenaugh happy working here?"

Flores asked, pursuing the disgruntle worker angle.

"Detective… No one's always happy in their job… Are you? Peter is, was, a perfectionist. So much so, he was recognized universally for groundbreaking advancements in high-tech field uniforms, ordnance, satellite telecommunications (SATCOM), even communications security (COMSEC)," said Ito proudly.

"What about Cavenaugh's coworkers? They feel the same? Maybe he stepped toes? pushed Flores.

Suggesting Ryan Ito's rosy picture had some thorns.

"From time to time. But look… ours is a cutthroat business. Furthermore, everyone here thinks he or she is a wunderkind. Funny thing though, almost everyone on my team is. So yes, some took offense," admitted Ito.

"Including you?" asked Flores bluntly.

"Me?" replied Ito, taken aback.

"I don't like your implications detective," snapped Elizabeth Donovan coming to Ito's defense.

"If Peter Cavenaugh was the driving genius you say... Weren't you worried he'd overshadow you, maybe replace you?" proposed Flores.

Suggesting to Ito he was jealous or threatened by the Carpstra golden-boy and might have taken it a step too far.

"Maybe you were into something not quite legal and Cavenaugh got wind of it... I mean, how else do you explain his disappearance right before your big deadline, and you not concerned until I showed up today?" accused Flores.

Wondering if Ito's first reaction to Cavenaugh's death was sincere or faked.

"Don't be absurd!" spit back Ito, outraged.

"You are way out of line detective... Ryan don't say another word. We're done," erupted the Carpstra lawyer.

"No, Beth. Wait... It's okay," asserted Ito.

No longer playing games, Ryan Ito locked eyes with Michael Flores and said.

"Did I feel threatened by Peter brilliance? Why should I? His ideas, his designs, they were eons beyond our fiercest competitors. He made Carpstra billions; and for some reason, Carpstra saw his successes as mine too. So no, I wasn't threatened... Quite the opposite," stated Ito emphatically.

Then Ito elaborated at length.

"Peter's absenteeism wasn't unusual. People in my department... how do I say this kindly... are eccentric, socially awkward, introverts. Why? Maybe because our brains process the world differently from others. We get inspired by the strangest things at the oddest hours. We push ourselves beyond physical and mental exhaustion. End up burned out, in poor health, alienating family and friends. And… I wouldn't trade a one of them," explained Ito.

Then he said of his deceased colleague.

"What made Peter so special was his ability to conceive and create ultra-sophisticated defense systems so user friendly, anyone could operate them effortlessly. Do you know what a rarity that is?" beamed Ito.

"So, if Peter did his best work at home when most of us slept, I let him… I didn't think it strange he hadn't come into the office, because quite frankly Detective Flores, unless he was working on a Department of Defense (DOD) contract mandating he work on site, it would be strange if he did," disclosed the manager.

Then, grabbing a sheet of printer paper off a counter, Ryan Ito jotted down several names and handed it to Flores.

"Here are some people who might have seen Peter this week. They'll be at the department meeting this afternoon. Now if you'll excuse me… I have to figure out how I'm going to replace someone who truly was irreplaceable. Ms. Donovan… I leave the detective in your most capable hands," said Ito dejectedly.

Rising to his feet Ryan Ito then walked out of the room, leaving Elizabeth Donovan and Michael Flores staring at each other in silence.

"Any chance I can hang around and compile my notes?" asked Flores sweetly.

Twenty minutes later Detective Michael Flores unknowingly found himself at the same True Brew coffee shop where Peter Cavenaugh and his killer had argued, sitting in the exact same booth.

Quietly organizing his materials for his afternoon interviews; among the many documents in Flores' possession was a copy of Peter Cavenaugh's Carpstra personnel file. This, plus Ryan Ito's information, had given the detective insight into who the man was. Unfortunately, it offered nothing as far as what got him killed.

"So, says you excelled as a radio and COMSEC technician while with the 187th Airborne Regimental Combat Team... The Rakkasans... Why does that nickname ring a bell? Deployed 1990, Operation Desert Shield," he digested; the information presenting more questions than answers.

"Honorably discharged, 2002... Earned degrees at Carnegie Mellon University, Moffett Field... Hired by Carpstra in 2006. Added more degrees. Specialized in Global Positioning Systems (GPS). Spy satellites?"

Seeing a possible a thread in the dead man's profession which might have led to motive.

"Hey there. I'm Zoe... I'll be taking your order. What can I... Oh, wait... Today's pastry special cranberry and walnut muffin," announced the perky pony-tailed brunette in her True Brew café's black uniform.

Startled, Flores looked up from his notes while simultaneously closing the folders in front of him; concealing Peter Cavenaugh's photo.

Grateful for the break, Flores smiled at the attractive server and engaged in a bit of harmless bantering.

"Let's see... How 'bout a large double-shot cold brew with low fat milk," he ordered, needing a caffeine jolt.

"That's it?... I dunno, you look pretty peaky to me. How about something substantial with that... Help you tackle whatever, all that is... A sandwich? My treat," flirted Zoe acknowledging Flores' large pile of papers with a wave of her hand.

Completely mesmerized by the striking woman, Flores made a counter offer.

"I look peaky, uh? I don't think anyone's ever described me as looking peaky before. Okay, sandwich it is. But only if you let me buy you dinner later tonight," he posed.

Admitting to himself he needed to recharge. And after all, he did have to eat.

"Thanks. But… no thanks," replied Zoe politely, erring on the side of caution.

"I understand… Really I do. What if you pick the place and time? We'll be like two friends running into each other… Nothing more," suggested Flores.

"I'll think about it," replied Zoe, cracking a noncommittal smile.

Then, pulling his wallet from his suit breast pocket to pay for his entire meal, Michael Flores allowed his police badge to not so subtly fall into plain view.

"See… You can trust me."

***

An hour before the department meeting, Detective Flores met Ryan Ito and Elizabeth Donovan back at Carpstra's main lobby to coordinate their efforts. The two then escorted Flores into a tiny second-floor windowless room with an adjoining door leading to a huge conference room where Ito's gathering was to take place.

The sparsely-decorated breakout room was perfect for Flores' purpose. To begin, upon each wall hung one, simple black-framed color photograph of a different Carpstra product. Squarely centered within the room was a small oval coffee table with four, barrel chairs evenly spaced around it; with the only other piece of furniture being a lonely standalone water cooler with attached paper cup dispenser gurgling ominously in the darkest corner.

Setting his paperwork atop the table, Flores invited Ito and Donovan to sit. He began by apologizing for his earlier heavy-handed tactics which the other two seemed to accept and became more at ease.

"So… What's your excuse for sending people in here to talk with me?" asked the detective, genuinely curious.

"Time Card infractions," replied Ms. Donovan crisply.

"Time Card infractions… You're kidding?" chuckled Detective Flores, not quite understanding the seriousness of the violation.

"That's brilliant, Beth," applauded Ryan Ito; impressed by her solution.

"Really?" snickered the doubting Flores.

"Don't laugh. When the United States Government's your customer, accurate timecard reporting is a strictly-upheld contract requirement… Every employee must maintain exact, up-to-date logs of the projects they work on… Every start time… Every stop time. No matter how often work on various projects change within a day… Even if only for six minutes. No guessing. No estimating. No projecting," informed Ito emphatically.

"The smallest of improprieties can cause Carpstra LLC massive legal and financial penalties; even mark them ineligible for future Government work. The impact would devastatingly impact our entire corporation," interjected Elizabeth Donovan.

"Detective, it's like this… Our people know a time card infraction can result in their immediate termination. It's that serious," declared Ryan Ito.

"Okay… So, where do I fit in?" asked the detective.

Having experienced his own form of career bureaucracy.

"I'll introduce you as a Government representative during our meeting; which you are," began Ito.

"And, I'll inform them during the meeting some will be randomly selected to participate in a surprise external audit. It will be assumed you, Detective Flores, will be holding the audit in this room. As you finish with your questions, each employee can exit out this hallway door unseen," interjected the lawyer.

"Sounds good… Uh… Mr. Ito. One more question for you," proposed Flores; his demeanor more toned-down.

Hoping Ryan Ito had become more ally than adversary.

"I read Cavenaugh's performance reviews. The guy had everything going for him. He could have…" the detective began saying.

"…run the entire corporation. Or at very least this division," finished Ryan Ito. "Even the bigwigs tried promoting him up the ranks, several times. He had reached the highest senior position in my department years ago. He refused."

"Who does that?" laughed Flores in dismay.

Not understanding anyone who would turn down a promotion, or more pay.

"Peter… He'd say he had enough upheaval to last a lifetime. He just wanted to be left alone to do his work," recalled Ito.

Just then a diverse group of noisy Carpstra employees filtered into the adjoining large conference room through an opposite-side hallway door. While certain people rushed to grab the cushy chairs around the long, highly-polished conference table in the front of the room, others fought over the few folding office chairs in the back. Still others chose to stand, or lean against a wall.

"Ah, here they come," announced Ito.

Watching the group jostle for position, Flores was given a kind of snapshot into the department's hierarchy. Their conversations reminding him a lot of whining high schoolers. Many speculating why the disruptive meeting had been called. Some complaining about the harsh overhead florescent lights hurting their eyes. Still others grumbling, "How long's this shit supposed to last."

Ryan Ito, Elizabeth Donovan, and Michael Flores stood at the front of the room waiting for the masses to quiet down. Those fixating on the stranger did just that; curious to learn who he was. As for the others, Ito had to insist on their attention.

"I appreciate you dropping everything on such short notice," began Ryan.

"We had a choice?" piped in a smart-ass programmer at the back of the room.

A few coworkers chuckled; most, however, shot the disrespectful bozo a look of disdain. Wishing he would shut the hell up and let Ito talk so they could get back to work.

"Folks... You're here for two reasons," announced Ito; ignoring the programmer's impudence. "First, this is Michael Flores from the Government. He and Elizabeth Donovan from Legal will be conducting a random external timecard audit during this meeting in the adjacent breakout room."

Immediately several groans and long-winded expletives erupted.

"Take Kerry first," shouted a woman. Directing her suggestion at the rude programmer.

"All right, all right... Quiet down please. I expect your full cooperation... Look people, this is nothing new. It's part of the job, so deal with it. Any information you miss, you can obtain from a teammate," declared Ryan Ito with an authority which Flores guessed was rarely challenged.

"Second... Guys... An unexpected situation has occurred which requires me to make major reassignments to the Mark5. And yes, I'm afraid it's going to impact most of you," he announced above several gasps.

The room fell silent as all eyes and ears focused on Ryan Ito diagraming the reorganization on a whiteboard; allowing Flores and Donovan to slip out the adjacent door and prepare to call the first employee.

***

Clarence Johnson surly crossed his massive arms over his large rounded chest and stuck his thumbs up into his armpits. Glaring at the detective, whom he believed was a pain-in-the-ass bean counter, the disheveled middle-aged man with bags under his eyes and ill-fitting wrinkled clothing maintained a minimal level of civility, but just barely. Not looking forward to the imminent bullshit, beneath his calm surface the man was boiling mad.

"You guys… Always look'n to nail some poor bastard like me."

Muttered Clarence Johnson, a 20-year Carpstra senior employee who had experienced too many of these senseless Government audits.

"And the real screwup… The guy further up the food chain… He gets reassigned and promoted," complained Johnson.

"Sorry… Didn't quite… Can you repeat that?" inquired Flores a little too politely, as if he had not heard.

"Noth'n. Just… Get on with it," huffed the Carpstra employee.

Adjusting his wide frame to fit the physical constraints of the uncomfortably compact barrel chair.

Feeling out-of-sorts himself, Michael Flores wondered if the man was hiding something, or if acting pissy was his normal modus operandi. Either way, after shuffling a few papers, Flores pulled out his notebook and began his interview by unnecessarily tormenting Johnson with a couple timesheet questions; to which the overworked, underappreciated man responded tersely yes or no.

Enjoying pushing the tough guy's buttons, the detective soon realized it was because he too was tired and needed to blow off some steam. He had just spent the entire day chasing leads that went nowhere, and he was feeding off this man's frustration.

"Cut the guy some slack," thought Flores, admitting he had no good reason for tormenting the man.

Too, Elizabeth Donovan had shot him a look which said, "Enough… You've had your fun."

Knowing she was right, that he had been acting like a prick, the detective turned the conversation to the real reason he was there.

"Why are you asking me about Pete Cavenaugh?" snarled Johnson, completely caught off guard.

Then, realizing the stranger was not really interested in him, Clarence Johnson's resistance vanished.

"Are you aware of any issues Mr. Cavenaugh might be having?" Flores asked him. "Say with friends, colleagues?"

"Friends? Pete? Pete's actually a very likeable guy… for an introvert. I don't know. Who's got time for friends… Look, when you're not here working, you're at home thinking about work," explained Johnson.

Checking his wristwatch with a look of concern the large man began fidgeting in his uncomfortable chair.

"What about weekends?" probed Flores, ignoring Johnson's desire to leave.

"Weren't you listening? There's product development, startup, deadline, debrief, updates, then new development. There're no weekends," declared Johnson.

Finally grasping the high-stress culture Carpstra's employees worked under, Flores now regretted giving the man a hard time earlier. Having no doubt Carpstra was the cause of Clarence Johnson's unkept appearance, negative attitude, and more than likely poor health.

"Seize the Stars, Detective Flores… Our dedicated employees go all-out to develop and create the world's most innovative high-performance, intelligence technology and products for our Nation's rapid security dominance solutions… for this century, and future centuries," chimed Ms. Donovan smiling before adding. "Which you… Mr. Johnson… and your coworkers, are sizably compensated. Isn't that so?"

Yet instead of agreeing, Clarence Johnson remained miserably silent.

"That's for now it… But Mr. Johnson, do not discuss any portion this meeting with anyone, got it? Ms. Donovan will tell you the gag order has been lifted," cautioned Flores, scribbling down the last of the man's statement.

"Who's got time to blab," retorted Johnson.

And with that, Clarence Johnson stomped out of the room without looking back.

Daniel Martinez, Cassie Kwok, and George Joz followed Clarence Johnson in turn. It was Flores' hope that at least one of them would offer something more tangible about Peter Cavenaugh's last days on earth than their predecessor.

When Daniel Martinez entered the room, he looked to Detective Flores as if he belonged to a high-school geek-club instead of being the senior development analyst on a top-secret NATO project. Then, when during his questioning Flores fabricated a story about sensitive materials going missing from their department; instead of talking about a possible Peter Cavenaugh connection, the goofy Martinez became quite nervous.

Normally high-strung, Martinez vehemently protested any wrongdoings; reciting Carpstra's work ethics regulations regarding company information and products verbatim. Swearing he followed every rule to a T, the young man's words did not seem to jive with his odd behavior; leading Elizabeth Donovan to devise an internal investigation of her own.

Next up was Cassie Kwok, a tough young woman who had clawed her way out of a dangerous neighborhood in South Phoenix. Feeling totally devalued, Cassie Kwok was not shy about sharing her opinion that Peter Cavenaugh's skills and reputation were overblown and far beneath her own. When asked if she had ever seen him act unethically or suspiciously regarding sensitive materials, Cassie eagerly chimed in.

"Carpstra's golden boy? Shit. Wouldn't put it past him... Hides out in his home, or lab... Guy's got such balls. He changes my code without asking. My code," she snarled. "Like I'm some shoddy neophyte."

After releasing her grievances about Peter Cavenaugh to a Carpstra higher-up other than Ryan Ito, Detective Flores watched Kwok leave the interview in a huff and remarked slightly sarcastically to Donovan.

"Carpstra... Just one big happy family."

Then, exhausted, the two took a five-minute break before summoning George Joz, the department's ASU intern. Figuring because the kid was a grad student he probably knew less than nothing, Flores was surprised when Joz provided him with the first real piece of information.

"Peter's a legend. I've been here, about six months... He's always in high demand. Works on key projects all over the state... Is that why he's not here now? asked George, with immense admiration.

162

Something in the young man's candor galvanized Elizabeth Donovan to act on a hunch. Bringing up Peter Cavenaugh's worklogs for the past year, she soon realized several of his charges did not add up.

Leaning close to Flores, intending her words for his ears only, Donovan said.

"If what George is saying is true, Peter was charging to programs which he was not assigned. See these projects… Each has a top-secret designation which requires all work be performed inhouse in our lock-down areas. You can't even bring a cellphone into these rooms. Was he mischarging, or working on these projects elsewhere? We need to ask Ryan," insisted Beth Donovan with a concerned look.

"Just maybe whatever it was he was doing, he wanted to get caught," theorized Flores with a new respect for timesheet accuracy.

Both completely bewildered as to how Peter Cavenaugh was actually spending his last days… and nights.

Their last interview was with a young woman named, Olivia Ash.

The stylish twenty-something with her trending bob hairstyle and perfect posture sat at the small round table across from Michael Flores and Elizabeth Donovan. Radiating with self-confidence, Olivia Ash removed her crisply-folded timesheet log from the pocket of her wrinkle-free khaki-colored pencil skirt, and placed it on the table in front of her.

All too eager to answer any question about herself and her work; what Olivia Ash was not prepared for were Flores' queries about Peter Cavenaugh. Her keen, natural aptitude for analytical analysis immediately telling her the initial questions put forth did not add up to the stated purpose of the meeting.

"Did Peter Cavenaugh ever talk about issues? With the military?" she repeated. "Sorry. We rarely spoke beyond a polite hello… Anyway, that's just not Peter's style. He's very tightlipped about… Say, what's this really about?"

Ignoring her query, Flores asked a few more questions before ending their disappointing conversation with his pat closing remarks and gratitude.

Maintaining perfect posture, Olivia Ash gathered her things as she rose from her chair and gracefully promenaded to the door. Placing a delicate hand on the doorknob she paused in deep thought before slowly pivoting to face them.

"Unless you mean when he actually served in the military," she reflected.

"He talked to you about his time in the Army?" asked Flores in utter shock.

Giving the young woman his undivided attention as Elizabeth Donovan, likewise, stopped writing and put down her pen.

"There was this one time… I remember because it was so unlike Peter… He just started talking to me," recalled Olivia.

"It was weird that he talked to you, or that he talked to you about being in the military?" probed the detective.

"Well… Both… For one thing, Peter never shared personal stuff. And two, it was lunchtime. He rarely worked in the lab during daytime," she disclosed.

"But on that day?" urged Donovan; encouraging Ash to elaborate.

"That day I was in the lab desperately trying to fix a bug in a military legacy system. Peter must've seen the unit, or me struggling… Anyway, he comes right up and starts talking," she said; lost momentarily in deep thought.

"And this was unusual," acknowledged Flores; grasping the significance from what others had said about the introverted Cavenaugh.

"Well, yay. He says, Olivia what's the problem? Olivia what's the problem? I didn't think he even knew my name. I was so honored," she exclaimed bursting with pride.

"Then he fixes the bug in like two minutes. I was so impressed… He's literally a genius. Anyway, he tells me he had a similar problem with an older version during Desert Shield. That he and his buddies were taking fire… and, he almost got his ass blown off because the damn things weren't working right. Oh… And, he learned a big lesson that day," she said; trying to recall the smallest detail.

"What lesson was that?" asked Elizabeth Donovan.

Anxious to get to the bottom of Peter Cavenaugh's timecard discrepancies.

"How did he put it? Oh yeah… Peter said, 'Make sure it works the way its suppose to… Learn all its quirks. Its glitches. Don't assume it's fine just because it came right out of the box. More often some moron before you has rendered it N.F.G… No F-ing Good,'" reflected Olivia; trying to use Cavenaugh's exact words.

"Then he said to me, 'If you don't… people die.' What do you think Peter meant by that?" she asked Flores, looking quite puzzled.

"Do you remember the exact date of your conversation? asked the detective, impressed by the young woman's recall.

Intuitively Flores knew what her response would be.

"Actually, it was three days ago. Come to think of it… I haven't seen Peter since," she confirmed with a raised eyebrow.

Then Olivia Ash said solemnly.

"You might as well tell me… What happened to Peter?"

Just then Ryan Ito entered the room and joined the meeting.

"Ms. Ash… If you would… I have a few more questions for you and Mr. Ito," requested Detective Flores politely; motioning for her to return.

Warily eyeing the stranger Olivia Ash quietly retook her seat sensing things were about to get very interesting.

"I'm sorry to inform you that Peter Cavenaugh has died," disclosed Flores gently taking out his police badge. "And, that you and Ryan Ito were possibly the last two people to see him alive… Except for the man who killed him."

***

At long last the ballgame miraculously ended when the Arizona Diamondbacks came from behind in the bottom of the ninth to prevail seven to six after a single brought home the winning run. Fans who had not left earlier hurriedly filtered out of the stadium into emptying parking lots. Many leaving in single vehicles while others were being urged to carefully step up and take a seat on a city bus, or community van. Almost everyone fighting some degree of frustration while moving bumper-to-bumper in a single-file crawl towards the exits. Painstakingly following directions from bored attendants dressed in reflective jackets as more than one driver was forced to take a direction they never wanted to go. Still others consciously choosing to creep onto the Arizona State Route 101 Pima freeway; then, immediately regretting it. Wishing they could magically whisk themselves out of the gridlock.

Back inside the baseball stadium Officer Mitzy Burton remained on high alert. Stating she would relax when her peahens were tucked back inside the safe house in the quiet Phoenix bedroom community of Ahwatukee.

For security reasons, and because of Esther's limited mobility, Officer Burton ordered both Esther and Mattie to remain seated until the entire stadium and parking lot had emptied. Turning a deaf ear to the women's protests, Burton then directed Officers Brian Warner and Jeffory Fenton to retrieve the two unmarked police cars and rendezvous at the stadium's main entry. Sending her remaining detail to secure their route while she escorted the women out.

"Okay ladies… Time to go home," announced Officer Burton to her charges.

Carefully ascending the stairs, Esther gingerly tackled one step at a time; grabbing the center banister with one hand, while with the other, using her walking stick for added stability. All the while Esther vehemently protesting any assistance from Mattie or Burton; and insisting everyone should just back the hell off.

When eventually they did reach the main concourse, Mitzy Burton appeared immensely displeased.

"Shit. Where the hell's my ride?" exclaimed Burton. "We parked the damn thing right here."

The four-seater golf cart in which they had ridden earlier was supposed to be available the entire day. Now it, along with any form of transportation and stadium personnel, was nowhere to be found.

"What now?" inquired Mattie, concerned.

"Murphy… Find me a damn golf cart or wheelchair ASAP," commanded Burton into the microphone hidden inside her baseball jersey.

"On it," garbled the overly-loud response in her earpiece; causing her to wince.

After lowering the volume, Burton turned to Esther and explained.

"There's no way to sugar coat it… Our transport's gone and I need to get you out of here right now. We've been lucky so far, but I'm done taking chances with your lives. If something doesn't arrive soon, I believe our best option is to carry you out."

"The hell you will!" defied Esther.

Limping off down the corridor with Mattie and Mitzy Burton chasing after her begging her to stop; Mattie because of Esther's sprain, Officer Burton because out in the open they were easy targets.

"Tante... Let them," pleaded Mattie.

"Look Mrs. Hausman... It's a hard trek cross the concourse and up that steep incline on the outer path to the long walkway leading to the curb," informed Officer Burton, hoping her charge would see reason.

"So? You coming?" asserted Esther humiliated; continuing to walk.

With neither golf cart nor wheelchair in sight, Officer Burton reluctantly joined the petite older woman and her niece.

"Murphy... Anytime now," she barked into her shirt; maintaining a keen vigilance as they ambled down the corridor.

The women's voices and footsteps echoing loudly inside the facility.

Then, seeing her aunt beginning to falter, Mattie pulled up.

"Tante... Sorry. Do you mind? I need to a moment," insisted Mattie lowering herself onto one of the top row seats.

Although fully aware she was the real reason they paused, Esther played along. Secretly grateful to rest her throbbing limb, she settled onto the seat beside her niece and involuntary sighed.

"So ladies... Where're we going for dinner?" asked Esther impishly.

Dabbing beads of glistening perspiration from her forehead; her suggestion immediately met with lively rebukes from both Mattie and Burton. That is until angry voices erupted nearby grabbing the officer's attention.

"Quiet... Quiet! No one's supposed to be in here but us," snapped Officer Burton, searching every crevasse of the stadium.

"Maybe they're your people," implied Mattie.

"No. I'd hear their chatter in my earpiece," disclosed Mitzy Burton.

Motioning to Esther and Mattie to quietly follow behind her, the women silently proceeded towards the exit in an effort to slip by the unidentified disagreement. It was Mitzy Burton who first spied the two, barely discernable silhouettes standing uncomfortably close to each other on a dark stairwell leading to the upper deck. Each man completely unaware he had an audience.

"Coincidence or ambush," weighed Burton tensing.

Treating the encounter as a worse-case scenario, Officer Burton gestured to the women to hide behind a wide concrete pillar.

Unable to clearly see the men's faces on the dark landing, Burton could tell one wore a ballpark vendor jacket, and the other, a taller man, was dressed in a light long-sleeved shirt and trousers. Determining whatever their heated dispute was had nothing to do with her charges; Officer Mitzy Burton opted to step in anyway on the chance they were armed and words turned into shots being fired.

"Excuse me gentlemen," she said in her best badass voice. "There a problem?"

Taken by surprise, the two silhouettes seemed to merge into one mythological monster as they simultaneously turned their icy glares upon her. Standing her ground, Burton raised her police badge high in front of her so there would be absolutely no doubt and reiterated with authority.

"I said… Is there a problem here?"

Instantly recognizing the badge, the two adversaries toned down their rhetoric.

"Tante… Stop!" shouted Mattie.

But it was too late. Esther's insatiable curiosity had gotten the better of her and she stepped out from behind the pillar to get a better look at the strangers.

Never once thinking these men might harm her; presuming instead those around her were overly protective. However when both men's burning eyes shifted to her, Esther immediately knew she had been mistaken.

No longer hearing Mattie and Burton's urgings to return to safety, Esther ears deafened with the same heart-pounding fear she felt the night Peter Cavenaugh was murdered. The night she swore she was being watched from her orchard. No, not watched… stalked.

Seeing Esther's traumatized expression, Mattie quickly stepped in front of her.

Meantime, while the strangers downplayed their dispute; one of the men decided to go a step further in amiably placating the officer.

"Yes Officer. Sorry Officer… Our behavior? Yes, inexcusable," capitulating; yet keying in on Esther.

Remaining at ease in his anonymity.

"How easily he deceived them. All except for her, the old woman," he thought. "I can see it on your face… She knows."

Still, for what it was worth, he enjoyed seeing her squirm. So much so he could hardly contain his exhilaration. Finding the paradox utterly laughable until something appeared on the old woman's face… recognition.

His suspicion had been right; she had seen him that night. Had she witnessed the kill too? Why had she not said anything to the police officer?

"Cat got your tongue, sweetie. Too scared to talk? You should be."

Her noticeable anguish causing titillating chills to surge throughout his body as he imagined himself pulling Peter Cavenaugh's firearm from his pocket, and bam! With the old woman gone the police had no witness; no witness, no case.

There had been one other brief opportunity earlier that afternoon; but, he had lost the old bat in the crowd. Later he spotted her sitting in the stands;

however, he had no clear shot. It then occurred to him the police had counted on him being there. Why else use their star witness as bait unless the bastards were positioned to move in and arrest him as soon as he exposed himself?

"Pretty ballsy... Who came up with that idea, sweetheart? The suit?" ridiculing the lead detective's feeble attempt to capture him.

After the ballgame he had all but decided to resume his mild, average-Joe facade and try another day when he noticed the women still in their seats. When eventually they began walking towards the emptied baseball stadium's exit, he had stealthily moved ahead; finding an elevated vantage point within a darkened stairwell where he could lie in wait. His hand inside his pocket resting on the gun.

What he had not expected was a confrontation with a ghost from his past. Keeping the gun hidden while dealing with his adversary the man sensed his time had run out; anticipating both the women and the calvary would be arriving momentarily.

Incensed, he would bide his time. Never doubting his ability to find the cops' precious witness any time he wanted; just as he had that second night in the orchard, and the next day when they had whisked her away into protective custody. All he needed was the opportunity.

As for Esther, immediately after stepping from behind the pillar her lightheadedness and weakened body necessitated she lean heavily on her walking stick. However, it was the shadowy figures' glares which really caused her to sicken.

"He's here... The man who going to kill me," her head screamed; yet said nothing. "Arrest them! One of them is the murderer. I can't tell you which... But it's him."

However just like that night, Esther's courage failed her and she froze. Collapsing as she lost her balance and involuntarily let go of the walking stick.

Horrified, Mattie grabbed the ashen woman in midair and searched for the nearest chair. As she assisted Esther onto the seat, Mattie followed her aunt's terrified eyes back to the menacing strangers. It was all she needed to know.

"Burton!" yelled Mattie, desperately trying to get the officer's attention.

But her shout was drowned out by the high-pitch whine of a golf cart speeding towards them. As the cart screeched to a halt between the women and what looked like a potentially dangerous situation, three members of the security team jumped out and immediately surrounded their charges.

"Gentlemen… that's our ride," declared Officer Burton fixed on the men. Then turning to Esther and Mattie she added.

"Ladies… Time to go."

Once the women were firmly seated, Mitzy ordered Murphy to vacate with all speed.

"Later old gal," snickered the man under his breath; glaring at the golf cart as it rounded the corner and disappear.

***

He had been sitting in the last row of the upper deck watching the explosive situation unfold. Having changed into his street clothes, from the safety of his high perch Terco closely observed the drama playing out between a stranger and his boss. Their angry shouting, he suspected, pertaining to some lucrative deal gone bad.

"What the hell, Jefe?" exclaimed Terco laughing.

It was not often he got to see his steadfast manager erupt with such uncharacteristic fury. He had decided to enjoy the show until he noticed three women heading straight for the hot-blooded dispute. Worse, he recognized the youngest dressed in her oversized D-backs jersey carrying that extraordinarily large floppy hat. Having been royally humiliated by her earlier his first thought was, she deserved whatever trouble she was walked into.

Then he saw the struggling older woman and remembered her kindness. Rolling his eyes, Terco swore under his breath and raced down the stairs towards them. Abandoning his rule of staying out of other peoples' affairs, he stopped in his tracks when the third woman began interfering in the men's argument.

"Hey lady… Get out of there!" yelled Terco.

Believing she was crazy, until he saw her hold something in the air and identify herself clear as a bell.

"Police."

Not wanting to have anything to do with cops, Terco stayed well-hidden and watched the tense standoff from afar. Suddenly several men, whom he presumed were police backup, noisily arrived on the scene in a speeding golf cart and whisked the women out of the stadium.

Turning his attention back to the two men, the adversaries appeared to hold their ground for what seemed an eternity; then backed away from each other. As the men exited in opposite directions, Terco's first thought was to follow the intriguing new stranger.

His instincts told him to stick with Silva, for now.

Chapter 10

"The meaning of life is that it stops."

~ Franz Kafka

Happy hour at the bustling Backstop Micro-Brewery and Grill in Old Scottsdale overflowed with customers looking for a little fun… a little, companionship. Bar hopping cohorts noisily drifting in and out of the establishment enthusiastically pushing open the heavy, stained-glass double doors with vertically elongated solid brass baseball bat handles; eager to sample the bar's specialties before moving on to their next watering hole, or home.

Lovers, or those soon-to-be, huddled together in quiet private corners. Hidden away from the rest of the world to concentrate solely on each other. Family and friends, coworkers and new acquaintances alike gathered around tables, wooden barrelheads, and makeshift surfaces, or bellied-up to the elaborately-carved massive oak bar. Their glasses filled to the brim with lip-smacking elixirs clinked, and spilled… and sometimes shattered. All while servers scurried about delivering trays piled sky-high with mouthwatering, greasy, comfort foods to ravenous guests. Vegetarians gleefully rubbed elbows with carnivore pals; all while resenting the owners' patronization and indifference toward them with their overpriced, meager meatless menu, thoughtlessly prepared and proportionally sparce.

The place rocked with approving cheers, disappointed groans, and a clamor of exuberant handclapping and tabletop fist poundings. Adding to the joint's jazzed ambiance, extra-large screens broadcast a wide variety of sporting events nonstop throughout the building; even in the bathrooms. Thus lessening the chance of missing that once-in-a-lifetime play, or up-to-the-minute fantasy league analysis.

It was during this time Homicide Detective Michael Flores entered the Backstop Micro-Brewery feeling both pleased and uncharacteristically nervous.

Pleased because his afternoon meetings at Carpstra had yielded significant information in the Peter Cavenaugh murder investigation; which he planned on analyzing later that night. Nervous, because the meetings ended later than expected and caused him to hit heavy rush-hour traffic; making him extremely late for his date with the vivacious True Brew employee, Zoe Bookman.

Praying the attractive café server had not given up on him and left. Doubt loomed over Flores as he stood at the hostess station searching the jammed-pack room for the adorable Zoe. When finally their eyes did meet, her face lit up; warming his heart and sending his spirits soaring.

"Over here!" shouted Zoe, enthusiastically waving to him.

The True Brew employee radiantly beaming as she patted an open barstool she had been saving for him. She, watching with delight as the handsome police officer broadly smiled at her while smoothly navigating through the crowd.

For his part, Michael Flores was caught completely off guard by the young woman's transformation. Although stunning dressed in the café's casual T-shirt, jeans and wrap-around apron; Zoe Bookman had metamorphosed into a classic vision of femininity draped in an elegant, pale-peach vintage cotton sundress which clung to every curve of her well-toned figure. Her previous pulled-back ponytail had since been released, allowing her thick dark caramel locks to gracefully fall in loose waves around her shoulders.

The look on Michael Flores' face told Zoe all she needed to know. Her efforts to impress had been an undeniable success; not that she really needed to try.

"Sorry. I got hung up. I know... I should've called... I hoped you'd wait. Honestly, I'm not sure I would have. You have every right to be angry and, well,... Anyway, I'm really glad you did... wait I mean," he stammered, feeling like a school boy.

Taking the seat beside her, Flores was unable to take his eyes off the breathtaking young woman. Zoe, amused by the towering detective's sincere groveling, eventually took pity on Michael after a bit of teasing and convinced him all was well.

In truth, Zoe had almost left several times. It had been a long day and she still had hours of graduate school studying ahead of her that night. She had given him 15 minutes more before heading home when he showed. She had almost forgotten how devilishly handsome and irresistibly funny the detective was. Now, spellbound by his impish grin and dry sense of humor, Zoe Bookman was very glad she stayed.

Soon the two were conversing with the same easy-going bantering they had established earlier. With the surrounding chaos and racket a viable excuse to surrender to their undeniable mutual attraction, Zoe pulled Michael closer to her ear to hear him better.

Breathing in the clinging aromas of warm roasted coffee beans and sweet pastries lightly brushed with cinnamon on Zoe's soft skin, long after her shift ended; in that moment, Michael Flores felt all was right with the world. Something he had not felt since his investigation into Peter Cavenaugh's gruesome murder began.

Having arrived at the bar mentally exhausted, Michael could think of no better way to set aside the grueling case, if only for a few hours, and recharge. Feeling too he would be a damn fool not to establish a relationship with this extraordinary woman, and see how far it might go.

"So… How'd the meeting go?" she asked sweetly.

The simple question asked in a voice so disarming it melted on Flores' ears like soft butter on a hot muffin.

"Oh… Right. The pile of papers… Not particularly interesting. You know… police stuff," steering the conversation back her. "I'd really like to hear about your day. If that's okay."

During the next few hours the two shared glimpses of their lives; telling amusing stories about jobs, family, even childhood pets. Both intuitively feeling safe revealing their imperfect selves; neither feeling the need to impress, or exaggerate. Then, halfway through a large platter of fried pickles and sliders Michael's phone rang; rudely reminding him why he was in town.

"Flores… We had a small incident," stated Mitzy Burton coolly.

Filtering out the restaurant noise, Detective Flores gave all his attention to the officer' account of the event after the ballgame.

From the moment he answered his phone, Zoe watched Michael's entire persona change. Gone was the charming, easy-going guy with the dry sense of humor. His posture became more rigid; his voice more authoritative, official. Before long Zoe found herself sitting next to a completely different person, Homicide Detective Michael Flores of Tucson's Violent Crimes Division.

Guessing her handsome lawman would soon leave her and return to the mysterious investigation now consuming his life, Zoe's heart sank. Wondering, sadly, if she would ever see him again; hoping with all her heart she would.

"During the Carpstra meetings. And, you're sure everyone's okay. What do you mean yes and no? Esther recognized who? He… recognized her," his calm voice unable to hide inflections of concern.

Stepping down off the elevated barstool, Flores slowly, gently, intertwined Zoe's fingers with his. Looking into her warm eyes he saw her acknowledgment; their wonderful evening had come to an end.

"I'll be right there… What? I need to wait? Why? Who's coming? Glee Piozzi? Who the hell is Glee Pio…? Oh right, Dr. Singh's… Seriously?" he exclaimed, baffled by Officer Burton's instruction not to leave the bar.

In the past, the detective had found the quirky doctor's assistant to be reasonably amusing; attributing her eccentricities to too much time spent locked up in her lab with the dead. Tonight, however, he believed Glee Piozzi had crossed the professional line. Flores could think of no possible reason why the Tucson lab assistant was driving over 120 miles to speak with him in person. Especially since face-to-face meetings were just as easily accomplished with a cellphone.

Suspecting Glee's need was not as urgent as others were led to believe, and resenting her for delaying his departure to the safe house, was the proverbial straw. Then he realized the longer he had to wait, the more he could rationalize spending that time with Zoe, he became somewhat placated. Nevertheless feeling the time had come to insist Dr. Singh assign another forensic technician to his future cases.

Flores was still conversing with Mitzy Burton when he watched the stylish hostess briskly walking towards him. As she did, he barely made out the out-of-step gait of the shorter Glee Piozzi following closely behind her. Tightly clutching a brown pocket expansion file folder against her breasts, Glee seemed to be protecting its contents with her life.

When at last the hostess reached Michael and Zoe, she stopped so abruptly Glee was caught completely off guard. Quickly side-stepping to avoid a collision with her, Dr. Singh's assistant awkwardly stumbled into a group of men and their generously filled pilsner glasses. Three of the men regained their balance without incident; unfortunately, a fourth man spilled the contents of his glass on both himself and her.

After profusely apologizing and handing him a fist-full of napkins, Glee insisted on paying his cleaning bill and bought the group another round before turning her attention to her favorite Tucson police detective.

"Glee. What you are doing here?" demanded Flores; exasperated with the lab assistant on so many levels.

"He didn't call? Detective Rub... He said he would call," responded Glee, answering a question with a question.

Clearly not the entrance or the greeting Glee had hoped; even so, she knew once Michael Flores saw what she brought he would be thrilled with her initiative. Then, positioning herself between the detective and an unknown woman, Glee turned her back on his more-or-less attractive companion and faced only him.

"Not since this morning," snapped Flores; his chocolate eyes hardening.

"Hi there... I'm Michael's friend, Zoe... Zoe Bookman," said the friendly woman with a smile; tapping Glee on the shoulder.

With a backwards glance Glee quickly sized up her competition; then unapologetically returned to Flores.

"Pardon me... Must've been something I ate," Zoe said contritely; her suppressed giggle morphing into a rather loud snort.

Glee's rudeness could have bothered her, but she let it slide.

Seeing the poor woman's one-sided infatuation, Zoe sensed that despite her handsome detective's extensive criminal behavior training; when it came to Glee, he was completely clueless. Michael, on the other hand, was trying his best not to laugh at his date's goofy expression and ignored most of the doctor assistant's jabbering.

"That's what I'm trying tell you. I have something you need… For your investigation… I took it to your desk not knowing you weren't there. Next thing I know, Officer Pawlak sends me to Detective Rub," babbled Glee.

Hearing Vernon Rub's name, Flores made immediate eye contact with Glee.

"Detective Rub said he uncovered key evidence. He said he was going to call you… He didn't call you? Turns out he found the victim's glasses and something else of great interest. He was emphatic you get this ASAP… So, I volunteered. Anyway… Here… You should call him," she suggested; glad to finally be taken seriously.

From inside the protected brown expansion folder Michael Flores pulled out a clear evidence pouch and returned the folder to its keeper. Peeking inside he found a mud-stained, silver polyethylene terephthalate antistatic case housing a green, broken printed circuit board.

"He said, tell him I found it ride'n the range. Does that make sense?" she asked, repeating Rub's message verbatim.

With great satisfaction Glee watched a broad smile appeared on Flores' face; followed by the detective suddenly excusing himself. Which Glee supposed was to find a quiet place to call his colleague.

"Wait, Detective… I have something else… for you," shouted Glee; her voice trailing off as the preoccupied Flores hastily stepped away.

Finding themselves left alone, the two women quietly looked around the room for a legitimate distraction. When none appeared, they found they had no choice but to strike up a cordial, yet restrained, conversation.

"So… How do know Michael? I mean, Detective Flores," inquired Glee in a way which implied the two were more than work colleagues.

"We're friends," responded Zoe, letting on little else. "You?"

"Shit... I really need to give this to him," Glee asserted anxiously; purposely avoiding Zoe's question.

Pulling a photo sheet from her folder, Glee searched the crowd for Flores.

"Those are really quite interesting," acknowledged Zoe; glimpsing at the two images.

One color image was that of an intact, complete tattoo. The other presumably the same tattoo, but partial, on a horribly disfigured arm. In other words, Peter Cavenaugh's arm after a pack of hungry coyotes dined on it.

"Wow... This one looks like it was ripped clear off the bone. What happened?" asked Zoe wide-eyed.

Glee, not believing for one moment Zoe's interest was real or that she had the slightest idea as to what she was seeing, replied mockingly.

"Oh really... You think so?"

"Do you know what it means? So bold... Many tattoo artists have a signature style and make their own stencils; customizing a traditional image. You can pretty much recognize their work," stated Zoe; tracing the intact tattoo with her index finger.

"Mine was designed. Want to see?" she offered.

Before Glee could think of a legitimate reason as to why she would not, Zoe gracefully lifted her ample waves off her slightly tanned shoulders; revealing an exquisite violet, iris bloom with a soft green, three-leafed stem.

"It symbolizes faith, courage, wisdom, respect... Qualities I admire. I know... Corny," she laughed sweetly; her face lighting up as she made fun of herself.

"No, it's absolutely... stunning," remarked Glee sincerely.

Likening the tattoo to the beautiful artistry of Monet. Noticing too, how the flower simply, delicately, adorned the curve of Zoe's swan-like neck.

181

"Shit... Even her tattoo's perfect," thought the miserable Glee. "No wonder he's fallen. Who wouldn't?"

In the past when Glee Piozzi truly wanted something she rarely stopped until it was hers. However after finding herself warming to the aethereal beauty, she realized it was time to give up.

"May I... Take a closer look?" Zoe asked politely; her thick locks flowing back into place.

"Sure. What the hell," replied the lab tech resigned; handing Zoe the sheet.

"What's Rakkasans?" she asked, reading the top of the intact tattoo.

Having done extensive research on the Asian-styled name, Glee felt she was now an expert on both the Rakkasans and their insignia.

"Bet there's a good story there," prodded Zoe; hoping Glee would tell it.

"I wish. But...," her words trailing off; not wanting to share this with the gorgeous woman too.

Furthermore, along with her broken heart and immense disappointment, Glee Piozzi did not want to add getting fired for sharing information of an ongoing murder investigation with Michael Flores' date.

"Here's what I think," conjectured Zoe; trying to lighten Glee's forlorn mood.

Appreciating she was contributing to the lab assistant's unhappiness, if only by association, Zoe concocted a series of ridiculous theories surrounding the tattoo. After a while Glee's spirits were somewhat lifted and she joined in. Before long the two were exchanging silly hypotheses, one more ludicrous than the other; roaring with laughter and truly enjoying the other's company.

In fact, when a tall man who had too much to drink lost his balance almost fell into their laps, without missing a beat the two cheerfully pushed him upright and sent him on his way. Resuming their crazy anecdotes as they ordered another round.

At some point over a shared basket of fries, the striking tattoo became oddly familiar to Zoe. Although concentrating as hard as her fuzzy mind allowed, she was unable to pull back her cerebral veil; yet continued trying as she shared her suspicion.

"Glee... This is going to sound crazy... But... I've seen this tattoo before," asserted Zoe loudly over the noisy room.

"Hey Bookman," called out Michael Flores.

Upon hearing her name, Zoe's hazy recollection vanished back into the dark recesses of her mind as she watched the handsome man saunter to her; his face full of regret.

Yet before Michael speak, Glee Piozzi chimed in.

"There's more... It's why I tracked you down in the first place," exclaimed Glee, showing him the tattoo photos. "It's all here with my notes."

Slipping the photo paper into a manilla folder, then inside the brown accordion file organizer, Glee patted the bundle before handing it over to an elated Flores. Hoping she had, at last, redeemed herself in the detectives' alluring eyes.

Placing the circuit board into the pouch, a strong sense of remorse washed over him.

"Glee, listen... I, uh... This is a great... really. Uh... Are you heading back now? Look, I've got to go. But hey... let me walk you both to your cars. It's the least I can do," he offered in a softened voice, not quite sure what else to say to her.

It was probably the longest, kindest exchange Michael ever had with Glee; and it sent her soaring. Even so she was not an idiot, accepting things as they were.

Still, his sincerity had brought her a joy she had known only in her dreams. She would replay this scene in her mind tonight, tomorrow… perhaps for weeks.

After texting Mitzy Burton he was on his way, Flores asked the women to gather their belongings.

"You know, thanks anyway… You two get going. I'm going to grab some caffeine before hitting the road. And, this place… well, it's as good as any," stated Glee, appearing completely done in.

Taking Flores' previously occupied stool, Glee swiveled the seat to face the bar and picked up the shiny menu. Pretending to read, still flying high, she was resolved not to let anything bring her down; especially the romantic couple's imminent goodbye.

"Know what? I'm going to stick around too… Just a while longer," added Zoe; wanting to make sure Glee was all right.

Beaming at Michael, Zoe squeezed his hand and called to Glee.

"Mind if I join you… My head needs clearing too. How 'bout we dump these nasty cold sliders and soggy pickles for some nachos?" she suggested in an upbeat tone.

Considering Zoe's proposal to commiserate Michael's departure by consuming mass quantities of unhealthy high-caloric comfort food a great idea; Glee, her nose still deep in the menu, gave a thumbs up.

Then, walking into Michel Flores' open arms, Zoe Bookman gently nestled her head against the detective's muscular chest. Trying to remain cheerful, she gazed up at him finding it impossible to hold back a tear.

"You going to call?" she uttered softly, forcing a smile.

"Absolutely… Soon as I can," assured Michael tenderly.

"Well, as they say… You've got my number. Don't wait too long," she kidded giggling. "I just might buy a sandwich for some other handsome customer."

Teasing him one last time as she gently thumped his muscular chest.

With a boyish grin Michael playfully pulled Zoe closer, pressing his body to hers. His hand lost in her thick, caramel waves as his mouth softly parted her silken lips. Warmly, gently caressing, their passions ignited. Neither wanting to let go, both lamenting their brief time.

When at last they separated, Michael tenderly cupped Zoe's chin and smiled; lightly tracing her moist lips with his fingertips. Then, after embracing one last time, Detective Flores gently squeezed Zoe Bookman's hand goodbye and disappeared into the crowd.

Speeding west on the 202 interstate, Michael Flores estimated he had about 35 minutes before arriving at the safe house. As he maneuvered the light traffic, try as he may, his feeble attempts to concentrate on his murder case failed. His thoughts of the irresistible Zoe Bookman, even now, proving too distracting.

Believing his investigation had already suffered, Flores categorically vowed to put his personal life on hold until Peter Cavenaugh's murderer was behind bars and Esther Hausman and Mattie Kaplan were safe.

***

Zoe Bookman and Glee Piozzi stayed behind at the Backstop Micro-Brewery and Grill much longer than intended. Ever since the dreamy Detective Michael Flores had left them to their own devices, the women threw caution to the wind; deciding, unwisely, to choose food as their way of lifting themselves out of their doldrums. Consoling each other long into the night, Zoe and Glee's final order in their ill-advised food orgy included an ample slice of freshly baked hot apple pie and a medium hot fudge sundae. Deciding too, no debauchery would be complete without an Irish cream liqueur cappuccino mounded sky-high with whipped cream and generously sprinkled cinnamon.

Comforted by each tasty morsel of over-indulgence, the two eventually found that like most highs, their euphoric mood was merely temporary. And, that by the time they decided to stop their teeth ached, bodies tingled, and stomachs bloated from massive quantities of simple carbohydrates.

A bright spot in their evening was their newfound friendship.

"I just don't mean guys who are single… I mean guys who aren't lying on Doc's slab. You know… alive," shared Glee laughing about her nonexistent love life.

Zoe, speaking of her creating beautiful self-sustaining outdoor environments where humans and wildlife peacefully coexisted. Overjoyed at receiving a grant to turn a neglected Phoenix urban area into such a place. Working at the coffee shop until she finished her thesis.

"Yep… Next month… I hang up my apron for good. Not that I minded… Most of the time I've met nice, interesting people," she giggled thinking of Michael. "But there's always knuckleheads… You know what I mean?"

"More than you know," snorted Glee; commiserating with Zoe.

On and on they chatted until after finally running out of things to say they called it a night. Which was about the same time they scraped the last bits of sweet whipped cream off their plates. Each complaining about paying for their sins for the next several weeks at the gym. Then, wishing each other goodnight outside the bar. A goodbye hug and promise to stay in touch. Parting as friends as they headed in opposite directions to their cars.

Not surprising since her arrival at the micro-brewery, the temperature had dropped substantially. In the Sonoran Desert, daytime blazing heat often turns pleasant by dusk; then, after the sun disappears behind western mountain ranges the air can become downright cold. This is especially true during winter months when temperatures can dip below freezing anytime of the day.

In her haste to get to the bar, she had regretfully forgotten a jacket and was now paying the price for her absentmindedness. The brisk night air, which nipped at her good mood, causing goosebumps to annoyingly tickled her arms.

Quickening her stride, she wrapped her arms around her chest and raised her shoulders in a failed attempt to block the chilly breeze from assaulting her neck. Doing her best to convince herself she was not freezing; her body unmercifully contradicted her with shivers and chattering teeth.

To make matters worse, because of the bar's overcrowded lot and Old Scottsdale's insufficient street parking, her only option had been a nearby residential area which did not post towing signs. Envisioning the car a few blocks away, she focused on how good it was going to feel once she got in and cranked up the heater.

When at last she reached the weakly-lit narrow road in the vintage 50's, southwest neighborhood; she began berating herself for giving in to every cheesy nacho chip, every forkful of apple pie, and every spoonful of hot fudge sundae. Still she had to admit, it had all tasted so damn good. Admitting too, there were worse ways to drown her sorrows.

A loud yawn escaped her lips.

Shaking the cobwebs from her brain she picked up the pace, contemplating stopping for coffee once she got going. Knowing she was not going to be worth a damn in the morning, she considered calling in sick; then recanted the idea. People depended on her to show up, she would tough it out.

Giddily envisioning sweet images of him, she pushed on until suddenly finding herself confused by the unfamiliar surroundings. Wondering if she had taken a wrong turn; or, if because it was light when she parked the street only seemed different in the dark.

Trying to get her bearings, she noticed how the crowds had dwindled to groups, then couples, and now, just her. Stopping, feeling a bit unnerved in her solitude, she automatically retrieved the old key she kept and placed it downward between two fingers.

"Better safe than sorry," she said to herself; feeling somewhat better.

Unaware of the figure hiding in shadows.

Never suspecting she was being hunted.

Never hearing the muffled footsteps stealthily drawing nearer, then directly behind her; until it was too late.

Too late to escape the hot lips pressing against her ear.

Too late to fight off being pulled off her heels. Clawing at her assailant's face. Targeting the menacing pale blue eyes as she desperately kicked and thrashed.

Unable to escape the large masculine hands from placing the deadly steel wire around her neck; squeezing tighter, still tighter. Too late to escape the vise-like grip dragging her into the dense oleander thicket.

Relentlessly struggling, her dizzy head screamed as she gasped for breath; ultimately fading into nothingness. Surrendering her limp body to death.

Chapter 11

"Carve your name on hearts, not tombstones..."

~ *Shannon Alder*

Driving aimlessly on the Valley's congested city streets, he aggressively weaved his RAM pickup among the dense traffic challenging fast-changing erratic stoplights and cutting off dawdling snowbirds. Stewing over the turn of events at the ballpark that day, he attributed his now soured stomach and splitting headache to his still unresolved problem. He felt absolutely no remorse or responsibility for his former associate's demise. In fact, he blamed his entire current predicament on his pal and now, the old bat.

The woman who witnessed him kill Peter Cavenaugh, Esther Hausman, was still alive and could finger him. He suspected the authorities were on to him; or at least had his description if not yet his name. However, without her testimony, they had no real proof.

Arriving early at the ballpark, he had covertly positioned himself to take his shot using a silencer on Peter Cavenaugh's revolver. Taking every precaution to ensure his fingerprints would not be on the gun in case he had to ditch it on the premises. Confident if the authorities did find it, they would trace it to a guy already dead.

But the cops had been lying in wait for him. Set a trap. Used the old woman as bait. Waited for him to make the attempt on her life. He had been too clever for them; seen her heavily guarded. When his plan proved too risky, he moved to his secondary location.

"Then, 'Mother Efer In Charge (MFIC) shows up again, after 20 years," he screamed; slamming his fist on the wheel.

His ire exploding, remembering the last time he and MFIC tangled. Finding out after decades they both lived in the Valley blissfully ignorant of each other.

Now, he needed to raise the stakes. Devise a more daring initiative to free himself of their witness without putting himself in further jeopardy. Yet despite his best efforts, his pounding head made inspiration impossible.

The more he rambled the more his reality became twisted, erratic. One second he was belittling the idiot cops for their lame efforts to connect him to Peter Cavenaugh. The next he was cursing the same people for not recognizing his brilliance; his art of deception, execution. Completely ignoring the messy trail of evidence he, himself, had left which pointed to his complicity.

"Assholes… They never proved anything… neither will you," he boasted; laughing.

Wincing as a sharp searing pain in his temple spoiled his elation.

"You think I'm some dumb grunt? Huh… By the time you figure it out it'll be too late for you… And your witness," he promised the cops.

Adding to his list of expendable people those who forced him to miss yet another opportunity to rid himself of the annoyance; just because they had ticked him off.

He had overheard the woman deny seeing anyone other than Pac Man that night. Yet, he knew the truth. He had been there, in the orchard. His eyes had locked onto hers. It was only a matter of time. She would cave, identity him, testify. It would be enough to send him to the chair.

"Who else knew, Pac Man?" he growled.

Recalling Peter's so-called run-in a few weeks earlier.

"Why didn't I see the red flag?" he questioned. "Faked… for my benefit."

Wondering if he had grown too complacent over the years, lost his edge.

"This is your fault Pac Man… If you weren't already dead… I'd kill ya. Now that asshole's back… Sticking his big nose in my business… Again!" he snarled.

Rubbing his aching temples as he complained to his invisible companion. Then snickering about how much fun he had maliciously liquidating his ex-associate.

Killing, anything, had never bothered him; in fact he rather enjoyed it.

There was something mesmerizing, even erotic, about watching the light go out of corporal beings. Like the intense power, gratification one got from watching porn, sexual and otherwise.

"Maybe that's why I hung around in those damn trees Pete," he admitted. "Watching you bleed out… A fête de jour… Pure ecstasy."

The images of the coyotes ripping apart his old friend still bringing him sadistic pleasure. Then, as if Esther was also there, he said.

"Scared you shitless today didn't I sweetie," letting out an unhinged chortle.

He had almost smelled the fear dripping off her clammy, wrinkled skin. Her ashen face, her terrified eyes; the remembrance making him shiver with delight.

Unexpectantly, a silver luxury sedan veered into his lane, cutting him off. Its driver purposely braking in front of him, slowing the sedan dangerously below the pickup's current speed.

Quickly reacting, he swerved the RAM onto the freeway's narrow shoulder; successfully avoiding crashing into the car as he rode out a skid.

Seething, he pressed down hard on the pickup's horn; taking the driver's careless action as a personal affront. Then, steering the RAM back into the flow of traffic, he stepped down hard on accelerator.

His only thought now… Payback.

On the attack, he maneuvered his RAM slightly ahead of the sedan in the center lane. Then he forced his pickup in front of the car; barely missing the offender's front bumper. Forcing the sedan driver to immediately slammed on his brakes.

The sounds of screeching tires and crashing metal was unmistakable.

Roaring with laughter he sped away, thoroughly gratified that he had left the sedan with a car up its ass. Continuing down the highway cheerfully, as if nothing had happened; calmly resuming his conversation with his invisible passengers.

"And you just stood there… Cops around you… All you had to do was open your big yap," he declared; perplexed by Esther's silence, and his good fortune.

"By the way, did you ever wonder if everyone was so hell-bent on keeping you under wraps, why they let you go to the game?" he asked invisible Esther. "Because you were bait… How's that feel sweetie? A piece of raw meat to flush me out."

"But how'd they know I'd show," he considered. "Somebody ratted."

His realization leading him to reconsider his associates' loyalties.

"Who's got the guts?"

Knowing of his reputation for harshly dealing with traitors, regardless of who.

With traffic thinning out, his calmer mind began making two mental lists; those he trusted, and those who might double-cross him. There were, of course, names on both. After all, he never figured Peter Cavenaugh had the balls to do exactly that.

"How'd that turn out, Pac Man?" he huffed. "You tell MFIC? Doesn't matter. He couldn't save you… And the cops can't save her."

Then switching gears he thought about the policewoman heading the old woman's security team.

"She… might prove problematic," he thought; then chuckled. "But then what do we say gang? We have no problems… Just opportunities."

His words reminding him of his decisions that night in the orchard. Initially, he had not deemed the old woman a threat. If he decided to kill her it would have merely been precautionary; intending on making her death swift.

Then he watched the cops whisk her away from her home and knew. She had become their witness against him; was holding all the cards.

His existence, his very life was in her feeble hands; and that kind of power over him would not be tolerated. He could feel her laughter, her disrespect. And because of it, he would make her last moments on earth a living hell.

***

For now he needed to calm down, cool off. Heading for one of his favorite watering holes, he decided to would work off his pent-up frustration by sweet-talking some cutie into a quick hookup. Soon he was tucked away in a corner booth sipping a warm Glenmorangie single malt. Allowing the melded flavors to caress his well-educated pallet as he savored the smooth aged whisky.

Hunting the crowd for that night's quarry, he became fixed on a hardedge brassy blonde with razor-cropped hair and multiple body piercings. Letting the warm liquor slide down his throat, he closed his icy-blue pale eyes; imagining the many ways he would use her.

He was all set to make his move when an attractive brunette caught his eye. Sitting alone at the bar, her young face projected the perfect mixture of self-conscious vulnerability and embarrassment.

"Easy pickings," he thought; suspecting she had been stood up.

Smacking his lips, he began familiarizing himself with every detail of his tasty next meal. He would let her stew in her own juices a few minutes longer; then, he would rescue her from her pitiful existence.

It was time.

Slinking out of the booth, as he took a step in her direction a broad-shouldered man in a dark blue suit pushed by him.

"Damn!" he cursed, glaring at his prey warmly greeting the man.

Annoyed, he scowled at the couple one last time before resuming his hunt. The second glance rendering him utterly speechless. He had seen the man once before; yet, immediately knew it was him.

The suit was the same man who had been in the old woman's driveway the second night he had hidden in her orchard. There was no mistake. The neglected young beauty's date was none other than the Tucson cop spearheading the witness's protection, murder investigation, and apprehension of… him.

Howling at the absurdity, a few bar patrons turned in his direction. He ignored them. The game had gotten a lot more interesting.

Pushing back into the recesses of the booth he observed the couple's predictable mating dance undetected. The suit gliding onto the barstool, leaning in close. His lips pressing against her delicate earlobe as they conversed in the noisy tavern.

"True love," he retched. Unaware the couple's romance was in its infancy.

Then came another startling realization. This one making the hairs on the back of his neck stand on end.

"Son of a bitch… True Brew," he exclaimed, stupefied by the coincidence.

The brunette was none other than the pony-tailed café server who had waited on him and Peter Cavenaugh the morning of their attention-grabbing argument.

Unable to think of anything noteworthy other than the brief, initial tiff. Once he and Cavenaugh had poured into that booth nothing significant or damning occurred. Leading him to wonder what exactly it was that True Brew was sharing with her cop boyfriend. And, if there were now two witnesses.

"Okay… Who the hell is this?" he growled.

Half rising in his seat, he watched with fascination as the clumsy new arrival waddled like a duck behind the tall graceful hostess walking briskly to the lovebirds. Not altogether unpleasing; still, it was quite obvious the odd little creature was not at all comfortable in this crowded pond. Then, upon reaching the couple, the hostess stopped short; the duckling, however, did not.

It was a spectacle worthy of a scripted comedy. In her vain attempt to avoid the hostess, the duckling tripped over her own feet. Stumbling into a group of men minding their own business she instinctively grabbed one man's arm, causing him to splash his golden ale over the lot of them. The beer-soaked men cursing their displeasure as the suit looked on mortified.

"C'mon suit… Where's your sense of humor?" he chuckled; enjoying the folly.

The cop, not so much.

Yet, whatever euphoria he felt quickly vanished as the new arrival pulled out a familiar plastic pouch from the brown accordion pocket organizer she held. Handing over the pouch to the suit, he carefully removed a rectangular-shaped green object.

It was a circuit board much like the one lost in the desert during his fight with Peter Cavenaugh. Unable to tell if it was the same one, he knew he had to move closer and get a better look. However, before he could figure out just how to do that, the suit rushed out of the room taking it with him; leaving both women behind to gawk at each other.

It was True Brew who opened her mouth first.

Whatever she said must have defused the tension, because before long the two were behaving like long lost friends.

"Shit… Now what?" he uttered under his breath.

Apparently that was not all the quirky duckling had hidden in her folder; because the next thing she removed was a letter size sheet with photographs on it.

Rising inconspicuously, he strained to see the images. When that failed, he slipped out of the booth pretending to be slightly drunk. Staggering towards the women, he lowered his head to avoid eye contact with True Brew and purposely stumbled into her companion.

"Sorry ladies… Really crowded," he slurred contritely.

Leaning over the duckling's shoulder.

To his delight, the women were so completely engrossed their conversation they scarcely noticed him and jointly pushed him on his way. However before they did, he had gotten a glimpse of two familiar tattoos. One, Peter Cavenaugh's half-eaten arm; the other, a perfect tattoo exactly like his own.

It was after taking a seat on the opposite side of the bar that he remembered.

On the morning of the heated exchange in the café, he had been unaware that his cuff had caught the edge of the table as he and Cavenaugh slid into the booth. That snafu had caused his button to unfastened and his shirtsleeve to slide down around his elbow; clearly exposing the identical tattoo on his inner forearm. Now remembering it was True Brew's staring that brought the wardrobe malfunction to his attention.

"Did she remember? Connect the dots to him?" he wondered.

Tormented by the thought of yet another setback, he slammed back his drink. Then, before he could move closer to the women to hear what they were saying, the cop returned.

"Damn," he uttered.

Remaining seated, he did not want to chance the suit noticing he looked like someone the old woman picked out in a police photo gallery. Or, True Brew remembering him from the café. Anxiously, he watched the brunette passionately kiss her cop boyfriend goodbye and his quick departure.

Suspecting the cop was acting on the newly acquired information about him; he felt it essential to find out exactly what that information was.

With the women remaining behind, he sipped another whiskey hoping the warm liquid would dull his throbbing head. Impatiently tapping a finger against the bar top, he examined his options. Deliberating which of the two was the greater threat, he concluded both held secrets he desperately needed to acquire.

When at long last the women called it a night, he followed them outside. Holding the door open for a few party goers cheerfully getting out of the chilly night air; he cunningly blended into the crowd while the new friends said their farewells and left in opposite directions.

"Who to choose?" he asked himself; savoring his next move.

Following her into a quiet residential neighborhood, its sleepy streets devoid of sidewalks and streetlights more than met his needs. Completely deserted, the only sounds were the loud echoes of her heels striking the asphalt.

Purposely she quickened her pace. Defensively positioning a key between her index and second fingers; mindful to keep its pointed steel edges exposed, ready to strike.

"Had she seen him?" he wondered, keeping to the shadows.

Undeterred, he silently closed in on her with the nimbleness of a mercenary. Mimicking her steps passed drawn curtains and dimly-lit windows belonging to homeowners tucked safely behind insulated stucco walls; passed front yards of thick flowering barriers and old-growth scrubs and trees. The mature vegetation hiding the owners from overly-curious onlookers. Insulating the residents from whatever unpleasantness occurred beyond their property lines.

This time, there would be no witness.

Moving quietly behind her, in one swift move he looped the garrote's snare around her neck and tightened the sharp wire.

Frantically kicking and thrashing against her assailant, she fought with all her might to loosen the unescapable wire tightening around her throat. Dropping the key out of reach; fighting until no fight was left.

Brutishly he dragged her limp body into a dense oleander hedge; its broken branches oozing poisonous sap onto her torn flesh. Still alive, barely conscious, he cruelly punished her for information; stopping only when satisfied nothing more could be learned. After which he quickly, efficiently, let the lethal weapon finish its job. Leaving her broken body in the thicket, where it remained undetected until an unsuspecting dog walker found it the next day.

"Thanks sweetheart. It's been fun," he whispered, patting her lifeless cheek.

Moments later, behind the wheel of his parked RAM, he felt an exhilarating gratification he had not felt for years. Broadly smiling, he lovingly curled the garrote back into its natural position and then, like a father tucking his child into bed, tenderly placed the deadly snare into the driver side door well. There to sleep peacefully until needed once more.

Next, with his head against the bullet-holed headrest, he breathed a sigh of relief and drove away. Never giving another thought to the lifeless young woman he had just left in the brushes.

Later, heading south on Scottsdale Road, he called one of his cronies and calmly dictated new orders.

"Maintain surveillance. I'm on my way," he commanded.

Finding Peter Cavenaugh's replacement had not been all that difficult. Perhaps that was because in the back of his mind he always knew his relationship with Pac Man would come to an abrupt end, and had always kept an eye out.

True, this new man was not the genius Peter was, hardly from it. But what he lacked in brains he more than made up for in balls. Plus, the guy got the job done without questions; and ultimately that was all that really mattered.

"What's the expression? Next man, or woman up. See Pac Man… I told you I'd all work out," he crowed.

Again pretending the dead man was seated beside him.

"Now… Now it's time to take care of the old woman."

***

"You okay Mrs. Hausman?" he inquired; still on the road to the safe house.

"Esther," she insisted on the other end of the line. "Yes Michael, I'm fine."

Although she forcefully denied it to anyone who asked; the fact was, underneath her cool exterior, Esther Hausman was shaken to her core.

"I'm almost there," the detective assured her; not buying her story.

Exiting the I-10 freeway, Michael Flores was feeling guilty for both letting Esther Hausman and Mattie Kaplan attend the Diamondbacks game, and for leaving the charming Zoe Bookman with Glee Piozzi at the Backstop Micro-Brewery and Grill.

Admitting he had enjoyed Zoe' company more than he could have ever imagined. He also admitted it had been quite some time since someone had filled him with such amorous feelings. And, if he had had any qualms about her feelings for him, their passionate kiss goodbye had blown away any doubt.

Be that as it may, right now the job was all that mattered. Using all his energies to catch Peter Cavenaugh's murderer, and protect those he would harm. It also meant the captivating Zoe Bookman would have to wait, for now.

Approximately forty minutes after leaving the bar, Homicide Detective Michael Flores entered the bedroom village. Originally named Casa de Sueños in 1935, the area's second homeowner changed it to Ahwatukee; which supposedly is a Crow Nation Indian word meaning House of Dreams. Since then some have disputed Ahwatukee is an actual word; yet regardless, the name stuck.

Serenely cradled in a desirable valley surrounded by the South Mountain range to its north and west and its neighbors, the Wild Horse Pass Gila River Indian Community to its south, Ahwatukee was annexed by Phoenix in the 1980's. Even so a decade before, land developers had already begun transforming the picturesque desert, dairy farms, and cotton fields into another sprawling middle-to-upper class community.

It was there Esther and Mattie were hidden away on a dead-end street among a few neighbors on generously sized lots. A single-story house sparsely landscaped with medium-sized gravel, low-growing plants, and mature, extremely thorny bougainvillea and pyracantha hedges. The bougainvillea and pyracanthas were intentionally positioned against the home's perimeter to deter any sane person from entering the house through unconventional means.

Showing his badge, Flores walked into the front foyer and nodded to the security team. Each member of the detail acutely familiar with the Tucson Homicide Detective's image and his excellent reputation.

Taking a seat at the well-worn, Americana dining room table, Michael invited Esther and Mitzy Burton to join him. The weary Esther dropping her wise-cracking demeanor, sitting across from him eager to discuss her suspicion.

"So, was it him? The schmuck who killed Peter Cavenaugh," she asked.

"We don't know. We're still tracking the men down," disclosed Flores. "Could be they were two slobs in the wrong place… Could be the killer's long gone."

Hoping stress had impeded Esther's acute intuition; because if both their gut feeling were right, Esther most likely had literally dodged a bullet that day.

"Michael… If I'm so damn safe, why squirrel me away hundreds of miles from my home? Why all these armed guards? Surrounding me like I'm the Queen of Sheba," she exclaimed; demanding the truth.

"Esther, would I have let you go to the ballgame if…" he began saying.

"I forced you," interrupted Esther. "Look… You know I didn't see that guy get killed… or anything else that night."

"Michael… Tell her," pleaded Mattie, taking the seat beside her aunt.

"Okay, you're right," said Flores slowly. "I believe you… All of it. The problem is when you went outside with Tashia, I also believe the killer was in the orchard and saw you. And, I'm convinced he thinks you saw him too. That you're a witness… A threat… Today's encounter was probably innocent…

But, it also could have been a botched attempt on your life. Until I know for sure, I have to assume the latter."

Silence overtook the four as the detective's words sunk in. Michael Flores purposely leaving out the part that he expected another attempt to occur soon; one even more aggressive. Unaware at that moment the killer was doing exactly that.

"Can you stay awake awhile longer?" asked Flores, seeing Esther's eyes drooping.

"Let's get to work," she replied, straightening in her seat.

"Right... You suspected the taller of the two men. Why?" encouraged Michael.

As Esther spoke Flores noted the substantial credence he now placed in her words. It was quite different from their first contemptuous meeting. Her account of the incident collaborated by Burton, holding his complete attention.

Somewhere in the middle of Esther's story Mattie rejoined the group from the kitchen; adding her two cents as she set a cup of hot coffee on the table beside Flores' brown pocket organizer.

Slowly sipping the warm stimulant, Michael nodded at Mattie appreciatively. She, returning his smile, retook the seat beside her aunt; casually tucking her foot underneath her as she leaned back against the chair.

"She's gotten used to me," he thought; amused.

Recalling the tumultuous day she and her aunt had come into his life.

Since then he had become acutely aware of breaking his cardinal rule of getting too close to the people involved in the crime he was investigating. Fearing it was because of his leniency towards Esther she had her brush with danger.

"Okay... Assuming the tall guy is our killer... There's no way he'd know you'd be at the game. Unless," deduced Flores uneasily. "Unless he has help."

Thinking now it would have been nice if Burton had arrested the men for say, disturbing the peace. Then, they could have obtained fingerprints, shoe sizes, DNA; even interrogate them as persons of interest. Yet the prime directive had always been to keep the women safe; and that's exactly what she did.

"Esther… If you didn't see anyone that night," he restated. "How can you be so sure it was him?"

"I know it sounds crazy, but it was the look he shot me… Like I was hasenpfeffer. And if you remember… I did see something move in my orchard. Could've been four-legged… Could've been two… Could've been him," she whispered.

"Yeah… I beginning to think so too," replied Flores soberly.

"Look… a police sketch artist is coming tomorrow. While images are still fresh in your mind maybe we'll get lucky creating composites of both," he said optimistically.

"Wait… It was very dark… The men's faces were fuzzy… Like old photographs," protested Esther. "I may not be able."

"It's okay Tante… We'll talk it out. Don't forget Mitzy and I were there too," Mattie reassured her. Adding, "Michael, we've got this."

"Anything will help," affirmed the detective.

Trying his best to be supportive as he stifled an insistent yawn.

"It's like Tante said… The stairwell was dark," confirmed Mattie. "In fact, we actually heard the men before we saw them."

"Yeah… Like they were ready to duke it out," added Esther; her memory suddenly sparked. "Their voices… very distinctive. Those I'd recognize."

As the energized women began pooling details, Mattie quietly rose from her chair and left the room for a few moments. Returning shortly with a long green tray brimming with mugs, a carafe of hot coffee, four small plates, and a wide variety of pastries and berries. Certain the sugar jolt would sharpen their memories.

It was the break each needed to lighten the mood.

As soon as Mattie placed the tray on the table the four jovially attacked its contents. The chaos prompting Michael to recall the dinner he shared with Mattie, Esther, and Kyle the night prior to leaving for the safe house. Then, just as now, Michael Flores was certain no one ever left a Hausman gathering with an empty stomach, or empty hands. Reminding him in so many ways of his family in San Diego.

Rejuvenated, Flores smiled as he reheated his coffee. Then, after popping a few bites of apple crumb cake into his mouth he asked the group.

"What about skin tone, hair color, markings?" he inquired. "Anybody?"

"The tall guy, very light skinned… And, he was a lot taller than me," recalled Esther, refilling her mug.

Stirring ample liquid creamer into her dark brew until it had turned almost beige, Esther was about to take a sip when Mattie burst out laughing and chimed in.

"Tante… Almost everyone's taller than you," she teased affectionately before interjecting. "But he was… Tall. Maybe, close to six feet."

"Listen kid, I do okay," retorted Esther chuckling.

Squeezing Mattie's hand gently; discovering she too had gotten a second wind.

"They're both right," piped in Officer Burton. "I estimated the guy to be six feet one, maybe two. The other guy, maybe five nine, ten."

Adding to their observations as her own memory sharpened.

"It was dark. Hard to pinpoint features. Both men balked when asked to step forward. However, sometimes they would accidently lean into a lighter area. To me, the tall guy seemed middle-aged. Lean…. Short light hair…. Maybe blonde, sandy brown, a little gray. Dress… Business casual. Typical white long-sleeve shirt…. Not really a good choice for a day in the sun in my opinion," she commented.

Then pausing, Burton glanced at her notes and proposed.

"I'm not saying the tall guy shouldn't be our focus… But who's to say the shorter man's innocent in all this. They obviously had history… Friends? Enemies? Regardless, they were definitely arguing," affirmed Mitzy Burton. "And the shorter guy was wearing a red and white striped jacket. Maybe he works at the ballpark. Or, maybe he's an accomplice, trying to fit in."

"Find the vendor… ID our mysterious tall man," proposed Flores. "Think you can recognize the vendor from an employee badge?"

Each woman nodded enthusiastically.

Now, no one was tired.

"Mitzy, contact the stadium… Let's get copies of their employees' badges," requested Flores enthusiastically.

"On it," she replied; glad to do something constructive.

Unfazed it was outside regular business hours, Officer Burton immediately stepped away to call in a few favors.

"Anything else? Eyes color? I know it was dark," encouraged Michael; looking for any glimmer of recollection on their faces.

"Sorry… I was watching Mitzy for our next move. The situation had gotten pretty scary," Mattie admitted.

"The lightest blue I've ever seen," whispered Esther slowly; gazing into space.

The look of dread on her face giving Mattie and Flores only a small sense of how truly terrified the older woman still felt.

"Light blue, Esther?" encouraged the detective gently.

"Icicles. Barely a hint of color. I saw them when he leaned into the light. They pierced right through me like daggers," she recalled. "Daggers."

The three remaining silent until Esther returned to the conversation; noticing Flores' expandable brown folder.

"What's in there?" she asked, cocking her head.

Her insatiable curiosity peaked.

Flores removed the photo paper of the two tattoo images and handed it to her.

"Look familiar?" he asked calmly.

Hoping the images would jog her memory further without upsetting her.

Esther's eyes widened.

Looking first to Michael, then Mattie, Esther looked closely at the intact tattoo; then, the one of the shredded half-eaten arm. Shuddering, she pursed her lips in disgust.

"Tante's not a particular fan of tattoos," stated Mattie without further elaboration.

However, before Flores could inquire why, Esther scolded him.

"Son of a gun Michael! You've had these all this… Okay kid… Spill the beans."

Handing the sheet back to Flores.

Seconding her aunt, Mattie grabbed the photo sheet from Michael and compared the two images. Both women insisting he tell them about the tattoo and if he thought it had something to do with Peter Cavenaugh's death.

He was just about to explain when Officer Burton rejoined the group. Now, with all eyes glued on him, no one was going anywhere until he talked.

"Okay, first let me say I got this tonight. Honestly. Second, I'm not sure there is a connection. What I have is a hunch. And by the way, what makes you think I'm obligated to share any of this with you two," he laughed; their eyes riveted on him.

"Start talk'n Michael," demanded Esther.

Locking her hands together atop the table as she leaned forward.

Recognizing he was outnumbered, Detective Flores agreed to an abridged version.

"The tattoo's an older style insignia worn by some in the 187th Infantry Regiment… Part of the U.S. Army's 101st Airborne Division Air Assault," paraphrasing Glee Piozzi's research.

Suddenly the room went quiet. Almost everyone around him waiting for him to continue.

"So… Apparently the 187th originated as a World War II glider infantry unit. After the war, the Regiment was posted in Honshu and Hokkaido in northern occupied Japan. There, residents gave them the nickname, Rakkasans. Which in Japanese loosely translates to falling umbrella… Uh, guess there wasn't a word for paratroopers," he conjectured.

Taking a sip of coffee to quench his throat, Flores chuckled lightly as he watched the women pour over the photographs.

"Go on," ordered Mattie. "I can research it too, can't I?"

Snapping a photo of the intact tattoo with her phone.

"Sure… Why not," he smiled.

"Anyway, the name stuck… The Rakkasans are the only airborne warfare regiment in the Army's history to fight in every war since the development of airborne tactics including the Persian Gulf Wars. There… they were part of an airborne regimental combat team," he read; intrigued by its history.

"That's where Peter Cavenaugh comes in… He was there. Pretty cool, eh detective?" he read aloud accidentally.

The unofficial comments a token of Glee Piozzi's quirky sense of humor. However, having acquired a bit more respect for the lab assistant's expertise and tenacity that evening, he cut her some slack.

"The report also says this Rakkasans tattoo appears to be slightly customized for reasons unknown," added Flores. "From gliders to parachutes to air landings to helicopter air offensives… The Rakkasans have pioneered and mastered every airborne assault mode of its time."

"Very cool," commented Officer Burton with admiration.

"Tante K. A. Just as you said. RAKKASANS. The type matches Cavenaugh's," acknowledged Mattie; pointing to the intact tattoo.

"That's probably a parachute. And this… a bald eagle's wing," offered Burton comparing the images. "It makes sense."

"So, what happened to the Regiment?" inquired Esther.

More interested in the people who wore the tattoo than the tattoo itself.

"There's a final note. The 187th's still part of the 101st Airborne Division's Screaming Eagles… And with that ladies, I'm calling it a night," announced Flores; stretching as he drowsily rose from the table.

"Now we know the tattoo's history. What we don't know is if it had anything to do with Cavenaugh's death," added the homicide detective. "I hope to figure that out… tomorrow."

Leaving the photos for Mattie to mull over, Michael scanned the living room for a spot to bed down for the night. Spying a worn cloth-covered couch in a dark corner, he removed his wrinkled suit jacket and tossed it on a cushion staking his claim.

"You're not sleeping on that lumpy thing?" cautioned Thom Murphy, a senior member of Mitzy Burton's security detail. "I don't envy your back tomorrow."

The ill-fitting cushions suggesting to Flores that not only would he wake with a sore back, but a stiff neck. With a wily smirk and raised eyebrow, Flores was about to search for another, more comfortable option, when Mitzy Burton distracted him.

"Michael, let me introduce you to tonight's detail. You've met Thomas Murphy. This is Brian Warner, and over there, Jeffory Fenton," she said.

"Guys… A minute," requested Flores; gathering the team.

Speaking to the group, he and Burton verified their evening assignments. Assessing each man as a seasoned pro, Flores learned two were ex-military before joining the force, and the other came from several generations of lawmen. After which, Michael Flores pulled Mitzy Burton to one side, requesting quietly.

"Walk with me."

His desire to converse with her privately not lost on their two charges.

Grabbing a couple of flashlights off the counter, Detective Flores and Officer Burton exited the house. Walking the home's perimeter to check the residence for security breaches. Stopping midway, Flores took a leap of faith.

"Mitzy. Here's the thing… I don't know who I can trust," he confided.

Evaluating her body language for signs that she too might be involved.

"I was thinking the same thing, detective," she replied uneasily; holding his gaze.

"We've got a mole," the two uttered simultaneously.

With their mutual suspicions voiced, for the moment both decided to trust each other and form an alliance.

"How else did he find her more than a 100 miles from her home? In that ballpark among the countless stadiums in the Valley. Among all those people?" asserted Flores, frustrated. "He knew exactly where she was... Does he still?"

Believing the killer was not acting alone opened a whole new dimension to Flores' investigation.

"If your lunatic has an accomplice watching our every move, that's bad enough. If that person's a member of my team, not someone on the outside... we've got big problems," suggested Burton.

"Regardless, someone tipped him off. Until we find out who... Trust no one," Flores stressed.

"Agreed... So, this killer of yours... Top man, or flunky?" Burton wondered.

"My guess... the boss. Maybe head of some crime organization. Which makes me wonder why he got his hands dirty? He's no amateur. Unless... The profiler's report stated the killer shows indicators of severe Narcissistic Personality Disorder (NPD). A psychopath... If so, killing Peter Cavenaugh was personal."

"Oh... I got word. The sketch artist and vendor badge photos will be here tomorrow morning. Maybe we'll get lucky," broke in Burton.

"Great... From now on, they don't leave the house," ordered Detective Flores. "At this point Mitzy... expect anything."

Besides Vernon Rub, Flores felt Mitzy Burton might be the only other person on the case he could trust. He was certain about Rub; the jury was still out on Burton.

Returning inside, the two said goodnight to Esther and Mattie as the women waved back and ambled down the hall. Leaving Thomas Murphy, Brian Warner, and Jeffory Fenton to assume strategic positions before turning the house completely dark.

Satisfied knowing a fresh security detail would relieve them at dawn, the team settled in for a long night. Equipped with elite night vision goggle, the three conducted a steadfast vigilance at the windows searching the darkness for anything that could be interpreted as a threat.

Two of the men completely unaware the third had already betrayed them all twice that day.

***

"Michael, my mind's made up. I'm going home," professed Esther Hausman out of the blue.

Esther's emphatic proclamation causing space and time to stand still as all eyes in the room fixed on her. The only sound, coming from the living room television.

"Breaking news. We interrupt this program...,"

Sipping a glass of chilled ruby-red grapefruit juice, the older woman braced for the storm which was about to ensue. What she did not expect was the harshness in which all parties concerned pelted her.

"What? Absolutely not," protested Michael Flores.

Choking on his words as he spat bits of cream cheese covered bagel.

"Mrs. Hausman, you are some kind of crazy," scolded Mitzy Burton.

"Kids… I mean it…. I can't stay here forever. And at some point, your bosses are gonna want you back. So, what're ya gonna do? Quit your jobs? Move in with me and we'll all live happily ever after?" she argued.

As Esther ranted Mattie Kaplan slowly set down her spoon and quietly folded her trembling hands in her lap. Her pursed lips struggling to hold back words she knew once uttered she would live to regret.

"Sooner or later, he's gonna get me… Or you… Or you… Don't get me wrong. I don't want to die. But I refuse to let any of you die because of me," Esther asserted.

The visible dark circles under her eyes betraying her sleepless night; accentuating the petite older woman's drained features.

"Esther, it's only been a few days. We're making progress. We'll get him soon… I promise."

Flores' assurances having little affect.

To those who had met Esther Hausman in the past, unflappable, was a word they used to describe her. A formidable woman of great resilience and undeniable inner-strength, people felt Esther could always be counted on when needed. To take charge, protect the weak, provide a refuge. Tenacious from an early age, her mother had nicknamed her, Cookie; as in, one tough cookie.

Even so, like most, Esther had her demons. Those which had appeared in her golden years, like growing old without Max, loss of health and independence, she tackled head on. Yet some demons had persisted since youth.

One such particular concern, that she would be a burden or cause harm to another. This was the fear now cracking Esther's impenetrable armor.

Since the dreadful night she found Cavenaugh's rotting body, Esther had tossed and turned. Terrified Mattie, Kyle, even Michael, would fall victim to the deranged murderer while trying to protect her; the ballpark incident had torn her apart.

"You can't protect me forever!" she yelled at Michael.

Mattie's stormy gray eyes welled with tears as her despair turned into a seismic meltdown. Clenching her fists she forcefully struck the kitchen tabletop causing several items to topple. Then, rising to her feet, she erupted.

"Enough Tante... Enough! What? I should just let this piece of shit kill you? How dare you give up. How dare you... You're all I've got," she cried.

Hurling the hurtful words at her beloved aunt between gasps of air. The very thought of losing her only family member, shattering the young woman.

In many ways, the similarities between Esther and Mattie were uncanny. Silently admonishing the other with their glares, the undeniable clash between the two generations was painstakingly entering new phase. A familial crossroads in that age-old struggle of family order dominance between the matriarch and the young lioness.

Watching the standoff from the sidelines, Flores and Burton wisely chose to remain quiet. Keeping their heads down, they concentrated on their breakfast; both hoping Mattie could talk sense some into her stubborn aunt and change her mind.

"I'm tired... I miss my home. I miss Tashia. I miss..." vented Esther; now more as a desperate plea than demand.

"I know," replied Mattie somewhat empathetically; seeing her aunt's pain. "But you can't go home if you're dead."

The room remaining awkwardly quiet for some time. When someone did speak, the words spoken were so sugary-sweet it most likely made their teeth hurt. "Would you please pass… Could I possibly bother you for…"

It was more than Michael Flores could bear.

Deciding to take matters into his own hands, he attempted to deflate the passive-aggression tension in the room by disclosing a new lead in his investigation.

"Mmmm… Better get going," he said coolly; looking at his watch. "I'll be late for my meeting about the evidence we recently found on your place."

"Evidence. Found at our place? When? Where? Why didn't you say something? Who found it? Your Detective Rub? Kyle? How is Kyle?" The women probed excitedly; bombarding Michael with numerous questions.

It was as if the two had never quarreled at all.

Once again absorbed in theories about the crime, the Esther and Mattie badgered the poor detective with questions and hypotheses until he gladly succumbed to their interrogation.

"Whoa ladies… Whoa!" laughed Michael, raising his hands in total surrender.

"So where is it?" insisted Esther; glancing at brown folder. "In there?"

"Uh huh," he teased.

"C'mon… Don't be an idiot, let's see," demanded Mattie.

"Okay, okay… Look, but don't touch. I mean it… I can't have you two tainting the evidence."

After removing the plastic pouch containing the circuit board from the organizer, Flores answered the women's many questions until he had to leave.

"Could be this little green board's tied to Cavenaugh… Could be trash. Either way, I should find out this morning," he declared; stowing the object.

Then he added.

"Meantime, you three have a busy day. I expect a full report," he ordered.

Driving away from the safe house, Detective Flores felt upbeat. That his charges were in a much better mindset, and there would be no further talk about leaving protective custody. As for him, he was hopeful. Certain today would finally yield a major breakthrough.

Chapter 12
Loose Ends

Driving to Carpstra's Queen Creek facility, Detective Michael Flores lowered his SUV's windows and drew in a deep breath of cool, March desert air. Completely ignoring the brown haze of pollution hovering over the Valley, until an annoying tickle developed at the back of his throat; forcing him to down several substantial gulps from his water bottle to alleviate the persistent irritant. Despite that, and the full knowledge the day's temperature was expected to climb from its current tepid climate to an ungodly swelter, the Tucson homicide detective remained optimistic.

As he closed in on Carpstra, he pondered several unknowns in his murder case which he hoped to resolve by days end. First, there was the origin of the newly discovered printed circuit board; his strong feeling that it was somehow tied to Peter Cavenaugh. Second, the identities of both the supposed stadium vendor and the creep with whom he was arguing.

"Was the ballpark incident coincidence or, staged?" reflected Flores.

Leaning more to the latter the hairs stiffened on the back of his neck at the idea of the safe house being vulnerable. His knee-jerk reaction being to immediately return to Ahwatukee, grab the women and go... where?

"The identity and whereabouts of the deranged killer was still unknown. Did he have help? Someone on the security detail? Outside, keeping surveillance on the house?" Also unknown... More than one? Possibly."

Ultimately Flores decided unless he could flawlessly sneak the women out and go completely off grid, the safe house was still their best option.

"Besides, given the women's interest in the case… There was no way he could keep them from doing their part to identify the two men and help the sketch artist. Not unless he wanted an earful," he admitted.

Pulling into Carpstra's fabrication parking lot, Flores marveled at its sheer size. The enormous compound, even larger than the last, contained several multi-storied buildings over vast acres. After checking in with security and taking a seat in the main lobby, he noted several bold signs warning employees about strict adherence to cleanroom protocol.

"I agree… We should move the women… Maybe Flagstaff," suggested Rub; hearing about the ballpark incident. "All new security… Start fresh with our people."

The daily calls between Michael Flores and Vernon Rub had become invaluable in keeping their investigation teams equally updated. Weighing heavily on both their minds that morning was Esther and Mattie's safety.

"If we go the official route and the mole is ours… we've got no guarantee the killer won't be told our new, more isolated, location. I say we stay totally off the grid," suggested Flores. "What'd say cowboy? AWOL… Tomorrow?"

"Bright and early. Our little secret," Rub confirmed.

Then Vernon brought up the new evidence he found.

"Ito concurred. It's Carpstra's. Only… He's not sure its origin. Says it's circuitry pattern's extremely unique… Yeah… The Queen Creek facility… Hey, someone's coming… See you tomorrow," affirmed Flores; cutting their conversation short.

Noticing a tall, thin woman in a white lab coat striding purposely towards him from across the dazzling minimalist lobby, Homicide Detective Flores respectfully rose to his feet and straightened his suit jacket. A confident, striking figure with white hair cut fashionably short, rimless glasses and a perfectly aligned Carpstra badge on the crisp edge of her lab coat pocket. Everything about this woman screamed, "Don't mess with me, I'm the boss."

"Had to be," he snickered to himself.

Denoting yet another security level on her badge. Wondering too, if Carpstra ever ran out of color-coded designations.

She had just reached the detective when a call came through on his phone identifying Dr. Warren Lee Singh, Tucson Chief Medical Examiner.

"Sorry Doc. Have to get back to you," he thought, pressing Decline.

"Elise Holbrook, PCBA Engineering Director. You asked to speak with me?"

Asserted the woman, trying to grasp why on earth she needed to be bothered with the inessential disruption.

"PCBA?" inquired Flores.

"Printed Circuit Board Assembly," she responded condescendingly.

Expecting no less, Detective Flores introduced himself and got to the point.

"Recently a circuit board was found in the vicinity of a crime scene I'm investigating. It's possible the board's tied to the incident… It's also possible, it's one of yours… Carpstra's. Sorry… What is it you do here?" he asked Holbrook.

Interrupting himself to make damn sure the self-absorbed woman was the person he should be speaking to; and, that he was not wasting his time.

"I head the PCBA Engineers, Assembly Technicians, and Quality Control activities for the fabrication and shipping of new and improved technologies and products," she rattled off.

Tired of explaining herself to people who barely had a clue, Elise Holbrook impatiently tapped her toe against the hard floor waiting for the detective to digest the information and get on with it.

Neither impressed nor intimidated, Flores probably would have snoozed off at, I supervise PCBA Engineers, had talking to her not been important.

"So, it's safe to say you're familiar with all of the Carpstra's circuit boards manufactured at this facility? Who designed them… The employees who assemble them?" he pressed, ignoring her arrogance.

"Products… Production logistics. Yes… Lower-level employees… Project managers handle our workforce. Look, I'm really very busy. Can you get to the point?" she demanded, growing more annoyed.

It was then Detective Flores removed the labeled plastic evidence pouch from his organizer and handed it to her.

"Wherever did you get this?" she asked wide-eyed.

With renewed interest, the Director took a seat on the nearest chair; examining the green board through the clear bag. Pulling up a chair beside her, Flores nodded his permission and the director conducted a closer analysis.

Slipping her elegant hands into the pair of ESD anti-static gloves she kept in her lab coat pocket, Holbrook delicately removed the circuit board by its edges. She then proceeded to meticulously inspect its entire configuration; including its soldering flow and assembly.

As she did, Flores used the time to listen to the earlier voicemail from Dr. Singh.

"Michael. When was the last time you spoke to my assistant, Glee Piozzi?" asked a worried-sounding Chief Medical Examiner.

"Last night. Why?" he texted back.

The uneasiness in the doctor's voice nagging him to excuse himself and called the medical examiner when Elise Holbrook spoke.

"This PCBA's identification number and assembly configuration is congruent with one of our newest, highly confidential prototype of great promise. Again detective... How did you get this?" she insisted.

"Shouldn't your question really be, how did your revolutionary prototype slip out the doors of this fortress under your noses? Being the Government's your largest customer and all... I would think strict protocols would be place against such a theft?" goaded Flores.

"There are," she insisted; her certainty waning until realizing. "Mmmm... This specific assembly is quite interesting. Unique."

The director was about to elaborate when she was cut short by another Carpstra employee who seemed to appear out of thin air. Dressed just as immaculately with the same security designation, the woman in the blue lab coat would not be ignored.

"Elise... Your presence is sorely missed at the K45M briefing," interrupted the woman behind them.

Sizing up the new arrival who appeared a few years younger than Holbrook, the woman's badge identified her as Patricia Sawyer.

"Very smooth Patricia," thought Flores; her deliberate disruption derailing the director's train of thought.

His first thought was, the two women planned it; like a ploy to get out of a bad date. Then, something about Patricia Sawyer's manner compelled him to include her in his questioning.

"What can you tell me about a Carpstra employee named, Peter Cavenaugh?" he asked; paying close attention to their reactions.

Whereas both women denied knowing Cavenaugh, Flores noticed Patricia Sawyer's complexion paling. He pressed harder.

"Neither? I find that interesting since I heard Peter Cavenaugh is an internationally renowned design engineer. A rock star in your industry... I also heard he works in this facility from time-to-time. Sure you don't know him?"

Unsure if the later was true, Flores figured a little elaboration would not hurt.

"Well, yes, of course I've heard of him. But I don't know him... Mr. Flores, which question would you like me to elaborate? Your original question, or this? As you can see, I'm needed elsewhere," retorted Elise Holbrook.

Weary of his do-you-know game, Holbrook purposely negated Flores' rank and authority by referring to him as mister; a slight not lost on the detective.

"And you?" he inquired.

"No... Never met him," insisted Patricia Sawyer a little too forcefully.

Returning to the board's design Director Holbrook repeatedly examined both sides of its printed circuit. Carefully inspecting the substrate of its fiberglass epoxy resin, copper foil pattern and numerous components.

Catching Patricia Sawyer gawking, Flores likened the object's effect on her to that of a ghost having risen from a grave pointing a reproachful bony finger directly at her. Feeling the detective's eyes on her, Sawyer pretended to turn her attention elsewhere.

"You involved in this, or innocently nosy?" he wondered.

"Patricia... Go to the meeting without me," commanded Holbrook.

Her abrupt dismissal prompting the subordinate to leave without further delay.

"Wait, Ms. Sawyer. I have a few more questions," called Flores.

But by then the woman had vanished as quickly as she had arrived.

"Sorry… Ms. Holbrook, you said the circuit board was unique. How?" he inquired.

Unable to stop himself from giving the director a taste of her own medicine.

"Dr. Holbrook… First it's a PCBA not a PCB," she touted; critical of his ignorance.

"The difference?" he asked; believing the distinction inconsequential.

"Think of it this way… A PCB is a blank printed circuit board with conductive patterns… It's the backbone for an electronic device, a foundation, nothing more. A PCBA, printed circuit board assembly takes the PCB and makes it into a functional circuit, a turnkey… Partially or fully ready to use," explaining as it related to the evidence in her hands.

"This high-performance, double-sided PCBA uses our surface mount technology. The printed pattern's solder flow lines conform to our prototype's design… as do the plug-in integrated circuits and electronic components attached here and the diodes there. It's absolutely groundbreaking technology; which, if used against us could cripple our Government… I was quite concerned," declared Holbrook.

"You *were* concerned?" repeated Flores.

Puzzled by Holbrook's now, cool demeanor after finding out their ground-breaking product had gone missing.

"Yes, absolutely… Until I noticed this… Its deviations are brilliantly subtle, and… completely flawed," grinned Dr. Holbrook; pointing to a tiny area.

"Flawed… It doesn't work? Why would someone go to all the trouble of stealing it?" asked Flores, baffled. "Unless… they didn't know it was inoperable."

"Oh it'll work Detective... But, it will instantly, irrevocably, damage any device or unit that uses it," Holbrook said confidently; placing the PCBA back inside its pouch.

Then, deciding she had nothing further to contribute, Elise Holbrook abruptly stood up and handed the PCBA back to Michael Flores. However before leaving, she proposed an interesting hypothesis.

"Detective... Perhaps espionage was not the objective," she conjectured; bringing up an excellent point.

"Dr. Holbrook, who could create something like this?" Flores inquired; almost certain he knew the answer before asking.

"Our engineers and technicians are remarkedly skilled. However, to create something this intricate... this deceptive... requires someone well above the gifted people in this facility," she offered as her parting words.

Michael Flores knew exactly who she meant.

"It would require, Peter Cavenaugh."

***

The rest of the afternoon Detective Michael Flores continued playing phone tag with the elusive Warren Singh. Determined to speak with him after receiving the medical examiner's cryptic message, he texted Singh he would call him immediately after his meeting with Cavenaugh's wife, Taylor. After which, he listened to a voice message from Officer Mitzy Burton saying the three were making progress with the sketch artist creating a composite of Esther's creepy mystery man.

As for Burton, the morning was proving fruitful. She was eager to share with Flores all they had uncovered.

Scattered haphazardly atop the dining room table were numerous photographs of ballpark vendors wearing the familiar red and white stripe jacket. Included with each photo, the name of the person who worked for the Salt River Fields at Talking Stick facility since its doors opened on February 26, 2011. One particular photo, deliberately set aside, was that of a person of interest now being sought by the police for questioning, Antonio Luis Silva.

***

Taylor Cavenaugh led Detective Flores into a multi-purpose room at the opposite side of her home. More an attached casita than bedroom, the substantial space with its own bathroom, walk-in closet, and small kitchenette also contained a private entrance. Explaining the room had been both her husband's office and a refuge for his exclusive use. It was a creative blend of functionality and old-world charm serving as part workplace, part man cave.

Perfect for a recluse hiding from the world.

Usually blasé about such things as décor, Detective Flores found himself blown away by the room's high-tech, innovative layout. Cavenaugh's massive desk and generous counters, devoid of clutter, provided ample space for supercomputer workstations and what appeared to be top-of-the-line CAD and 3D printers. Three walls, with floor to ceiling built-in bookshelves, were stuffed with various reading materials and models. Its large walk-in closet, a massive storage area providing an abundance of meticulously organized drawers, shelves, and cabinets.

The room, however, was not without its creature comforts. A cozy pullout couch with a multi-drawer coffee table was position in front of media wall exquisitely decorated with natural stack stone and illuminated shelving. A fanatic's paradise containing entertainment systems, expansive music and movie collections, and centered, an extra-large television screen.

Even so, with all its sophisticated equipment and all its electronic gadgets, what Flores noticed most were the family photographs and treasures purposely arranged in every nook and cranny of the room. Each a telling reminder of who Peter Cavenaugh was; yet, failing to reveal why he died, or, who killed him.

Taking their seats on the couch, as the two made small talk Taylor turned on the television; using its broadcast to act as soothing background noise before their conversation turned serious.

"This room was for Peter's exclusive use. Outsiders were not welcomed… including me… He stocked it with his favorite junk foods… Even cleaned it," she said; then laughed lightly. "The fact is, it's probably the cleanest room in the house."

Then, fiddling with the papers and file folders she had stacked on the table to show Flores, Taylor's resolve collapsed.

"Do you want to look at these? Peter was the family bookkeeper," she disclosed; fighting back tears. "I haven't a clue if I found everything, or when things are due."

With overwhelming despair, Taylor longed for her dead husband to walk into the room and return her to the mundane world she once knew.

"Sorry," she sniffled. "Seems I have control issues. Peter hated that."

Dabbing her eyes with a tissue, she took a moment to compose herself.

"How are your kids?" inquired Flores; pointing to a family photo on the table.

"Jocelyn's too young to understand. Maggie's… struggling," confided Taylor; her voice cracking.

"Mind if I look around while we talk?" he asked her gently.

With Taylor's consent, Detective Flores respectfully ambled about the room asking his questions. Stopping now and then, marveling at the complexity of technical drawings on counters as well as Cavenaugh's wide-range of reading materials in his bookshelves.

Not surprisingly, when he entered the converted walk-in closet Flores found cabinets and shelves packed with a wealth of data, design schematics, and models. He also found drawers and drawers filled with soldering equipment, flux containers, substrate spools, blank PCBs, and hundreds of various components and diodes.

Peter Cavenaugh did not need to steal Carpstra's finished products. All he needed was the schematic to build what he wanted from inside his own home.

"Your husband often brought work home?" Flores inquired nonchalantly.

Trying to figure out why a guy, who was well-off and seemly had everything, would take such a risk.

"No. Not at all… For product security reasons and Government contract regulations Carpstra doesn't allow it… Yes. He tinkers… tinkered here. Invented many things which Carpstra bought from him. These, are Peter's own concepts… His designs… His fabrications. He built those computers… Hardwired boards… Programed software. He learned a lot during his time in the military. But it was afterwards, at Carnegie Mellon, where he excelled," she said with pride.

The two sat for a moment silently absorbing the room; the only sound, a soft murmur from the television.

"Next up… A new development in the case of a young woman found murdered in a Scottsdale neighborhood last night," reported the local newswoman.

The reporter's words catching Flores' attention. Watching the screen as the news camera panned the crime scene, a familiarity washed over him.

"Looks like every place else up here," he thought; dismissing the broadcast.

Returning to the widow, pausing; then asking Taylor a question which had been plaguing his mind.

"Mrs. Cavenaugh… A co-workers of your husband's mentioned Peter once spoke of an incident while in the Army. She said he seemed extremely troubled by it. Do you know what she was referring to?" he asked cautiously; suspecting it a sensitive issue.

Surprised, Taylor stared back at him flabbergasted.

"Yes, I do… But he rarely spoke of it… even to me. The times he did, he'd get so angry… At night, sometimes he'd wake shivering, soaking wet… Haunting him for years," she divulged.

Greatly relieved to at last confide that which she promised to keep secret for so long. Taylor walked to a shelf, then returned with a framed photo and handed it to Flores.

The photograph showed a group of US soldiers dressed in standardized desert battle dress uniforms. The exceptions being a man and woman, who both wore only a white T-shirt and pair of chocolate chip pattern military shorts. All but one, had assumed a silly pose and were pointing to a different spot on their body where a Rakkasans tattoo had been inked. The tattoo, identical to her husband's.

As Taylor Cavenaugh's fingers lightly traced her husband's face she again welled up.

Never comfortable in situations such as these, Flores gave the widow a moment and turned back to television. This time catching the tail end of another broadcast about a woman gruesomely slain in Old Town Scottsdale.

Michael Flores's gut tightened envisioning the worst. It took all his self-control not to bolt from the house and demand to speak with Warren Singh.

"Mrs. Cavenaugh… The incident oversees… What can you tell me about it?" Flores asked instead; gently handing Taylor another tissue.

Determined to stay on task, and not allow his imagination run wild.

"Who told you? Oh, what does it matter, now… One night in our backyard we were looking through our telescope and Peter started talking… babbling really. It was so unlike him. He said shortly after his Desert Shield deployment, his squad was ordered on a night mission. Supposedly, they were to use some new field equipment… helmets I think… He said because he was their IT expert he was ordered to inspect each helmet's Global Positioning System recognition feature. Make sure it worked… Sorry, I really didn't understand what it was," she admitted; stopping to sip her water.

Flores remembering the essence of Olivia Ash's conversation with Cavenaugh shortly before he was killed.

"Don't assume equipment works… Someone's probably screwed it up before you got it… Test it… Learn its secrets. If you don't… people die."

Flores' heart sank guessing the ending of Taylor Cavenaugh's story.

"Anyway, Peter said the helmets had just arrived. Still in their original boxes. He said the few he checked worked fine. Then, there was a commotion in the compound. He got pulled away to help contain it," she remembered him saying.

"Delaying him from inspecting the rest," acknowledged Flores.

"Right… And before he could finish, the mission was underway with them wearing the helmets… At some point, his squad came under attack," she said; biting her lower lip.

"And the helmets… They didn't work." Flores asserted.

"Some did… But I guess others had a defective… recognition sensor, I think? Whatever it was, it went bad… identifying friendlies as hostiles and vice versa. Peter said he realized it after he accidently shot at one of his own men."

Desperately needing the detective to understand after her husband's discovery he acted heroically, Taylor stressed.

"He tried warning his people… But it was chaos. No one listened," relayed Taylor of her husband's horror. "He said he shoved his sergeant behind a jeep and yanked off his helmet. Screamed at him what was happening before switching off the man's helmet and giving it back to him."

Watching Taylor get up and refill her glass, Flores asked gently.

"How many?"

"Five… Five of his friends… Kids, like him. Killed by friendly fire. He never stopped blaming himself," she exclaimed.

"He was all of what… Twenty?" guessed Flores sympathetically.

Knowing full well how it felt to be blamed for something beyond your control.

"Nineteen," she replied softly.

"Was there an investigation? The company… Was it held accountable for the defective equipment?" asked the detective.

"No… It was covered up. Peter was told to shut up, or they'd make sure he was convicted of dereliction of duty," added Taylor; repulsed.

"He wasn't at fault… Who told him he was?" spat Flores.

Furious for the young Peter Cavenaugh, who obviously had been manipulated to take the fall.

"That's what I told him. No charges were ever filed. But Peter truly believed his friends died because of him… If only he had checked all the helmets… I tried to convince him that even if he had, it could have been years before the defect occurred, or was detected. He wouldn't listen," she asserted.

Saying his decades after, living with the guilt, had turned him into an emotionally detached recluse.

"The company… It was Carpstra, wasn't it?" Flores reckoned.

Guessing revenge might be a great motive for corporate theft.

Taylor nodding. Admitting she never understood why he agreed to work for the company. Never thought him ever to be involved in anything illegal, until recently.

"You know as smart as Peter was… he wasn't what you'd call people savvy. He'd always say his pals had his back… Though, he wouldn't say how… He all but admitted to me he only took the Carpstra job because of some pact he'd made. To make Carpstra pay. Then, I believe he had a change of heart," she said pensively.

"What makes you think so?" probed Flores.

Wondering if it was this change of heart which had gotten him killed.

"Because, Peter dedicated his life to emerging security technologies. And in doing so, he inadvertently became Carpstra's golden boy. But what he created was not for Carpstra. It was for his fellow soldiers, first responders… So they'd have their best chance to return home… unlike his friends who didn't," she replied sincerely.

"This pact… The pals he spoke of… Are they military, Carpstra coworkers, like-minded political friends? Perhaps a leader he mentioned?" Flores asked; working on a theory about the murderer and his possible minions.

Seeing Taylor's exhaustion Flores knew he should stop; yet kept pushing. Certain she knew something, even if she did not know it herself. Certain too, until her husband's murderer was captured, nothing would prevent him from killing again.

"Sorry… Our small social circle consists of my friends, and relationships formed around our children. The few friends Peter had fell by the wayside the more reclusive he became. Sharing very little with us his life outside our family," she said of her husband's struggles with his mental decline.

"Okay, let's take a step back… The people in this photo… Do you know who they are?" he asked gently.

"Yes… Early in our marriage Peter told me. He was so happy then. Later, when things became worse, I'd sometimes hear him talking to them through these closed door. That's when he started drinking… Refused help… This, detective, is where it began," she admitted; venting her anger at the photograph.

Taking the photograph from Flores, Taylor sat beside him and pointed.

"This, you know, is Peter… They called him Pac Man… Don't ask. Most of them had silly nicknames," she laughed, circling the younger image of her husband with her index finger.

"Good look'n guy," replied Flores smiling; noticing the happy, carefree pose.

Noticing too the tattoo on Cavenaugh's forearm looked very different from the last time he saw it.

"That's Tyrell Bloggs… Toro. Hayde Ward, she was Lark, because she sang like a bird… William Lopez and Bobbie Myers. I don't know why, but they were just Willie and Bobbie. And Woody, David Woods… These were the five didn't make it."

Closing her eyes, Taylor leaned against the couch. The toll of collateral damage from that one horrific incident long ago having proven more than her family could bear.

"Who's this?" Flores asked reluctantly.

"Oh, Sarge… And that's Bro hanging on him. Hah… Always thought Bro was taking his life into his own hands. It's just not something a sane person would do. Nobody messed with Sarge," she replied brightening up with genuine affection for the gruff-looking man.

"He definitely does not look too pleased," agreed Flores with a laugh.

Recalling how his own sergeant did not have much of a sense of humor either.

"Who took the photo?" asked Flores, interested in the group's faceless member.

"Oh… Xander. Peter always said Xander was a total control freak. But then, I guess we all have our quirks… He did say Xander was smart enough not to tangle with Sarge though," she said; obviously disliking the faceless member of the group.

"Now she looks familiar… Where have I seen her?" noted Flores with surprise, pointing to another servicewoman.

"Taylor… Can you copy this for me? he asked politely.

Rising from the sofa, Taylor gave Flores a nod and willingly placed the photograph on the printer glass; handing him a copy a moment later.

Upon a closer look, Flores was positive he had seen the servicewoman somewhere. Clearly compensating for the extreme heat; with short hair and minimally dressed in her military t-shirt and shorts, she looked tough as hell.

Then it hit him. In the photograph she looked nothing like Elise Holbrook's pristine assistant in the blue lab coat. Regardless, he was sure that was exactly who she was. Then he saw it plain as day; above her right wrist, a smaller Rakkasans tattoo just like Peter Cavenaugh's.

"Is this Patricia Sawyer?" he asked Taylor; looking for confirmation.

Mindful that just that morning Sawyer had vehemently denied knowing her old army buddy, Peter Cavenaugh.

"Yes. That's Sis… But Sawyer's her married name… Her maiden name's Fenton. She's Bros sister… I mean Jeffory Fenton's sister."

Explained Taylor, her finger sliding across the photograph from the woman's face to the man annoying the sergeant.

Recalling Mitzy Burton's words, Michael Flores' body immediately tensed.

"Michael, let me introduce you to tonight's security detail. This is Thomas Murphy, Brian Warner, and over there, Jeffory Fenton."

***

"Mitzy pick up. Fenton… Jeffory Fenton's the mole," he screamed into his phone as his police SUV sped towards Ahwatukee.

Calling for backup, Detective Michael Flores activated the SUV's siren and stepped on the gas. Praying that when he arrived at the safe house he would find the women just as he had left them that morning.

It all made sense. Jeffory Fenton had been a member of Mitzy Burton's detail from the very beginning. The question in Flores' mind now was, was Fenton the boss, or a stooge following orders? That Fenton felt secure in his cover and had orchestrated the necessary countermoves in plain sight; Flores also wondered if the man was that brazen, or extremely lucky. Either way, this was how Peter Cavenaugh's killer had stayed a step ahead. Either way Flores had no doubt Fenton too, was trained to kill.

"Mitzy... Where are you!" he yelled; his attempts to contact her in vain.

Thirty-five minutes out.

Terrified, Flores' last communication with Officer Mitzy Burton had been earlier in the day. She had left a message on his phone saying the three were working with the police sketch artist and having success creating images of the two strangers.

All had seemed fine.

Yet in reality, the women were unknowingly keeping company with a mercenary.

Taylor Cavenaugh's photograph was proof that Jeffory Fenton and his sister, Patricia, had been in Peter's squad. Furthermore, neither one had mentioned they previously knew the victim.

All this time, Fenton had been pretending to protect them; living with them. Maybe even browsing vendor photographs with them, or sitting with them as the police artist created computer-generated composites of the two men. Wondering how far Fenton was willing to go to protect himself.

***

The sketch artist had been refining the second person of interest's features when Jeffory Fenton received a call. Excusing himself, he found a secluded area in the house where he would not be overheard.

"A Detective Flores' got our assembly, and Holbrook identified it. Not only that, I'm pretty sure he suspects I'm involved," shouted a panicked Patricia Sawyer. "Jeff, he's at Taylor's right now… It's only a matter of time before the cops puts it together.

"Pat, calm down… We planned for this… I'll leave soon. You know where to meet," directed Fenton; keeping his voice low.

Patricia Sawyer had always been more reactionary to volatile situations than her brother; even in combat. Yet, Jeffory Fenton knew immediately after seeing the police artist's sketch that their window for escape was closing fast. Peering round the corner from his hiding spot, Fenton closely observed his fellow lawmen to see if anyone was acting differently.

"Geez… You're still in the house? Are you crazy. Get out!" screamed Sawyer.

"I'm going to… But first, he needs to be updated," Fenton insisted.

"What? No. Don't be an idiot. We… You… don't owe him anything… Leave… Get out while you can," pleaded a breathless Patricia.

Scared her brother would cause both their capture, or worse; Patricia Sawyer's mind had been made up the day she learned of Pac Man's death. Refusing to go down as an accomplice to murder. She also knew if she turned state's evidence against the unstable demagogue; when she least expected, someone would repay her betrayal by inflicting unspeakable horrors. Her only recourse now was to reluctantly abandon him and save herself.

"I'm not waiting… Bye Jeff," she said with finality.

Hearing a car door slam and engine engage before the line went dead, Jeffory Fenton realized there would be no rendezvous. Immediately after, another call came in.

"Stay put… I'll coming," commanded the all too familiar voice.

Feeling he had no choice, Fenton did as he was told; occasionally glancing out the windows for the predetermined signal.

Attributing his restlessness to his job, Fenton periodically interacted with the women while checking the sketch artist's progress. Smiling perhaps a little too broadly as he spoke. Fenton applauded the group for their ability to remember the smallest details as one portrait took on an uncanny resemblance to the man now hiding outside.

When at last the signal was given, Fenton slipped out the backdoor and met the man at a previously discovered surveillance blind spot. Had it been anyone else, Fenton would have refused such a fool-hearty daylight assault. However, he had known the man far too long to think anything he said would matter.

"Don't worry Jeffy. Piece of cake," reassured the man.

Their objective was clear; no witness, no proof.

The man's ruthless plan to eliminate everyone in the safe house, grab the police sketch and computer, and get out fast was not so dissimilar to the covert operations they had jointly executed over the years.

Armed, the two silently entered the house and hid inside the main bedroom's dark walk-in closet. Assessing their pistol silencers would not completely muffle gunshots and would alert others; they opted to use close-quarters combat skills to systematically neutralized each member of the security detail before taking out their main target; using guns as a last resort.

Their first victim was a plainclothesman making indoor rounds. By the time the lawman realized the house had been breached, it was too late.

Quietly dumping the policeman's lifeless body inside the closet, the two assassins closed the door; then, worked their way down the hall. Fenton took the lead so as not to alert his fellow officers when approaching. His skills proving equally as lethal as the taller man who wielded a deadly garrote.

Silently moving from room to room, the two eliminated the second officer coming out of the bathroom, and the third in the kitchen sipping coffee. All that remained were the completely oblivious women in the living room.

Glancing from the police sketch to Esther, the tall man made his presence known with chilling calmness and a macabre grin

"Looks just like me. Doesn't it sweetie?" he remarked.

Recognizing his voice, Esther turned towards the tall man horrorstruck. The other three women gasping as the figure in the police sketch stood before them. Even more shocked to see beside him someone they trusted with their lives pointing a gun directly at them.

Instinctively Mattie screamed for help as the sketch artist, panicking, dropped her drawing pad and jumped to her feet. Officer Mitzy Burton immediately realizing why Mattie's pleas had fallen on the quiet house.

"It's you, Fenton? You're the maggot," confronted the incensed Burton.

"Look buddy… You want me, you got me… Let them go," pleaded Esther.

Suspecting their situation would become dicey if they lingered, enjoying the witness's distress, the man decided they should acquire the information he desired elsewhere. Then, finish the job once and for all.

"We don't need the baggage," he said to Fenton with a surly grin.

As the women stared in horror, Jeffory Fenton pointed his gun directly at the police sketch artist and pulled the trigger. The suppressor, not completely muffling the gunshot, flashed as the bullet left its barrel; penetrating the artist's forehead. Striking the woman dead before she hit the ground.

"No!" screamed Burton.

Helplessly watching her colleague crumble to the floor; instinctively stepping in front of Esther and Mattie to shield them with her body.

"Assholes... Headquarters received those sketches electronically half hour ago. They know who you are, you piece of shit. If you get going now, you both can be in Nogales... four hours tops," urged Burton.

"Nice try," sneered the man slightly amused.

Then he gestured to Fenton.

Quickly his crony snatched each woman's cellphone and tucked the sketchpad and laptop under his arm. Returning to the man's side like a well-trained monkey.

"You know... Regardless of the trouble you've caused me, I think before you go and meet your glorious makers we all should have a party. Don't you?"

Proposed Cavenaugh's killer; looking forward to making all three woman suffer.

"We don't have time," protested Fenton. "Let's do them now."

"Jeffory... Neither of us knows what the cops know. Maybe we have to shut down operations, maybe not. What we need is a little tête-à-tête... Now... Get the ropes."

***

As Detective Michael Flores approached the Ahwatukee safe house his heart sank. Warning red and blue flashing lights atop multiple police cruisers continued slicing the warm desert air as yellow crime tape was strung around the parameter and a few uniformed officers held back inquisitive neighbors behind police lines. All concerned acutely aware the media would soon be arriving to create a circus-like show; detailing the gruesome carnage inside.

Officer Thomas Murphy, a member of Mitzy Burton's security team, had been off duty when the assault on the house occurred. Meeting Detective Flores at the front door, Murphy handed the detective a pair of police shoe covers and cautioned him about the bloodbath inside.

"It's not pretty... Medical team says judging by body temperatures, livor mortis, and tissue discoloration, they were slaughtered around two hours ago," reported Murphy.

With the brutal assassinations of his fellow officers, disappearance of their witness, her niece, and his close friend Mitzy Burton; Thomas Murphy was clearly struggling.

"Who were they?" demanded Murphy.

Every fiber of his being telling him the massacre was not caused by one person.

"Fenton was the inside man," Flores replied forcefully. "I've yet to identify his partner... Maybe his sister... More than likely, there were others."

"His sister? Son of a...," swore Murphy; his face reddening. "What do you need?"

"Anybody talk to neighbors? inquired Flores, seeing the fire in Murphy's eyes.

The detective barely finishing his words before Murphy bolted from the room to take on the task.

Searching the house, Michael Flores examined the aftermath. Wishing the women were inside hiding, unable to hear them calling. Soon, he had no illusions. They had been taken. If they were alive, he was certain they would not be for long.

He began searching for clues inside the living room near the blood-soaked carpet from the sketch artist. Suspecting this was the last place Esther and Mattie were before their disappearance, Flores was disheartened that nothing pointed to where they had been taken. His eyes falling on the dining room table, recalling breakfast. The hullabaloo after revealing the circuit board; their laughter, teasing, the optimism.

Then, something on the table grabbed his attention. Among the coffee mugs, half-eaten pastries, and several piles of photographs; one headshot of a man wearing a red and white striped jacket had been set aside.

"The ballpark vendors," he uttered.

Studying the man's face, Flores felt a nagging familiarity.

"Excuse me... I believe you're looking for me," interrupted the stranger in the adjacent foyer.

Taken aback, the detective shot the weathered, gray-haired man a look of disbelief. Not only was he the man in the photograph he was holding; he was the same no-nonsense soldier in the photograph Taylor Cavenaugh had given him.

And although presently dressed in a light-blue western shirt and faded worn-out jeans, the perfect image of an aging cowboy just off the range. The stranger's determined expression told Flores if anybody could help him find the three missing women, it was him.

Holding the man's steely gaze, Michael Flores straightened and said.

"Hello Sarge... What took you so long?"

Chapter 13

"There's Always Hope Until There Isn't."

~ Sakshi Arora

The noisy garage door slowly squeaked and groaned down every inch of its tracks until, ultimately, the thick steel door butted against the concrete slab with an all too familiar groan. As two men stepped from the RAM pickup into the dimly lit garage, the taller coolly demanded of his accomplice.

"Jeffy… Show our guests to the workout room. The hooks on the equipment wall should prove, eh… extremely useful."

His cagey smirk reflecting his recent triumph.

"So… I do the heavy lifting while you're doing… What?" complained Jeffory Fenton; getting stuck with grunt work once again.

"Me? I'll be putting in my welcomed appearance," replied the man arrogantly.

Gesturing in a way which had always rubbed Fenton the wrong way.

Removing a trash-filled plastic bag from the receptacle, the man cheerfully exited the garage side door. Then, rolling a larger garbage container down to the curb for the next day's pickup, the man mischievously sang the wrong lyrics to a well-known Creedence Clearwater Revival tune. Taking great pleasure knowing he was grating on his associate's already strained nerves.

Listening, Fenton shook his head.

"Teflon," he uttered to himself; marveling.

No matter what the misdeed, culpability slid off the man and inevitably into someone else's lap.

Counting himself lucky, 'til now; Fenton was feeling less and less confident about their present circumstance, and his part in it.

He had met the man decades earlier during Army basic training. Both he and his sister, Pat, had been immediately drawn to the charmer's flagrant disregard for boundaries and authority; as well as his brash, unorthodox outside business dealings.

Yet for all the entitled latitudes the tall man felt due him, the blind loyalty, obedience; the man felt none of the same was due others. Fortunately, Fenton had never bought in to the man's grandiose delusions. He did as he was told because it had afforded him a sizeable, hidden nest egg and comfy lifestyle above his lowly police salary.

As for others who chose otherwise, did not fall in line, disrespected him; it was none of his business what happened to them. Besides, as far as he knew it had been ages since anyone had tried… until Peter Cavenaugh.

Pac Man's demise had been a sobering reminder of the man's wrath.

Furthermore ever since that night, the man's standard modus operandi and need to blame others for his own missteps worsened. His uncompromising edicts, bizarre idiosyncrasies, and excessive need for revenge had taken on a crueler, macabre, twist.

"Don't go out tonight… It'll cost you, your life. There's a badass out tonight."

Sang the man, removing his mail from the box at the foot of his driveway.

Meanwhile, Jeffory Fenton begrudgingly walked to the rear of the pickup. Folding back the truck's collapsible hard panel bed cover, he exposed the three women they had just kidnapped from the Ahwatukee safe house. Trussed like Thanksgiving turkeys, their mouths sealed shut with baby chick decorated duct tape, Esther Hausman and Mattie Kaplan stared at Fenton with wide-eyed terror. Officer Mitzy Burton's eyes, however, flashed with rage.

Unable to squash his laughter; yet, having seen the very capable senior police officer in action. Fenton looked around the garage for something to both impair Burton's vision and help subdue her, if needed. Then, spying a large green cloth sack with drawstring cords sewn into the hem gathering dirt on the floor, he opened the dense bag and roughly shoved Burton's head inside it. Forcefully tightening the cords around Burton neck until she gasped for air. Then, before knotting the lines, he delivered a blow to her midsection for good measure.

"Nothing I'd like better than to finish you off," Fenton whispered in her ear. "Lucky for you, he's got other plans... Or, maybe not."

With a final yank on the ropes, Fenton shoved the officer back onto the truck bed. Her unprotected body landing hard atop the metal going completely limp.

Next it was Esther's turn.

Ignoring her cries of pain, Fenton grabbed Esther's ankles and slid her petite frame toward him onto the tailgate. Easily hoisting her over his shoulder like a sack of potatoes, he carried the older woman down a long unlit hallway to what the man had called his workout room.

There, lifting her above him with all the emotions of a robot, Fenton secured her wrist bindings to a sturdy hook anchored on the wall. Abandoning the dangling Esther as she struggled to touch the floor with the tips of her toes. Returning moments later with a groaning Mattie who was drifting in and out of consciousness.

After eventually securing Mattie's limp body onto a second wall hook, Fenton stomped back to the garage for his final, mundane task. Pausing briefly when a slight separation in the living room window's vertical blinds caught his attention. Although dusk was rapidly transitioning into nighttime, Fenton could still discern the man's figure standing in front of the house talking to four other people.

And, although he was unable to hear their conversation, Fenton chuckled at the man's pleasant expression as he shuffled through his mail and gossiped.

"Teflon," he uttered once more.

Watching the clueless dolts succumb to the man's charm, much as he initially had. They, thinking how fortunate they were to have such a perfect neighbor; always ready to lend a hand to human and animal alike.

"Great... You'll bring the can up, Friday," confirmed a balding man; looking as if he just finished eighteen holes of golf and several margaritas.

"Absolutely. No problem... That's what we do for each other," replied the man smiling broadly.

It was then a woman walking her dog approached the group on her nightly stroll. Stooping, the man greeted her apricot miniature poodle by name as he tousled the soft curly fur behind its ear. The owner, laughing heartily as her pooch happily shook its entire body after the tickling. Wishing everyone a nice evening before continuing on her way; her attentive poodle prancing obediently at her left side.

When the man ultimately made his appearance in the workout room, it was just in time to see Jeffory Fenton hang Mitzy Burton onto the final hook.

"What's all this?" he asked casually.

Tilting his head at the dark green sack shrouding Burton's face.

"I didn't like the way she was looking at me," replied Fenton bluntly.

Leaving any further explanation unsaid.

Shrugging off Jeffory Fenton's peculiar way of dealing with his former superior, the man announced his plans for the evening.

"Well Ladies… I'm sure you're in suspense so, I won't keep you hanging," he began; giggling bizarrely at his absurd pun. "Tonight we're all going to have a nice little chat. Won't that be fun?"

His hair-raising announcement ending with another sadistic laugh.

"What are you waiting for?" demanded Fenton; his patience growing thin.

Now regretting not having escaped with his sister; contemplating his own vanishing act at the next opportunity.

"Come on Jeffy… A little delay's not going hurt. Anyways, there's still a few good neighbors outside. No use rousing suspicions if our little party becomes too loud. Sides… Can't you feel the excitement building," cajoled the man.

Intent on extracting information from the women by whatever means necessary later on, the man vacated the room leaving a dumbfounded Fenton to guard the three bound and gagged women.

As he entered his study the man made a beeline for his well-stocked bar; pouring himself a full Snifter of bourbon. Then, falling into an overstuffed leather armchair, he slowly sipped the smooth ambrosia; allowing himself the luxury of losing himself in the dancing flames of his gas-lit fireplace. By the time the mantel clock's melodic chimes heralded the hour his plan was set. Deciding, for now, to continue enjoying the palatable spirit until it was time for the evening festivities to commence.

***

As for the three kidnapped women, their traumatic journey to their abductor's lair had shaken each to their core. Hogtied, gagged and blindfolded,

Esther, Mattie, and Mitzy Burton had been forced into the bed of the pickup and its hard cover tightly fastened-down over them. Trapping the women in a pitch-black abyss as if they had been buried alive inside a metal vault. Unable to see or speak, let alone protect themselves; the three had been unmercifully tossed about at every turn, abrupt stop, and aggressive acceleration. Colliding not only into each other, but the utility chest bolted behind the truck cab and the secured tailgate.

Through it all Officer Mitzy Burton had done her best to focus on their whereabouts and free herself from her bindings.

Grateful the Valley's urban planners had adhered to a traditional north-south-east-west street infrastructure grid. She tried to visualize the kidnappers' route; committing every smell, every straightaway, every turn and road condition to memory. Looking for any opportunity to escape.

Almost certain they were traveling east on local streets; a semi-truck's horn blasted overhead alerting her to an I-10 freeway overpass. Similarly, familiar smells like gasoline, fast-food grease, and sweet grasses informed her of passing specific businesses and intersections. Using every stop to kick or head-butt the pickup's collapsible bed cover. Hoping to detach the panels from the truck and draw enough attention someone would notice; and, with any luck, do something about it.

Likewise, although Esther and Mattie were unfamiliar with the terrain they somehow understood Burton's intentions and joined as best they could.

Yet despite their best efforts, the only person who noticed was a sleepy 6-years-old boy in the back seat of his family's Honda when the car pulled alongside the RAM at a stoplight. The youngster, watching with fascination at the panels popping; much like hot exploding popcorn kernels trapped inside a pan, pelting the underneath of the lid. And, although curious as to what was causing the phenomenon, the drowsy boy opted instead to drift off to sleep with none the wiser.

After traveling the same road for quite some time, the pickup eventually drove over a small incline embedded with railway ties. It was just the clue Burton needed to pinpoint their current location.

"Gilbert! Got to be," she thought.

Her backbone repeatedly bouncing off the pickup's metal bed.

With renewed exuberance, the officer intensified her efforts. Unfortunately, soon after the truck made a series of quick sharp turns, drove up what seemed to be a driveway, then stopped. That, together with the sounds of the engine shutting off and a garage door closing made every idea she considered vanish.

"Great. Now what?" Mitzy thought.

Certain their situation was about to get a lot worse really fast. Because now, not only was she bound and gagged with her head stuffed inside a damn bag, she was also hanging from some kind of hook like a slab of beef.

Sensing it was Esther and Mattie hanging beside her, Burton had no clue as to their condition. And, since her lips were duct taped shut, asking was not an option. Cunningly picking at the knot the officer figured if she could break free, she would just have to wing it.

It was then Burton unexpectedly found a small rip in the bag's fabric. Peeking through it, she first saw Jeffory Fenton sitting on a flat utility bench obsessing with his phone as if trying to contact someone. Noticing too, his neglected gun was a good foot or two in front of him.

"Now we're talk'n," thought Burton.

Intent on seizing the firearm as part of her plan. She also noticed a stack of metal weight plates and a rack of barbells beside an exercise machine on Fenton's right.

"Well those look promising," noted Mitzy optimistically.

Becoming aware of several items in the room she could use as effective weapons.

"Okay… Time to get off this damn hook."

Forcing her body to appear limp in hopes the men would ignore her, Burton carefully increased her efforts to loosen the knot; extremely cautious of the wall mirror showing her movements.

Meantime, exhausted and aching, Esther Hausman was still struggling. Barely able to touch the floor with her toes for stability; even so, Esther was determined to get free.

"How do I get to that gun first?" Esther wondered; staring at Fenton's gun.

Realizing too if she did, she had no clue how to fire it.

Attempting to loosen her restraint, Esther awkwardly pirouetted right using her big toes; coming face-to-face with a groggy, yet alive, Mattie. Anxious about her niece's condition, she then accidently overcompensated; twisting to her far left and finding the hooded Mitzy Burton hanging like a rag doll.

Shocked, Esther's toes lost their grip on the slick tile floor.

"Just ain't your day Granny," laughed Fenton watching the dangling Esther helplessly swaying.

Crying out from the excruciating pain, Esther used what little strength she had left to stabilize herself. Comprehending too, somewhere in the house Peter Cavenaugh's murderer was devising horrors much worse than a couple dislocated limbs.

"Michael… Where the hell are you?" whimpered Esther; the ropes tightening around her wrists.

Coming to terms with the realization that no calvary would be arriving in the nick of time to rescue them, Esther thought of that night in her backyard when she found Peter Cavenaugh. How her fears had uncharacteristically gotten the better of her. Determined no matter how scared she became this time would be different, she dug in deep. Remembering too, Michael telling her he was going to use the man's idiosyncrasies, sensitivities, against him to undermine him; to try and force him to make a critical mistake.

"He's got no concept of right… wrong… Of other people's feelings. He blames everyone else for his own failings. Writing alternate realities to augment his own image and self-importance."

Michael's words of wisdom actually paraphrasing a psychological evaluation from an expert he had referred to as a Dr. Singh; also saying.

"This guy's an extremely dangerous psychopath. He possesses both Antisocial Personality Disorder (ASPD) and Narcissistic Personality Disorder (NPD) predatory traits and behaviors liken to dictators and serial killers… Definitely not someone you bring home to the family."

Now determined to mess with the killer's head, Esther began planning how best to get under the bastard's skin.

"Pride…? Intelligence? Manhood. Asshole, I'm gonna be the scab you can't stop picking… You're going to kill us anyway… Might as well risk causing you to lose your cool. It might just create an opportunity for us to escape."

***

"His name's Oliver Alexander Baring... but he prefers to be called Xander. I call him a rabid S.O.B. who should've been put down years ago," said the retired sergeant with utter contempt.

From the foyer of the breached Ahwatukee safe house, Antonio Luis Silva approached Homicide Detective Michael Flores. Everywhere were gruesome signs of the carnage carried out by Oliver Baring and Jeffory Fenton.

"Tell me," insisted Michael Flores somberly.

Trying to make sense of the pointless slaughter of so many good people.

"I had the misfortune of serving with Oliver Baring in my squad during Desert Shield and Desert Storm. From his first day to his last, that pond-sucking amoeba was pure poison."

"Yours being the 187th Airborne Infantry Regiment," affirmed Flores.

"Right. In some circles we're called the Rakkasans," professed Silva with pride.

"Baring and his cronies weren't merely corrupt. They were merciless profiteers who were never held accountable for anything; infractions, illegal activities... worse," claimed the retired noncom.

"Why's that?" urged Flores.

"Slippery eel slithered out of every charge... Something always happened to the case, or witness. He'd get off scot-free. Leaving a path of destruction and shattered lives. And still, the bloodsucker's wreaking havoc. Had I'd known about Pete sooner. I would've...," said Silva; his remorseful words trailing off.

Sympathetic, Flores handed Antonio Silva the group photograph he had gotten from Taylor Cavenaugh and asked.

"Oliver Baring... Xander... He's the elusive photographer?"

"Yeah... Never liked being photographed himself. No surprise... Evil manipulative bastard pied piper our most impressionable soldiers. I must've warned those kids hundreds of times 'bout him," professed Silva.

"Where'd you get this? Oh... Right...Taylor," he began to inquire. "She's a good kid... Didn't deserve this. None of them did."

"The Cavenaughs... You've stayed in touch?" delved the detective; needing to fully understand their relationship.

"No. Not really... Ran into Pete and Fenton a while back. First time in years. Something seemed off... Both were strained, tight lipped. Two weeks ago I bumped into Pete again. Then Baring shows up look'n all surprised... Thinking 'bout it now, Pete must've orchestrated it. Told me afterward we needed to talk. It was the last time I saw any of them," declared the older man.

"Until the ballpark," interjected Flores. "You were the person arguing with Baring after the game."

"Yeah... Warned him to leave the kid alone. He played dumb... When I learned about Pete's death I had my suspicions. But like always, no proof... Then today, after you left Taylor, she put two-and-two together and found me in Pete's contacts. Begged me to help you catch her husband's killer. Believe me, I didn't need persuading. So...," offered Silva.

The Sergeant's steely eyes conveying years of frustration watching Oliver Baring evade prosecution.

"Mr. Silva... Oliver Baring and Jeffory Fenton just slaughtered several police officers and abducted three women. If you have any ideas as to his whereabouts, now would be a good time," pressed Flores.

"Like I said, it's been years... However, bottom feeders like Xander hide where they feel most safe... In his case, it's probably right underneath the noses of people he's conned into believing he walks on water," affirmed Silva. "Having said that, if the women are alive, I agree they only have hours."

Just then Officer Murphy rushed into the room to provide Flores with an update; sidestepping the medical team removing the police sketch artist's body.

Jeffory Fenton and his pal had slaughtered his friends and kidnapped women he had sworn to protect. Struggling to stay objective, Murphy knew he would not rest until they got the son of a bitches. And, at that moment, he was not very particular as to how that should, or would be done.

"Murph… Add the name Oliver Alexander Baring to the Jeffory Fenton, Patricia Sawyer all-points bulletins. He's the ringleader. Arizona driver license photo and description. Every media… Also initiate Amber and Silver alerts. Kidnapped… Esther Hausman, Matilda Kaplan, Mitzy Burton. Photos of all three. Oh and Murph… Suspects are armed and dangerous," directed Flores; emphasizing the need for extreme caution.

"Stick around Sarge," requested Detective Flores. "We're not done yet."

***

"Ladies… It's show time," announced Oliver Baring giddily.

Rubbing his hands together as he entered the workout room, the bourbon he had so liberally consumed earlier heightening the psychopath's macabre cravings. Reeking, the man known to his followers as Xander, eagerly approached the three tethered women. Standing toe-to-toe in front of Esther, his sickening-warm breath caused her to involuntarily cough as she fought back the sour bile rising in her throat.

Grinning, Xander leaned in closer; taking his time pulling off the wide duct tape across Esther Hausman's mouth. Carelessly, recklessly ripping strips of dry skin off her cracked lips; delighting in the blood trickling from the new wounds.

"Jeffory... Does our special guest look comfortable to you?" he asked rhetorically. "I don't think so either. How about helping her... say over there."

Motioning to a vinyl seat attached to a large, multifunctional exercise machine.

Xander, smitten with his own brilliance, continued to carry on as if he were a game show host entertaining his personal audience. His obedient co-host, Fenton, following his orders; releasing Esther from her unyielding wall hook.

"Tante!" screamed Mattie horrified.

Landing on the hard tile, Esther screamed in agony as she curled up into a protective ball; grateful for the nothingness overtaking her.

"Well that won't do, Jeffy," declared Xander; watching Esther slip into unconsciousness.

Grabbing Esther by the shirt collar, Fenton then heartlessly dragged the woman to the metal apparatus. After shoving her small limp frame onto the unyielding flat seat, he easily caught the roll of white athletic tape Xander flung at him.

"Wakey, Wakey sweetie. That's right... Jeffy, start with say... a 150 pounds," suggested the psychopath; filled with anticipation.

"You don't have to do this. I'll tell you. Anything you want," pleaded a groggy Esther.

"I know you will... But in truth? What's the fun in that?" laughed Xander.

Desiring to break the old woman while learning what he could; then, make her pay for all the trouble she had caused him.

After binding Esther's ankles against the seat's metal legs, Fenton walked behind the fitness machine and shoved the weight stack pin into a hole which joined several black cast-iron weights into one extremely heavy block. Pulling down on the shiny metal triceps bar attached to the lift cable pulley, he then positioned the long bar below Esther's chest. Tightly taping each wrist to an opposite end of the bar; creating a quasi-medieval torture rack.

Finally, grinning, Fenton looked into Esther's eyes and released his grip.

Instantly Esther was jerked upright, yet her feet remained fixed to the seat's legs. The metal triceps bar colliding with the top pulley wheel with a loud crash as its cables brutally stretched the older woman's limbs in opposite directions.

Wailing, Esther feared her poor body would soon give out from the psychopath's brutal abuse.

"Now that I have your attention," said Xander somberly. "At the ballpark… You recognized me from that night."

"No, I never…," gasped Esther. Horrified watching Xander approach Mattie and Mitzy through her blurring vision. "Wait! It was because of… your stare. The way you looked at me. The hatred. I… I just knew."

Refusing to believe he had been wrong, all this time, Xander maintained his present course; hell bent on forcing Esther to confess the truth… his truth. That she had watched him kill Peter Cavenaugh, had seen him again in the orchard. That the police had placed her in witness protection because she could identify him, and would testify against him.

"Eh… Wrong answer," he asserted loudly.

Then using his index finger, he pointed back and forth between the fettered Mattie Kaplan and Mitzy Burton.

"Eeny, meenie, minie, mo," he sang.

"Wait! You have to believe me," sobbed Esther breathlessly.

Desperate to convince her tormentor she was telling the truth.

"You had a feeling... You just knew. Like the cop just knew... And the girl just knew," mocked Xander; refusing to believe Esther's ridiculous story.

"What girl?" cried Esther; truly confused.

Positive the completely delusional psychopath was imagining people.

"Dear, dear, Esther I'm so disappointed... Now, who to call on first? Mattie? Mitzy? Who best to convince you?" baited Xander; tapping his chin with his finger.

Wide-eyed, Esther stared at Mattie, then Mitzy. Her terror further satisfying Xander's sadistic needs as he lingered before the two tethered women prolonging his choice.

Meanwhile, unknown to the two men, the sack obscuring Officer Mitzy Burton's face had worked to her advantage. Pretending to still be unconscious, she had duped Xander and his henchman into believing they could ignore her. It had given Burton's nimble fingers time to blindly pick at the knots securing her wrists to the hook. Allowing too, for her to rub her mouth against the fabric; dislodging the tape and making it possible to communicate with Esther and Mattie.

Suddenly Burton's loosened ropes slipped, dropping her body a good three inches. Her heart pounding, she stilled herself; listening for the men's reaction.

Nothing.

"A couple more minutes," she anticipated; resuming her undertaking.

It was then Burton heard the sound of a cable rapidly recoiling for a second time. Esther's suffering was heartbreaking. Unable to remain silent, Burton confronted their sadistic captors; drawing attention away from the older woman onto her.

"Look you shits... She doesn't know anything," asserted the policewoman.

Immediately regretting her decision not to keep her big mouth shut, Burton's skin crawled as she felt Xander and Fenton's eyes upon her.

"Well, well... You are with us, Officer Burton," exclaimed Xander.

Delighted to have another guest available to play his games.

"Picking on a little old lady... What's the matter boys? 'Fraid she'll hurt you?" mocked the officer.

Hoping the slight at their manhood would suspend Esther's vicious torment.

"How the...? Shut up Burton, maybe you can take her place," warned Fenton.

Furious his former out-ranking officer was had removed her muzzle, Fenton sprang to Burton and delivered a powerful blow to her midsection.

Caught off guard, Burton struggled to recover. With the wind painfully knocked out of her she tried her best not to vomit.

"Now Jeffory... It that any way to treat our guest?" snickered Xander.

Pleased that Fenton had finally gotten into the spirit of things.

The women, realizing the longer they withheld information the longer they would survive, resigned themselves to the horrors coming next.

Ignoring the high-pitched ringing in her ears, Mitzy Burton resumed working on the knot. Deliberately groaning now and then to convince her captors Fenton's fist had done its job.

"Your turn darling Mattie," mocked Xander. "Jeffory, if you'd be so kind."

To distract them, Esther decided to pick Xander's scabs.

"Look bud... You want to blame me. Fine... But we both know you're the real screw up... You got away with murder, dumbass. And you're too stupid to know it. No one had a clue about you... till now," chided Esther.

Xander's pale eyes filled with hatred as he turned from Mattie to the old woman.

Gambling on the psychopath's instability, Esther relentlessly pushed Xander's buttons as the sweat-induced moistened athletic tape binding her wrists to the triceps bar loosened.

"Just a bit more," she guessed; leveraging her forearms against the bar.

The tape gave way.

Right under their captors' noses Esther cagily inched her hands to the opposite edges of the metal, just shy of sliding off. Her feet, however, were another story. The tacky mesh binding her legs to the seat's steel leg refused to budge. Furthermore, the tools to cut the tape were too far from her grasp.

"Good girl. Stick it to him," cheered on Burton silently as Esther mouthed off.

Ignoring the bantering between Xander and the old woman, Jeffory Fenton brazenly approached Mattie; his intent all too apparent.

Standing but inches away from her, Xander's henchman raised his arms above Mattie's head and loosened her bindings. Next, tightly gripping her under her arms, he easily lifted her off the hook and wickedly slid her body down his until face-to-face, his mouth forced her lips to separate.

Biting down hard on Fenton's lower lip, Mattie drew blood.

"I enjoyed watching you when you slept… dressed… Especially in shower," laughed the voyeur; tasting the trickle of blood.

"Always knew you were a perv," retorted Mattie with disgust; struggling to release herself from Fenton's grip.

Distracted, Xander ignored Esther's blabbering to become a willing participant in Fenton's erotic melodrama.

"Now Jeffory… Don't hog," insisted an aroused Xander; his energy renewed.

Grabbing Mattie's thick auburn hair, Fenton hauled the young woman to Xander; laughing as she tripped over the several barbells on the floor beside the flat bench.

"Have fun boss," he snickered.

Forcing Mattie to straddled the utility bench directly in front of Xander. Then ambled to another seat where he casually reclined; eager to observe.

Exuberantly pulling Mattie's body against his groin, Xander placed a muscular arm across her ample chest to restrain her. Next, he produced a shiny red box cutter from his pocket and freed the sharp, deadly blade from its sheath. Deliberately pressing its shiny flat surface against Mattie's silky skin.

"Sshhhh… Sshhhh," cautioned the psychopath; tightening his grip as Mattie tensed. "I wouldn't fidget if I were you. You never know when this little blade might accidently… slip."

Amused at Mattie's precarious predicament, Fenton hooted.

"Look familiar old woman? Almost exactly like the one I borrowed from your barn," giggled Xander. "You know… The one I used to carve up our mutual friend."

Esther gasped, sickened at the realization that the knife used to kill Peter Cavenaugh belonged to her. Xander burst into laughing seeing her tortured expression.

"Pretty little thing… Be a shame to mar such delicate skin, or those stunning eyes," threatened Xander.

Without missing a beat, the murderer slowly pressed the tip of the sharp blade into Mattie's upper arm. Reveling in the rush as Esther's resolve crumpled.

"Oops… How clumsy," professed Xander, ignoring Mattie's gasp.

Esther unleashed a barrage of profanity, promising to repay him in kind.

"Now there's an intelligent response," Xander remarked with a bizarre giggle.

His sadistic grin and cold pale-blue eyes confirming Esther's fear; Xander was done playing games.

"Here's the deal sweetie. I ask you a question. You answer correctly. Nobody gets hurt... Answer wrong... Well, you get the picture," he asserted. "Now, that night in your backyard. I know you saw what I did... Why come outside?"

"Yes... I saw," agreed Esther. "But I thought you'd gone."

Hoping if he heard what he wanted she could buy them a little more time.

"Ding... Right... Now wasn't that easy," he declared; probing further. "You told the cops what I looked like. But not having my name, the ballgame was a trap."

"No. Yes. Maybe... I don't know," faltered Esther.

Confused how to answer because why then the employee badge photos, why the police sketch artist?

"Eeehhhh," Xander shouted; mimicking an incorrect buzzer.

Applying pressure, the blade slicing deeper into Mattie's delicate skin.

The bright ruby-red fluid immediately oozing from the open wound; trickling down Mattie's arm until it dripped off her fingertips onto the floor.

"Stop! How could I know," pleaded Esther.

"She doesn't... But I do," interjected the hooded Mitzy Burton belligerently.

Then, with undeniable conviction, the police officer warned her captors.

"Hurt either again... You'll never know," promised Burton.

"Mitzy... What do you mean, you do?" demanded Esther; scarcely believing her ears. "You... Michael... You knew who this monster was... All along?"

No longer thinking rationally, an enraged Esther let lose all her pent-up furry. She had trusted the law with their lives and the law had intentionally, callously, used them as collateral damage.

"No wonder nobody trusts cops these days," sighed Xander with false empathy.

"Not so high and mighty now, are ya Burton?" crowed Fenton.

With Mattie trapped against Xander and Esther tied to the exercise machine, Jeffory Fenton placed his firearm on the floor beside the mirrored wall and sauntered to Mitzy Burton. Eager to abuse his former female boss, Fenton cruelly demonstrated the power he now held over her. Maliciously probing every inch of the officer's well-toned physique before grabbing the delicate area between her legs.

Burton gasped and lowered her head; whispering sweetly into the Fenton's ear.

"You want to grab someth'n Jeffory... Grab this."

Fenton's cocky leer instantly vanished as Burton unleashed a ferocious offensive against the henchman. Pushing off the wall with her strong legs, Mitzy catapulted atop the traitor; using his body to cushion hers as they both crashed to the floor.

Quickly on her feet, having tossed both the sack and ropes, Burton kneed Fenton in the gut as he attempted to rise; then, delivered a solid blow to his left eye.

Stunned seeing the wind knocked out of Fenton; Xander suddenly found himself struggling to retain control of Esther's niece.

Mattie, following Burton's lead, turned on Xander with all the fury of a caged cougar. Repeatedly jerking her head back towards him until she heard the distinct crunch of his nose breaking followed by a primal scream; telling her she had hit her mark.

The dazed killer's hands instinctively releasing her to protect the fracture.

Wasting no time, Mattie tumbled off the bench narrowly avoiding the psychopath's wild lunges with the box cutter. Countering his attack, she seized the hand holding the blade and pulled him off-balance towards her. Biting down hard on the inside soft flesh of his wrist, and causing him to drop the knife. The weapon clattering somewhere beneath the flat bench.

"You're so dead!" roared Xander.

Grabbing Mattie's shirt; yanking her off the floor.

Howling insanely at his conquest, Xander never saw the dumbbell in Mattie's hand until it connected with his lower jar. Wailing, the killer crumbled to the floor cradling both fractured mandible and nose as he wafted in and out of consciousness.

Meanwhile across the room Burton and Fenton desperately tried to overpower the other and reach the gun beside the wall mirror.

"Mattie, get Esther out! Don't wait for me," screamed Burton over her shoulder.

Xander's henchman suddenly ramming his body into hers. Slamming her against the wall. Burton, in turn, hooked Fenton's knees; sending him falling flat on his back. His head smacking against the tile floor.

Obeying Mitzy's orders, Mattie kept one eye on Xander's altered state of consciousness as she retrieved the knife and ran to free Esther. Unfortunately in doing so she accidently kicked Fenton's gun out of Burton's reach just as her fingers were about to grab it. Sliding the weapon across the room to the opposite wall with both Burton and Fenton in hot pursuit.

Vigorously, Mattie cut through her aunt's leg bindings as Esther slid her wrists off the triceps bar. Esther, plopping onto the seat with a jarring thud as the bar and weight stack loudly crashed into the machine. Mattie gently assisting the freed Esther to her feet; then turning to help Mitzy Burton.

A loud groan resonated behind the work bench as Xander's hand rose up and grabbed the seat.

"Where's the gun!" cried Mattie panicking; searching for the firearm.

"Never mind the damn gun," yelled Burton. "Get out!"

Her right cross barely grazing Jeffory Fenton's face.

"We're not leaving you," protested Esther, stepping towards Burton.

But then the faltering Xander, clinging to the bench, zeroed in on Esther.

"Run. Now!" screamed Burton.

With a firm arm around her aunt's waist, Mattie dashed Esther out of the room just as Jeffory Fenton knocked Mitzy Burton to the ground.

Racing to the front door the women found the deadbolt locked with no key in sight. Frantic, they bolted to the kitchen; to go out the same way they came in. As they did, shots rang out from the dark hallway.

"Mitzy," cried Esther, turning to help the officer.

"Tante, we have to go!" insisted Mattie, urging her aunt forward.

Determined to get her aunt to safety, yet racked with guilt leaving Burton to combat Xander and his henchman on her own, Mattie hurried her weakened aunt through the kitchen into the adjacent laundry room and the door leading to the garage.

Without warning, a crazed Oliver Baring lunged at them from behind. Seizing Esther's ankle in his massive hands, and jerking her back with such force both went tumbling backwards into the kitchen.

Thrashing wildly, Esther kicked at Xander using her free foot. Mattie, jumping atop his back pounded the killer with her fists. Yet in spite of their valiant efforts and his significant injuries, with a burst of adrenaline Xander flicked Mattie off away as if she was an annoying flea.

Stumbling, Mattie fell hitting her head on the corner of the kitchen table; collapsing like a Raggedy Ann doll.

With the younger woman out of commission, the psychopath gleefully threw Esther onto the floor roaring with unbridled delight as he straddled her body. His substantial size crushing her ribs, hindering her breathing.

Then, giggling as drool from his fractured jaw dribbled onto the older woman's chest, Xander pinned Esther's shoulders against the cold floor with his knees. Encircling her neck with his massive hands, sadistically tightening and releasing his grip. His lust for vengeance taking precedence even over his enormous pain. Unaware a woozy Mattie had gotten to her feet.

Grabbing a greasy skillet off the stove with both hands, Mattie awkwardly swung the pan at Xander head; flimsily making contact above his ear. It was enough to knock him out cold.

Pushing the unconscious Xander off Esther, Mattie helped her woozy aunt to her feet and hurried her into the laundry room. Forcefully pushing open the door to freedom, the elated women stepped inside the dark garage. Their euphoria short lived as the door slammed shut and locked behind them; trapping them in darkness.

Frantically searching the wall for both the light switch and garage door opener, unable to find either, a resigned Esther calmly pulled Mattie to her; lovingly cupping the young woman's face.

"Mattie, if for some reason we're separated, get to Ida's... Hear me... Ida's," pleaded Esther.

"Why? What do you mean? Tante we make it together or not at all," argued Mattie.

Worried her aunt was about to do something rash.

Yet before Mattie could get an answer, a clamor and deafening bellow erupted in the kitchen. Oliver Baring was very much alive. And now, it was only a matter of time.

Then, recalling having seen a side door when Jeffory Fenton carried her into the house earlier, Esther grabbed Mattie's arm.

"This way!" she screamed; pulling her niece.

With outstretched fingers the two felt across the dark garage until bumping into the exterior wall and finding the door. Their good fortune turning at finding the knob uncooperative, making freedom or death a toss-up.

Purposely avoiding the war zone down the hall where Fenton and Burton were battling, Xander staggered to his study to retrieve Peter Cavenaugh's NAA Black Window .22 revolver. Returning, he yanked open the door and stood in the archway squinting into the hazy garage.

The laundry room eerily backlit Xander's grotesque silhouette as a small patch of light streamed across the darkness; exposing the women standing beside the side door. Alarmed at seeing the psychopath alive, yet alone cognizant, Esther stepped in front of Mattie; shielding her.

"Hear that? Police sirens… on their way here. A good neighbor probably heard your gunshots. Better run while you still can asshole," asserted Esther defiantly.

Instead, glaring, Xander directed his gun at her and mouthed one word.

"Goodbye."

However before pulling the trigger, a loud crash resonated from the kitchen. Startled, Xander dragged his damaged body back inside intent on defending himself. There, Officer Mitzy Burton had unselfishly willed her pummeled body into the kitchen. Intent on saving Esther and Mattie, Burton belligerently called out their names. Hearing the women scream back to her the killer was armed and on his way.

First came the shouting, then a series of pop, pop, pop. Finally, an eerie silence.

It was then the door lock unexpectedly gave way, surprising them both.

"Remember, Ida's… Don't stop… I love you kid. Always," declared Esther.

Throwing open the door Esther shoved her niece outside and closed it between them, deliberately locking it once again. Determined, if Xander was still alive and intent on killing her, no one else would die because of her.

"Be safe my beautiful child," prayed Esther; still clutching the knob.

"Tante, no! Open the door," cried Mattie on the other side. "Open the damn door!"

Pounding the barricade with her fist Mattie attempted to twist open the knob, but the lock held firm. Wasting no further time, she turned her back on her beloved aunt and bolted to a neighbor's for help.

Hearing the garage side door slam from inside the kitchen, Xander stumbled back and flipped the wall switch. Shocked to see Esther there, standing alone. Wobbling, he stumbled towards her; intent on finishing her off.

Esther, evading his grasp, fell against the RAM driver's side door. Finding it open she quickly hoisted herself behind the wheel while slamming and locking it shut.

Furious, Xander stepped back unsteadily and squared off in front of the windshield. Slowly he raised the .22 revolver; struggling to steady his weakening, shaky hands.

At the same time Esther caught sight of the key fob in the cup holder. Punching the ignition button, she shoved the truck into Reverse and stepped down hard on the accelerator. With screeching tires, the RAM plowed through the garage door with a deafening boom, shattering its panels and sending the splinters sailing in the air.

Thrown to the ground, gawking, Xander watched as his pickup burned rubber.

Speeding down the driveway, Esther was caught off-guard when the RAM bottomed out where the sharply sloped drive met the street. The impact forcing the pickup to momentarily defy gravity before crashing back to earth and stalling out.

Behind the wheel of the stalled truck, a stunned Esther saw house lights turn on as curious neighbors spilled into their front yards. Then, she heard distant police sirens.

"If those sirens aren't headed this way, we're all dead ducks," she thought.

Considering the innocent bystanders as she searched the crowd for Mattie.

"Cookie… Run," she decided; certain if able, Xander would pursue her.

It was then, emerging from the shadows of the garage, that Xander slowly serpentine down the driveway towards her with gun in hand. No longer caring about neighbors, or police; his only thought, desire, was to destroy Esther.

Standing in front of the windshield, locking his eyes onto hers as if in some bizarre western standoff, Xander glared at the old woman seated behind the wheel.

Then, raising the NAA Black Window .22 revolver, Oliver Baring lined his sights on Esther Hausman's forehead and pulled the trigger. The shot barely audible over the deafening wails of police sirens closing in.

Chapter 14

"If anyone could have saved me it would have been you."

~Virginia Woolf

The bullet expelled from the NAA Black Window .22 revolver barrel and its attached suppressor at a speed of more than 1,200 miles per hour (mph), and sped towards its target at an approximate speed of 1,500 feet per second (fps). The likelihood that Oliver Alexander Baring's shot would miss hitting Esther Hausman squarely between the eyes was nearly impossible.

If she had purposely tried to dodge the projectile hurling toward her, she would have needed to react to the sound of the gunshot 0.20 seconds faster than the fastest Olympic springer. And, since sound travels at 768 mph, which is 1,126 fps, or roughly half the speed of a bullet, Xander's bullet should have struck Esther before she ever heard the gun fire.

It then seemed incomprehensible that two random acts would occur simultaneously and cause the deadly projectile to miss Esther by mere inches; embedding deep into the driver's seat headrest just a tad below the bullet hole previously made the night of Peter Cavenaugh's murder. Even more unbelievable was the fact that it was Esther herself who unwittingly set one of these anomalies in motion thus saving her own life. But, that is just what happened.

After the RAM bottomed out on the street at the end of Xander's driveway, it remained motionless for several minutes. However inside the cab, a breathless Esther was anxiously fumbling with the knob used to reposition the driver seat closer to the wheel to compensate for her much shorter legs.

Panic further set in when the bloodied, disfigured killer appeared from garage waving a gun he intended to use on her.

Then, when Xander's trembling hands did pulled the trigger, the .22's spring mechanism hammered the firing pin discharging the bullet at that same time Esther's foot accidently slipped off the gas pedal. And, with her badly bruised hands and swollen fingers unable to grasp the steering wheel, Esther went into an uncontrolled freefall; sliding off the slick upholstery onto the floor where she became wedged under the steering column.

Esther's second saving grace could only be attributed to a basic physics anomaly.

As the bullet pierced the windshield, the glass's thickness altered the projectile's trajectory; deflecting the bullet's path enough so that it veered wide of its intended target. And although the round missed Esther when the bullet penetrated the glass, thousands of dangerous lacerating shards showered upon her. It was because of the seat mishap and her quick duck and cover; Esther's life was miraculously saved.

Hastily pulling herself back onto the driver's seat, shocked, Esther peered through the windshield hole with splintering web-like glass emanating from its round void. There, only a few yards in front of the hood stood the monster, glaring at her.

Not waiting for Xander to get off another round, Esther shoved the RAM into Drive and stomped on the gas. With a loud squeal the powerful machine jerked forward, bouncing over the curb onto Xander's desertscape front yard; surging on the same path as the killer. Forcing him to either dive out of the way of his beloved truck, or be run over by it.

As he lay on the ground racked with pain, Xander watched his pickup speed away with his nemesis behind the helm. By the time he had pulled himself together and fired several more rounds in her direction Esther had driven 1.2 miles; too far for the bullets to hit its intended target.

However just because the deadly projectiles did not hit the truck, it does not mean the bullets did not find other, unintentional targets.

It was not too far away for two of Xander's stray bullets to travel before embedding into the foundation of 9-years-old Kelly Martin's home directly below her open bedroom window as the child innocently slept in her bed.

Or, from entering Phillip Bloom's living room and shattering a treasured religious heirloom on an end table next to where the unsuspecting retired firefighter was reading the Arizona Republic newspaper. Sending colored splinters of the cherished crystal in all directions; including Bloom's eyes.

Slowly rising to his feet, Xander tenderly cradled his broken jawbone and assessed his situation. While most of his neighbors had hurried back into their homes and bolted their doors, not wanting to get involved, a few others remained; unable to take their eyes off the man they had always regarded as a model citizen.

Of the many gawkers was the man in golf attire who Xander spoke to earlier and, his wife. The third, a stranger, apparently had just delivered their pizza. Petrified, the threesome watched in horror as the grotesque figure covered in blood staggered in their direction supporting his fractured mandible with one hand while waving his menacing gun at them with the other.

"Oliver… What the hell's going on?" blurted the man in plaid shorts.

The man assuming Oliver Baring had been a victim of a horrendous attack and was injured standing his ground defending himself. It was not until Xander placed the .22 to the pizza deliveryman's forehead that the confused neighbor realized his error.

Not sticking around for an explanation, the terrified golfer grabbed his wife by her collarless peach-sequined T-shirt and hastily dragged her toward their house. Crushing the pizza box against his chest as if its doughy contents would shield him; and, leaving the poor pizza man completely at the killer's mercy.

Paying no heed to his fleeing neighbors, Xander pressed the gun barrel harder against the frightened man's temple.

"Keys," demanded Xander.

Slurring his word as drool dripped from his lower lip.

"In the car... Take it. Please... Just don't shoot," begged the ashen-face man.

His trembling knees buckling.

Gingerly sliding behind the wheel of the pizza man's faded Indigo Dodge® Challenger, Oliver Baring opened the Recover My Ride GPS tracking system on his phone. Clearly in unbearable pain, he took a moment. Amusing himself by watching the panic-stricken pizza man banged on the front door of the very customers who abandoned him; and they, yanking him inside before again slamming the door.

The tracking system beeped twice letting the killer know it had located his moving vehicle with a red dot representing his truck.

"Got you... Bitch," Xander sputtered; the flashing dot on the screen crossing a familiar intersection.

The police sirens were becoming ear-piercing. Soon they would arrive at his home; yet, he no longer cared they knew who it belonged to. Nor did he care if they captured his long-time associate Jeffory Fenton, or found the cop lying on his kitchen floor, or, the escaped auburn-haired niece.

The only thing the enraged killer cared about now was the woman behind the wheel of his pickup. His deep hatred for her negating any rational thought he had left.

With a single-minded purpose, Xander stepped on the Challenger's accelerator. Burning rubber, the muscle car sped after Esther Hausman; its illuminated pizza chain car topper attached to the faded roof disclosing the direction he was traveling to overtake his next kill.

***

Even with a generous head start, Esther's escape was in serious peril. Frustrated, unable to operate the truck's navigation system, it was one of those rare times in Esther's life she wished she was more tech savvy. Now, totally confused by the unfamiliar surroundings with so many houses and strip malls looking amazingly alike. Esther was unwilling to wrongly guess where police stations might be, and continued driving as if on the verge of a major meltdown.

Furthermore, completely clueless as to whether Xander was dead, incapacitated, or, hot on her trail; it was for this later reason she refused to stop at any late-night businesses still open and ask for help. Terrified Xander might recognize his truck in a neighborhood parking lot and slaughter every man, woman, and child inside the establishment before killing her.

Exasperated, making another wrong turn, Esther decided the best way to attract police attention would be by violating the most basic traffic laws. Thinking at least one of her infractions would trigger a traffic camera and spur whoever was monitoring the feed to either send help, or throw her in jail.

"Geez... Arrest me already," she shouted; running another traffic light.

Then, taking a calculated risk, Esther pulled into a moderately crowded parking lot where similar trucks faced the street.

"Well if it's one thing Arizona's got plenty of... it's pickups," she snorted.

Squeezing the RAM among the other trucks, Esther shut off the engine. Taking a moment after to look in the rearview, she probed a mean laceration on her forehead.

"You'll live... For now," she remarked cynically.

272

Shifting her priority back to the elusive escape route, Esther scoured the night for something familiar; ultimately recognizing two silhouettes in opposite directions.

It was in the western sky the heavy cloud coverage parted long enough for the crescent moon to peek through; softly illuminating the South Mountains cradling Ahwatukee. That meant the mountains far-off to her right had to be the eastern Superstition range near Apache Junction. Both were viable routes back to Tucson. Yet there was also a third, faster, option which she now knew how to get to. And although this route had its unique challenges, this it was what she chose.

At the Gilbert Road, Route AZ-87 intersection stop sign, Esther drew a deep breath.

"Florence first... Then 79... Then, Ida's."

Daring to hop her plan to reach the cabin and elude Xander for good might actually work. Knowing too if the killer caught her there, in the middle of nowhere, no one would ever find her body.

"Here goes nothing," she whispered nervously.

Turning left, Esther drove into a pitch-black wilderness which had changed very little since 1939.

Long neglected, the narrow two-lane historical state highways, or backroads as the locals called them, were often favored over congested I-10 interstate for various reasons. Traveling the rustic thruways meant crossing vast undeveloped Sonoran Desert to reach Florence; then, much the same from Florence to Tucson.

These were roads where humanity's existence was almost nil. Where the rough blacktop, littered with axel-breaking pot-holes, merged with meandering hills of sharp curves and limited visibility. Where unpredictable wildlife wandered; and, if an accident occurred, someone might be stranded for a very long time.

Relying on her memory and broken reflective white lines to identify where the highway's lanes and shoulders converged, a determined Esther eased the truck's right-side wheels back onto the road after accidentally having veered too closely to an irrigation ditch.

"You gotta be nuts, Esther," tersely chiding herself.

Ignoring her common sense she increased the pickup's speed.

Unconvinced she escaped Xander's wrath, Esther continued checking the mirrors; imagining Peter Cavenaugh's killer was behind every wheel.

If lucky, she would reach Ida's cabin in the 8,000 feet high mountain community of Summerhaven sometime that night. Still almost 200 miles away, to get there meant driving the truck up the unpaved Old Mt Lemmon road which snaked the Santa Catalinas' northeastern slopes, in total darkness.

"Madness," she admitted.

Knowing under the best conditions even the top off-road vehicles broke down attempting the climb. But that, was a problem for later.

Driving onto the Gila River Indian Reservation, Esther's muddled brain insisted on evoking the events which led her to this very moment. Back to Peter Cavenaugh's mangled corpse, the ballgame, and then the safe house. Next, Xander's personal torture chamber, demanding, "Do the cops know about me?" And finally, Mitzy Burton's confession, "She doesn't... But I do."

Still shocked at Mitzy's declaration, Esther now bitterly suspected everything she had been led to believe about the murder on her property.

"She doesn't... But I do."

Burton's words had stung.

If what Mitzy said was true, was the ballgame the first time she and Mattie were used as bait, as Xander claimed? Had her trust in the police been misplaced? She had trusted Jeffory Fenton; look where that had gotten her.

"You too, Michael? You promised to protect us," she said sadly.

Reality, however, had proven quite different.

***

About the same time Esther Hausman was crossing the Gila River Indian Reservation, a black unmarked police SUV screeched to a halt in front of Oliver Baring's Gilbert residence. Silencing its siren, Homicide Detective Michael Flores purposely left the vivid blue and red emergency lights flashing as a warning to the curious to keep their distance as he bolted from the car. His slightly younger passenger immediately joining forces with him; the two working alongside each other as if they had been a well-seasoned team.

Cautiously approaching the house, Flores attempted to evaluate the hostage situation. Having no idea what transpired before their arrival, or what conditions were behind the locked doors, he grabbed a bullhorn.

"Oliver Baring, Jeffory Fenton… This is Detective Michael Flores. Talk to me."

Endeavoring to open a dialogue with the killers; yet, cautious not to escalate already heightened emotions.

Meantime his passenger was diligently coordinating with Gilbert police backup, evacuating civilians, and directing a newly arrived American Medical Response ambulance behind police lines. Soon it became quite apparent to all, the brash young man in the rumpled T-shirt and torn jeans was not the bystander he initially seemed.

"Baring… Nobody else needs to get hurt. Call me…," assured Flores.

Holding up a large piece of cardboard displaying his number while still trying to ascertain the hostage dynamics.

Suddenly without warning, a woman ran from the dim garage with hands held high.

"Don't… Don't shoot!… Michael, Mitzy's been shot. She's unconscious, bleeding… The kitchen… Tante… He's going to kill Tante. Save her!" begged a frantic Mattie Kaplan stumbling towards him.

"Where are Baring and Fenton? What rooms?" demanded Flores, steadying the young woman. "Who's holding Esther?"

"Rooms? Fenton's inside, dead… Tante's not… Wait… Who's Baring?" she asked, utterly confused.

Unaware Xander was Oliver Baring's name of choice, Mattie thought Flores was referring to another of the killer's henchmen. Someone unaccounted for who was all too willing to carry out the psychopath's bidding. However before Mattie could ask for clarification, a somewhat familiar stranger joined them. Addressing Mattie with a wirily grin as he gestured to the EMTs to follow him, the man interjected.

"Kitchen. Right? I'm on it," he asserted; his voice also a recognizable puzzlement.

Immediately disregarding the distraction, Mattie turned to Flores and unloaded.

"Listen! Tante's gone, Xander's after her. He's going to kill her!" she screamed.

Grabbing the detective's suit jacket, Mattie pulled Flores towards his car giving him an abridged version of what happened; including Esther's escape. Then, adding a complete description the killer's pickup, Mattie told him Esther's exact route and destination. She also described the car Xander stole, right down to its pizza topper delivery sign.

"Tante counted on Xander going after her and not me. She's sacrificing herself. Michael... Go. Now!" pleaded Mattie.

Leaving the newly arrived Officer Murphy to spearhead the crime scene, Detective Michael Flores sped after Esther Hausman. Unaware until he reached the Highway 87 turnoff that he an uninvited guest was hiding on the floor behind the driver's seat.

***

Hot on Esther Hausman's trail, Homicide Detective Michael Flores could not shake the sinking feeling that for the first time in his career he failed to bring the perpetrator to justice. Much worse, he failed to protect Esther and the others involved in his murder case. Earlier the day had yielded promising information, leading him to expect a prompt resolution; but that was before the slaughter at the safe house, before Esther, Mattie, and Mitzy Burton's abduction.

Standing amid such carnage, fearing the women were dead, hope had come in two forms. The first was Peter Cavenaugh's retired Army sergeant, Antonio Silva. The second was an observant Gilbert police dispatcher. It was the quick-thinking dispatcher who notified him of a possible hostage rescue situation at a residence belonging to Oliver Alexander Baring.

Aware of an all-points bulletin on Oliver Baring as the prime person of interest for both murder and kidnapping, she immediately sent officers to the home. After, she contacted Flores and the Phoenix Federal Bureau of Investigation office about the hostage crisis.

Apparently, a call had come in from a neighbor walking his dog who had surprised a family of javelina trying to overturn a garbage can placed on the street. Glad when the cantankerous and often dangerous javelina scurried away, the good citizen decided to right the trash can and pick up the rubbish.

It was then he caught a glimpse of suspicious activity inside Baring's house through the front window's parted vertical blinds. Curious, the man said he looked around to see if anyone was watching him; not wanting to be tagged as the neighborhood peeping Tom. Then, when he felt the coast was clear, he nonchalantly approached the house and peered through the window.

What caught the neighbor's eye was a reflection in a hallway mirror. Thinking at first he was watching some kind of kinky sex play; it was not long after the man realized it was an old woman being tortured and called the police.

Standing within earshot of the call, Antonio Silva overheard Michael Flores' conversation with the dispatcher. Not waiting for an invitation, Silva easily kept pace as Flores sprinted to his SUV. Demanding the detective take him along.

"You're a civilian," protested Flores. "I can't protect you if you get in the way."

"I won't," insisted Silva. "I know how these creeps operate. Do you?"

"You not planning on going vigilante on me are you?" accused Flores; to which Silva solemnly replied.

"Detective, you need me... What's more, you know it."

Unable to argue with Silva's logic, Michael Flores once again found himself bending rules he never would have considered on any other case. Certain if the three women were alive their time was growing short, he decided to take the chance and picked up the pace. In the back of his mind still questioning how far the retired noncom would go to seek overdue justice.

Suddenly Flores stopped dead in his tracks.

"You... Move that damn rig. Now!" barked Flores.

Flashing his police badge at the sleepy driver behind the wheel of a large news van blocking his vehicle.

Startled, the driver quickly turned on the engine and lurched the van forward. As he did, his vehicle exposed a casually dressed man a few years younger than Michael Flores leaning against the detective's shiny-black police SUV as if he owned it.

The punk's arrogant expression was the last straw.

"Off asshole!" ordered the detective.

At that point, wanting nothing more than to wipe the egotistical grin off the moron's face, Flores grabbed the wise-guy by the shirt and strongly assisted him off his car. Not caring one iota that his immature, unprofessional behavior only served to feed his own foul mood, Flores tossed the stranger onto a large section of common area landscaping stones.

"Look pal... Unless you're police or FBI get lost. Or, I'll arrest you for obstruction," threatened Flores.

Gathering himself into a relaxed sitting position on the rocks, the unruffled man smiled broadly at the two men standing over him.

"Terco?" exclaimed Silva, completely mystified.

The conniving low-life from work being the last person Antonio Silva expected to see that evening.

"You messed up in this, Jefe?" Terco asked smugly.

Still grinning at his boss from the ground.

"What? You know this knucklehead?" snarled Flores glaring at Silva.

Not waiting the detective climbed into his SUV, intent on leaving both men in the dust until Terco called Flores by name; demanding he stop.

"That's just it... I'm your knucklehead," replied Terco glibly; flashing his FBI shield at the annoyed detective.

Rising from the ground, Terco indifferently brushed away the pitted gravel imbedded his palms. Then without further explanation, he climbed into the backseat of Flores' SUV and buckled his seatbelt.

"We going?" he asked coolly; folding his hands in his lap.

Reports of shots fired at the Gilbert residence of Oliver Baring blared across Flores' police radio.

"Get in," shouted Flores to Silva.

With police lights flashing and siren screaming, Michael Flores accelerated onto the eastbound 202 Santan Freeway towards Gilbert with two unlikely passengers in the backseat. Having no desire to make small talk with either, he remained silent; his head swimming with worst-case scenarios.

Barely noticing Flores' excess speed and aggressive maneuvering the two men effortlessly maintained their balance as if expertly riding a wild bronco. All the while quietly sizing up the other until Silva broke the silence.

"So, Terco. I mean Renan... You're FBI?" commented Silva suspiciously.

From the moment the kid had been assigned to his team Silva had pegged him as a hustler, a total screw up. Now scrutinizing him closer than even, Silva was still convinced the kid was a screw up.

"Actually Jefe it's Collins... FBI Special Agent Aiden Collins," replied Terco with the same wiseass smirk.

"Really? Not Renan Cardoso?" asked Antonio Silva with a quizzical brow.

Cocking his head at the disheveled ballpark employee in disbelief.

"Long story for another time Jefe," answered Terco, tight-lipped.

The young man giving Silva the impression the two still had business.

Just then Flores' SUV squealed to an abrupt stop close to Oliver Baring's house. With Gilbert police backing them up, Michael Flores and FBI liaison Aiden Collins left Silva in the utility vehicle and immediately initiated the hostage rescue protocols for which they had been highly trained.

It was then a familiar auburn-haired woman suddenly ran from the open garage screaming; her hands high in the air.

"Don't shoot!" ordered Michael Flores.

Chapter 15

The Town of Florence

Preferring the backroads over the hectic I-10 interstate, Esther had always suspected these original Arizona highways and the vast lands it crossed had changed very little since the blacktop was first laid in the late 1930s. The roads opened to all who traveled its path spectacular panoramic scenery with few human structures to obscure the one-of-a-kind splendor known as the Sonoran Desert.

Reaching the outskirts of the town of Florence, Esther slowed the pickup to the specified 35 miles per hour and turned into the BURGER KING® parking lot. Certain at that late hour only essential businesses were open; and, the fast-food chain was not one of them. She chose a secluded space behind the building where tall shrubs somewhat concealed the truck, and shut off the engine. Figuring the chance of anyone noticing her, or pulling into the lot, was almost nil.

Staring into nothingness, unable to drive another block, Esther rested her forehead against the steering wheel and closed her eyes; silently giving thanks for being alive. After saying the same for Mattie, she then asked more as a plea than a prayer to smite the son of a bitch, Xander; or at the very least render the psychopath completely harmless for the rest of his sorry-ass life.

It was then her thoughts turned to Mitzy Burton and what the officer had told Xander and his henchman while they were held captive. Realizing now Burton's tale had been a convincing act which she had foolishly believed. But that was then. Now as tired as she was, Esther recognized the truth. That Mitzy Burton's story was a ploy to buy her time to get them all free of their vicious captors.

Then standing in the garage, the ruckus in the kitchen. It was Mitzy who had lured Xander back inside; Esther was sure it was. Mitzy, who had bought her and Mattie time to escape. Then the gunshot, and absolute silence.

Esther's heart wrenched, feeling utterly ashamed for her last words to the fallen officer. Begging forgiveness, Esther then said a fourth prayer, Kaddish.

"And you Michael… Did you abandon us? Or did Xander kill you too?"

Not knowing whether to be furious or grief-stricken. Unaware at that very moment Michael Flores was speeding in her direction, determined to find her before Oliver Baring did.

Laying back against the pickup's bullet-riddled headrest, Esther let out a heavy sigh; the emotional and physical abuse she had endured at the hands of Xander and his henchman having taken a great toll.

Feeling her adrenaline subside and intense pain retaliate in its place, the lightheaded Esther used her shaky, inflamed fingers to vigorously push down on muscles that were strongly knotting. Kneading the protesting tissues like malleable dough until the spasms relaxed. Then tentatively, she tilted the rearview mirror downward, shocked to see a brutalized stranger staring back with tears pouring from swollen, glazed eyes.

"I give… You win. Your secret's safe with me," blubbered Esther; wiping her runny nose on her shirt.

Yet, knowing her vow of silence would never appease Xander's blood lust, Esther blinked away her tears and snorted back the dripping snot.

"You done? Get going," she scolded.

Resolved to reach the remote cabin where Xander would never find her. To beat the bastard at his own game. Admitting, with a loud drawn-out yawn, she had absolutely no idea what that game was, or how to play it.

Another intense spasm; this time seizing her lower back.

"Shit!" howled Esther, cringing.

The sharp surge akin to a lightning bolt streaking down her sciatic nerve to the tips of her toes.

"Maybe a sprained ankle is not so bad," she said, punch-drunk tired.

Needing to sleep, or risk doing so behind the wheel of the pickup, Esther grudgingly reversed her decision not to stop for long periods. Closing her heavy eyelids; yet, unable to sleep. The images dancing in her head were not those of the psychopath, but rather, her much-loved desert creatures. Coyotes yips and owls hooty-hoots sang to her on the winds of the arid, unspoiled earth. Their nocturnal songs eliciting visions of home, treasured pets, dear friends.

Then one special night of stargazing, a delicious meal, and a couple bottles of Sonoita wine. She and the Tadais took turns identifying celestial objects visible with the naked eye; Mars and Venus, the constellation Leo. Each sharing stories about their family, and how they settled in this awe-inspiring land.

Joseph started by saying over 6,000 years ago, before Christ, this region was home to numerous cultural groups. One group, prehistoric farmers known as the Huhugam (Hohokam), arrived more than 1,200 years ago.

Explaining it was the Huhugam who built a comprehensive irrigation agriculture throughout the Phoenix area using only sticks and stones for digging, and baskets to carry out dirt. Yet somehow they managed to create the largest, most complex and sophisticated system of canals in ancient North America. Portions of which are still evident today. Their canals brought water to countless villages and thousands of acres of fields. However for all their technological advancements, the entire Huhugam nation, its people, mysteriously vanished by the 15th century.

Emily then said Joseph's ancestors, the Tohono O'odham, arrived in the early 1700's; followed by the Apache, Papago, and Pima along with Franciscan Missionaries hell bent on saving souls.

Always curious about life in these communities whenever she drove across lands belonging to the Gila River Indian Community's two distinct tribes; the Akimel O'odham (Pima), and the Pee-Posh (Maricopa). Esther ashamedly admitted she would rudely stare into tribal neighborhood yards situated alongside the highways; trying to catch a glimpse of the people living there in their unique sovereignty designed homes. Vowing not to peek the next time; each time failing miserably.

This was especially true of the charming Spanish-style Saint Anne Catholic Church Mission set off the AZ-87 roadway. Probably an early-twentieth century construction which always seemed in need of repair; yet, compared to its adjoining graveled-covered cemetery, the tiny white-stucco structure appeared quite perky.

Every time driving by, she would envision the people who worshipped there, and those who chose the desolate location as their final resting place. Finding it hard not to gawk at the small stars and stripes flags attached to diminutive poles sprouting from the rock-hard earth beside the heads of honored graves.

"Gas," Esther declared a little too loudly; noticing the nearly empty tank.

Having no money of her own, Esther diligently searched the crevices of the cab.

"Shit… For a killer, you keep a pretty tidy car," she remarked sarcastically.

Smirking as she blindly rummaged through the driver's door well until something sharp stabbed her hand.

"Damn… What the hell?" she cried.

Quickly retracting her fingers from the dark abyss.

Sucking on a trickle of blood oozing from a cut on her index finger, Esther carefully lifted the deadly garrote from its hiding place with her other hand.

"Well, this can't be good," she exclaimed, examining the weapon.

Sickened as she speculated how such a device was used, Esther carefully replaced the sharp object back from where it came and continued searching. Then, after lifting the black cushioned armrest between the front bucket seats, she slid open the center console privacy slot. There, hidden under a package of travel hand wipes, was a large shiny paperclip securing two neatly folded twenty-dollar bills and a fiver.

Driving down Main Street, Esther dug crusts of sleep from her weary eyes as she passed the municipality sign welcoming her to the Town of Florence, founded 1866.

"Damn... Civil War barely ended," snorted Esther.

Recalling what she and Max learned when they moved to the state. That Florence was established when Arizona was still a territory and is state's sixth oldest non-Native American settlement; ultimately flourishing into a thriving agricultural center.

"Nine years before, this was all Spanish, Mexico territory... The US bought it... 1854, the Gadsden Purchase." she acknowledged with a slaphappy wave of her hand and a suppressed yawn.

"Before that, Mexico took it from the Indians... US settlers crossed their border, seized their land, and took their jobs... Making us illegal immigrants," she snickered.

"Forty-two years before Arizona officially became the last contiguous state in the union... Valentine's Day, February 1912... Two years before World War I... And, 45 years before... Me," she giggled. "Mattie's right... I am a relic."

Pulling into a dimly-lit gas station, Esther noticed the place was empty except for the teenaged cashier sound asleep inside the station's tiny convenience store. Slumped in a tattered vinyl chair behind the register, the kid was using the countertop as a pillow and his dirty cap to lessen the fluorescents.

Feeling safe, Esther shut off the engine.

As she opened the door and gingerly slid to the ground, she took a deep breath of cool night air. Then, with great effort on wobbly legs, she set off in search of the women's bathroom. Her annoyance at finding that door locked somewhat mollified after discovering the men's door slightly ajar.

Carefully rinsing her wounds with the bathroom sink's lukewarm water, Esther gritted her teeth as she applied the cheap liquid soap to her stinging cuts and bruises. Leaving the bathroom with water dripping off her body; preferring her enflamed tissues air dried rather than irritate them further with the rough paper towels.

Seeing the young cashier's head still glued to the countertop, Esther contemplated waking him to pay for the gas. Deciding instead, she needed the money more than big oil at the moment, she pocketed the much-needed cash with every intention of returning later and making things right.

That was, of course, if she was still alive.

Climbing behind the wheel Esther took comfort in the quiet night and empty streets. In some ways the serenity gave her a sense of hope. That perhaps she had out-foxed Xander, or he had given up. After all when last she saw him in the pickup's rearview mirror, he was badly injured; and, he had no clue where she was going. And, given the police were probably closing in on him, he would have been a fool not to run for the border.

On the other hand, she had both hurt and humiliated him; unforgivable sins in the narcissistic psychopath's eyes. If able, Xander would demand his ounce of flesh.

Torn, she had to decide.

Although an agricultural town, Florence was actually better identified as Arizona's Pinal County administrative center and county seat. Given its strong police presence and correctional institutions, including the State's primary prison, it was no surprise Florence was one of the safest places in Arizona to live.

Even so, turning herself into the police did not necessarily guarantee her safety. Her abduction from the Ahwatukee safe house was proof of that.

Plus she felt safer, more in control, on her own.

Still, it was the best way to find out about Mattie. If she was alright.

"Should I stay or should I go," sang Esther softly to herself.

The lyrics of The Clash popular tune playing over and over in her head as she tapped the catchy earworm's beat against the steering wheel with her swollen, achy fingers.

Ten minutes later the Florence Police Department's night duty officer, Sergeant Daniel Tucker, watched with great interest as a tattered older woman covered with cuts and bruises approached him.

Straightening her posture, Esther stood firm before the sergeant and looked directly into his eyes.

"Good evening officer… I am in need of assistance," she declared a bit too formally.

Looking as if she was ready to collapse, Sergeant Tucker quickly pulled a chair close to his desk and helped Esther into the seat; patiently waiting for her to explain.

Not knowing where to begin, Esther took a moment to brush a clump of dirt off her ripped jeans. Then, with a weary sigh, she said.

"My name is Esther Hausman. And, in all likelihood... I'm about to be murdered."

As the floodgates opened, Tucker listened intently as Esther described her situation and all its horrors. At one point, the kindhearted officer politely interrupted her long enough to escort her to the station's break room. Where, after getting comfortable in one of the cushy chairs around a long conference table, she continued.

While she spoke, Sergeant Tucker poured Esther a hot cup of coffee; then, pulled a paper sack from the refrigerator with the letters DT written in thick Sharpie. Next, after grabbing two dishes from a rack beside the sink, he set the plates down on the table and spread the contents of his bag to share.

Beyond grateful, Esther plucked a red seedless grape from the ample bunch before her. Biting into it, the cold succulent fruit splashed its sweet juices onto a particularly sensitive spot at the back of her throat, causing her to repeatedly cough. Ignoring the slight inconvenience, at that very moment Esther would have sworn to the almighty that she had just eaten the best tasting grape ever grown on Earth.

The urgency of contacting Tucson Homicide Detective Michael Flores had not been lost on Tucker. Activating the conference speakerphone on the table, after several attempts to patch him through to Flores, they were finally connected.

Upon hearing Michael's voice Esther's heart melted; completely forgetting her anger.

"Mattie's fine... Annoyed she has police protected... but fine. Mitzy, I don't... She's still in surgery. At least she's alive. Esther... Listen to me... I'm on my way to you. Stay with Sergeant Tucker... Understand," stipulated Flores.

"Why? What aren't you saying? Michael... You got that bastard, didn't you?" Esther asked; demanding the truth.

"Fenton's dead; but Oliver Baring… that malignant narcissist you know as Xander… He's still at large. Esther, this guy's completely out of control. You're safe there, with the sergeant. Stay put," urged Flores; his tone conveying what his words did not.

Nevertheless, his message was crystal clear. Xander was coming for her.

Rising from his seat, Sergeant Tucker immediately instructed his fellow officers to initiate security protocols; leaving Esther alone in the room to speak privately with Flores. It was then she asked the question which still plagued her.

"I get it… He's still after me," she acknowledged. "But what I don't get, is… Michael… The ballgame… Did you use Mattie and me as bait?"

"Bait? No… Never… Who gave you that idea? Fenton… Fenton and Baring have… had a long association which I recently discovered. Decades. Fenton wormed himself onto our security detail and kept Baring informed of our every move. Esther, I'm truly sorry… I…," he uttered; the guilt eating him up.

He had failed to protect her, and Mattie. Failed to quickly solve Peter Cavenaugh's murder and identify Baring. Failed to connect Fenton and Baring's association. Failed to prevented the lives of so many from being brutally wasted.

"Esther I'm asking you to trust me, one more time. I'll be there. Forty minutes, tops. Please… Stay put. I won't let that monster hurt you again. I promise," begged Flores. Feeling their relationship strained. "Just wait."

"Michael I do trust you… But if he's out there, nobody's safe," replied Esther wearily. "Not even you."

"Wait, Esther!" pleaded Flores.

But the line went dead.

"Sergeant… Everyone… I can't thank you enough for… well, everything."

Esther said with sincerity as some of the officers rejoined her in the break room.

"Mrs. Hausman, stay here. Stretch out until Detective Flores arrives," suggested a kind policewoman.

"Yes... I'd like that. Uh, but first, where can I clean up a bit?" Esther asked politely.

Dragging herself out of the chair, she followed the officer's directions to the women's bathroom; thinking about the fate of her security detail and Mitzy Burton. Vowing to herself silently as she entered.

"No one else dies cause of me."

After dawdling inside the restroom until it was completely empty, Esther peeked into the hallway. When absolutely sure the coast was clear, she stealthily slipped down the corridor and out the side door.

Then, back inside the RAM, she promptly started the engine and nervously checked her surroundings one last time before turning the truck south. She was well beyond the Florence town limits before any of the officers realized she was gone.

Chapter 16
Highway 79

Night was its darkest when Esther Hausman turned south onto Arizona State Highway 79. Taking a huge gamble, she turned off the headlights to shroud the truck under a nocturnal cloak and deliberately picked up speed. Fully aware she increased her chances of both driving off the road and colliding with unsuspecting wildlife; nevertheless, she counted on the ploy to improve her odds of reaching Summerhaven where not even Oliver F**ing Baring could find her.

Having driven Highway 79 more times than she could count; this was the first time Esther had used it as an escape route. The humming, thumping of its degrading asphalt beneath the pickup's wheels urging her to drive faster. Her frazzled mind concocting all sorts of absurdities to keep awake; her most bizarre creation, a scenario much akin to a Stephen King novel.

"Cursed to travel Highway 79 for eternity, *Tormented Tilly*… Dah, dah, dddaahhh."

Her voice theatrical, much like telling a ghost story. The tale, an old Ford 150 taking on an evil life of its own whenever traversing the ill-fated road.

"Tilly… You got noth'n over this horror story," Esther scoffed; checking the rearview mirror.

Her sour mood somewhat lightening after passing a large road sign; certain this particular stretch habitually confused unfamiliar travelers.

Whereas the large sign proclaimed she had entered the Pinal Pioneer Parkway; numerous metal posts which followed identified two more, conflicting names as the road's designation. The posts' top sign being the official Arizona Route

79 highway shield; and the one below it, a Historic US 80 brown and white marker. All three identifiers claiming the same 58 miles between Florence and Oracle Junction as their own; and all three, absolutely correct.

Originally part of The Dixie Overland Highway, the name was changed to US 80 in 1926 when the United States Numbered Highway System was created. And, like its more famous northern sister, Route 66, in its heyday US 80 became a major, southern, transcontinental route.

"Still a damn wagon trail," she mocked; hitting a bumpy patch.

Remembering her Arizona history and how the road originated during the Mexican-American War. Recalling too it was nicknamed The Mother of Highways because of its economic impact on towns. Then, when super highways became preferable, US 80 was decommissioned; yet, because Pinal Pioneer Parkway remained a viable artery for Florence, it was reinstated as Arizona SR 79 in 1992.

"Well, you're certainly a mother," snorted Esther, hitting another pothole. "Or maybe it's Lucifer… Beelzebub."

Its worn road reflectors and broken lane lines adding to Esther's exhaustion and eye strain; making it extremely difficult to tell where asphalt ended and soft shoulder and irrigation ditches began. And, with few streetlights, passing zones, or safety barriers as well as winding hills; Highway 79 was an accident waiting to happen.

Struggling, unintentionally giving in to her fluttering eyelids, Esther began nodding off; veering the speeding pickup straight towards a watery grave. As the tires slipped onto the shoulder, loose gravel and debris pelted the truck's underbelly creating enough racket to rouse her just in time.

Quickly jerking her foot off the gas instead of slamming on the brakes. Esther let friction slow the speeding machine to a stop, then shut off the engine.

"You're okay, Cookie," she reassured herself.

Her trembling hands refusing to grasp the steering wheel.

Desperate to reach Ida's cabin where she could finally sleep, Esther shook the cobwebs from her brain and guided the pickup back onto the highway. Now, barely able to make out the Santa Catalina Mountain range in the horizon against the star-studded black sky. The vague peaks gave Esther a sliver of hope, even though she knew full well she still had a long way to go.

Nervously increasing the pickup's speed Esther checked the mirrors for vehicles approaching from behind; as well as for suitable terrain ahead to hide, if need be, and animals meandering along the roadside's thick vegetation.

Just imagining she might injure or kill of any creature straying or bolting onto the highway made her want to retch. Therefore it was not surprising that somewhere in her frazzled mind she got the idea that if she straddled the yellow center dividing line instead of staying inside her own lane she would have more time to react and avert colliding with an unsuspecting creature.

At least that was her theory; however flawed, or not.

Weepy-eyed exhausted, driving down the middle of the road, Esther thought about the lack of cellphone service on Highway 79 between Florence and Oracle Junction, ironically, not being one of her problems. Since what few calls and bandwidth did get through quickly dropped or crackled; any connection was more or less a crap shoot.

"No phone… No problem," she chuckled.

Knowing it would not have worked anyway.

***

Minutes before Esther Hausman had slipped away from the Florence Police Station, a Dodge Challenger parked on a side street beneath a row of generously endowed Mesquite trees. His pale blue eyes glued on the station, the well-hidden Oliver Alexander Baring carefully sipped a large frozen slushie through a wide plastic straw, deciding his next move. His obsession with the old woman providing him remarkable clarity and fortitude, considering.

"Really? How stupid," he grunted; his fractured jaw drooping.

Watching the old fool clumsily exit the well-fortified sanctuary and hoist herself into his pickup, Xander was glad to confirm his belief that the woman's ability to stay alive was due more to dumb luck than intelligence.

"Well sweetie… Your luck's just run out," he thought; sipping the icy-cold liquid.

Welcoming the slushie's numbing effect on his throbbing temples and swollen face.

As his prey pulled away from the curb Xander watched the blinking red dot on his phone brainlessly track the old woman, just as it had done when she stole his truck. It had given him the time to stop at a Germann Road pharmacy first and grab a basketful of medical supplies; stabilizing his broken jaw and nose, and stocking up on a candy store full of heavy opioids.

"Ding… Cleanup on aisle three," he had sputtered ghoulishly.

His debilitating pain dulling as he stepped over the bodies of the dead pharmacist and her equally dead assistant lying on the linoleum floor in their own pool of blood.

His next stop proving equally rewarding when the nervous security guard at the closed big-box superstore was all too willing to show him the sporting goods section. The man insisting he take all the ammunition he wanted for Peter Cavenaugh's .22 revolver, free of charge.

Then, after depositing the silenced guard behind an outdoor dumpster on the loading ramp, Xander finally acted on the blinking red dot showing him the RAM's exact location in the town of Florence.

And so he sat.

Staring at his once prized pickup from inside a stolen Dodge Challenger that reeked of souring tomato sauce and Italian spices underneath a Mesquite canopy.

Opening the windows, Xander welcomed the cool breeze airing out the car's stench. Then, after adjusting the jaw stabilizing bandage, he popped another oxycodone and followed it with a slushie chaser. Next, grabbing a syringe and glass vial from the back seat, he puckered a muscle and injected himself with a dose of Ketorolac for good measure.

The combination of potent pain drugs kicked in.

Never considering in his half-crazed mind that his target was anywhere other than inside the police station, Xander planned his next move. His car door was barely opened when the old woman unexpectedly appeared outside completely alone.

"Silv'a plat'a," mumbled the killer.

Amazed when instead of returning inside the police station the old bat headed straight for his pickup.

"I could take you out right now?" giggled Xander eerily. "But then… Where's the fun in that, sweetie?"

Allowing the old woman to drive away as part of his new plan; one which he hoped would have a more thrilling, satisfying, end. And so he sat, memorized by the blinking red dot moving on his phone app. Much like an eager cat ready to snare a mouse; his entire body excited to play with his new toy.

"Talley-ho!"

Screamed Xander, stepping down hard on the gas. The Challenger's tires squealing, spinning, before finally burning rubber and peeling away. Racing after the red blinking dot. Occurring to him suddenly, the last time he had driven this highway his passenger was none other than Peter Cavanaugh. The very notion feeding his hysteria. Giggling until the red dot suddenly vanished from his phone and in its place two words, "No Service."

***

Miles away an unaware Esther Hausman too was riding high. However, unlike Oliver Baring' bloodlust, Esther's high was due simply to hope. Hope, that after seeing no sign of Xander or his henchman since Gilbert, she might have given the killers the slip. That she might actually live to see another day.

"Everything's coming up roses," she sang loudly, giddy with optimism.

Belting the show-stopping classic from the Broadway musical *Gypsy;* Esther gingerly tapped the steering wheel with her swollen fingers. Scanning the radio for any music in which she could join a boisterous celebration of life. What she found instead was the obnoxiously-loud cackle of static on every station; compliments of Highway 79's ever-present dead zone.

"Who needs you!" she yelled at the radio; switching off the irritating noise.

Opening the windows, cool fresh night air filled every nook of the stale cab with clean desert aromas helping her clear head. The sounds of nature's serenades along with the tires soft humming against the road relaxing her. Bothered only slightly by the occasional thud, thud, thud whenever she accidently drove over a lane stud, or two, or five.

Lazily she glanced into the rearview mirror. Becoming complacent at once again seeing darkness and empty road behind her, Esther sensed she was finally out of harm's way. Even so a small voice kept nagging, stay vigilant, keep the headlights off.

She checked again, only this time was different. This time she caught sight of a tiny glow dancing, floating, above ground in the far distance.

At first Esther thought it was the crescent moon reflecting off the metal mile markers; yet soon realized it was not strong enough to cause such luminosity.

"What the hell is that?" she asserted, studying the orb.

Her gut telling her the light was something menacing, something she should fear.

Wide-eyed, her breath quickening, the threatening phenomena grew brighter, larger. Gripping the steering wheel, Esther increased the RAM's speed; dangerously fixating on the object behind her instead of paying attention to the road in front of her.

Suddenly catching sight of a young doe strolling along the shoulder, in a knee-jerk reaction Esther yanked the truck into the oncoming lane. Blasting the horn as the truck flew by the timid creature.

Fortunately for Esther, the panicking deer leapt safely into the tall grasses instead of the road. Even so, fearing the doe might change direction, possibly flee to the other side of the highway, Esther slammed on the brakes. The pickup fishtailing; ultimately coming to a screeching halt, spanning both lanes.

"Idiot!" she screamed at herself.

The glow was gaining.

Quickly straightening the RAM, Esther pushed the pickup faster than she ever dared; hugging the yellow centerline, determined to outrun the dancing light.

Then, as quickly as it appeared, the orb vanished.

Heaving a sigh of relief, Esther returned the pickup to a manageable speed; yet, kept one eye on the mirror. Lulling herself into believing the strange light must have belonged to a local who lived in a remote trailer. And, the person must have simply turned off road, or onto one of the few hidden dirt lanes leading who knows where.

An elongated green sign caught her eye.

Mile marker 123.

"Okay... You got this," she told herself; squaring her shoulders.

For some reason this stretch of Highway 79 had always been maintained better than the previous. Flanked with wide flat shoulders and substantial pullouts, the downside to this long straightaway was Esther's extreme vulnerability if another car wanted to pull alongside her, or ambush her up ahead.

Having driven several miles further, each time Esther glanced in the mirror the road had appeared empty. Only this time, the orb was back; bouncing in midair like the Grim Reaper's lantern.

"Xander!" cried Esther horrified.

No longer mistaken as to who was really behind the wheel, Esther punched the accelerator. Pushing the RAM dangerously faster, her only thought... Run.

Still, the bobbing light began overtaking her. Closer, still closer, until she clearly saw the bright yellow dome atop a massive muscle car roaring up behind her.

***

Drunk with revenge, an exhilarated Oliver Baring shrieked with delight watching the old woman bolt like a terrified cottontail. The thrill of the chase taking his bloodlust to a new fever pitch.

"Run lil' bunny," he garbled.

His fractured jaw just one of his many reasons to kill Esther Hausman.

One moment howling triumphantly, tickled to soon be rid of the proverbial thorn in his side. The next screaming in sheer agony; cradling his traumatized face with his free hand, pulling off the highway. Idling the car long enough to wash down a few more opioids; not caring his pickup once again sped out of sight.

His pain easing, becoming more manageable; the psychopath slid the gear shifter into manual mode. Revving the engine to over 3,000rpms, Xander restrained the muscle car until its whine turned into a fierce high-pitch scream. Then, let it fly.

Shifting gears the turbo boosted Dodge hit 100mphs, cutting the distance between the two vehicles in no time.

Nostalgia washed over him as he began experiencing the same exhilaration he had as a child at the local amusement park; releasing his pent-up hostilities on unsuspecting people and their bumper cars. The joy he felt seeing dread, even hate, on his victims' angry faces right before delivering the defining blow.

"I'm com'n sweetie," he roared.

Now intending on inflicting the same kind of torment. Deciding he would tap the truck's bumper a couple times to let the old woman know what was coming next. Then, pull alongside her, and kiss her goodbye.

***

Mile marker 120.

As soon as the tires touched the particular patch of rough pavement Esther knew Highway 79 would shortly transition from smooth straightaway to brutally problematic asphalt. So familiar was she with the highway's quirks, that regardless of the darkness her mind's eye instinctively saw where the blacktop was vulnerable, the bridges narrowed. Where shoulders were weakest and watery irrigation ditches hid beneath dense vegetation. Yet it was after this flat stretch ended and the scenic rollercoaster with its sharply-banked blind curves began which most concerned her.

"This should be fun," she grunted.

Weighing her chances of successfully driving the treacherous hills at night without shoulders, passing lanes, or for that matter, streetlights.

Knowing if she continued driving without headlights it would probably be suicidal. Knowing too her best chance, her only chance, of getting to the cabin unseen was to remain cloaked and get through the hills as fast as possible. Hopefully without plunging into a deep gorge along the way.

However, none of that mattered now.

Because there, in her rearview mirror, was the orb.

Switching the headlights on Esther gunned the accelerator, realizing it was only a matter of time before the crazed lunatic caught her. Realizing too, she had to use her knowledge of the highway against him if she had any chance of surviving.

In a matter of minutes Xander was a meager three miles behind her, then twelve car lengths, then eight, three. The Challenger's high-intensity beams ricocheting off the pickup's mirrors; refracting burning white-hot light directly into her eyes.

Salty tears streamed down Esther's cheeks as she fought the powerful beams blinding her.

Squinting, she quickly flipped the rearview mirror to night vision mode neutralizing the unbearable brilliance. Then repositioned the angles of both side mirrors until they acted like a boomerang; reflecting the strong high-beams away from her and back inside the Dodge, straight into Xander's coldblooded eyes.

The Challenger swerved sharply left, then overcorrected right before backing off.

"How'd you like them apples?" screamed Esther into the rearview.

Only now understanding the psychopath would readily torpedo the larger pickup with a car in order to kill her. His unhinged mind failing to take into account they both would die in the collision if he did.

Approaching mile marker 118.

Dogging his prey from a safer distance, Xander never expected the old woman had it in her for such an inventive counterattack. Her resilience surprising him, he begrudgingly chucked his initial plan of bumper tag and decided to go straight to force the old bitch off the road.

Moving into the opposite lane, Xander closed the gap between them.

Immediately Esther jerked the pickup into his path, narrowly missing colliding with the car as she cut him off.

"Son of…," he howled incomprehensively.

Slamming on the brakes; the screeching muscle car billowing clouds of smoke.

Furious at another botched attempt, Xander slid the muscle car back behind the RAM; drafting mere feet off its bumper.

Proving much tougher than she looked, Esther continued fighting off Xander's advances. Each time jockeying the pickup into a defensive position, even using the highway ditches to hinder him. Forcing him each time to retreat or crash.

"Where is he!" she screamed.

Unable to locate the Challenger's menacing roar in the pickup's blind spot. Frantic, Esther veered the RAM too far to the right; creating just the opening the psychopath needed.

Taking full advantage of Esther's blunder, Xander excitedly targeted the area around the truck's gas lid. Then, the crunch of metal striking metal. The contact enough to force the pickup sideways, off the road towards a steep embankment.

Miraculously retaking control of the pickup before it slipped off the bank's edge, Esther braced herself for the next attack. Instead, surprised seeing the car behind her spinning to a halt in the middle of the road with Xander trapped inside.

Seething as the old woman sped away, Xander impatiently grinded the ignition; its stalled engine taking its sweet time before it suddenly engaged. Then, revving the motor until confident the Challenger would not sputter out, Xander stepped on the gas. The car's hanging front bumper sparking every time it struck the ground.

This time Xander would not be denied.

Again moving into the oncoming lane, Xander pulled alongside the pickup's driver side window. Feverishly glaring at Esther, daring her to look at him. Xander's unhinged mouth howled with delight as foam drooled off his limp chin. Regaling in her horror when at last their eyes did meet.

The vehicles, speeding side-by-side down the two-lane highway, dangerously close to both each other and the road's paralleling irrigation ditches.

"How are you alive!" she screamed, terrified.

Trying her hardest to concentrate only on the highway; yet, unable to keep Xander's crazed expression out of her mind. Esther slammed on the brakes, bringing the pickup squealing to a halt, and causing Xander overshoot his target.

Scrambling for ideas, Esther stared ahead at the idling muscle car. Scared out of her wits, she considered making a run for it back to Florence. Then, realizing the road was too narrow for the pickup to perform a U-turn in one motion; she knew her only option was forward, through the monster's trap.

Xander, savoring his triumph, revved the engine again, then again. Toying with the old woman just as he planned, calmly waiting for her to make her final, futile move.

"Cookie… It's now or never," she declared; gathering what little courage she had.

Filled with both overwhelming dread and determination to survive, Esther punched the accelerator. However within minutes the muscle car caught up; first right behind her, then beside. She, resolved to live. He, intent on exacting his pound of flesh.

Feeling Xander's blistering rage burn into her flesh, Esther turned her head to give the sadistic lunatic one last hard look of defiance and indeed saw a monster.

Covered in matted blood with an ill-fitting medical head bandage barely stabilizing his gapping mandible, Xander was no longer the meticulously dressed, cool-headed leader of misguided men and women. Gone was the smug, steely-eyed strategist who cunningly manipulated, bullied, even buried his foes. Instead, glaring back at her was the true malignant narcissist, showing the Gollum he always was.

For his part, Oliver Alexander Baring was having the time of his life. High on pain killers, on the verge of total retribution, the madman let out an insane yowl. Then, drove the Dodge straight into his beloved RAM.

***

Mile marker 116.

There have been rare occasions in Esther Hausman's life when this world and the next world eerily entwined. Just as some people have said they felt a chill the exact moment a loved one died, or swore they saw a dearly departed walking the halls of their home. On the few times something like that had happened, Esther's logical mind denied what her heart knew had been real.

It therefore came as no great surprise to her that at the precise moment Xander crashed the muscle car into the pickup such a phenomenon occurred. The fact that it happened approaching the Tom Mix Memorial made the event that more surreal.

For what seemed like an eternity after impact, both out-of-control machines pulverized everything in their path. Yet, inside the pickup, Esther peacefully watched the devastation unfold in silent slow motion.

Keenly aware of the chaos outside; behind the wheel Esther calmly called on what she remembered of geometry and hazy rules of inertia, force, mass, velocity to subdue the wild steel beast's out-of-control trajectory. Never once conceding her situation could be fatal.

However in reality all hell had broken loose.

The collision sending the RAM airborne; then, crashing back to earth with a boom.

Its badly damaged chassis sparking as it crunched against ground; followed by an immediate, kkkeeerrrunch, as strained suspension coils compressed.

The pickup's chassis again bouncing into the air; lifting off-balance as it tilted onto its left set of tires. Then teetering like a pendulum swinging back, teetering on its right. The vehicle's perilous balancing act defying gravity until eventually plopping on all fours; sliding on Highway 79 sideways.

Still during all the madness, Esther remained oddly serene.

Feeling, or rather sensing, a pair of familiar loving hands holding her shoulders gently, yet firmly, against the driver's seat. Esther believed unequivocally that she would be safe, that she would survive. Never once questioning its absurdity as the Tom Mix Memorial slowly, silently, passed before the bullet-holed front windshield.

Clearly recognizing the distinct metal cut-out statue symbolizing the legendary Western movie hero's devoted steed, Tony the Wonder Horse. The riderless equine's mournful head hung low above a patch of chiseled bright green grass fixed atop a tapered stone-stacked pillar. The historic marker commemorating the silent-film star's end reading, "Tom Mix whose spirit left his body on this spot."

Esther's sharp presence of mind correcting the marker's accuracy.

"Did not," she said with conviction.

Certain the film star had not actually died on that spot.

BAM!

A second collision, more violent than the first.

Whereas the two heavy-bodied vehicles had been performing their own independent death dances; they converged a second time, then ricocheted in opposite directions.

This second impact causing Esther's limbs to fling about the cab like a raggedy doll, even though the seatbelt had automatically seized up after the first impact. Securing her small body against the seat; and thereby protecting her from the inertia which would have otherwise thrown her through the windshield.

Unfortunately, the seat belt system was not designed to prevent the side of Esther's head from smacking into the driver side window an inch above her ear. Rendering her both unconscious and incapable of fending off the forward thrust which slammed her chin into the steering wheel.

As for Oliver Baring, he too had not been left unscathed. Unresponsive inside the destroyed muscle car; the probability that he sustained life-ending injuries in addition to serious ones he had already incurred was almost certain. The fact that very few people walked away from such a high-speed collision. If Xander was not dead now, he soon would be.

As for the mangled steel which once was the stolen Dodge Challenger, the collision had blasted the vehicular murder weapon across the road and off the shoulder.

Now, with wheels spinning on wobbly axels, the car dangled over a murky irrigation ditch. Its crushed chassis seesawing on the weakened embankment's dirt edge; guaranteeing a nose-dive into a watery abyss with Xander trapped inside given the slightest shift in balance.

Inside the pickup, Esther struggled to shake off her massive headache and blurred vision. Sluggish, she chose the windshield bullet hole as a focal point until finally grasping not only was the bullet hole gone, but the entire windshield as well. That in all the turmoil her foggy brain had interpreted the trillions of tiny lights she was seeing as stars; instead of correctly identifying them as sparkling shards of windshield scattered across the highway. And, that both the pickup and she were upside-down.

"Shit... Now what?" moaned Esther.

Tightly trapped by the retracted seatbelt and its plate latch jammed inside its buckle. Grateful the belt had kept her alive; yet, anxious it was now keeping her a suspended prisoner completely vulnerable to attack.

Unfamiliar noises outside the pickup sent her panicking, imagining the worse.

"He's coming," she cried.

Then all went quiet.

Taking a needed pause, Esther noted how utterly dark and silent her world had become without piercing headlights and roaring engines. Straining her ensnared body to get a bigger picture of the collision's aftermath, Esther's limited vision glanced at the mangled muscle car on its side oddly rocking over a ditch.

"Not so scary now are you?" she mocked wearily.

Chuckling at the thought that she had been terrified of a car with a plastic pizza slice fixed to its roof.

Suddenly hot searing pangs surged from Esther's neck; running down her shoulders, then throughout her entire body.

Holding her position until the pain became intolerable Esther noticed besides the muscle car, the pizza dome too was totaled. The menacing orb now looking more like a broken, cracked-open egg shell unable to illuminate anything inside the Dodge.

After resting her neck, Esther again turned her head toward the car. Only this time the excruciating pain was back within mere seconds bringing her to tears; signaling her numb body was waking from its trauma.

"C'mon give. You blessed piece of shit!" shouted Esther; struggling with the buckle.

Her pain level rising to a point she feared she would soon become an emotional mess, or worse, go into shock.

Frustrated, giving up on the jammed latch, Esther looked for another way to escape. Using her right hand to grab the hand grip above the door window, she tried pulling herself closer the roof; hoping to slacken the strap so it would loosen its constriction.

It did not.

Her next idea was to squirm out from behind the seatbelt and let her body drop. This too had its drawbacks, but she decided to give it a go anyway.

Unfortunately, when trying to raise her hands above her head her previously numb left arm woke with a vengeance where the seatbelt pressed against her shoulder. Crying out, she was immediately overwhelmed with nausea and lightheadedness.

"Well, this isn't good," she shuttered.

Trying to keep a level head, Esther lowered her arms and looked away. Knowing if she saw a bone piercing through skin she would in all probability black out.

Laboring to catch her breath, Esther searched the cab for a third option.

Seeing a large piece of broken glass within her grasp, she braced her shaky legs against the steering wheel for stability and used her good, right hand to cut the belt until it hung by a thread. Then, wrapping the thick nylon webbing around her hand she made a fist and leaned forward using all her weight, snapping the final threads. Next, using the broken strap, Esther gently guided herself into a sitting position on the soft-upholstered roof. Freed at last, she inhaled a deep celebratory breath of cool night air which triggered an uncontrollable cough that rattled her ribcage.

"Ooowww!"

She cried mournfully in agony.

Feeling sharp pangs as her lungs compressed. Suspecting a rib and probably her collarbone were broken, Esther purposely shallowed her breathing; supporting her aching torso with her one good arm. Then, after sobbing like a baby for a few minutes, which only intensified her pain, Esther put an end to her pity party.

"Enough," she scolded.

Wiping her tears and dripping snot on her shirtsleeve. Knowing she was damn lucky to be alive.

Suddenly realizing the force of the crash had pushed the pickup beyond the Tom Mix Memorial closer to its equally historical Tom Mix Wash and bridge, Esther chuckled wickedly. Grasping the irony of the destruction all around her, she asked for advice from the departed soul who died there decades earlier.

"Well Tom… Any thoughts?"

It was October 1940, when famous silver screen Western star, Tom Mix, left friends at the Oracle Junction Inn and rushed to an afternoon family event in Florence. Driving at extremely high speeds, Tom neither saw the washed-out bridge nor the road workers trying to flag him down. Leading him to fatally crash his yellow Cord 812 supercharged phaeton convertible in the riverbed which now carried his name.

Although the coroner attributed the actor's death to the excessive speed; he also reported an unsecured metal suitcase contributed to the Tom's demise. Apparently after the crash his heavy suitcase unexpectedly became untethered striking the western star's head, fracturing his skull and breaking his neck.

Sometime afterward, to honor their famous resident, Arizona constructed the memorial rest stop; naming both it and the wash in which he died after him.

"Didn't I teach you idiots anything?"

Esther imagined the cowboy saying to her, looking down from his heavenly cloud.

Just then an unexpected horn-blast broke the night's silence.

Turning toward the noise, Esther was shocked to see a small beam of light flickering inside the Challenger.

"Xander," she whispered; horrified.

Her distress rousing her to vacate the pickup before it became her coffin.

Grappling with her pain, Esther carefully wiggled her injured body over the pickup's splinter coated dashboard and through its glassless windshield frame. Then, gently sliding to the ground, she slinked commando style over the glittery shards. Her fingertips grabbing the asphalt as her right leg pushed her body forward to the dense roadside vegetation. Ultimately concealing herself beneath the thick wild oat grasses; combing back the disturbed foliage to cover her tracks, making her getaway parallel with the highway.

Then, taking a moment to catch her breath, Esther peeked back at the crash site through a few carefully parted blades. Immediately clasping her hands over her mouth to muffle her gasp.

The shadowy figure slowly slithered out of the Challenger's driver-side window and slid into the watery irrigation ditch. Unable to tear herself away from the hideous sight, Esther watched as the monster's soggy silhouette pulled himself from the murky water and emerged onto the highway.

"You dead old woman?" grunted Xander.

The psychopath's hatred spewing his from his hanging jaw.

His loud rantings muffling the rustling undergrowth as Esther labored to escape him. Her damaged body begging for mercy as she serpentine the unforgiving terrain.

"You can't hide!" shrieked Xander.

Dragging his left leg as he hobbled to the middle of Highway 79. Then, squinting into the dark cab of his once cherished RAM, Oliver Baring pointed his revolver at the gutted windshield and fired repeatedly.

"Pretty smart, eh?" he sputtered.

The sight of the empty cab sparking his heavily opioid mind's need to hunt his victim. Melodically singing Esther's name again and again as he capriciously directed his flashlight into the dark in search of his quarry.

"Come out… Come out wherever you are."

Finding no place in the open brush to hide, Esther finally keyed in on the dark crevasses beneath the Tom Mix Wash bridge. With her strength all but tapped, Esther reached the dry riverbed and pulled herself over embankment; slowly inching her way down until halfway the earth suddenly gave way beneath her.

In an out-of-control headfirst slide, Esther found herself lying completely exposed in the river bottom unable to go on. Praying Xander did not hear her less than graceful decent and find her trail. Praying the night would continue hiding her. But mostly, praying she would not end up dead like poor Tom Mix.

"Here lies Esther Hausman. She died from her injuries before a crazed murderer could kill her," she whispered.

Writing her epitaph as Xander incessantly bellowed into the night.

Then, gathering her last vestiges of strength, Esther pushed her broken body along the riverbed's embankment slope; hoping to make her tracks less noticeable. When at last she reached the bridge's underbelly, straining, she pulled herself onto the abutment ledge and scooted her body under the bridge joints where it was darkest.

Bracing herself against the support, Esther half listened to Xander's unrestrained tantrum growing closer.

"Well, guess this is it," she acknowledged.

Able to take only shallow breaths now, Esther slipped in and out of consciousness; welcoming nothingness and its great relief from her torturous pain. Reconsidering if survival was all it was cracked up to be; Esther made peace with death. Then, a familiar sound triggered that stubborn, innate desire within humans to live. Heeding words of warning in her head, Esther stiffened.

"They don't, usually, strike unless given reason," Joseph Tadai had snickered; emphasizing the word, usually.

Determined not to give the viper's hypersensitive pit organs any reason to consider her a threat; wide-eyed, Esther held perfectly still as the Western Diamondback rattlesnake slithered toward her.

Yet despite her efforts the poisonous serpent persisted. Its long heavy body laterally undulating, silently gliding towards her. Its specialized brain and sensory organ interpreting its world from the microscopic airborne particles on its flicking tongue and ground vibrations. Nature compensating the snake for its limited hearing.

Stopping short of the abutment, the rattlesnake became curious about an inviting depression in the sand with a partial border of rocks. Coiling its massive diamond-shaped pattern inside the cozy dimple, the snake settled; contently nestling its spoon-shaped head atop its rattle's black and white bands before drifting off to sleep.

Having an inkling as to how serious her injuries were, Esther remained completely still. Certain in her weakened state she would never survive the rattlesnake's venom.

"You want a piece of me? Get in line," she whispered defiantly; hazily sinking into oblivion once more.

Nevertheless upon awakening Esther was alarmed to find the irked Diamondback's head raised high in a defensive posture; its steely elliptical pupils fixed on her.

Immediately disengaging eye contact, Esther could almost feel the snake's flickering tongue probing her moist skin. Its sensitive night vision shifting between her and the threat directly above them on the Tom Mix Wash bridge.

Completely unaware of Esther Hausman's proximity, Oliver Baring popped the last of his oxycodone and arbitrarily called into the night.

"I know you're here old woman."

His shouts antagonizing the agitated Diamondback further; provoking the viper to refocus on Esther.

As the last of his potent drugs kicked in, Xander retraced his steps using his phone's flashlight to search the wreckage a second time. Only this time he noticed the line of shattered glass leading from the pulverized windshield to the irrigation ditch.

Following the shards to the exact spot where Esther entered the underbrush, Xander expertly tracked the old woman's trail of broken shrubbery to the displaced dirt on the embankment; then, into the river bottom.

Esther had not counted on Peter Cavenaugh's killer finding her so soon.

With no place to run and no strength to do so, she anxiously pushed herself further back onto the ledge. Moments later, she heard Xander clumsily slide down the sandy slope into the dry river gorge.

Esther realized she was not ready to die. That the thought of no longer existing in this world, leaving all she loved, terrified her beyond belief.

But then, a dim flashlight penetrated the ravine. Then, the sound of shuffling steps in the rocky sand. A dark figure drawing nearer.

Any second her executioner would discover her hiding place. There would be no calvary coming to her rescue. No Michael Flores swooping in at the last minute.

She prayed her body would fail before Xander discovered her. Or if not, the psychopath would get little gratification out of torturing her mere shell.

"I com'n fo ya old woman," he garbled; sadistically giggling.

Her only thoughts now of Mattie.

And then, there he was.

Xander's grotesque figure was barely discernable in the night, yet she could smell the familiar stank of clotted blood, rotting decay. Directing his glaring flashlight beam directly into her eyes he let out another of his sickening giggles.

"You lose 'ol gal," he sneered.

Eager to finish the game.

Hearing the cock of the revolver, Esther instinctively shut her eyes and feebly pushed away from Xander. Her shoe scraping the ground, flinging pebbles and sand down the rocky incline.

Laughing at the old woman's pathetic attempt to evade him Xander adjusted his stance. Then, taking one more step, he aimed the gun directly at Esther's forehead and enunciated perfectly.

"Time to die."

It was then Esther's world went dark. Never hearing the blast of the gun being fired. Never feeling the weight of the Western Diamondback's heavy body against hers as it struck.

Chapter 17

"The reports of my death are greatly exaggerated."

~ Mark Twain

The highly-trained Golder Ranch Fire District paramedics exchanged doubtful glances as they feverishly administered life-saving aide to an unconscious Esther Hausman. When at last the ambulance pulled up to the Tucson hospital emergency entrance, they were extremely glad to see the four-member trauma unit rush towards them. More so after sharing their patient's status and the hospital team took over; dashing the critically injured woman inside.

Watching Esther being wheeled out of sight behind sandy-colored double doors, Homicide Detective Michael Flores felt helpless. That all this, Esther, Mattie, Mitzy Burton, the security team; all of it could have been avoided had he just discovered the killer's identity faster, the mole sooner.

He had almost arrived in Florence when police Sergeant Daniel Tucker contacted him that Esther slipped away from their custody. Figuring she was heading for the cabin, he continued following Mattie's directions until happening upon the Highway 79 accident scene.

Shouting to Antonio Silva to wait in the car, he joined two Pinal County Sheriff's Deputies who had come across the crash minutes before him at what looked to be a war zone. Understanding as soon as he saw the vehicles involved.

Wasting no time, Michael Flores and senior Deputy Austin Williams instructed the younger deputy, Morris Dipp, to secure the area as they sprinted through the minefield of spewed debris, each choosing a different vehicle. Michael Flores heading straightaway for the demolished pickup, Williams the Dodge.

Both bracing themselves for the gruesome task of finding bodies in god-knows-what condition.

Dipp calling for backup and an ambulance as he strategically positioned the two police cruisers at opposite ends of the site. Keeping the red and blue emergency lights active to alert motorists while placing flares around the perimeter; glancing at his colleagues to see if they needed help.

Tensing, Flores approached the upended RAM. Resembling a desert tortoise on its back, he immediately noticed the Toyo off-roading tires; leaving little-doubt in his mind it belonged to the murderer Oliver Baring. The vehicle which Peter Cavenaugh had ridden in to his death. The vehicle Esther Hausman was driving.

"Esther... Why didn't you wait?" he whispered forlorn.

Assessing the fastest entry into the truck, Flores entered the cab through the missing windshield opening with extreme caution. Shining his flashlight, expecting to find Esther Hausman's lifeless body wedged inside the wreckage; he quickly exited the pickup both stunned and elated.

"Holy Shit!" escaped Michael's lips in disbelief. "She's gone."

Never occurring to him that Esther might not be inside. Or, she might be alive.

Struggling to access the Dodge Challenger, which had taken a nose dive into the watery irrigation ditch with its trunk now duck-butt up, Williams paused to give the detective his full attention.

"Sorry Detective. I know she was...," began Williams sympathetically.

Misinterpreting Flores' odd expression for one of grief.

"No... I mean... Esther's literally not in there. It's empty," interrupted Flores.

Enthusiastically climbing out of the cab, Flores quickly searched around the chassis to see if Esther might be pinned beneath it. After finding no trace of her, he allowed himself a sliver of hope.

"Esther… It's Michael," he shouted repeatedly into the night.

Hastily extending his search into the desert brush, Michael Flores was several yards away when he turned back and saw Austin Williams crawling out of the destroyed Challenger's passenger window. The deputy, looking just as confused as Flores felt, having difficulty squeezing his large frame out of the opening.

"What's up?" yelled Flores to Williams.

"I got zilch… Nada… I mean the car's empty too," shouted back the puzzled deputy. "Who survives a crash like this?"

"Satan," said Flores under his breath.

Seeing the lawman successfully extricate himself, Flores yelled.

"Williams, check up the road. I'll go this way."

Hoping the monster was so badly hurt he slinked off somewhere to die. If not, there was only one reason Oliver Baring would end his hunt for Esther Hausman. She was already dead.

"Esther… Where the hell are you?"

His optimism dwindling until his flashlight caught the pickup's shattered windshield trail. Tracking the glass shards, Flores's fears amplified at seeing a large shoe imprint disturbing the glittery path where the trail and broken vegetation met. Clearly suggesting the trail of glass was Esther's, and the shoeprint, Baring's.

Meanwhile, not one to sit by, Tony Silva had completely ignored Detective Michael Flores' order to stay inside the SUV. First, helping Dipp secure the area, then helping Deputy Williams in his search. Having picked up Oliver Baring's shoeprints near the Dodge, the killer's trail soon led both Silva and Williams to Flores.

"Think Baring got her?" asked Williams tentatively.

Having little hope they would find Esther Hausman alive.

The three men spreading out along the irrigation ditch.

"Over hear," yelled Williams.

Finding Baring's partial shoeprint on the edge of the Tom Mix Wash bridge.

"Which way?" called Silva, looking to Flores.

"Fan out on the road," directed the detective.

Then on a hunch, Flores changed his mind.

"No wait... The wash."

Rushing down the unstable slope into the sandy riverbed the three men split up; searching in different direction to cover ground more quickly.

Suddenly the faint, distinct sound of a rattle caused each man to freeze.

It was Deputy Williams' flashlight that first settled on the irritated reptile tucked among the deep fissures of a pile of large sedimentary rocks.

Still uneasy from its earlier encounter with humans, the Western Diamondback rattled once more; deciding it had had quite enough. Not happy to have the flashlight blinding its sensitive eyes, the rattlesnake contorted its shimmering scales onto the opposite-side embankment. Its serpentine movements into the underbrush a sobering reminder to all three that Oliver Baring was not the only dangerous creature lurking in the desert.

Cautiously resuming their search, the men continued shining their torches along the brush and inside the ravine; this time more conscious of their steps.

Suddenly Michael Flores' flashlight caught of what looked like an old shoe tucked beneath the Tom Mix Wash overpass on the abutment ledge.

"Here!" shouted Flores; running up the incline.

Finding Esther motionless, Michael checked for a pulse. She was alive, just barely; but alive. As for Oliver Alexander Baring, he was nowhere to be found.

***

Hours after the rescue, standing in the hospital's emergency lobby, Michael Flores wondered if they should have done anything different to help Esther. Then, they had been concerned of doing more harm than good if they tried to move the older woman before the medical team arrived. Flores had remained by her side monitoring her pulse while the deputies had flagged down the ambulance on the bridge. At that point, each followed the EMTs' directions in securing the critical Esther onto the backboard and getting her off the difficult ledge and out of the wash. Once inside the ambulance, the paramedics had struggled to keep Esther from coding during transport. Then in the hospital driveway, he had overheard a staffer say as they whisked Esther to surgery, "She probably won't survive the table."

Sometime after that a pleasant hospital worker escorted both him and Antonio Silva to the more comfortable surgical lounge on the fourth floor. Reserved for family and friends; there, the two men had laid claim to a secluded area of the room where they could talk discreetly and gather additional seating.

"Coffee?" offered Silva quietly.

Handing Flores a waxy paper cup filled with dark, lukewarm brew.

321

With a subtle nod of thanks, Michael Flores clasped the cup and took a large gulp. Unprepared for the horrendous swill which assaulted his tastebuds, he immediately spat the disgusting sludge back into the cup. Coughing into his phone as he attempted to clear his throat of the lingering aftertaste while conversing with Detective Vernon Rub.

"Didn't know you'd be so choked up hearing my voice Mikey," joked Rub.

Chuckling as he listened to his pal gag on whatever disgusting thing he was attempting to ingest.

Already feeling the onset of heartburn gurgling deep inside his unhappy gut, Michael Flores glanced sideways at Silva. Noticing the retired sergeant's scowl while nonchalantly crinkling his empty paper cup and tossing it into the trash. Flores surmised the soldier probably pegged him as a total wimp; incapable of handling anything stronger than skim milk.

Shrugging off the assumption, Flores returned to his conversation with Rub and the more pressing matter of apprehending Oliver Baring.

"Always the comedian, Vern," mocked Flores; ignoring the jab.

Glad to hear his friend's voice, although he would never admit it to him for all the antacids in the world. His protesting stomach gurgling once more.

"Look... Between the injuries you said Baring sustained in Gilbert and what he most likely suffered in the crash... Well... The guy has to be lying in some hole dead, or soon to be," speculated Rub.

"I dunno... Either way, Sherriff's got his people combing a fifty-mile radius around Tom Mix. But in case he's alive... Breached their net... Get Border Patrol on this. Cause if it's me... I'd head south," coughed Flores; trying to clear his raspy throat.

"C'mon Mikey… No way in hell he walked from that crash without major damage. Border's three hours… You really think he can make it that far?" questioned Rub.

"Vern… If anyone can its Baring… This guy's… He's like one of those reptiles that loses its tail and grows another. Just when you think you got hold of the slimy bastard, he slips away," cautioned Flores. "If Oliver Baring's still alive… He'll happily kill anyone who looks cross-eyed at him. Believe me. Cavenaugh's death was nothing compared to the Ahwatukee slaughter. No one's safe."

Digesting Michael Flores' words, Vernon Rub was about to comment but then abruptly changed the subject.

"Oh, hey. I forgot. The Lucas kid and their neighbor…," began Rub, then hesitated.

"Joseph Tadai," affirmed Flores.

"Yeah, Tadai… They're on their way. Kid's pretty shook," added the former New Jersey cop as they finished their conversation.

The fact that his tough east-coast friend had developed a soft spot for the quirky veterinarian student, slash, ranch hand caused Flores to smile. Knowing Rub would deny it, swear he was just doing his job… To serve and protect.

"No wonder we're friends," thought Flores; grinning. "It's our modus operandi… Pretending we don't care. Only this time… it's not working."

Flores glanced at his watch.

It had been more than an hour and a half since Esther was wheeled to surgery. Since then, no word had been forthcoming about her condition. However, considering the extent of her injuries neither he, nor Silva, really expected anything different.

Fidgeting, his leg having developed an annoying twitch, Michael Flores decided to stroll around the room and look for a much-needed distraction.

Finding himself at the lounge information desk, he inquired about Esther's status. To which a kind woman, whose nametag read Ciera, wrote down an eight-digit number for him to use to track his friend's progress on the monitors positioned around the room. Assuring him someone would be out as soon as there was anything to report.

Searching the status display screen, the detective found Esther's identification number six rows from the top in the first column. That screen remaining visible for nearly thirty seconds before cycling to another and the next group of patients.

"In Surgery," read Flores to himself.

The words burning into his exhausted brain as he retook his seat near Silva. Deciding to check back in a few minutes in case he read it incorrectly, or Esther's status changed; maybe sooner.

"Docs did get to her quick," he considered. "But then, if she hadn't been so bad off they wouldn't have had to."

The longer they waited, the more each man became lost in his own private world.

For Michael Flores, it was a simple round clock yellowed with age which hung on the opposite wall high above a watercooler. Distracted by its quirkiness, Flores found the timepiece an interesting contrast to the sleek, noiseless, chronometers integrated into the patient monitors.

Whereas the second hand's circular rotation felt like an eternity, its minute hand became a form of entertainment. Immediately hooked, Flores became fascinated watching the minute arm jerk, jerk, jump, from bar to bar and number to number. Its aged mechanism producing a strange, irritating, off-key melodic tic, tic… twang much louder than expected as it advanced.

Esther's status remained the same. "In Surgery," Flores read again.

As time dragged on the men's restlessness worsen. Only now the muscles which they strained during Esther's rescue had stiffened greatly. Not to mention the soreness of their buttocks pressing against the hard lime-green vinyl lounge chairs.

Although he appeared tranquil, his hands folded in his lap, Michael Flores' mind was racing; second-guessing every decision he had made since taking charge of the murder investigation. His hindsight blaming him for things he should have foreseen, done differently, or done better until the guilt-ridden knot in his stomach tightened to the point of nausea.

A clear ding in the ceiling audio system announced a surgeon's noisy entrance into the lounge from an area marked, Staff Only.

Grateful to be focusing on someone other than himself, Flores gazed around the room; noticing almost every eye fixed on the doctor in scrubs. Guessing, that like himself, each person was desperately hoping their loved one's name would be spoken along with good news.

Following the doctor's wandering eyes, Flores first noticed a large family huddled in a corner of the lounge. Collectively holding their breaths, the group of six dabbed their red swollen eyes and noses with wadded-up tissues clutched in tight fists as they clasped each other's free hand.

In the same section, a frail senior citizen was seated on a small loveseat against the windows with a younger companion who looked as if she could be her granddaughter. The younger's loving arm gently wrapped around the elder's shoulders; both displaying the same resigned expression.

Then across, at the farthest end of the room, a middle-aged man sat by himself working on a laptop. He had abruptly stopped typing and looked up; telling someone on his cellphone a doctor had just come into the room and he would call them back.

"Family of George Martin?" called the weary surgeon; searching for his patient's contact.

Timidly the young woman by the window raised her hand; still keeping her arm wrapped around the elder.

Promptly walking to the two women, the doctor sat down and began speaking softly. Instantly the others, as if an unwritten rule, collectively averted their eyes and returned to their own private hell.

Antonio Silva choosing to focus on the room's television which was broadcasting local news. He supposed the contraption was there to help those waiting, mindlessly pass the time.

It did not.

Drowsily staring at the newscasters moving their lips, Silva did not care one iota about anything they were saying. Admitting to himself that not only was he bushed, but that he felt much older than his 59 years.

A lifetime ago the youthful 19-years-old Antonio Luis Silva had taken the US Army Oath of Enlistment to protect and serve his country. Sometime later, after making Sergeant, he proudly served with the regiment affectionately dubbed the Rakkasans; part of the 101st Airborne Division of the 187th Airborne Infantry. It had been his greatest honor.

During his time in the military, Silva had felt a certain protectiveness towards the men and women under his charge. A commitment which extended even after his retirement. Although he had not seen or spoken to Peter Cavenaugh for decades; when recently his former private sought his help, he never once thought to refuse. Then when Peter confessed Oliver Baring was involved, enough was said.

Both men had served under him during Operation Desert Shield and Storm. It was there Silva had seen first-hand Baring's bizarre narcissistic traits and questionable activities. A master at getting people to blindly follow him. Baring would skillfully deflect blame onto others while escaping any responsibility for his wrongdoings.

So this time, after hearing Peter's story, Silva decided he would personally bring Oliver Baring down once and for all.

Now in the waiting room the retired sergeant deeply regretted that decision. Admitting he should have gone directly to the police from the start; because in the end he had failed. Baring had won, Peter was dead, those poor souls at the safe house were slaughtered, and an innocent woman was fighting for her life.

Turning to Michael Flores quietly sitting across from him, Silva recognized the dejected expression on the detective's face. He could keep quiet no longer.

"It's not your fault Detective," stated Silva. Saying what he had wanted to tell Michael Flores earlier. "It's not Pete's fault… If anything… It's mine."

It was as if Silva read his mind. Slowly raising his head, Michael Flores locked onto the older man's weather-worn face and waited for an explanation.

"Oliver Baring, or Xander as he likes to be called, is an egotistical parasite with no moral compass… He'd kill his own mother if it got him what he wanted. In Kuwait, some of the more insecure kids in my unit fell prey to every word of his bullshit. They became brainless zombies around him… The soldiers who didn't buy his crap… The ones he couldn't control…. Well, let's just say our unit suffered unusually high accidents," disclosed the former sergeant.

"But why's Baring…?" Flores started to ask.

"My fault," finished Silva. Then explained. "I'd always suspected Xander was behind the mayhem in our compound one particular day. Then after returning from a disastrous mission, I was certain."

"The helmets?" asked Flores.

"Yeah," affirmed Silva.

Surprised the detective knew. Then elaborated about the incident.

"I learned Jeffory Fenton pulled the kid… Peter… from our equipment room during a bogus disturbance. I suspected the order came from Xander, who had somehow slipped in and sabotaged some new, high-tech helmets. Xander's not stupid. He's got electronics skills. Then the bastard got the higher ups to believe the mission calamity was Pete's fault. The kid bought it too… I knew better. But knowing it…"

"And proving it," asserted Flores.

Saying out loud what he surmised all along.

"Well like a lot of scumbags, Xander can be… What's the word? Charismatic. Had a lot of em fooled. Those who tagged him for the pond scum he was… Is… Ended up with targets on their backs one way or another," confirmed Silva.

Implying Oliver Baring's unscrupulous time in the Army went beyond verbal persuasion, trickery, and bullying.

"The helmet fiasco," reiterated Flores.

"Yeah… Five of my guys bought it on that mission… Tyrell Bloggs, Hayde Ward, William Lopez, Bobbie Myers, Davy Woods. Each had publicly chastised Xander. Called him toxic to his face. Warned his groupies to wise up… Curious don't you think… they were the soldiers wearing the defective helmets. The ones who died that day," said Silva; not expecting another explanation.

"You too, Sarge," stated Flores; recalling Taylor Cavenaugh's version.

Reminding Silva he was Xander's most outspoken critic, and also was targeted.

"Yeah. Well... Probably. I was lucky. Pete yanked mine off. Kept screaming, 'Shut 'em down!' That wasn't the last suspicious incident either. Yet every damn time I thought, I got you bastard dead to rights. He'd beat the rap," Silva added; shaking his head in disgust.

Then Silva went quiet and turned back to the television as if say, "I'm done, I've said my piece."

"I know exactly what you mean, Sarge," Flores agreed pensively.

Realizing Sergeant Antonio Silva was as much a victim of Oliver Baring's madness as were all the others.

Squirming in his seat, Michael Flores could no longer endure his aching left buttock against the hard chair and gingerly stood. Clasping his hands behind his neck, he was about to stretch when he was distracted by loud, animated chatter in the hallway. His grin broadening as a familiar voice insisted on immediate answers.

"So here you are! How's Tante?" demanded Mattie Kaplan; rushing into the lounge.

"Hey stranger," replied Michael Flores gently. "This is all I know."

Hanging on Michael's every word as he ushered her to the nearest monitor, Mattie's eyes glued to the yellow-coded line showing Esther's status.

"See there... In Surgery," said Michael, pointing to the line.

Suddenly realizing how long it had remained unchanged.

Mattie whispered the words again as if somehow that would force the designation to magically change to, In Recovery.

"Sorry…," she inquired; still fixated on the monitor. "I never asked about Mitzy?"

Ashamed for almost completely forgetting about the policewoman who had sacrificed her herself to save both her and her aunt.

"She'll make it… And so will Esther," he assured her.

Suddenly, as he gazed upon Mattie's lovely face, it hit Flores that he had not actually seen, or spoken to her since yesterday in Gilbert. Even then their exchange had been quick, focused on rescuing Esther. Now standing beside her, Michael was shocked by the numerous wounds she tried to hide.

Looking more like a war casualty than the dust devil who kicked open her jeep door, pushing pass everyone to protect her aunt when first they met. Michael became conscious of Mattie's stiff posture. Her need to sit down slowly. Her smoky-gray eyes dull, absent of their fiery flecks. Then there were the multi-colored bruises which covered her body. Particularly the nasty ones blooming on her swollen cheek, lower chin, and around two sets of painful looking stitched lacerations.

Fuming inside, certain her injuries and Esther's were courtesy of Oliver Baring. Michael Flores began entertaining ideas of how to pay the killer back for his cruelty which didn't entail breaking the law.

Certain too, that Mattie had allowed only minimal medical attention before demanding she be taken to Esther.

"You know… You may have internal injuries. How about letting a doc check you while Esther's still in surgery?" he thought about proposing.

Instead, knowing full-well the fury Mattie would unleash upon him at the mere suggestion; the tall, rugged detective pursed his lips and chickened out. Stepping away to call Vernon Rub for an update on their manhunt while keeping one eye on the monitors and the other on Mattie.

In Surgery… Hour five.

"Well at least she's alive," Flores thought; trying to stay optimistic.

Still, with no medical person able to tell them about Esther's condition, all they could do was standby and silently pray the older woman would make it.

Like most hospitals, this facility was wickedly frigid.

Unable to escape the countless ceiling vents blowing icy-cold air down upon their heads, several people in the surgery lounge wrapped their arms around their core and tugged whatever apparel they had up around their chilled necks and frozen ear lobes.

Some in the room cupped their freezing hands around their drippy noses, rapidly exhaling to generate heat. Complaining caustically that their snouts were likened to a dog's on a frosty winter morning. Others caressed steamy hot liquid in paper cups to ease their aching fingers, noting even plain hot water was a blessing.

With the arrival of Joseph Tadai and Kyle Lucas, their group had more than doubled.

Kyle had thoughtfully brought a red and blue University of Arizona fleece hoodie. Assisting Mattie, he gently helped her first pull the sweatshirt over her head then recline on a small double-chaired loveseat. Afterwards, purposely taking a seat next to an interesting, newly arrived stranger.

Introducing himself, the young veterinarian student casually started up a conversation; curious about how this person was involved. Finding out the man had driven Mattie to the hospital from Gilbert, but not much more. The still curious Kyle gestured to Joseph to join them once his call with Emily finished. Hoping the two of them could worm a little more information out of the newcomer.

Feeling cozy inside the hoodie, Mattie gently rested her head on Michael's scrunched-up suit jacket and curled her knees up on the loveseat. The jacket's scent of dry-cleaned fibers mingled with the detective's masculine aroma relaxed her, made her feel safe.

Careful not to disturb her stiches, she rested her throbbing arm on her middriff and pulled the sweatshirt hood down over her face. Pretending to have fallen asleep; Mattie figured it was the politest way of avoiding her well-meaning friends' many questions about how she felt, or what she needed. Because right now, what she needed most was time to process all the horrible things that had happened since the night Peter Cavenaugh was murdered.

"We've become quite eclectic," she thought; squinting at her little group mingling.

Some she considered family, others acquaintances; and one, a total stranger, who seemed to know an awful lot about her family. Then, there was the handsome, yet annoying wise guy speaking with Kyle and Joseph.

Earlier she had watched this man expertly control the chaotic situation in Gilbert. Directing teams, giving orders, making decisions; as if he had been doing it for years.

"He's the beer guy from the ballgame for God's sakes!" Mattie's head screamed. "But now… Now he's an FBI agent? Furthermore, his name's Aiden Collins… Not Renan Cardoso like his badge says… And not Terco, the name everyone calls him."

Marveling at the guy's many convoluted identities.

"Arrogant… Self-centered… Yet, he drives me over 100 miles to be with Tante. And, he's still here waiting with us."

Blushing, feeling both confused and guilty, Mattie recalled how rude she was to him at the ballgame. Remembering too his touch; electric, strong, yet gentle.

His alluring voice, now conversing with Kyle. How drawn she was to it the first time she heard it.

"Who are you Aiden Collins?" she wondered; drifting off.

It was sometime later, Mattie opened a drowsy eye just in time to see an older man cover her with a thin, royal blue hospital blanket. Thinking him to be a hospital volunteer, when he sat down next to Aiden Collins she became quite puzzled. Sitting up, she was about to speak to him when Michael Flores distracted her.

Greatly agitated, the detective paced back and forth in an isolated area of the lounge.

"Well he didn't just disappear into thin air," growled the homicide detective; realizing he had spoken a little too loudly into his phone.

Frustrated by the manhunt's lack of progress, Michael Flores found himself overacting to the slightest irritants. Especially aggravating at that moment was Aiden Collins' legs. Stretched-out in the middle of their limited space, his chair leaned back against the wall, the kid reeked of arrogance and rebellion. Serving only to add to the Flores' ire; and increasing his desire to kick the chair legs out from underneath the punk all that more.

"Pain in the ass," spat Flores under his breath.

Recognizing the worst qualities of himself in the younger man.

Deciding to step into the hallway to finish his conversation; Flores promised himself that when he did return, it would be with some semblance of professional decorum.

"So, Mr. FBI man... Why me?" demanded Antonio Silva.

Confronting Aiden Collins calmly as to why he was suspected of criminal activities.

"Your watch," replied Aiden.

"My what?" Silva exclaimed.

Looking at the young man as if he were nuts.

"Watch... Your watch," repeated the younger man unequivocally.

Nodding towards Silva's shirtsleeve as he tapped his own wrist.

Rolling up his sleeve, Tony Silva exposed the elaborate black MTM multi-functional wristwatch which had evidently put him at the top of FBI agent Aiden Collins' suspect list. Not understanding the connection, Silva insisted on an explanation.

"Okay... The Cactus League owners asked us to step in. Seems somebody's been making off with a ton of high-price sports memorabilia and selling them on international black markets," explained the agent.

"And that's FBI's business?" inquired Silva.

"Yep.... Network trafficking and interstate transportation of stolen property is a major theft crime... Well, that and other stuff," replied Collins.

Giving Silva the abridged version in crime jurisdictions.

"You swallow an FBI textbook Terco? Just so's you know... I didn't steal the watch," retorted the older man.

Still not understanding what his timepiece had to do with the agent's assignment, or why the kid zeroed in on him.

"Okay, okay, I believe you. But the watch is just one of your tells," smirked Collins.

Pausing, still uncertain he should confide in the man.

"It's like this, Jefe... Transnational and national regionally based crimes impact our economy... Lost revenue. Rising consumer prices. Taxes... Plus, money from stolen goods fund terrorists... Organized crime. Traffickers, gangs... You know, bad guys," explained Aiden condescendingly.

Terco's transition from arrogant street punk to arrogant commerce law professor grated on Silva, yet he continued probing; needing to find out more.

"I get it... It hurts the country. Not to mention the owners' pockets," replied Silva just as sarcastically.

"Jefe... You're not stupid. You know there's tons of money in autographed sports memorabilia. In some countries, prices go crazy for certain athletes," added Collins with enthusiasm.

Then, checking himself, he returned to his laidback, bad-boy persona.

"So that's why you act like a street thug look'n to score," grasped Silva. "But why me?"

"Yeah... Well, unless my cover's blown," declared the FBI agent. "Look... You have to know you're suspiciously quirky as hell... You really don't?"

Silva's eyes hardened. With a raised eyebrow he lowered his voice, angrily accusing the kid of racial profiling. Of twisting facts so he would fit the perpetrator's profile.

"So, I'm a thief because I'm Hispanic... I own an expensive watch, which of course, I can't afford? Wait... What tells?"

Deciding he wanted to see Silva's reaction, Collins indulged his old boss.

"I can see how you might think that... But no," refuted Aiden Collins calmly.

"Then explain," snapped Silva.

"Mr. Silva, it's not because you're Hispanic... Which you clearly are... It's because you're... Well, because you're just plain... weird."

Then Collins set the old man straight.

"Jefe, everything about you screams guilty… Of what, I don't know… Yet. You conceal an expensive watch up underneath a five-dollar, thrift store shirt. And if someone makes a comment about it, you overreact. Bite off their heads. You order your crew like… Don Corleone. And, oh yeah… you come into work with cuts and bruises, constantly … Especially your knuckles… Like you used some guy's face as a punching bag?" touted Collins with a wiseass smirk. "Want more?"

"For your information dipshit… My unit gave me this watch when I reentered civilian life," proudly retorted the retired noncom. "Not that it's any of your damn business or anybody else's… And yes… I did use some guy's face as a punching bag earlier this week… Jeffory Fenton's."

"What's that?" piped in Michael Flores; catching the end of the conversation. "When'd you have a run-in with Fenton?"

However before Silva could explain further, a weary surgeon wearing dampened scrubs entered the lounge.

"Family of Esther Hausman," she called in a tired, husky voice.

"Here… Esther Hausman. We're here," panicked, Mattie standing little too quickly. "I don't understand… The board says Tante's still in surgery."

The surgeon always hated this part of her job; talking to humans who were not under anesthesia. Not her greatest strength, she strolled to the group averting their eyes.

Mattie's heart sank as she braced for bad news.

"Listen, I know it's been quite some time since someone's…," began the surgeon.

"Someone?… No one! No one's told us anything all day," vehemently reprimanded Kyle, cutting off the doctor's planned speech.

"Kyle, please… Doctor, is my aunt alive?" Mattie asked apprehensively.

"Mrs. Hausman is still in surgery... She's hanging in... And, we're doing all we can for her... But, even if your aunt survives surgery you have to be realistic... She may not... Your aunt's in pretty bad shape," asserted the surgeon.

Her voice trailing off as soon as she realized the bluntness of her words. However acknowledging even if the older woman survived surgery; realistically, she might die trying to recover from it.

It was like her mother and Uncle Max all over again.

Concentrating on the surgeon's lips, and not so much on what she was saying, Mattie hoped the others were absorbing information she could not.

"...Mrs. Hausman suffered three fractured ribs. One severe enough to need a plate to secure it. She also suffered a broken clavicle which required fixation... Reconnecting the collarbone surgically," disclosed the surgeon.

Hesitating once more before divulging Esther's most serious injury.

"...But right now Mrs. Hausman is undergoing a splenectomy. There was no choice... Her spleen was incredibly damaged. About to rupture. If that happened, massive internal bleeding would ensue. We couldn't risk it. We would have lost her on the table," explained the doctor; incapable of softening the blow.

Tearing, Mattie nodded in affirmation; looking to Kyle and Joseph, then Michael, then back to the surgeon.

"Can she live without a spleen?" Mattie asked soberly.

"People do. Full lives in fact. However... given the massive traumas your aunt suffered... And her age. Well, if she does recover. She could live a fairly normal life," offered the surgeon as delicately as she was able.

"Doctor... Given Esther survives the surgery... In her weakened state. Without a spleen. What are her chances if she incurs an infection?" interrupted Kyle.

"I won't sugar coat it… The spleen's an important part of the lymphatic immune system. It fights bacteria and infections by filtering bodily fluids. Without it, your aunt's at greater risk of life-threatening infections. She'll need to take medications and precautions the rest of her life… But first, let's get her through surgery," asserted the surgeon.

Then, after handing Mattie a pamphlet entitled, *Living Without A Spleen*, the surgeon began to walk away. Turning back to the group briefly to offer a bit of hope.

"Look, I'm not going to minimize the seriousness of your aunt's condition. But listen… If your aunt's proved anything; she's proved she's a fighter. Don't give up."

***

Beep… beep… beep.

Midnight.

The heart monitor and intravenous (IV) bag alarms simultaneously blared without warning; spoiling what little serenity there was inside Esther Hausman's Intensive Care Unit (ICU) room. Each deafening alert bleeping one after the other, after the other; until eventually the night nurse came in to check on her patient, and shut the damn things off.

Regardless of the commotion, the heavily-drugged older woman remained in a comatose-like slumber in her hospital bed. However, to the seasoned nurse, her patient's unresponsiveness to all the clatter was anything but blissful.

Scooting pass two groggy people who chose to sleep in the room's chairs, the nurse went about her duties while making notes in her patient's chart. This included adjusting the older woman's immobilized left arm inside the black shoulder abduction sling. And, repositioning the attached rectangular, contour foam pillow against her patient's small frame for better support. After which, she examined the urine bag hanging off the side of ICU bed for cloudiness, blood, and other signs of kidney malfunction; suggesting her patient had taken a turn for the worse.

When satisfied all was as it should be and the older woman was at least stable, the nurse disappeared; the door closing quietly behind her.

***

Beep… beep… beep.

Four a.m.

Having just fallen into a deep sleep for the first time in days, Mattie Kaplan was more than displeased when the unsettling high-pitched monitor rudely woke her. Instinctively grabbing the cold, faux-leather armrests of a recently acquired, deficiently-padded, hospital recliner; Mattie jolted upright with a gasp. Her heart wildly thumping; she glared angrily at the source of the disturbance and in a raspy voice demanded.

"Flores… Give me your gun. I'm going to shoot that mother."

Michael Flores, who had been half-dozing in a much smaller, much harder visitor's chair, slowly rose to his feet smiling back at her.

339

Gingerly twisting his tall athletic frame within the limited space he let out a huge yawn. Then, slipping into the hallway as a nurse entered the room, the detective acknowledged the police officer stationed outside Esther's door and strolled to an area marked Cell Zone. Settling in, he kneaded his stiff neck while calling the police station for an update on the hunt for Oliver Baring.

Meanwhile, back inside Esther's ICU room; glassy-eyed, Mattie stared at the night nurse pressing multiple buttons on the offensive monitoring unit.

It had been hours since the second surgeon lifted everyone's spirits with the news that Esther was out of surgery and resting in recovery. And although he had immediately cautioned, "But understand, she's far from out of the woods." Their entire group had risen to their feet in quiet celebration.

Now half awake, sitting beside Esther, her face felt sticky from the salty tears she had shed; blubbering and hugging the surgeon with gratitude. Recalling too, giving uncharacteristic bearhugs and profuse thanks to everyone in their little cluster. Even kissing the gray-haired stranger on his cheek; yet, she had absolutely no idea why.

Only now did it occur to Mattie that Michael Flores had not been among those celebrating. That because he had left minutes before the doctor's arrival, arranging an officer to stand guard outside Esther's ICU room; Michael, was the one person she had not thanked.

Filled with regret, it was because of Michael that anyone thought it necessary to protect them from the murderous psychopath. Michael, who found them in Gilbert; who immediately set off after Esther. Michael, who had rescued her barely alive aunt from underneath the Tom Mix bridge.

"That's no excuse," she scolded.

Attributing her omission to her jubilance at the surgeon's good news. The doctor's words lifting her so high she could hardly restrain herself. Exuberantly ordering Joseph to return to his family, almost pushing him out the door.

Demanding Kyle, too, go home and take the FBI agent and older man with him.

Commanding Kyle, "Don't let these guys drive to Phoenix without first eating a really good meal and resting."

Refusing to take no for an answer.

Then another round of spontaneous hugs as the group disbanded. Finding herself in Aiden Collins' arms. Feeling the same sensual pull she felt when first they touched at the ballpark. Wondering as she studied his engaging features.

"Why on earth would I ever be dumb enough to trust you?"

From the moment they met the mysterious stranger had been a cocky smart-aleck, lounge lizard, liar, and all-around jerk. Yet, he also showed himself to be a respected leader, intelligent, brave, caring.

Skillfully working with Michael to resolve the Gilbert hostage conflict. Leading the medical team to the fallen Mitzy Burton. Remaining behind when the scene was secured and the others left. Insisting on driving her to Esther; but only after she received medical attention first.

Now hours later, lingering in his embrace, Mattie searched the handsome face for answers. Ultimately deciding although sometimes extremely annoying, Aiden Collins was a very good man.

Oblivious to the others uneasy glances. Mattie also failed to notice Joseph Tadai distracting himself by tidying their area. Or, the gray-haired stranger sitting down, leafing through inconsequential pamphlets. But mostly, she was unaware of the fidgeting Kyle Lucas trying not to gawk.

Kyle, feeling his allegiances divided between Mattie and Michael, had for a long time suspected the detective's interest in his friend was not purely professional. Admitting although Mattie's obvious affection for this new man was none of his business; he did not want Flores to be ambushed either.

"Like I don't have enough without running interference for you three," thought the veterinarian student; rolling his eyes.

Completely unaware of Michael Flores' budding romance with Zoe Bookman. Or, that when Mattie and the FBI agent had met earlier literally sparks had flown. It was up him to diplomatically break up the intimate hug before Flores' returned.

Still, it was Tony Silva who stepped in; deciding enough was enough.

"Okay Terco... Let's go," demanded the hard-edged retired noncom.

"Terco? Not Aiden? Or Renan?" Mattie asked the gray-haired man.

Giving the stranger her complete attention.

"Nah... Terco... Means stubborn... Or in his case, pigheaded," chuckled Silva nodding towards the FBI agent.

Laughing heartedly, Mattie had no doubt the virile young man before her had well-earned the nickname many times over. To which, red-faced, Collins was about to protest when the exhausted Antonio Silva again interrupted. Expressing his desired to leave; this time a bit more forcefully.

"Now Terco," asserted Silva with a raised eyebrow.

Nodding goodbye to the group, Kyle and Silva headed out; leaving behind a dawdling Collins.

"Right behind you Jefe," called Aiden as he gently squeezed Mattie's hand.

Then, flashing a wise-ass grin, he left.

Watching Aiden Collins quicken his steps round the corner to catch up with the two men, Mattie doubted she would ever see him again. Then, feeling Michael Flores' warm hand upon her shoulder, she turned away from the door.

"Ready?" asked Flores tenderly, extending a steady arm to Mattie.

Moments later, she and Michael stood silently outside Esther's ICU room preparing themselves for what was next.

***

Agreeing not to leave Esther unattended until she was stable, Mattie and Michael took turns sleeping in the hospital recliner and visitor's chair. Often in a stupor, the two would fixate on the slumbering woman's rising and falling chest while equally glued to her heart rate monitor vector lines and numbers. Neither of them completely understanding the data; yet both extremely grateful the sensitive equipment showed Esther was still alive.

As Mattie stared lethargically at the monitor's spiking lines and changing numbers her muddled brain chose that particular moment to dredge up the day her father disappeared from her life.

Having never come to terms with his abandonment. Sitting there, Mattie confessed the day her father left was the day she vowed never again to trust the opposite sex. A promise, that other than Uncle Max, Kyle, and Joseph, she had kept all these years; sabotaging every male relationship she had ever since. Recognizing now, how utterly impossible those convictions had become.

All because Peter Cavenaugh was murdered in her backyard.

When first they met, she and Michael Flores had clashed head-on; she treating the brusque, irresistibly handsome homicide detective with utter contempt. Which in retrospect, she admitted, he had deserved. However later, when he joined them for dinner, his brashness vanished. And although he maintained a professional decorum, his manner had become caring, his conversation engaging; finding herself surprisingly comfortable in his presence.

Feeling a friendship evolving, she began looking forward to Flores' appearances. Noticing whenever he entered the room her heart fluttered with joy, wondering if he felt the same; sensing he did. At a loss of direction, never having allowed herself such emotions.

Then she and Tante attended that damn ballgame. Her attraction to that annoying beer vendor, who in actuality turned out to be a just as annoying undercover FBI agent. It was like she had let the floodgates open.

"Geez Mattie… That's what I call stick'n to your guns," she chided herself.

No longer able to deny she was drawn to not one but two men; confused as to which feelings were true, or what to do if both were. Then realizing whatever her feelings, they were completely irrelevant. The mysterious FBI agent had disappeared out of her life. And Michael, although he had not left her side at the hospital, had more pressing issues of his own; like capturing a murderer.

Perfectly happy maintain a stagnant status quo, Mattie decided the only thing in her messed-up life that mattered was Esther. For now, she would ignore the rest.

***

As Mattie and Michael moseyed over to the room's bathroom sink they took turns splashing water on their faces. Sleep deprivation was now their new norm. Chatting, they soon found themselves playfully flicking drops of water at each other. Teasing as if they had known each other for years.

"Well, you were behaving like a pompous ass," proclaimed Mattie.

Alluding to their rocky first meeting; flinging a towel at him. Then, curling up in the recliner, Mattie pulled the thin hospital blanket up to her chin and tucked the edges around her body. Shuddering from the room's bone-chilling temperature.

"Yeah... I get that a lot," admitted Michael chuckling. "What can I say... I'm a work in progress."

Grabbing the pillow off a second chair they had pinched, he lightly tossed it to her. Then hunted for the other blanket.

Not giving Michael the satisfaction of acknowledging his kindness, Mattie applauded his enlightened assessment of himself; breaking into a smile, then light laughter.

Their easy-going bantering continuing until Flores found the second blanket wadded up. Carefully shaking it out, he gently added the blanket to hers and sat down. Clearing his throat, he wanted to ask Mattie a sensitive question, yet was unsure how to broach the subject.

"Mattie... Something I've been curious about... But it's got nothing to do with the case. It's personal... And well,... I don't want to seem rude," he began cautiously.

"Rude... You?" poking fun at Flores' obvious discomfort.

Then, gently invited his query.

"No, really Michael... Ask."

"Well, it's about Esther... and tattoos. How should I say this? Umm... Your aunt seems to have more than a run-of-the-mill dislike for tattoos. Am I right?" he asked tentatively. "How come?"

Watching Mattie become somber, Flores was certain he had overstepped. He was about to change the subject when Mattie spoke; choosing her words carefully.

"Esther's mother, my Bubbie... Uh, grandmother, had one... A tattoo," she said hesitantly.

"Your grandmother?" he repeated cautiously, not understanding her uneasiness.

"Yes... So did our Synagogue's Cantor Lieber... and my friend Adel's mother... But the tattoos weren't artistic creations, or symbols of love or respect. They were numbers... Here," she explained touching her forearm.

The color drain from his face. Michael knew what Mattie was going to say next.

"These tattoos were carved into the flesh of Jewish civilians... Nazi prisoners at the Auschwitz-Birkenau concentration camp during the 1930's and 40's. Numbers. Used to catalogue the people like livestock... Dehumanize them... They represent Hitler's Final Solution to rid the world of Jews," she affirmed with unwaveringly frankness.

The full weight of her words sent Flores reeling. Suddenly the oxygen in the room felt too thin to breath.

Staring at his scuffed oxfords, unable to meet Mattie's eyes, Flores recalled Esther's account of finding Peter Cavenaugh in her backyard. The half-eaten corpse had sent many of his seasoned investigators puking their guts out that morning. Yet, Esther had not seemed affected.

First he thought the older woman suffered from dementia. Then, he entertained the notion that she knew more about the deceased than she was saying. It only occurred to him much later that Esther Hausman was made of tougher stuff than he had given her credit for.

Then, at the safe house, it puzzled him when Esther became unsettled looking at the photos Glee Piozzi brought him. What he did not understand then, he did now.

"As unnerving as the corpse was… It was the Rakkasans tattoo itself," he grasped.

Although still not fully appreciating the emotional impact, Flores' heart went out as he fondly gazed upon the heavily sedated woman.

"I'm sorry. I didn't kn…," stumbled Michael.

"Stop… How could you?" interrupted Mattie.

The familiar, sheepish look of embarrassment on his face Mattie was used to seeing whenever the Holocaust came up in conversation among certain non-Jews.

"Growing up… Nobody was Jewish," he tried to explained.

"Michael, I understand… Jews barely make up two percent of the U.S. population. Never meeting a Jew… It's more common than you think," she reassured.

Overcome with a compelling need to continue apologizing, Michael added.

"The Holocaust… The Concentration camps… As a kid I was told it was a story… A hoax to make us, Christians, feel… guilty. It was never discussed in school, or church. What I heard was Jews harmed Christians… Jews killed Christ. Jews ran the banks, the world. Lies drilled into all our impressionable minds. Why? I don't know."

"Señor Flores… You had your own shit growing up," asserted Mattie.

"Yes… But," he inserted.

"But nothing," she insisted passionately. "You're not that kid anymore… You know six million men, women, and children were murdered during Hitler's regime. You're not a deluded Holocaust denier who thinks Nazis are misunderstood, fine people. Or an imbecile who labels anyone who disagrees with them a Nazi… You've seen the hate crimes, cruelty, jokes, stereotypes… You know anti-Semitism getting worse."

Then, taking a deep breath, Mattie returned to the subject at hand, Esther.

"Michael… Tante's the product of two camp survivors. Her parents' visible and invisible scars did not miraculously disappear once they were liberated. They carried them to their deaths," said Mattie seriously.

"And their scars became Esther's," acknowledged Michael sadly.

"Yes, my mother too… Tante's sister… Sometimes survivor's children identify so closely with their loved one's experiences, they too develop similar symptoms, phobias," she added.

The morning nurse briskly walked into the room to check Esther's monitors, interrupting their tense conversation.

"How's she doing?" asked Mattie.

"She's holding her own. Bless her," replied the nurse with a kind smile. "Considering all she's gone through… I think she's doing great. Don't you?"

Then, after changing Esther's IV fluids and verifying the devices were functioning, the nurse lifted the blanket around Esther's feet to examine her patient's ankles and output. When satisfied nothing was indicating heart, liver, or kidney failure, she wrote a few cryptic lines on the white board and quietly said goodbye.

"What symptoms? What phobias?" Michael asked hesitantly.

Knowing it really was not any of his business.

Mattie then recounted an instance as a teenager. She said it might better explain the demons which still plague her aunt.

"It was a sticky June night. Maybe 2 a.m. Uncle Max was snoring. I couldn't sleep. You're used to Tucson monsoons… But in Phoenix, nights rarely cool down. Must've been at least 100 degrees… I opened the back patio door. Tante was outside watching those breathtaking, panoramic heat lightning strikes. Some so close, you could hear the sizzle across the sky. The thunder so loud, it shook the windows."

"Tante had her favorite, heavy-woven Mexican blanket wrapped tightly around her like a cocoon. It's boiling hot, and she's shivering. I asked her if she was okay. She didn't answer… Her mind was elsewhere," said Mattie; making eye contact Michael.

"But she wasn't sick," reaffirmed Flores.

"No… In almost a whisper Tante said she had a reoccurring nightmare. I was shocked… Uncle Max knew, but she purposely kept it from me. She said it always began with her as a terrified child… She's walking hand-in-hand with her mother down a gravel path. There's hundreds of people shouting, crying… Being shoved into lines," described Mattie vividly.

Then, after taking a sip of water from a brightly-flowered paper cup, she continued.

"Tante said she never saw Bubbie's face, but knew it was her by the number tattooed on her forearm. That she has a similar number as well."

Flores sat completely still, not wanting to give Mattie any excuse to stop.

"A shadowy figure of a German soldier roughly yanks her away from her mother. Then, she's naked… Standing in a dark cement room packed with other naked people. She's terrified, crying… Foul air chokes her. She violently gulps for oxygen like a fish pulled from water. She can't breathe; collapses to the floor. She's staring at the ceiling, feeling her life ending… Then she wakes soaked; feeling guilty for living."

Cupping Esther's unresponsive hand in hers, Mattie leaned over and gave the back of her aunt's hand a gentle kiss.

"I think I'd hate tattoos too," Michael said softly.

"So do most Jews of her generation. And many of mine… See," said Mattie showing her bare arms and neck. "Out of respect. Not a one."

Silently Flores mulled the complexities of this older woman he swore to protect. Remembering how first he had misjudged her. How since then, she had won him over with her sharp wit, kindness; her sheer courage. Thinking too, what a shame it would have been had they never met.

It was then hospital attendant Charles Nuñez walked into the room with a new piece of equipment. With a pleasant greeting, he handed a folded note to the detective.

"Excuse me, Detective Flores… A woman's asking for you at the nurses station. She insists it's important. Asked me to give you this," informed Nuñez; wheeling the older unit away.

Yawning, Flores silently read note; then, with a surprised look, sprang to his feet.

"Back in a sec," he called over his shoulder; happily rushing into the hall.

Greatly interested in seeing who had elicited such joy in the detective, Mattie leaned as far as her chair allowed and peered out the door. Unfortunately, the nurses station's harsh florescent lights made the area around it dimmer, obscure. So, all Mattie could make out was a hazy figure dressed in what looked like a long coat.

"Glee Piozzi!" whispered Flores elated.

"Michael, I've been trying…," began Dr. Singh's lab assistant uneasily.

However, in his genuine happiness the detective cut her off.

"Glee… You've no idea how glad I am to see you," said Flores; grinning broadly.

"Michael wait," pleaded Glee.

Unable to stop the detective's rambling.

"I tried calling you, and Doc… But everything was happening so fast. I saw part of a newscast about a woman murdered near the bar where we met the other night. Well, let's just say my imagination… Anyway, you're here, safe, and…,"

"Michael, stop!" cried Glee; a little too loudly.

Tears welled up in Glee's eyes as she spoke more forcibly than she intended.

Mattie, curious about the who the person was and what was so urgent, stood in the room's doorframe; straining to hear their conversation after hearing the woman shout Michael's name.

Then, as she watched the person in the long coat grab Michael Flores' sleeve, she heard a familiar voice behind her whisper a familiar name.

Esther Hausman was at long last awake.

"Sarah?" hoarsely called Esther; confused and barely lucid.

Mistaking her niece for her younger sister, Mattie turned and replied gently.

"No Tante, it's Mattie… You're okay… You're in a hospital. No… Don't try to move. You're pretty banged up… But you're going to be fine," reassured Mattie; pressing the nurse call button.

Recognizing Mattie for who she truly was, the older woman relaxed her head back against the pillow and tried to swallow.

"Bet you're thirsty. Tante… Here, let's get you some cool water. Maybe start with a couple of sips. Later, I'll tell you everything," she promised.

Grabbing a plastic mug off the overbed table, Mattie took a look down the hall on her way to the sink. Stunned, the silhouetted Michael was clutching his middriff and grabbing onto the nearest armchair. His strong young frame hunched like a feeble old man; he then clumsily stepped backward causing the chair to tip.

"What the hell is she saying to him?" uttered Mattie; quite concerned.

The stranger, moving in quickly to steady him.

A nurse brushed by her in the doorway.

Mattie could hear the caregiver cheerfully welcome Esther back to the world of the living; striking up a conversation with her patient as she took her vitals. Lingering in the doorway, Mattie was torn between running to Michael and remaining with Esther. Then, putting on a brave face, she returned to her aunt.

"Zoe... It was Zoe. Strangled?" lamented Michael Flores.

Devastated hearing it was Zoe Bookman who was the murdered woman. Killed outside the Scottsdale bar that night he had left her, and Glee, to fend for themselves while he returned to the safe house.

"Zoe's death... It's my fault... I should have been there... Walked them," cried Michael's shattered heart.

Deaf to Glee words, Michael's mind filled with vivid images of Zoe's lovely face, captivating smile. The adorable way she tilted her head. The sound of her beguiling voice so intelligent, confident; her wit. Their warm embrace, passionate kiss; the sweet smell of confectionaries lingering on her soft skin.

"Don't be an idiot," she had teased before he left her. "No need to rush. I'll wait."

"Glee... Tell me again. Why contact you?" he begged; still foggy about the details.

"The police. They found Zoe's Backstop Micro-Brewery and Grill credit card receipt in her wallet. The date and time-stamp was near her time of death," explained Glee.

"I remember, she said you both were staying," he acknowledged.

"Right. After you left we hung out. Ate... Drank... We used our cards to split the bill. When the Scottsdale police questioned our server about Zoe, he remembered me and found my half of the payment. That's when they called."

"She was strangled," reaffirmed Michael quietly; choking on his own words.

"Yes," responded Glee gently. "And Michael... The murderer... He used a wire."

"Like the garotte used to kill the security men at the safe house? Baring... You're saying Baring did this? Why? Why kill Zoe? We just met... She didn't know anything... Unless... Unless it was a message to me... To back off... If that's true, Zoe really did die because of me," he sighed.

Glee's heart broke for Michael.

"Stop... Please... It's not true... Michael, there's another reason why he killed her... There has to be. You'll figure out. I know you will," implored Glee.

But nothing she said stopped him from blaming himself for Zoe's death.

Watching the handsome detective's chocolate-brown eyes harden, Glee Piozzi knew one thing for sure. If, no when, Michael Flores found Oliver Baring, it was going to end badly; perhaps for both of them.

After Glee left, Michael Flores walked the residential neighborhoods around the hospital for hours. Not wanting to talk to anyone, unable to hide his pain, he thought of nothing else but Zoe; her violent death, his life without her. Vowing he would find the sick son-of-a-bitch who destroyed so many lives, and make him pay.

When at last Michael did return to the ICU room, he held back. Crossing his arms as he leaned against the doorway, he observed the older woman sip ginger ale through a jumbo straw in a cream-colored plastic hospital mug; exhausted, yet smiling.

Mattie, sitting on the edge of her aunt's bed, happily chatting. Their hilarious comments about the goofy photographs of Taisha which Kyle recently sent. Him, truly amazed by Esther's resilience.

"Matilda... Now, tell me... What happened after I stole that asshole's pickup?" insisted Esther, patting her niece's arm.

As the recent dose of heavy pain medications kicked in, Esther snuggled her head against the thin hospital pillows and waited for Mattie to begin.

"Here's a watered-down version. Take or leave it," offered Mattie; just as stubbornly.

Unsure how much Esther could take; Mattie did promise her aunt she would go into greater detail when she was stronger. Then, she began disclosing the events of the past 48 hours. The attending nurse becoming so engrossed in Mattie's story while administering her duties, that she asked for permission to remain.

"...And that's when Michael and, uh... a Mr. Silva found you," she said with finality.

"So... First I thought he was a hospital volunteer... Mr. Silva. You know like one of those greeters at a big box store... Turns out, he works with Terco... I mean Aiden... Collins. You know him, Tante. The jerky beer guy from the ballgame... You liked him. Called him cute... Anyway, get this... Aiden's actually an undercover FBI agent. He was working another case and asked to join Michael when Xander held us at the house," rambled Mattie; turning slightly pink with embarrassment.

"Wait," interrupted Esther. "The beer guy's FBI? Who's Silva? He FBI too?"

A bit fuzzy on some of the facts, Mattie asked Michael to fill in the holes. When he remained suspiciously quiet, she added.

"All the time we were together in the lounge, I never recognized him. Later Aiden said it was Mr. Silva who was arguing with Xander on the ballpark landing."

This new information caused Michael to perk up and pay closer attention.

"Aiden… The jerky kid who's not a beer vendor, but a Fed. He says the second guy…," uttered Esther slowly; slurring her words as her eyes drooped.

"Okay folks… Time to go," ordered the nurse. "Mrs. Hausman needs to rest."

Mattie earnestly pleaded to stay with her aunt; vowing to be absolutely quiet.

Reluctantly yielding, the nurse issued a stern warning on her way out that she would be back to check.

"I get Collins knows Silva. Does he know Baring too?" whispered Flores.

Still shocked to find out it was Tony Silva who was arguing with Xander that day.

"I don't think so… Mr. Silva is Aiden's boss while Aiden's undercover. Aiden said Silva had no clue who he really was, until today. He said he did see Silva arguing with someone he didn't recognize during our incident… That Mitzy had things under control. And, he didn't want to blow his cover unless he absolutely had too… He also said he wasn't aware of the murder, or us in protective custody until today," she whispered back; then joked. "You know… You people really should talk."

Then, gently pulling the blankets up around her slumbering aunt's neck, Mattie kissed Esther softly on top of her head; then sat in the recliner.

"It's how she likes to sleep," relayed Mattie lovingly to Michael.

355

"Sounds like Special Agent Aiden had a lot to say," remarked Flores sarcastically.

Shooting Michael a playful look of reproach, Mattie gestured to him to take a walk with her. As they reached the door, Esther called out.

"Wait… Mitzy! How's Mitzy?" she demanded, fighting to stay awake.

"She's okay. Really Tante… Please, go to sleep," smiled Mattie sweetly.

"Xander… What about Xander?" she asked anxiously.

"Esther, don't worry. You're safe," reassured Michael.

His melancholy apparent, even though standing in a shadowy doorframe.

"Michael… What's wrong?" asked Esther; her hoarse voice filled with concern.

"Nothing. Nothing's wrong. Esther… Please. Sleep," urged Flores.

"Okay guys… Mrs. Hausman, they'll be back soon," said the nurse reentering the room; motioning to the visitors to take a break.

Walking side-by side Michael sensed Mattie knew something had happened earlier. Having no desire to fully discuss Zoe's death, or the circumstances surrounding it, he was glad when his phone rang.

Surprised to hear the unrecognized voice of Morris Dipp on the other end, Flores hesitated. This gave the younger deputy involved in Esther's rescue on Highway 79, the opportunity to jump in.

"Detective Flores, it's Mo… Uh, Deputy Morris Dipp from the other night… I'm at Impound. Our guys tore apart what's left of that RAM pickup like you asked," asserted the deputy getting right to the point.

"You found something?" inquired Flores, allowing his hopes to rise.

Grateful too, to be focusing on the case and not himself.

"Damn straight… I mean, affirmative sir. Jammed up tighter than snot inside the driver-side door. A real nifty garrote… Wooden handles and all. Looks like it's seen some recent action. I sent it to your lab for analysis. Hope your guys can get some decent evidence off it. Sure don't need any sleazy defense attorney convincing a jury its circumstantial," added the deputy with a measure of concern.

"Great work… Really, thanks… Hey, do me another favor?" implored Flores.

"Name it," offered Mo Dipp, happy to be appreciated.

"A young woman name Zoe Bookman was murdered the other night outside an Old Scottsdale bar… Strangled… Can you share this info with their investigators. Just might be a connection," requested the homicide detective; certain there would be.

"No problem. Oh… Something else Detective," added the upbeat Dipp.

As if waiting for a drumroll, the deputy paused before delivering the kicker.

"We dug two .22 caliber slugs out of the RAM driver seat headrest. I sent them to ballistics. Mean anything to you?" probed the curious lawman.

"Hell yes, Deputy! It means we finally got the son-of-a-bitch," replied Flores with great sense satisfaction.

Betting the headrest slugs matched the bullet removed from Mitzy Burton's body and those extracted at and around the Gilbert house. All of which came from the gun he believed registered to Peter Cavenaugh, which was used to kill him and several others. The gun which several neighborhood witnesses already testified seeing Baring fire. He now had his evidence.

***

The patient lying in Florence Hospital room 250B turned his head toward the large picture window and stared into oblivion. As an attending physician and his group of aspiring young medical students gathered round him, the man purposely avoided the doctor's superficial pleasantries and attempts to engage him conversation. Grunting one-syllable replies only when absolutely necessary; the man otherwise remained aloof and silent.

Overworked and exhausted from pulling a double shift, the attending physician reviewed his introverted patient's chart; not really caring he was being given the silent treatment. Just as happy to use the injured man purely as a teaching opportunity, the doctor decided at that moment a cadaver on a slab would have sufficed. The fact that this stiff was still breathing was insignificant.

"Okay folks… Our patient, uh, a Mr. Wade Stafford, suffered a broken mandible which required surgical wiring… If that wasn't enough, Mr. Wade obtained a nasty rattlesnake bite close to his left Gastrocnemius muscle, a broken nose, and multiple lacerations and abrasions. Lucky he had a driver's license As you can see, his facial injuries and swelling are so extreme; identifying him would have required other means," declared the seasoned physician.

"Gordon, impress me… Tell me about Mr. Stafford's condition?" he asked of a shy young woman hiding behind a much taller classmate.

"Well… Mr. Stafford's lower jaw was wired using the maxillomandibular fixation procedure. Given there's no complications, it should take about two months to heal. The patient needs to remain on a liquid diet until the wires are removed," she proposed succinctly.

Demonstrating her shyness should not be mistaken for ignorance, the medical student then slid back behind a classmate.

Satisfied with her answer, the attending nodded then changed the topic.

"People… Fact. Arizona's got a large population of assorted poisonous snakes. We know warmer weather makes these guys active. We also know if you happen upon one at any time, you might just tick it off," he said; peaking his students' interest.

"With that in mind… Mr. Dorsey, give me the recommended treatment for a poisonous snake bite," he asked a more outgoing medical student.

Positioning himself beside the attending, the aspiring doctor was all too eager to show his brilliance.

"Rattlesnake Antivenin Crotalidae Polyvalent is usually injected for a bite determined to be from the viper species such as a rattlesnake. However, because of Mr. Stafford's unstable condition when he arrived, he required an intravenous-drip prepared with a 1:1 to 1:10 dilution of reconstituted Antivenin in Sodium Chloride and USP, or 5 percent Dextrose," beamed the confident student with a toothy grin.

"Given Mr. Stafford's injuries, and the extreme toxicity of the venom, what's noteworthy here is that Mr. Stafford was able to drive himself here at all… Rattlesnake bites are both life-threatening and excruciatingly debilitating. The venom causes hot pounding pain, extreme swelling and often, tissue damage. The more you move, the faster the poison travels throughout your system. Increasing the risk it will kill you," stated the attending dryly; accepting the student's assessment.

Then, without actually addressing his unsociable patient, the attending let him know he was damn fortunate. His inference having little to no effect on the aloof man lying in the bed; the doctor then said straight out.

"Quite frankly Mr. Stafford… It's a miracle we could save you," he asserted, looking directly at his indifferent patient.

However instead of a responding with the slightest appreciation, a peculiar expression appeared on the stranger's face. One which left the medical team vowing never to be left alone with the man.

"Uh, let's move on," said the attending uneasily; motioning to his students.

Upon exiting the room in single file, the attending made a quiet comment meant only for his students' ears.

"One final note… We found substantial level of opioids in Mr. Stafford's system when he arrived. That's probably what masked his pain and enabled him to drive himself here. Guess you could say his impending drug overdose actually saved his life. Even so… I wouldn't recommend this course of treatment for everyone," he joked, trying to lighten the mood.

Xander turned his head towards the door just in time to see the last medical student file out of his room. Silently giggling to himself, he envisioned the aspiring doctors as waddling ducklings clustering around their mama.

"All little ducks in a row. Each with their spanking brand-new stethoscopes draped around their scrawny necks," he thought with a sneer.

Attempting to smile behind his heavily bandaged face; he then pictured a long rotisserie spit rod with each little ducky screaming its head off as he roasted them over an open pit of hot coals.

Chapter 18

"It's the bullet you don't hear…"

~ Unknown

The peculiar patient in room 250B, known to staff as Wade Stafford, stared contently out the large picture window from his hospital bed watching the antics of a tiny male Costa's hummingbird. Over and over, the agitated hummer zzzzip, zzzzip, zzzzipped up and down, forwards and backwards, in its attempt to intimidate its reflection in the windowpane. With its wings rapidly beating up to 70 times per second, it used every bit of its 3 1/4 inches length and 3 grams of weight to dart about, repeatedly charging its image. Each time stopping abruptly in midair inches from the glass and certain death.

Oliver Baring's life-long admiration for the diminutive species' biological engineering was totally uncharacteristic from his otherwise cruel, narcissistic self. Fascinated by the avian aerodynamic framework, he marveled at the little creature's ability to hover in the air and defy gravity.

Watching from his side of the glass where he lay confined to his uncomfortable hospital bed and lackluster sterile room. He yearned to be outdoors listening to the Costa's quirky song of raspy squeaks and chirps. The unique beating of its wings; a hum which sounded more like insect buzzing than traditional flapping.

Mesmerized too by the Costa's plumage, sparkling in the morning light. Its green back and vest outshone only by the shimmering brilliance of its rich amethyst cap and flamed-throat feathering. The tiny bird, for the moment, a welcomed distraction from his present situation.

Then, after a final, unsuccessful assault; the hummingbird veered away, vanishing for good. No doubt in pursuit of some fetching female, or to sip sweet nectar from a tubular lupine or desert honeysuckle flower. Leaving the psychopath alone in quiet solitude to ponder his next move. Which given his current physical condition left him few options.

It was then a sharp pain radiated from the deep puncture wounds where a rattlesnake's fangs had sunken into his calf. Wincing, Xander instinctively grabbed the bed siderails; bracing for the shooting agony which always followed. Trying desperately not to clench his broken jaw while riding out the surge.

His contempt growing for the medical staff, Xander seized the nurse assistance device and repeatedly pressed the button. Convinced the delays between pain medications were done on purpose, he waited fuming; cursing the person who caused his grief.

"Rot in hell old bat," he growled.

Glad to finally be rid of the old woman who he believed died on that ledge underneath the Tom Mix Wash bridge. Feeling no remorse for those who died, or accountability; he blamed the entire Cavenaugh debacle entirely on her, the state's witness. In fact, it was her fault he was in the hospital at all. That he had to climb that incline to get to where she was hiding; even that he encountered the snake.

In defense of the Western Diamondback, it had nervously watched the large creature approach and uncoiled itself from the shallow hollow where it had been resting. The very instant Xander planted a threatening foot too close for comfort, the snake struck without warning. Faster than the blink of an eye, the lightning-quick rattler lunged with an acceleration of 70 milliseconds. Its curved, cone-shaped fangs penetrating Xander's leg; injecting a dangerous mixture of hemotoxins and neurotoxins directly into the meaty flesh and veins of his inner calf.

Then, after releasing its vise-like grip, the rattlesnake swiftly slithered away under the cover of night. Leaving its intruder to suffer the consequences.

The excruciating pain which followed had been beyond anything Xander had ever experienced. Dropping the .22 handgun, he collapsed to the rocky soil wailing like a baby and cradling his calf.

Soon his vision blurred, his heart pounded wildly. In his weakened state the narcissistic psychopath became fully aware his own survival was at stake. Reluctantly, he abandoned his bloodlust to mutilate the woman's corpse to save his own skin.

Giving the motionless old woman one last glare, lightheaded, Xander attempted to rise on trembling legs; yet stumbled. Relying on his military survival training, he fought to keep his clouding mind sharp by utilizing familiar mathematical computations and elementary programming if/then protocols.

"You not the only genius Pac Man," he slurred pompously.

Conjuring Peter Cavenaugh's ghastly image, which seemed to be another motivator.

Gingerly stretching to retrieve the handgun, Xander tucked the .22 into his pocket. Then, calculating his odds of being found in the dry ravine was basically nil; he slowly, agonizingly, dragged himself out of the riverbed and over its embankment.

"If… the odds of someone finding me in pitch darkness… before I die… is less than zero. Then… I better get my ass to the road… and a hospital… Using as little energy as possible. Else… I die in this damn… desert. However… Even if… I get to the road… I'll probably get run over," he thought cynically; panting and grunting as he struggled to move.

Repeatedly slurring his go-to mantra to spur himself onward.

"No prob… just… opportunities."

Eventually reaching Highway 79, Xander pulled himself into the middle of crash site and collapsed on his back wheezing and coughing.

"Houston… We do have a problem," he thought; staring at the empty road.

Scanning the wreckage for anything he could use as a tourniquet, Xander knew it was imperative to apply pressure above the snakebite and slow his circulation. With no luck, he decided his only choice was to carefully remove the support bandage around his broken jaw and hope the filthy binding would suffice before the venom compromised his lymphatic system.

"Opportunities Pac Man… We have," he hallucinated.

Yet lucid enough to understand if he lost consciousness it might be forever.

Digging deep Xander pulled himself into a sitting position determined to stay awake, to stay alive.

"Shit… My luck… The cops find me before I croak… I survive… And get the chair," he thought.

Chuckling through his misery; trying not to jar his body.

"Happy Pac Man? You piece of… If you weren't dead… I'd kill you," he hissed inaudibly.

Coughing up blood.

Listlessly staring down the road Xander's first thought when he saw the bright light was, the end was near. Then, when the beam grew larger, he realized it was actually a pair of headlights.

Thankful his gritty phone's flashlight was still working. He limply waved the torch at the approaching car; hoping it would stop before it crashed into the wreckage and ran him over.

Moments later, a faded old Chevy Caprice® with numerous body dents and rusted chassis halted a few yards in front the crash site. Its yellowed headlights dimly illuminating the horrific two-car accident and seriously wounded man.

Sitting behind the wheel was a disheveled middle-aged man who had just completed a double-shift at the Florence GreenTree Suites. Sleepily on his way home, the hotel worker was totally unprepared for the devastation before him. Cautiously he opened the car door and warily emerged from the sedan; gawking both at the crash site and the injured man at the center of the disaster.

"What... The... Hell... You okay mister?" he asked nervously.

Feeling ridiculous immediately afterwards asking such an obviously stupid question.

Cradling his jaw with one hand, Xander grabbed onto what was left of his pickup and tried hoisting himself to his feet. Staring wildly, he wanted to scream at the dimwit; but instead, wheezed uncontrollably forcing out only one word.

"Hospital," slurred Xander; pleading for help.

The motorist, unable to understand what the injured man was saying, froze. Uncertain whether he wanted to get involved. But then, Xander pressed his hands together as if in prayer and begged.

"Hospital."

"You want me to take you to... I dunno... How 'bout I call you an ambulance instead? If I move you, I could get you paralyzed. You could sue me," replied the stranger; still resisting.

Torn, the motorist knew the Godfearing thing to do was to drive the badly wounded man to the hospital. However, his practical side was unable to shake the notion of the legal troubles he could incur if his actions permanently worsened the man's injuries; doing him more harm than good.

"You know, some people now adays…," declared the motorist with extreme apprehension.

Cursing himself for not taking that third shift his boss had asked him to work.

"Please!" cried Xander; sliding down the car back onto the asphalt.

"How 'bout that other car?" asked the motorist tentatively.

Trying to buy time to think as he pointed to the Dodge Challenger; its grill now submerged in the murky irrigation ditch water.

"One… Dead… Face… Gone," grunted Xander.

Painting a grizzly picture with his limited speech. Xander was hoping the motorist would be so repulsed he would change his mind about going over to it; and, find it empty. He also did not care to share the other driver, an old dead woman, was under the Tom Mix Wash bridge; or, having to come up with an explanation why. Unfortunately for Xander, his lie backfired.

The motorist took an uneasy step towards the muscle car.

"Dead… Need hospital… Now!" groveled Xander.

Well aware precious time had been lost to combat the poisonous venom.

Stressed, the motorist hurried back to his car. The situation proving too overwhelming for him to handle on his own, the man pulled out his cellphone and punched 911. Becoming further exasperated when he discovered there was no cell service, and the call did not go through.

Considering the best thing for all was to leave the wounded man where he was and go for help, the motorist slipped back behind the wheel and started the engine. Putting the car in Reverse, he glanced through his windshield one last time and saw the shattered man howling; begging for help.

His heart melted.

Against his better judgment, he left the car idling and made his way through the rubble. Gently putting his arm around Xander, the motorist helped the injured man into the backseat of his Chevy.

"Name's Wade Stafford."

He said, gently pulling the seatbelt across Xander to secure him to the seat.

Moaning softly as the seatbelt crossed his chest, Xander closed his eyes and replied.

"Oliver."

"Well Oliver… Florence Hospital's back a ways 'bout 30 miles. It's the closest I know… Sorry. Just is," said Stafford apologetically.

Thinking he'd have quite the tale to tell the missus when she came home next week after visiting her sister in Utah, Wade Stafford began to gently close the car door.

It was a tale he would never live to tell.

***

It was 6:45 a.m. when Ellen Franks walked out of the elevator and onto the Florence Hospital second floor, eager to begin her four-day morning rotation. The thirty-one-year-old nurse and single mother of three was thrilled to finally be on the same schedule as her young school-aged children. She was also ecstatic not to have to listen to her mother complain about the burden being put upon her babysitting her grandkids every time Ellen was assigned nightshift. Or how Ellen's youngest, who insisted on using grandma's newly purchased couch as her personal jungle gym, needed more discipline.

After greeting her sleepy colleagues, she placed last night's spaghetti leftovers into the staff lounge refrigerator along with a tall mug of iced coffee; then, took her place behind the central nurse's station counter.

Contently checking her assignments, Ellen's short-lived bliss lasted barely fifteen seconds before an out-of-bed status alarm flashed on the computer screen. Apparently, the odd patient in room 250B had once again defied doctor's order and gotten out of bed by himself.

"Were the orders rescinded?" she wondered.

Checking the patient's medical chart; not in the least surprised it still read, OOB with Assistance.

No longer feeling cheery, Nurse Franks promptly rose to respond to her patient's needs. Not at all pleased that the enigmatic man in room 250B had a history of being a pain in the ass; and, that he had been assigned to her.

"Apparently, Mr. Stafford has a problem with rules," she remarked to a fellow nurse.

Then, noticing a coworker snickering and a few others blushing as they busied themselves with supposed tasks, Ellen Franks headed down the hall. Speculating bad luck had nothing to do with her getting the second floor's most undesirable patient.

As the last nurse assigned to the current dayshift schedule, she expected to be assigned some of the more difficult cases. But Mr. Stafford, that was downright cruel. Gathering her inner strength Nurse Franks opened the door to 250B, greeting her patient in her very best Florence Nightingale voice.

"Good morning Mr. Stafford... Now you know, you're not supposed to get out of bed without ass...," stopping short her gentle reprimand.

"Oh... shit," she uttered; staring at bed.

Turning to the white board for the name of the previous night nurse, Ellen Franks called the nurses station and demanded immediate assistance.

"Natalie, has Stacy Miller left for the day? Good... Have her get down to room 250B, stat. Yes. Now! And Natalie... have Dr. Richards and security join us," she insisted in her cool, matter-of-fact tone.

In least than two minutes, Nurse Stacy Miller abruptly opened the door closely followed by the floor's nursing supervisor and the senior resident, Dr. Alvin Richards. Bringing up the rear was one of the hospital's seasoned security guards.

"Ellen... Can't this wait? I was almost out the d...," Nurse Miller vehemently protested.

Stopping her rampage in mid-sentence, Stacy Miller glared at the person lying in the hospital bed. Although the man was familiar, he definitely was not the patient she had taken care of the previous night.

He was, however, most definitely, dead.

"Hey Stace... When was the last time you checked on Mr. Stafford?" Ellen Franks asked Nurse Miller, a little too sarcastically.

Even though the thin sheet had been pulled up around his ears, it was apparent the young man lying face-down in the bed had met a ghoulish fate. With his now bluish-purple skin showing definite signs of rigor, the gawking medical staff conjectured the man had probably died a good six hours earlier.

The most logical cause of death was obvious. The young man's throat had been cleanly slashed from ear to ear with a sharp instrument.

As if one, all eyes followed the generous stream of blood. Starting at the wide gap above the Adam's apple, the blood had trickled down onto the bed where the excess spillage dripped off the bedframe and, ultimately, puddled on the floor.

Interestingly enough, the out-of-bed sensor, which usually was fastened to a patient's hospital dressing gown, now dangled precariously from the tip of the deceased's left earlobe. As the hospital team stood there trying to make sense of the horrific deed, the metal sensor clip slipped off the deceased's stiffening tissue and bounced onto the floor several times with a cheap-sounding ting, ting, tang.

It was then both nurses recognized the unfortunate corpse as a hospital employee who, just yesterday, had boasted about coming into big bucks and a new career.

***

Four and a half days before the young hospital worker was found dead in room 450B, Oliver Baring had groggily woken from the rigid fixation jaw surgery which used plates and screws to put his broken mandible back together. Initially uncertain where he was, once Xander's head cleared he remembered giving hospital admissions a false name. Figuring by now some local, who was probably missing the person whose name he had stolen, had probably called the police and local hospitals. He became concerned at any moment Florence Hospital personnel would alert the authorities that a patient with that name was there.

Immediately he put a plan into action. First, because he was too weak to get out of bed by himself he purposely behaved nasty and aloof towards hospital staff. Hoping by doing so they would leave him alone unless absolutely required. He also figured the less they saw of his extremely swollen face, the less likely they would link him to a police's inquiry or a missing person's photo.

Next, at his first opportunity, Xander swiped a pair of medical scissors off a tray after a nurse changed his bandages; tucking the shiny razor-sharp instrument safely inside the guts of his polyurethane-coated pillow to keep it within reach. And, although racked with pain, he began squirreling away highly-effective pills for whenever he was able to hit the road. Encouraged further after finding the Chevy car keys at the bottom of his patient property bag.

His strategy for breaking out of the hospital was simple. All that remained was his ability to discreetly leave the facility under his own power and find the car. It was this last piece of his plan that was proving harder than he expected; and finding help to do so was proving quite difficult.

He tried enlisting the services of part-time maintenance worker, Bert Phillips; targeting him specifically because he dressed like a man in need of money. Assuming Phillips would jump at the chance to perform simple tasks outside his mundane job description and earn extra cash, Xander surprised when the man turned him down.

His second choice was 18-years-old Scott Evans.

Part of the second floor ICU janitorial crew, Evans was responsible for daily basic cleaning, emptying trash, and mopping floors. Whereas other hospital staff kept clear of room 250B's unnerving Mr. Stafford and his legendary sour temperament; yet for some reason, Scott Evans was drawn to the mysterious man like a moth to a flame.

Hanging on Xander's every word, Evan's would sit spellbound by the patient's side and listen to his account of how he survived both the horrific car crash and deadly rattlesnake bite. Wowed by the man's story of his courageous struggle to reach Florence Hospital, and likening it to that of an adventure hero.

In turn, Xander purposely remained aloof to others; yet, made Scott Evans feel as if they shared a special connection. Repeatedly flattering the young man so that in no time Evans fell for the killer's irresistible guise hook, line, and sinker.

Unable to keep their unique relationship a secret, Evans was all too happy to boast to anyone who would listen. Suddenly the young man went from a nobody going nowhere to a pseudo celebrity. Small crowds would gather round him at the end of his shift to hear about his daily interaction with the enigmatic patient. Most of the time his accounts were true; other times his stories were exaggerated, even completely fabricated. Regardless, for a young man desperately craving attention and validation, Evans had at last attained a prominent status.

As for Xander, learning Evans was an unhoused high school dropout crashing on a friend's couch for twenty dollars a week was all he needed. At first he had asked for simple favors, which Evans had eagerly performed. Eventually his requests became larger, more daring. Xander even convinced the young man to spy on fellow hospital employees; asking him to report if security or the authorities showed an abnormal interest. This allowed Xander to concentrate on regaining his health, giving him a better chance to escape.

Then came the news.

The hospital patient advocate assigned to him had stopped by to tell him Mrs. Stafford had been found outside the small, picturesque southern Utah town of Kanab. She apologized it had taken so long, but his wife and her sister had been camping in a remote area in Zion National Park. It had been very difficult to locate her. However, Mr. Stafford would be happy to know Mrs. Strafford was on her way back to Arizona and should arrive at the hospital no later than tomorrow afternoon.

It was all Xander could do to express his gratitude for their diligence in finding his wife. Whether he was ready or not, it was time to go.

Immediately after she left, Xander contacted Scott Evans to locate the Chevy; which apparently had been parked by an unknown hospital staffer the night he arrived outside the emergency entrance. Given Florence Hospital was a singular four-story facility with a parking lot flanking each of its sides; ultimately finding the car proved to be a doable task for young Evans.

Next, feigning claustrophobia, complaining about his doctor's unreasonable order not to allow him out of bed on his own, Xander begged Scott Evans to bring a wheelchair to his room around midnight and bust him out for a few hours of badly needed fresh air.

Appealing to the young man's fragile ego and need for cash, Xander told Evans that not only would there be a fifty in it for him; but if they succeeded, his new bad-boy image would be a sex magnet.

It was shortly after 11:50 p.m. when Nurse Stacy Miller left room 250B after taking her patient's vitals. Watching the night nurse round the corner, Scott Evans made sure the coast was clear and slipped into Wade Stafford's room with the wheelchair. Then, pulling the chair alongside the bed, Evans leaned over Xander and gently shook his shoulder.

"Ready to get out of here Mr. Stafford?" giggled Evans mischievously.

Looking up, smiling with gratitude, Xander allowed Evans to gently assist him out of bed and into the wheelchair. Then, as Evans turned his back on Xander to step away, before he knew what was happening the killer rose from the chair behind him. Forcing the young man completely off balance while wielding the hidden scissors with expert precision; slicing Scott Evan's jugular in one quick stroke.

Wasting no time, Xander shoved the young man onto the bed and exchanged his hospital dressing gown for Scott Evans' somewhat bloodied housekeeping uniform. Afterward, in a macabre act true to his callous nature, the psychopath positioned the young man in an unconventional pose face down. Smiling as he pulled the bedsheet over Evans' shoulders in hopes the swap would not be discovered for several hours.

Next, in one final bizarre act before leaving, Xander clipped the out-of-bed sensor onto Evan's earlobe. Quite amused at what he considered his own personal touch.

"Thanks for the help moron," whispered Xander sneering.

Then, shoving the scissors and pain pills into Wade Stafford's hospital possession bag, Oliver Alexander Baring silently slipped out of room 250B.

Using the wheelchair as both prop and walking aid, Baring grabbed a few bath towels off a housekeeping cart in the hallway and made his way out of the facility never to be seen again. Finding Stafford's car exactly where Scott Evans said it would be, he opened the driver side door and was instantly overcome by the obnoxious stench emitting from the real Wade Stafford decaying on the backseat floor.

It seems it had been so late the night he pulled up to the Florence Hospital emergency entrance, the tired hospital employee tasked with parking the Chevy had felt no need to inspect the car before securing it. Something Baring had surmised when he woke from surgery and not found himself handcuffed to the bed.

Given the Chevy had been parked in an open lot under the hot Arizona sun with the windows rolled up tight for close to a week, the real Wade Stafford had been growing riper with each passing day.

Retching several chunks of bile onto the pavement, Baring covered his nose and mouth with a hospital towel as he lowered the car windows. Breathing through the fabric, he got behind the wheel and lay another towel across his lap in case he needed to again vomit.

With tears pouring down his cheeks, Oliver Baring spat onto the ground one last time before closing the door and driving away from the hospital. Struggling to see the road through his stinging, blurry eyes.

It was somewhere between Coolidge and Casa Grande that Baring found the perfect spot to dump the overly pungent Stafford. Yanking the corpse onto the side of a rural road; Xander drove away overjoyed. That is, until he once again became soured by the bothersome motorist's lingering foul stench.

Spying a truck stop with full amenities off the I-10 freeway, Xander parked at the furthest car spot and waited for the convenience store customers to thin out. Then, using Wade Stafford's credit cards, he purchased several bottles of high-energy drinks, soft chewable foods, numerous scented air tags, and a variety of cleaning supplies before withdrawing the maximum allowed cash from the its ATM machine.

Covering his mouth with a towel, he took short breaths while opening the car doors to air it out. After completely dousing the interior with cleaning solutions, he hung several air fresheners off the front and back seats in hopes the rancid odor would quickly neutralize.

As soon as he could tolerate the aroma, Baring pocketed what little cash there was and tossed Wade Stafford's wallet into a packed dumpster. Then, merging onto the I-10 freeway he headed east; impatient to reach to the Interstate I-19 Corridor. Scanning the local radio stations as he drove for news reports about a fugitive at large. Comfortable in knowing if all went well, in a few hours he would be just another American expatriate living in Mexico.

***

Hours later, sipping a cold cerveza on the patio of the noisy La Chiquita's bar in the border town of Nogales, Arizona, a familiar figure slowly approached Oliver Baring's table. Although the burly, bald-headed man had been a business associate for years, Baring knew him simply as Vaxq.

If you needed anything smuggled anywhere or a buyer found, Vaxq was your man. In this particular situation, Vaxq had agreed to sneak Oliver Baring across the border into Mexico and drive him anywhere he wanted to go.

Not in the least surprised Xander was in trouble with the law. The fugitive's request for assistance, however risky, was a no brainer. Yes, their years of association and illicit deals had proved extremely profitable. However it was Xander's volatile, vindictive nature and insistence on having his own way that impelled Vaxq to stay on the narcissistic psychopath's good side.

Xander might be vulnerable now but Vaxq knew how quickly things changed; he did not dare disappoint. He had seen once too often what happened to those who did. Besides business was business, and he had expenses and creditors of his own. If helping Xander get into Mexico also meant he would be greatly compensated for his efforts, why not.

By late morning the two men had arrived in the beautiful, serene city of Puerto Peñasco on the Gulf of California.

Decades earlier Puerto Peñasco, or as it is commonly known in Arizona as Rocky Point, was a quaint Mexican fishing community. Then, rickety wooden motels, fish merchant shacks, and dingy bars lined its dirt roads. So too, did the village's abundant population of hungry brown pelicans. Their large bills and gular pouches nestled against feathery chests, the large birds would lazily perch atop wooden dock posts and weather-worn roofs.

Each day crews from shrimp boats would dump their catch from nets or large metal tubs directly onto the fish merchants concrete floors. Hundreds, even thousands of shrimp piled on top of each other in huge mounds. These crustaceans would then be sold fresh or frozen inside icy plastic bags, all for a mere pittance.

It became an "in" thing for Arizonans to do, especially on the weekends. The drive south to Rocky Point was pleasant and easy. Once there, barbequing fresh shrimp on the beach and camping on the sand became common practice. Also common was the return to the US side with unlimited pounds of fresh or ice-packed shrimp. Eventually, Mexico placed a limit on how much shrimp could be brought back into the States per car. Still, it was quite a deal.

As time went on the sleepy town flourished, transforming into a resort and retirement destination. Since then, more than a thousand US citizens have bought second homes or repatriated in Puerto Peñasco. Some have even purchased large boats which they dock and live on year-round.

Oliver Baring was one such American who did just that.

Waiting for him at the end of Muelle 8 (Pier 8) was Dulce Santuario (Sweet Sanctuary). A completely renovated, classic, 1980, 42-foot CHB Europa trawler. Exquisitely rebuilt from bow to stern with high-end modern decor and appliances, it sported luxurious living quarters and superbly crafted teak decks. Yet for all its glitter, Dulce Santuario's most important assets were its well-hidden, state-of-the-art engineering and navigation systems. That, and its bulletproof hull.

He had bought the boat with cash years earlier under an assumed name and continued to pay a hefty price to keep her secured, maintained, and well stocked. With a substantially large stash of capital in a local bank, Xander could set off for a long voyage in international waters at a moment's notice.

When finally they arrived, Vaxq assisted Xander down the steps to the lower living quarters. The two concluded their business, and went their separate ways.

Now alone, Oliver Baring kicked off his shoes and slowly stretched out on his lush, custom-crafted king size berth. Happy to be back on Dulce Santuario and living in the style he was accustomed, Baring heaved a sigh and smiled. No longer afraid of arrest, or extradition back to the States. From that moment on he would conduct his business from the trawler until he deemed it safe to return, on his own terms.

The gentle sway of his floating second home and distant cries of the gulls began lulling him to sleep. Wincing, Baring turned on his side and smiled; at last content. Asking himself why he would ever want to go back?

Yet, unable to shake the feeling of unfinished business.

Chapter 19
Legacy

"Detective Rub… It's been four months since the murder of Peter Cavenaugh took place at a rural home in northern Tucson. Where does this investigation stand today? Are you any closer to discovering the whereabouts of your primary person of interest… a Mr. Oliver Baring? And if so… do you expect an arrest anytime soon?" probed Caitlyn Zebrowski, rapid-firing questions at the lanky detective.

Sitting at a desk adjacent to Vernon Rub, the attractive young newswoman with medium honey-blonde hair blown out to perfection leaned in to the detective. Attired in an overly snug, slate-gray business suit which revealed just the right amount of cleavage, Zebrowski was the perfect image of what sold today on news stations across the country.

Even so, Homicide Detective Vernon Rub had her pegged straightaway as a mediocre opportunist hell-bent on making a quick name for herself. And so far, she did not disappoint.

A newly hired journalism graduate, Caitlyn Zebrowski had been assigned to create a good-will community piece highlighting the Tucson Police Department; a day in the life feature to be entitled, "To Serve and Protect."

Likewise, she had been directed to obtain interviews with noteworthy police officers in the Violent Crimes Division. Especially those involved in a recently thwarted kidnapping attempt of a local state representative's 7-year-old daughter. And in particular, the heroic lawman who had gone above and beyond to save the child.

In the midst of a heated gunfire exchange between law enforcement and her abductors; this officer had snuck into the building, then sunk out carrying the young girl. Once the child was safely back in the arms of her parents, the lawman returned to his fellow officers; playing a key role in apprehending the felons. As a reward for his quick thinking and valor, the police officer received an accommodation, a promotion, and a couple of days off.

As for Caitlyn Zebrowski, regardless of the fact that this was her first real job out of college, the ambitious reporter felt the assignment was beneath her talents. Deciding instead to use the public-relations piece as a ruse to enter the inner-sanctum of the Tucson police force and go after a juicier story. Further deciding to plead ignorance to her uptight by-the-book boss after the fact.

Not wanting to miss recording a single word of Vernon Rub's department-authorized bullshit, she moved her phone closer to him. Her plan, to catch the seasoned detective off-guard in hopes of obtaining an exclusive on the hottest local story of the year. That of the nationwide manhunt for a dangerous serial killer who has successfully evaded both Tucson police and the FBI for months.

And, given the police detective in charge of the floundering murder case and the officer who rescued the child were one in the same. What better way to sensationalize the narrative than to obtain soundbites from his investigation team.

Whether Rub was or was not happy about the way the manhunt was being conducted was completely irrelevant. She would make sure whatever he said would be slanted to reflect the disgruntled sentiments she intended.

"Heroic Cop Or Incompetent Bungler," she mulled; considering possible headlines.

Not that she gave a hoot about whether the Tucson Police's golden-boy did or did not mismanage the murder investigation. Caitlyn Zebrowski was determined to use Vernon Rub, and anyone else she could, to create a story that would attract the most audience. Even if that meant expanding her rhetoric by hinting the policeman's heroic act to save a young girl's life was fake news. Staged solely to make an inept officer and corrupt Tucson police force look good.

Scribbling a series of damming, contrived phrases in her notebook. Zebrowski knew if she created a catchy lead and parroted it each time she referenced the investigation; the public would buy her accusations as truth, without question.

"Serial killer thwarts wannabe hero. Not a bad hook," she decided.

Hoping other news outlets would use it; giving her reporting enormous credibility.

"People don't care about truth. Nobody fact checks. Rumors... Mudslinging... That's what they want," Zebrowski had argued with her editor. "Repeat a lie enough times... The mindless sheep will swear it's true."

It was a trick-of-the-trade Caitlyn Zebrowski learned early on from watching propaganda sensationalists who called themselves journalists. A strategy she believed would reward her with a long successful career in a top news market, fame, wealth; perhaps even earn her the Pulitzer Prize.

Repositioning her phone, Zebrowski was growing impatient for Detective Rub's reply to her last question.

For his part, Vernon Rub had grown weary of the duplicitous wannabe demigod.

"Ethical journalism my ass... What an oxymoron," he muttered to himself.

Expelling a huff, which he unsuccessfully disguised as a cough, Rub fired back. Ultimately bringing the unpleasant interview to an end.

"Unfortunately Ms. Zebrowski... Because you're new to reporting, you're probably not aware of the standard police policy not to comment about an ongoing police investigation," stated Rub rising from his seat. "Now, if there're nothing further."

In Vernon Rub's mind, his words meant he needed to get back to work. In Caitlyn Zebrowski's, it meant this cop's got something to hide.

"So you're saying Detective Rub... Not only are efforts to bring this serial killer to justice at a standstill... The same inept detective is still leading the investigation. Or, has he been reassigned? Terminated?" goaded the reporter.

Her gut telling her the detective was about to lose his composure and give her the soundbite she was looking for.

Instead, stone-faced, Rub looked Zebrowski directly in the eyes and addressed his coworker.

"Officer Pawlak... do me a favor. Escort our guest from the press out. Thanks for stopping by Ms. Zebrowski. You have a nice day now."

His voice so saccharin sweet, it would make a confectioner's teeth hurt.

Next, picking up his treasured Bruce Springsteen mug from his desk, Detective Vernon Rub ambled to the coffee station across the room. Stopping there just long enough to refill his mug before strolling out of the room.

"Detective... The good people of Tucson have the right to know their tax dollars aren't being wasted on blundering cops barely capable of watching a clock," rudely shouted Zebrowski in Rub's direction.

Her offensive outburst compelling some in the room to stop and smirk at who was making all the racket.

Not backing down, Zebrowski took a step in Vernon Rub's direction with the intent of dogging him. It was then an extremely annoyed Officer Pawlak stepped in her path causing her to abruptly stop. Using his index finger in a circular motion, one might use with a three-year old, Pawlak ordered the reporter to make an about-turn and leave the premises by way of the appropriate exit.

"Well that was fun," grumbled Rub to Pawlak.

Both listening to the incensed reporter's tirade as she vacated the building.

On his way back to his desk Rub again stopped at the coffee station; only this time to pick up an abandoned newspaper on the counter.

Thumbing through it for something to counteract his testy mood, he found exactly what he was looking for at the bottom of page 18 in bold type. There, the header read, "Heroic Officer Saves Child From Kidnappers."

Below the header, in the column directly right of the article, was a coffee-stained photograph of Homicide Detective Michael Flores receiving an award. The photographer had perfectly captured his friend's goofy half-smile as he stood there in his impeccably-pressed uniform surrounded by the Police Chief, the little girl's parents, other ranking officials, and a few friends.

Someone in their department had drawn a thick red circle around Flores' face with a marker; prompting others to creatively add not-so-subtle names and catchphrases with arrows pointing to it. Reminders to Flores from his coworkers that although he might have earned a new level of respect, they were not about to let it go to his head.

Tossing the paper onto the desk adjacent to his, Detective Rub smiled as he announced to anyone who cared that he was taking a very long lunch. Grabbing his car keys he stopped to glimpse upon the article one last time. Chuckling, suspecting Caitlyn Zebrowski had absolutely no clue she had been sitting at the desk of the very person she was intent on destroying all that time.

***

"Michael… Over here!" yelled Mattie Kaplan, waving to the detective.

Beaming at the auburn-haired beauty shaded under a ridiculously large-brimmed sunhat, Michael Flores cheerfully acknowledged her as he briskly crossed the now familiar gravel driveway and entered the fenced-in grassy backyard. Purposely stopping along the way to bend down and give the elegant borzoi, Tashia, a gentle scratch behind her significantly graying ear before continuing on to the farthest section of the yard.

Tashia, contently lying motionless in the lush, cool lawn, had raised her drowsy narrow-domed head in his direction when she heard his footsteps. Had she not, given her extremely streamline physique, Flores might have walked right by the gentle giant unaware she was there at all.

Marveling at the graceful sighthound's body, he wished he had seen her in her prime; flying through fields full stride at immense speed. Remembering before he knew better how he had mistaken the borzoi for long-furred greyhound. And, how Esther and Mattie had lovingly, yet thoroughly, schooled him about the aristocratic breed's glorious, yet tenuous, history.

"You can't look at humanity's evolution, history… without looking at the dog's," Esther had insisted. "Some breeds, particularly the ancient ones, have been around since before the written word. Barely unchanged from their original form. Bred by man for man's specific needs. Where would we be without them?"

"Where indeed," he thought giving Tashia one last tickle.

When at last reaching Mattie, Michael impishly grinned teasing.

"Hey… You got rid of the rosemary."

"Well… For some odd reason we thought gardens might make better use of the land," replied Mattie; equally flippant.

Sitting atop decorative tiles, like those used to cap all four raised gardens, Mattie leaned towards the sweet basil and snipped a few lush sprigs. Dropping them into a ratan basket already brimming with fruits and vegetables, she then moved her bounty to her other side and gestured to Flores to join her.

The new stucco structures had replaced the dense rosemary hedge which only months earlier had concealed Peter Cavenaugh's ill-fated body. Michael Flores not only understood the need for the change, he was the one who suggested it.

Having sorely missed the women, Michael's personal life had suffered miserably since his promotion. Now, sitting beside Mattie basking in the sun; he was overjoyed to spend the entire day with people he cared about and who considered him family.

As the two caught up, Flores studied the coop-like cages which encased each garden. Confident the superbly designed structure effectively kept hungry critters from munching on the thriving vegetation. He noticed too, the latching doors which offered easy accessibility; the special sunshade and built-in irrigation system which encouraged maximum growth. The entire system would protect the tender crops from the blistering Arizona sun; without which, most would turn into crispy stalks of dry kindling by the end of May.

"How 'bout some of these," Mattie asked.

Snipping glistening farmer's beans and sweet peas from the plants' sticky tendrils.

"Don't forget those," Michael requested wide-eyed.

Pointing to succulent deep-striped violet and dusty rose Cherokee Purples heirloom tomatoes thriving next to bright orange and yellow Brandywines; some flowering, some newly set, others ripe for the picking. Flores could still taste the rich tomato soup and decadent grilled cheese sandwich he had devoured that first night in their kitchen. Hoping both were part of today's lunch menu.

A sudden gust of cool air brought light whiffs of lemon and sugar off Mattie's glowing skin. His stomach growling as he envisioned freshly baked lemon bars and fluffy meringue pies. Then, slipping into melancholy; the aromas reminding him of Zoe Bookman. She too had smelled of sweet pastries, freshly ground coffee. He missed her terribly. Her engaging wit, alluring smile, soft body. He blamed himself for her tragic death. He blamed himself more for her murderer still being at large.

"Michael… Lunch will be ready in about an hour. Hungry?" inquired Mattie kindly.

Sensing the reason for his sadness.

"Hungry? Me? Nah," he denied playfully.

Refusing to allow his demons to spoil their day.

Just then Flores' stomach growled so loudly they both laughed.

Not letting the obvious go by, Mattie pulled a few more green beans off a bush.

"Here… Maybe these will tide you over," she giggled.

"Hey… Still want to go today? I mean… It's not major league," he inquired.

Gratefully snapping the largest bean in half and popping it into his mouth. His hesitation, thinking the women had accepted his invitation out of politeness and not because they really wanted to go.

"Yes! Stop. We'd love to," interrupted Mattie; giving his shoulder a slight push.

Flores' main reluctance due to the fact that Major League Baseball's All-Star Game and fan events were being hosted that week in Phoenix, of all places. He had first proposed they go there and join the festivities. To which both women had politely thanked him and emphatically declined. Esther adding she had no desire to visit Phoenix anytime soon; expressing her sentiments in much stronger language.

That was when Michael suggested the more subdued outing cross town at Tucson Electric Park stadium.

Years earlier, Tucson Electric Park had been considered an elite, hybrid spring training facility. Constructed so the stunning Santa Catalina Mountains could be seen from anywhere inside the ballpark, its design was a unique cross between vintage and modern ballfields. It was also the shared home field for the fledging Arizona Diamondbacks, Colorado Rockies, and the well-established Chicago White Sox.

In time the three clubs moved north to the Valley where the majority of Cactus League ball clubs already resided. The White Sox landed a sweet stadium deal in Glendale, Arizona. The D-backs and Rockies instead combined their resources to build a state-of-the-art, multi-functional complex within the Salt River Pima–Maricopa Indian Community near Scottsdale.

Still used for a variety of venues, that day Tucson Electric Park was hosting a charity ballgame comprised of retired A-list major leaguers and local celebrates. Billed as an afternoon of fun for the whole family. The game's proceeds were slated to provide much needed support to local community food banks.

"Okay. If you're sure," checked Flores; then changing the subject. "By the way, where's Esther?"

Expecting to see the other half of the dynamic-duo recouping on her cushy patio lounger and sipping a large mug of hot coffee; much as she had that first day.

"Down there... with her three amigos."

Smiled Mattie coyly; motioning to the barn.

"Three amigos?" repeated Flores.

Not certain he heard Mattie correctly. Wondering who the people were; and, if they were planning on joining them on their afternoon outing.

Greatly amused by the quizzical look on the handsome detective's face, Mattie gave Michael another gentle push. This time in the direction of the paddock.

"Michael… Go," she insisted; grinning sweetly.

Balancing the hefty bushel of fruits and vegetables against her hip, Mattie strolled toward the house. Stopping briefly, she watched Michael Flores making his way to the barn when suddenly it occurred to her that he had never actually stepped inside it. Thinking she should help him navigate the facility, she was about to put the bushel down and run after him then stopped; snorting mischievously.

"Hell… He'll figure it out… Eventually."

Smiling as she shifted the heavy basket onto her other hip. Then turning away, Mattie proceeded to the house with the inquisitive Tashia trotting behind her.

***

The closer Michael Flores came to the large structure the more the air filled with the distinct fragrance of newly cut pasture grasses. So enticing was the smell, in fact, that had it been another day he might have bedded down in the shiny green blades and taken a long nap. Be that as it may, excited to find Esther Hausman and her guests, Flores continued on to the red-oxide colored stable with its stark white trim.

His past impressions of the place had always been rather blasé. After all, it was just a barn. It looked like a barn should; or at least like every barn he had ever seen, or imagined. This time, however, he stopped to truly examine the building and found it anything but commonplace.

To begin, it was massive. He remembered a time in the hospital ICU room before Esther had come round. Mattie had said something like their home was more or less an afterthought. That her aunt and uncle had placed most of their efforts into the barn. At the time he thought she had misspoken, chalking up her error to exhaustion. Now, he was not so sure.

As gentle swirling winds grew into gusts, a persistent loud metal-sounding squeaking caught his attention. Spotting its source on the roof's apex, Flores paused to watch an ornate brass weathervane of a horse running atop a long arrow. Wabbling in the southeast breeze, the arrow's tip was seemingly pointing to a large door on his right.

Stepping inside, it took Michael's eyes a few moments to adjust to the dimmer light. However once they did he swore he had been transported through a magical portal to an exquisite equine facility akin to something found inside a Barns Beautiful coffee table magazine.

"Holy shit," exclaimed Flores. Letting out a long, low whistle.

Never suspecting from the outside anything like this. Everywhere he looked elegant pine-panels adorned walls, doors, rafters; beneath his feet, high-end shock-absorbent, slip resistant textured pavers. His eyes falling upon a stunning exterior door to his right; clearly meant to differentiated between the stable and Kyle Lucas' studio apartment.

Like his pal, Vernon Rub, Flores had become fond of the quirky veterinarian student and was genuinely disappointed to learn Kyle was spending the day on campus. However, that did not stop the detective from placing his hand on the doorknob of the living quarters to see if it was open.

Pausing, deciding his penchant for snooping was not a good enough reason to invade the kid's privacy, Michael backed off.

"Sorry… Force of habit," he said; as if Kyle was standing beside him.

Feeling his integrity still intact, Flores glanced at the massive equine arena occupying a good portion of the building's center. Having seen only the outside paddock before today, he now understood the extra-wide barn doors allowed indoors and outdoors to become one. Leaning against its wooden fencing he was impressed by its sheer size; yet, unable to fully comprehend the number of possibilities it afforded.

Soft nickering followed by a woman's gentle laughter echoed throughout the enormous cavity. The sounds stirring within Michael an excitement he had not felt since he was a boy.

"Esther… That you?" he shouted a little too animated.

Climbing over the railing into the arena, Flores stood atop the specialized sandy ground mixture brushing the soil from his palms; the sky lights' diffused shafts illuminating the dusty particles floating in air. Searching the hazy interior, he was still unable to find his older friend until she shouted with delight.

"Michael, over here. Middle stall. Ach… Where's my head. Come cross the arena… There's another gate on this side."

Following Esther's voice, Flores noticed a silhouette of a horse moving back and forth in front of a wide, open window. He soon found her speaking gently to some very anxious snorts and heavily pawing hoofs.

"I'm not intruding?" he inquired tentatively.

Looking for the people Mattie had called Esther's three amigos.

Whereas the three of them had gotten off to a rocky start, the two women now truly considered the detective family. As such, that meant Flores was now fair game when it came to a certain degree of Hausman family mischief.

"Intruding? Wha…? Matilda. Oy gevalt. Michael… Get over here," Esther insisted.

Shaking her head; not surprised her niece attempted to make the unsuspecting detective the butt of her joke.

Approaching Esther, Michael was shocked at how thin she had gotten. The physical trauma she had suffered at the hands of the murderer, Oliver Baring, had taken an undeniable toll. Now four months into her recovery, Flores wondered how much longer before her arm was out of the sling, before she would regain normal movement of it, if ever. Knowing too, parts of her would never fully heal.

Mentally, however, Esther was the same fierce, independent spirit. In spite of her pain she still insisted on doing things the right way, her way. And, woe to the person who got in her way. This usually meant no cutting corners and overexerting herself to the point of exhaustion; all of which greatly worried everyone concerned.

"Here you are… How are you?" Flores inquired, giving her a gentlest of hugs.

"No complaints… You know me. I just keep plugin," she responded lightheartedly.

Waving off any further attempt to ask her about her health.

"Still one tough cookie," he thought.

Smiling as he looked deeply into her twinkling eyes. Then searching, surprised not to see a small gathering around her; he asked.

"Hey… Where are they? Your friends?"

Not sure why Esther's complexion suddenly pinkened, or why she sidestepped his question, Michael instinctively changed the subject.

"You'd never guess from the outside this place…," he began saying.

Stopping mid-sentence as two nosey, majestic heads popped over half gate stalls to inspect the curious visitor.

"Will you look at these beauties," he declared softly; marveling at the horses.

Finding herself over the moon to share the Hausman dream with her favorite detective, Esther gestured for Michael to follow.

"C'mon kid... Let me give you the fifty-cent tour," insisted Esther cheerfully.

Tactfully placing her hand atop his forearm to aid her stability, Michael allowed Esther to slowly lead him to the first stall.

"This is Molly. Our resident Quarter Horse... She belongs to a friend, Fayleen Lambert... Funny little thing, Molly... Loves to brush you off against a tree or fence if she thinks you don't know how to ride. Horses are pretty smart about stuff like that," she chuckled; giving the little mare a pat on her neck while adding.

"But walk down to the pastures without her... Before you know it she's jumped the paddock fence and's by your side like an old school chum."

"Pleased to meet you Molly," grinned Flores; gently stroking her head. "Hope we become friends... We won't be riding off in the sunset together, however, you can join me for a stroll sometime if no one minds."

Molly nickered softly as if she understood his joke; leaning into Michael's soothing touch with pure contentment.

"This. Our dream...," she gestured. "Max, Mattie, mine... A loving sanctuary for abused, abandoned horses, dogs, really any animal. I don't have to tell you. Some people are less than pond scum... Here... We do our best to heal them physically, mentally... Rehome if possible. Otherwise, the place becomes theirs forever."

"How do you manage? The three of you," remarked Flores; concerned.

To which Esther said with pride.

"I know, we were crazy.... Max. Mattie. Me... Still are... But the animals we take in suffered terribly at the hands of humans they trusted or feared. By rights... each of 'em should have died... For those we could, can help, we make damn sure we make a difference."

Pulling a freshly harvested carrot from her pocket, Esther offered it to the little Quarter Horse. Gently curling her soft lips around the tasty morsel; Molly's nimble tongue maneuvered the treat and happily crunched away.

"Fayleen rescued Molly... Poor thing was all alone... Abandoned in a cold muddy field. A heavy link chain wrapped so tightly around her neck it literally embedded into her skin... The other end of the chain was anchored to a truck tire. She was so weak... More ribs than meat... Took a long time before she'd allow anyone to touch her. Now look," beamed Esther.

Laughing as Molly explored her pockets. Esther, rewarding the little mare's ingenuity with another carrot and final pat before motioning to the next stall.

"Look around... Whole place's solar. Heating. Cooling. Electricity... Even the aqueduct system which brings constant fresh water to each stall. My Max was an amazing attorney. He was also a brilliant, compassionate visionary," she said lovingly of her late husband.

"Sounds like you had a great marriage," remarked Michael; affectionately giving Esther's hand a gentle squeeze.

"We did Michael... That we did."

Patting his arm; still mourning her loss.

"Tell me more," he implored gently; fascinated by the entire operation.

"Well... The horses roam the fields during the day. There's plenty of shade, fresh water, grassland... They're a tight little band... People don't get that about horses. They're extremely social creatures... They form deep, long attachments to each other… Nighttime they're in stalls with wall-to-wall waterproof mats beneath bedding that mimics natural pasture. Each stall is extra-large, squeaky-clean, temperature controlled. Enormous exterior windows provide fresh air and cross ventilation. Oh, and interactive toys. Helps keep bored minds busy."

Slowly approaching the next stall Esther said quietly.

"Dora Crewe owns Trouble," she said; inviting Michael to take a peek.

Suspiciously eyeing the stranger's every move, a timid buckskin with a large scar across his left flank nervously backed up until his rear bumped the stall's far corner.

"That wasn't his name when Dora brought him here… He didn't have one. Some hikers near Sasabe. Found him near death in 112-degree heat. We suspect smugglers rode him across the border. Just left him to die… No water. No food. We didn't think he'd last the night."

The buckskin nervously took a step towards Esther then stopped, pawing his bedding as he glared at Michael.

"Dora had us set up a table and cot, here… She worked remote. Stayed day and night for months… Hand fed him… Nursed him back to health… Gained his trust," she said softly.

Patiently waiting for the horse to decide if it was safe to approach.

"Amazing he survived… So, Trouble, because of the effort it took to save his life?"

Michael surmised; it becoming quite clear the beautiful creature would never trust most humans ever again. Understanding too the buckskin's mindset, he took a few steps back giving the horse the space he needed.

Timidly the buckskin approached Esther; ready to shy at any moment.

"Not quite," she said grinning. "Trouble, because whoever's dumb enough to leave an open can or bottle of pop around unattended… he knocks it over. Or, tries to drink it… What's that saying, 'Payback's a bitch.' And I swear he snickers every damn time."

Esther, reaffirming her story as Flores' looked at the skittish equine in disbelief.

"Come on… Time you meet the three amigos," she chuckled.

Gesturing to Michael follow her.

"You made two stalls into one," he noticed; then looked around. "So, where are they? You're friends."

"Right here… Shimá," called Esther in a light, singsong voice.

Almost immediately the head of a striking red and white paint emerged over the stall half gate wanting… no, demanding attention.

"Hello my beauty… This is Shimá… Her name's Navajo. It means mother… I adopted her from a barren, overcrowded Mustang holding pen in northern Arizona," Esther stated; lovingly hugging the mare.

"Shimá, and hundreds like her, were separated from their harem bands during a U.S. Bureau of Land Management's (BLM) hellish helicopter roundup. It's BLM's long-standing inhumane practice for regulating and reducing native wild horse populations. Many die… Others live out their lives in horrible conditions," she declared with disdain.

"Isn't that the best way. To keep the wild horse population and environment healthy?" Michael asked innocently.

"Don't get me started on BLM's bullshit. It's a cruel, barbaric program," she countered a little too strongly. "There's other successful programs. Like Maryland's and nonprofit wild horse preserves. They humanely inject breeding-age mares with equine contraception for less births. Their wild herds are healthier, undisturbed."

Then Esther added sadly.

"The State Representatives I've talked to say their concerned. Then regurgitate the same BLM rhetoric. In the past, a few advocates have successfully gotten laws passed to end BLM roundups. Then, a new House or Senate comes to power and overturns it to appease well-funded interest groups."

"Putting BLM helicopters back in the business," commented Michael.

Silently watching Shimá gently nibble whisps of Esther's hair.

Without warning, a second Mustang emerged from the stall's shadows insisting on equal, if not more, attention. Surprised, Flores took a stutter-step back as the horse wedged herself between Shimá and the two humans.

"This is Yázhí. Navajo for little one," roared Esther.

"I didn't know Shimá was pregnant when I adopted her… Imagine running for your life, pregnant… Stunning isn't she… You know Michael… These Mustangs are our heritage. A symbol of freedom… The Old West. Yet one day, they'll only exist in old cowboy movies and as team mascots… At least you'll never have to worry," she promised Yázhí; giving the youngster's muzzle a kiss.

A protesting whinny followed by a couple excited snorts bellowed from the fifth stall. Drawing his attention away from the Mustangs; Michael looked over and saw two shining black orbs staring back at him.

"Who's the black?" he asked; memorized by the enormous creature.

"Drek… My third amigo… Magnificent isn't he? Sweetest Thoroughbred I've ever met. In his heyday, Drek earned his stable a pretty penny on the track. When age took his speed… Just like Kentucky Derby winner, Ferdinand, his owners repaid him by selling him off to a slaughterhouse to become horse burgers in some foreign country's restaurant," Esther explained.

The striking gelding lowered his head nudging Esther to rub his cheek.

"He was just being loaded into the meat truck when I spotted him... Bought him right then and there."

"I've never seen anything like him," said Michael awestruck; petting the giant steed's forehead before asking. "Drek? Am I saying that right?"

"Yeah... It's Yiddish... Means garbage. That's what they did. Threw him out like yesterday's trash... He's got lots of good years left... Don't you boy," insisted Esther. "He's actually a wonderful pleasure horse. Ride him anytime you want. Even if we're not home."

"Thanks. But... I, uh, don't ride," declined Michael politely; stroking Drek's gleaming body.

"Don't worry kid... He'll take good care of you," assured Esther.

Seeing the familiar look of love at first in Michael's eyes sight.

"You know. I.... might do just that," he replied candidly.

Accepting Esther's offer with a broad grin.

"Who's in there?" he asked; gesturing towards the sixth stall.

Still finding himself unable to tear away from the engaging Thoroughbred.

"Right now only fresh bedding. It's kept ready," Esther stated simply. "You know... Just in case."

Sensing the heartbreak, care, even danger involved in helping these animals in crisis, the detective was intrigued to see what else the facility offered.

"Hey... Mattie says you're grooming area...," began Michael.

"Is the envy of Arizona's swankiest spas," finished Esther smirking.

"Is it true?" demanded Flores, using his best interrogation voice.

"I dunno... You tell me detective," teased Esther; playing coy. "Come... Let's start with the tack room."

Locked arm-in-arm, Esther and Michael strolled back across the arena leaving the majestic black contently munching grain. His sensitive ears set forward, twitching slightly like a satellite dish fine-tuning its reception, Drek listened to the human voices grow softer as their footsteps became distant.

It was then suspicious movements within the dark shadows of stall six startled the Thoroughbred, throwing him into a panic. Quickly shying to the far side of his enclosure; his superbly sculpted muscles quivered as he nervously keyed in on the threatening source.

Terrified, ready to fight or flee; the Thoroughbred glared as the gate unlatch, then slowly with opened with a long creak.

Fixed on the emerging danger, the horse instinctively pinned his ears flat against his neck as he stretched his head upward to its fullest height. With eyes widening and nostrils flaring, the massive equine whipped his tail as he repeatedly struck the bedding with an angry hoof; warning the menace to back off.

Never once taking his eyes off the intruder until absolutely certain it was gone.

Chapter 20

"You should have a child named after you."

~ Yiddish Proverb

"Unbelievable," repeated Michael; his keen eye missing nothing.

Inspecting every nook and cranny of the barn, Michael Flores was convinced he was no longer in Tucson; but rather inside one of Kentucky's illustrious horseracing farms like Claiborne, or Calumet.

He marveled at the well-organized tack room with every kind of riding and interactive equipment imaginable. Yet, when he walked into the state-of-the-art medical and grooming area, it completely blew him away.

"Fridge for temperature sensitive meds," said Esther proudly.

Sauntering him around the large room like a game show hostess.

"Nonperishable medical, grooming supplies… Heavy-duty washer, dryer. Towels. Bedding. And in here… Our dog spa."

She announced, escorting Michael into the cheery side room. It's walls filled with photographs of recipients being pampered; quite a few which were of Tashia.

"Hydraulic grooming tables, washing, drying stations, sundries, toys," she beamed.

Flores excitedly exploring, asking questions. Then they entered the equine room.

Soft, soothing music filled its treatment and grooming areas; including wash stalls with temperature-controlled hoses and cross-water gentle sprayers, ceiling-mounted deluxe solarium-warm air dryers, and heat lamps. Overall truly a haven dedicated to healing and wellbeing.

In the back of Flores' mind he could not help playfully imagining urbanite Vernon Rub's reaction. Suspecting though, after the initial shock wore off, and after a long day mucking stalls; the tough guy probably pulled a chair under the heat lamps and baked his sore muscles.

"Adopt me Esther," begged Michael chuckling.

"You already are kid," she replied endearingly; gently squeezing his arm. "Time for one last stop."

Standing across the hall facing a closed door, Esther put her hand atop of Michael's to stop him from turning the knob. Then, dramatically set the scene.

"Inside are two adjoining rooms for food preparation… In this one, we store bulk feed, barrels, bales… Trucks drive under a fancy-schmancy ceiling-mounted electronic winch and unload really, anything. Another door inside opens to our full-service kitchen where we prepare food for animals and humans. From the kitchen, there's direct access to the stalls. So you see, my dear Detective Flores, we've come full circle."

With that, almost bursting, Esther led Michael inside the pitch-dark cavity singing as she flipped the wall switch.

"Ta-dah!"

Nothing.

Frustrated, Esther forcefully toggled the switch several times. However except for some diffused light coming from the hall behind them, they stood in darkness.

Suddenly, the hallway door slammed shut.

Caught off guard, both fumbled for the knob only to find the door firmly stuck.

"Well, shit. How the hell… Wait… Wait… There's a flashlight on the desk. I got this," declared an embarrassed Esther; stepping away.

"No… stop!" shouted Michael.

But it was too late; the darkened chamber had already swallowed the older woman.

"Wait a sec… I've got my phone," he implored. "Esther?"

"Oy!" she yelled; tripping on a bucket.

Remaining unfazed, finding the wall; Esther gently leaned her weak shoulder against the wooden panels. Guiding herself with outstretched fingers until ultimately bumping into the desk.

"I'm here!" she yelled; groping for the flashlight.

"Is there a chair? Sit down. I'm coming… We can check the fuses together," said the detective calmly.

Yet every inch of his body screamed with urgency; get out of the room.

"Damn… Where is it?" she grumbled.

Praying Esther would do what he asked; Michael's heart sank when, not surprisingly, the sound of determined footsteps echoed across the room.

Rushing, groping for his phone's light source, suddenly it slipped through his fingers; hitting the ground with a loud clatter. Fearing it skid out of reach, or worse broke, Flores' immediately crouched down, searching the floor.

"Michael… The far wall… Barn doors! You know, deliveries… Don't go anywhere," she reassured him.

Confident she had things well in hand, Esther shuffled towards what she thought was the exterior wall; extending her one good arm in front of her just in case she bumped into something else. However despite her best efforts, the darkness soon caused her to become disoriented.

"Almost," she declared nervously.

Not willing to admit her confusion as she gritted her teeth and pushed onward.

"Esther… Stay there," he shouted; recognizing the trepidation in her voice.

Taking a small step in the direction of her voice, Flores' shoe lightly brushed the side of his phone. Finding it working, he accessed the tiny pin light and searched for Esther inside the vast abyss; praying this time she heeded his plea.

She had not.

With her very next step Esther's right foot clipped a raised object hidden on the murky floor. Certain the older woman's cry meant she was headed for a serious fall, Michael rushed blindly towards her erratic footsteps. His phone's tight beam slicing the dark void; finding the petite woman just in time to miraculously scoop her up in mid fall.

Tripping over the same menacing object, struggling fiercely to maintain his own balance; when at last he recovered, Michael lowered Esther onto her feet. Taking great care not to further jar her arm in the sling.

"You Okay?" asked Flores; breathing hard.

Scanning the floor with the narrow LED for the cause of their near calamity.

Then, catching a glimmer of the culprit, Flores felt Esther shiver as she grabbed his arm. The two instantly realizing how close they came from being impaled on the tines of a razor-sharp pitchfork.

"Yeah… Thanks kid," she panted gratefully; still unnerved. "What idiot leaves that in the middle of the floor? We could've broken our necks… or worse. Michael, do me a favor… Put the damn thing against the wall."

"Sure… You know, Mattie's going to be furious. We're late for lunch as it is," he remarked; bending down to grab the pitchfork's long wooden handle. "Finish the tour another day?"

All too glad for the suggestion, wearily Esther let Michael take the lead.

Using his flashlight to find the desk, Flores gently escorted his exhausted companion to the chair. Then, after leaning the intimidating agricultural tool next to the faulty light switch he tried the hallway door again; discovering it still unyielding.

"Okay if I leave you?"

"I'm fine… Go… Barn doors aren't locked… Grab the handle… slide. You'll see," she informed Michael; still a bit breathy

Grateful for time alone to settle her nerves; Esther leaned back in the chair rubbing her weak shoulder blade.

Meantime Flores, barely able to see his hand in front of his face, cautiously traversed the shrouded room. Between half expecting some lurking danger in the obscure void to break his neck and the nagging sense of impending doom, every muscle in his body tensed. Then, by sheer luck, the narrow light landed on the door handles.

Taking a step forward, something popped beneath his shoe.

Directing his light down, several pieces glistened on the floor. He picked one up, examining it closely, feeling its sharp edges. That was when he knew.

"Shit," he whispered; realizing the glass was part of a light fixture.

Sprinting to the doors Flores slammed into a metal handle. Tugging with all his might to slide it open, when that door refused to budge he tried the other. Digging in he pulled back; his heels giving way as he slipped to the floor.

They had been caught in a perfect trap.

"You okay?" she called, unaware of the ominous situation.

Figuring the threat was hidden inside the darkened room with them, watching, waiting to strike; Flores rushed back to Esther.

"Is there another way out?

He whispered calmly without explanation; shutting off his phone light.

"Why? What's wrong?" she insisted; rising to her feet at Flores' silent urging.

"No time… Where?" he pressed.

Hearing the concern in Michael's voice Esther immediately replied.

"Kitchen door across the room… That way."

"We're going… Now," he insisted; not waiting for her consent.

With a firm hand supporting Esther's waist, Flores hurried them across the pitch-black room; bumping into a few more obscured obstacles along the way until ultimately reaching the kitchen door. Finding it too, shut tight.

It was then a squeaking sound of straining door hinges broke the silence behind them. Soft shafts of light entered the room from the hallway as sounds of hard soles striking the floor drew nearer. Their spirits lifting, welcoming being the punchline of Mattie Kaplan's wisecracking jokes, Esther and Michael turned to greet her.

"Matilda… Thank God. I'm so happy…," Esther began.

Stopping short as she and Flores came face-to-face with the haloed silhouette of Oliver Alexander Baring; pointing a handgun directly at them.

Horrorstruck, she tightened her grip on the detective's arm.

"Happy to see you too sweetie… Understand you had a few mishaps today? Poor thing. You really should be more careful… Lucky you didn't break your pretty little neck on that nasty pitchfork."

His facial bones now mended, Xander's sharp tongue and chilling titters sent shivers down the older woman's spine. Even so, Esther refused to give the psychopath the satisfaction of seeing how truly frighten she was.

"I knew an asshole had to of left it there. Didn't your mother ever teach you to put your toys away?" she retorted boldly, standing her ground.

Her ballsy response eliciting more bizarre giggles. Then, still in good humor, the psychopathic matter-of-factly acknowledged Michael Flores' existence.

"Well looky here… Been a while cop… Wow. The whole band, back together… No wait… We're missing that fine niece of yours, sweetie. No matter. Plenty of time… Later. That was her in the kitchen, right?" he leered.

Deriving great satisfaction watching the old woman's distress as he graphically informed her how he planned to payback her niece for clobbering him with his own frying pan. That was, after he finished up here.

"Oliver," interrupted Flores.

Trying to divert the killer's focus from Esther to him.

"Xander, " he corrected.

"Xander… Thought you crawled into a hole someplace and died. You know… maybe a better name for you is cockroach," sneered Flores.

"Tsk…tsk Detective. Now you've hurt my feelings," mocked Xander; ignoring Flores' obvious ploy.

Then, an odd moment ensued.

Cocking his head Xander paused; seriously studying his adversary he asked.

"How the hell are you still alive old woman?"

When he had found her under that bridge for all intents and purposes she was as dead as a doorknob. Limp, motionless, no signs of breathing; he had seen corpses look more alive. Then, learning the contrary, his curiosity got the better of him. Slipping back into the States to find except for a minor arm injury, the old bag was in amazingly good health.

Esther, refusing to give Xander the satisfaction of relishing in her near-death ordeal, or months of recovery defiantly countered.

"I'd ask you same, if I gave a shit."

"Now... After all we've meant to each other," he snickered.

Amused by the old woman's feeble attempt to appear tough.

Flores, convinced the only thing the murderer liked more than taking life was talking about himself, played on the malignant narcissist's ego.

"So, Xander... Before you crawl back under that rock, tell me... How'd you do it? How'd you out-smart us poor, brainless cops? Crystal ball?"

"Must've driven you crazy, uh," he giggled with superficial charm. "Me turning up again, and again, and again... Out of the blue... Poof... Like, magic."

Boasting on and on about his brilliance, his loyal minions. Letting the detective know in no uncertain terms he had always had eyes on their witness. It was like floodgates bursting open.

"Your days were numbered from the start, sweetie... Starting the night Pete left this world... to the moment I blew you off the road," laughed Xander. "Too bad too... I really liked that pickup."

"Keep yapping moron," thought Flores; squinting to find a weapon.

Regretting having left his firearm locked in his apartment safe.

"But you want to hear the best part? I'm sit'n, just down the street from the Florence police station... Watch'n... Pop'n Oxy... Sipp'n my slushy. Planning how to get to this one inside that fortress, and voilà!... She just up and walks out all by her lonesome," roared the killer with delight. "I mean... How stupid is that!"

"Hey, I don't pick assignments," chuckled the detective.

Engaging the psychopath; looking for a chance to overpower him.

"Didn't think anyone would find your decrepit bones on that shitty road," purred Xander to Esther; his tone turning ugly. "You should've died under that bridge old woman... Had I known otherwise... Should've emptied the whole cylinder into you... You know... Just for fun."

"So, why didn't you?" demanded Esther.

Then suddenly she realized what happened.

"You! The snake... bit you... Well, it takes one to know one," Esther blurted.

Laughing so hard several tears poured down her cheeks. Recalling the feel of the rattlesnake's heavy body on hers. No, not on her, lunging over her; striking him right before she blacked out.

"Shut up... Shut Up Bitch!" screamed Xander. "I'll kill you... I'll kill you both."

His fragile ego bruised. Xander extended his arm, tightening his grip on the handgun.

Esther fell silent. She had pushed him too far.

Pointing the .22 at Esther, then Flores, then, back at her; the psychopath cocked the revolver's hammer. Then, in a split-second decision, he let up. Stopping himself from pulling the trigger. Deciding their quick deaths would do nothing to satiate the justice he felt owed him.

He needed to hear from the old woman's own lips that he was right. That she had seen him execute Peter Cavenaugh. That she could identify him. And because of that everything that happened since was not his fault, but all of theirs. Afterwards, they would die. Of course the cop was just an appetizer, thought Xander; and the niece… dessert. The old woman… she would be his main course.

"Think that's funny cop?" seethed Xander with a spiteful grin. "You didn't think it was so funny when I snuffed out your little brunette girlfriend… After you left the bar… It was a hard choice… Her or that oddball… Guess I made the right one… She was vvveerrry nice… Her soft skin sliced so easily.

"Girlfriend? Michael… what girlfriend?" interjected Esther; meeting his pained eyes.

Clenching his fists Michael Flores fought to restrain himself; to keep his head. Even if that meant dying little-by-little as the psychopath went into great detail about Zoe Bookman's final moments. His heart ripping from his chest as the murderer's sickening giggles punctuated how easily Zoe dragged into the bushes. Her look of dismay as the garrote cut into her neck, strangling the life out of her.

"We're not so different, cop. You and me… Your eyes don't lie. You crave my death," egged the murderer. "You burn for it… I'm right here."

Yet it was Esther who launched the surprise attack.

"You son-of-a-bitch!" she screamed; rushing the killer.

Shoving Esther out of harm's way, Michael dove for Xander.

Anticipating an assault, the killer pivoted away from the detective's grasp. Regaining the upper hand on the situation as Flores crashed to the floor.

"You've slowed down cop… Too many frijoles?"

Grinned the deranged psychopath with satisfaction. Pointing his firearm at his attackers as he taunted Flores.

"Pretty brave with that gun... Afraid to take me on one-on-one? Yeah... You prefer defenseless young women," incited Michael. "She was an innocent, you coward."

Looking up at the murderer from the floor.

"You think I killed True Brew because of you? You... Numbskull! What makes you think I'm afraid of you... I've got news for you, cop. You're nothing but an insignificant gnat to be squashed anytime I want," he bragged.

Xander's emphatic denial and gut-wrenching laughter causing Flores to doubt. That perhaps Zoe really had been killed for a reason other than him. But why?

The fact was he had only met her a few hours earlier. What if she had been planted in the café shortly after his arrival? What if she had been a willing participant all along; part of Xander's gang like Fenton and his sister? Purposely keeping tabs on him, getting close to him, another informant. If so, why had she become a threat to Xander? Maybe she had second thoughts, wanted out like Peter.

Had he been played, or was Zoe Bookman exactly who she appeared to be? A lovely, vibrant young woman unknowingly caught up in something she knew nothing about.

"Then why? Why kill her?" insisting on hearing the truth.

"Consider this... my parting gift." Xander chuckled. "Why? Kismet... Serendipity."

Esther quietly moved to Flores' side; placing her hand gently in his. Her friend had never mentioned Zoe Bookman, or her tragic death. Gazing upon the detective's saddened face, she realized for the first time that he too had greatly suffered at the hands of this madman. Yet, never once did he mention it, or let it his job suffer because of it.

"It's like this… Your sexy little nymph just happened to be the café server who waited on Pete and me the very day I killed him… Quite the coincidence wouldn't you say. Not only did she see us arguing… She also saw this," Xander said seriously.

Bunching up his shirtsleeve against his body to reveal the identical Rakkasans tattoo as Peter Cavenaugh's on the inside of his forearm.

"So what?" protested Flores; gesturing at the insignia. "It would mean nothing to her. We never discussed the case."

"But that's where you're wrong… After that ballgame fiasco, I stopped by… wait for it… Backstop Micro-Brewery. I know. What are the odds? I saw you, True Brew… That weird chick," he exclaimed. "See… What'd I tell ya? Karma."

Utterly shocked Flores was about to speak; but Xander would not be interrupted.

"When you left the room talk'n on your phone, the gals compared the photographs… Pac Man's gnawed arm with the Rakkasans. Yeah… I got a good look too. I also saw that look on your girlfriend's face… The kind when you know you've seen something and are trying like hell to remember where."

"She never said," insisted Flores.

"It was only a matter of time… She'd hear a news report… See Pete's picture. She was bright. Too bright. I'd been in that café several times. I knew she'd put two-and-two together, eventually. Loose ends detective… loose ends," admitted Xander; justifying Zoe Bookman's death.

"That's why you're here. I'm a loose end too," affirmed Esther.

"That… And you're supposed to be dead… Wanna guess how I found out you weren't? Thank your cop," he exclaimed.

"Michael?"

Esther and Flores looked at each other, both completely puzzled.

"Yeah... Here I am liv'n the dream in Mexico and one day an amigo says, I brought you a present. Tosses me the Tucson Daily Star. So, I'm flip'n through it and... holy shit! There's this article about the cop saving a little kid," recounted Xander.

Pulling a folded newspaper from his back pocket.

"Even in the dark you can't miss that stupid grin... And look... Who's that? Why, it's you and your lovely niece. Friends of the officer the photo says," scoffing sarcastically.

Glaring at Esther as he tossed the paper on the ground in front of them. Then, aiming the gun at Michael Flores's head, Xander added with pure loathing.

"Now old woman... from your own lips... The truth," he said with finality. "You saw me that night... You saw what I did to Pete."

Esther began to protest. "Truth is not subjective. Just because you believe something doesn't make it true if it isn't."

Xander cocked the hammer.

"Okay... Yes... Everything. I saw everything. I told the police," she falsely admitted. "Got what you wanted? You have nothing else to prove."

Suddenly the kitchen door burst open, rebounding off the feed room's wall. Its significant force causing the hallway door to again slam shut as all eyes turned in the direction of the familiar figure entering the room while shouting.

"Why the hell's the kitchen door locked? And why's it so dark in here?" scolded Mattie Kaplan; miffed with the pair for ruining her lunch.

"Stop right there, cop," yelled Xander; catching Flores' sudden movement.

The monster's voice all too familiar. Mattie realized the silhouette was holding a gun on Esther and Michael and rushed to her aunt's side; pulling her close to her.

"Mattie no… Run!" shouted Esther.

Wishing her niece would have turned back an escaped. Yet knowing all too well Mattie would never abandon her.

"Well if it isn't our little fireball. Glad you could join the party," leered Xander.

"Enough. Whose fault is it? Yours! You're the screw up… You got away with murder… murders. You were living comfortably in another country and your absurd ego couldn't leave well enough alone," admonished Esther. "How stupid are you?"

Furious, the killer was about to shoot when Michael stepped in front of Esther.

"Better hope you kill me first, asshole. Cause if you don't, I'm going to break your neck."

"If he doesn't I will," promised Mattie with pure hatred.

It was then Esther Hausman quietly, defiantly, walked out from behind Michael Flores.

Staring directly into Oliver Alexander Baring eyes she uttered with great distain, slowly and succinctly in Yiddish.

"A kleyn kind zol nokh im heysn."

All of a sudden loud, high-pitched squeals emanated from two extremely annoyed equine followed by the booms of powerful hoofs striking stalls; breaking the silence. It was all the distraction Flores needed.

Lunging headfirst into the murderer's middriff, Flores sent Xander hurling backwards the same time he pulled the trigger. The gun letting out a deafening blast as it dropped to the floor; echoing throughout the room's darken cavity. Its projectile narrowly missing Mattie and lodging into a bale of hay directly behind her.

Viciously brawling, the two men fought for possession of the .22; blocking the women's several attempts to retrieve both the firearm and escape to the kitchen. Rushing back to the hallway door, Esther and Mattie collectively twisted and pulled on the doorknob with all their might, yet it failed to open. Unable to avoid the fighting, or find the gun in the hazy room, Mattie quickly ushered Esther behind several stacked bales. Hoping her aunt would be safe there, she gave her aunt a kiss on her cheek.

"Stay here," she ordered over her shoulder. "I mean it Tante. Keep down!"

Avoiding the men, Mattie bolted to the kitchen door.

However contrary to Mattie's wishes, Esther peered over the bale.

"Nnnoooo," screamed Esther.

Horrified to see Xander' punch send the dazed Michael to the ground.

Quickly regaining possession of the revolver, Xander spotted Mattie out of the corner of his eye. Catching up with her just as she was escaping into the next room, Xander seized a thick cluster auburn locks; sending Mattie backward, sprawling onto the feed room floor.

The strong torque as Mattie released her grab on the kitchen doorknob sending the door swinging back violently, bouncing off the wall, causing it to again slam shut. Plunging them all into obscurity.

"Not this time," bellowed Xander wildly into the barely visible room.

Attempting to rise, a hunched-over Michael Flores fought to steady his wobbly knees. Clumsily turning as Esther cried out to warn him.

"Michael! Gun!" she screamed, desperate to save him.

413

But her warning came too late. The bullet had already pierced Michael Flores' forehead before the detective ever spotted the spark from the .22's discharge.

Crashing to the floor, deep-scarlet blood trickled from the motionless young man's torn body. Marring his handsome features as the warm life-source oozed from his head; trailing down his rugged face.

"You bastard!" cried Mattie; rushing to the fallen lawman.

Her horror intermingling with the killer's sadistic laughter.

"Come out, come out wherever you are," tittered Xander triumphantly.

Motioning to Esther to step out from the shadows.

"Enough... Enough," said Esther calmly.

Emerging from behind the bale with her hands raised; joining her niece as she defiantly faced the psychopath.

"Don't fool yourself, sweetie. This... The safe house... The cop and his little girlfriend. It's on you. Should've minded your own business," accused Xander; waving his gun.

"Think so?" asserted Esther; determined to set the record straight before she died.

Even though she knew Oliver Alexander Baring was incapable of feeling remorse or of taking responsibility for his own actions. That he would never admit he could ever be wrong. Or, that absolute truth was true all the time. That once truth was manipulated, became subjective, twisted to support a belief or project an image; it was no better than an out-and-out lie. A lie, which in this case, had led to many unnecessary, tragic consequences.

"You idiot... Get this through your thick head. I never saw you kill Peter Cavenaugh... I never saw you in the orchard. I never saw you... Ever! You got away with murder and you're too stupid to know it," insulted Esther. "You inept, egotistical, pond-sucking moron.

No longer caring if Xander killed her then, or ten seconds later.

"Time's up, sweetie. I got a cold cerveza and hot mujercita waiting cross the border," declared Xander, turning his gun first on Mattie. "Darl'n, I owe you this one."

Delighting in the titillating shivers deep within his groin as he forced Esther to watch her niece's execution, Xander began counting to three.

"One," he said coolly.

"I'm so sorry Mattie," cried Esther.

Tears flowing down her cheeks as she hugged her niece.

"Two," giggled Xander.

Inhaling a deep breath before proclaiming his final decree.

"Three."

However instead of pulling the trigger, a look of utter shock appeared on the killer's face. Xander's eyes widened as he gurgled an exclamation from his pompous sneer; watching with detached amazement as three tiny crimson circles slowly appeared evenly spaced across his chest. Staring in disbelief as the circles grew larger, turning into droplets. The droplets becoming streams of blood; soaking his expensive shirt.

Then, as if taken over by a creature from outer space; three razor-sharp metal prongs protruded out from Xander's chest cavity. The pitchfork, which Michael Flores had leaned against the wall earlier, now deeply embedded in Oliver Baring's back; skewing him like a shish kabob.

As Xander eye's met Esther's in disbelief he grabbed his chest; allowing the gun to slide to the floor with a dull thud. Then, taking a jerky step towards her, he slumped to his knees. His head hanging low, the light behind Oliver Alexander Baring pale blue eyes grew fixed and dull... Finally, the monster was dead.

Frozen where they stood. Esther and Mattie stared at the lifeless murderer completely bewildered.

Suddenly, as if both regained their senses at the same time, they became aware of the person standing behind the dead man... former Sergeant Antonio Luis Silva.

***

The last thing Homicide Detective Vernon Rub expected that quiet afternoon was a call informing him an officer was down at the residence of one Esther Hausman; or the second call about a dead body at the scene. Immediately responding with red and blue emergency lights flashing and siren wailing, the seasoned detective sped to the rural estate he knew all too well. Parking alongside the familiar red-oxide barn, Rub sprinted to the paramedics standing at the rear of the Golder Ranch ambulance. As he rounded to the back of the vehicle, a sense of relief washed over him finding Michael Flores seated inside the open cabin arguing with EMTs about going to the hospital.

His friend was alive; ill-tempered, but alive.

"I'm okay. It's just a scratch," protested Flores.

Waving off the paramedics attempting to examine his head and take his vitals.

"Detective… You're not okay. You're lucky the bullet grazed you, and didn't penetrate that thick skull of yours," rebuked one paramedic; dismissing Flores' absurd self-diagnosis.

"A comedian," replied Flores; displaying his familiar surly grin. "I am fine."

"You lost consciousness. You lost blood," countered the exasperated EMT.

"Mikey… Shut up and let these guys do their job," scolded Rub.

Putting an abrupt halt to his colleague's asinine behavior.

After a brief exchange with the appreciative paramedics, Vernon Rub turned to Michael Flores and threatened.

"Here's the thing Mikey… Continue acting like the knucklehead you are, and these guys are gonna put you out. Think they won't? I told them I'd give you the juice myself," declared Rub unsmiling. "I'm tired of picking up dead bodies from this place. So shut up and do as your told."

Knowing his friend was quite serious about his ultimatum, Flores sighed with resignation; allowing the paramedics to proceed without further objection.

"Wait!" yelled Mattie Kaplan.

Sprinting towards the EMT as they began closing the ambulance doors.

"Hey Vern… Just wanted to check on this guy one more time before they took him away," she joked lightly; unable to take her eyes off Michael.

"Sorry. We've got to go," insisted the ambulance driver.

"Just a second guys… Esther okay?" inquired Flores drowsily with a small wince.

"She's fine. At least, she will be… She's a…" Mattie began softly.

"tough cookie… I know," joined Michael, gently squeezing Mattie's hand.

"She and Mr. Silva are in the house kibitzing, drinking coffee... Actually Tante's rambling... He, doesn't talk much... Seems nice, though. After all, he did just save us all from certain death. Anyway, promise to tell me where he fits in to all of this, later?" she insisted; her concerned voice slightly cracking. "Go... I'll be along soon."

"Wait... One more thing, Mattie... What did she mean?" he asked. "Esther... That thing she said to Baring."

Determined to get an answer before allowing the ambulance to leave.

"Now Flores," insisted Rub sternly.

"No, really. Just a sec.... Xander was about to pull the trigger and Esther said something like... A klei zo," trying his best to repeat the strange words.

"A kleyn kind zol nokh im heysn... It's Yiddish... It means you should have a child should be named after you... Soon," enunciated Mattie laughing.

Seeing the priceless blank expressions on Michael, Vern, even the EMT's faces, Mattie explained.

"It's something European, Ashkenazi Jews say to someone they wish ill, or bad luck," she said with a broad grin.

Believing her explanation was crystal clear.

"So, it's a curse?" questioned Rub, unable to help himself.

No one in the group, outside of Mattie, quite understanding the phrase's full implication.

"Guys... Look... In Judaism it's our tradition to only name a baby after someone who has died... So in essence, Tante told the bastard to drop dead," roared Mattie; unable to keep her laughter from exploding.

Pleased to see Michael and Rub smiling; grasping the expression's real meaning.

"That's it people," ordered the driver emphatically. "We're going."

As the ambulance doors closed on a still chuckling Michael Flores, Vernon Rub and Mattie Kaplan said their goodbyes; reminding their friend they would be along shortly. The two lingering a bit longer as the emergency vehicle pulled out of sight.

"When you're done here, come up," Mattie said to the detective. "We'll save dinner."

Then grinning Mattie turned and walked to the house, where Esther Hausman and Antonio Silva were still conversing.

As Homicide Detective Vernon Rub entered the barn it was as if he never left. The sights, the sounds, the smells, all came back to him.

"Only this time I'm not searching for clues, protecting veterinarian students, feeding animals, or shoveling shit," he thought.

Ambling up the familiar hallway to the bulk feed room, an officer raised the yellow crime scene tape for him to step underneath. Entering the room Rub noted several newly installed light bulbs brightly illuminating the corpse.

Listening with amusement as Dr. Warren Singh succinctly instructed his technicians on how to remove the pitchfork imbedded in the decease's back. Rub smiled as the doctor's dedicated assistant, Glee Piozzi, took notes and unzipped the body bag intended for Oliver Alexander Baring.

Chapter 21

"If There Are No Dogs In Heaven Then When I Die I Want To Go Where They Went"

~ Mark Twain

Towards the end of the third Tuesday in July, the golden hour arrived in an intensely dramatic fashion; magically veiling Tucson's valley and mountains in sheer iridescent rose gold. Time seemingly freezing as many of the human inhabitants stopped to gaze at its beauty. Welcoming too the relief it brought as the ethereal blanket dulled the blistering 105 degrees landscape to a more tepid, yet muggy, 92-degree temperature. The opening act leading into an equally spectacular show when the robin egg blue skies gave way to the night. Sharing its heavens with brilliant golds, yellows, and oranges as the sun's final flares, in a last-ditch effort, roasted the earth before dipping behind western mountains.

Dressed in a sleeveless cream-color tank top and pair of brightly flowered capris, the barefoot Esther Hausman placed the wooden tray containing mouth-watering snacks and dips atop the backyard patio coffee table. Pulling an icy-cold Corona from one front pocket and a Tecate® from the other, she set the bottles on the table. Then, changing her mind about waiting, she flipped the bottlecap off the Corona and took a good long sip before grabbing the remote control. As she turned the outdoor patio television to the local station's pregame show, Esther settled atop her favorite over-stuffed lounger and relaxed. Having bedded the animals for the night she now considered herself, officially off the clock.

Cooling beneath the ample ceiling fan's whirling blades, she eyed a particular lime slice in a brightly decorated ceramic bowl. Pressing the zesty fresh green citrus against her dry lips; she sucked the tart, meaty juice from its flesh as mild monsoon breezes rose from the southwest, tickling beads of sweat on her body.

With her arm no longer in an annoying sling and her collarbone officially healed, Esther felt better than she had in months. Smiling, blissfully content under the brilliant Arizona stars, she patted the cushion beside her.

"Tashia… Up, up," she said gently; encouraging the ancient borzoi to join her.

The old hound slowly hoisted one long leg after the other up onto the couch; her aged body wobbling a bit as she stood stiff-legged. Then, carefully circling a few times within the small space until satisfied with the accommodations; she lay beside her human taking up most of the space. Pressing her immense narrow frame against the back pillows while hanging her slender limbs off the cushions; Tashia nestled her narrow head in Esther's lap and fell asleep dreaming of chasing rabbits.

"And that's why we live in Arizona," Esther said softly; stroking her hound's long graceful neck.

She could feel her excitement building. Soon it would be time, the awaited event.

Oblivious to the hum and wiggling of the old fan's wooden blades above her, Esther found herself glued to the 55-inch screen as she shoved a fresh lime slice into the mouth of the Corona. Pushing down on the fruit with her finger until the wedge slid down the glass bottle neck; submerging deeply into the light-golden liquid.

"Aaahhh," she exclaimed after taking another generous swallow.

Giddy, anxious for the program to begin.

Tashia, lifting her long nose towards Esther's lips, whiffed her human's breath to see if what was recently ingested might be to her liking. Reacting to the undesirable alcoholic odor with a snort and hard sneeze, the borzoi instead

421

edged towards the aromatic morsels closest to her and placed a front paw on the coffee table. Then stealthy straining, tried to steal a more desirable tidbit off a plate.

"I know… Can't wait. He'll be here soon," responded Esther lovingly; gently rubbing the inside of the insistent hound's ear as she gave her a baby carrot.

As the program transitioned to a commercial a steel-gray RAM grabbed Esther's attention. Watching the montage wide-eyed, the larger-than-life pickup alternated between fast-pace city streets and rugged open terrains. The diverse family inside its premium leather cab living life to the fullest as energetic music underscored the deep-throated narrator; urging the audience to rush out and buy one before they are gone because, "The sale won't last."

Unfortunately, the advertiser's message had quite a different effect on Esther who shivered as the color drained from her face.

His had been almost identical to the one on the screen. And even though logic told her the butcher's RAM was now in bits and pieces atop some Florence junkyard scrapheap, Esther still felt a twinge of fear.

True, Oliver Alexander Baring had been dead for some months. Yet, much like a person who loses a limb sometimes feels immense pain where the appendage is missing; so too did certain sights, sounds, and smells trigger immense terror inside her; a desperate need to flee.

"Stop… You're fine," she insisted; scolding herself.

Another shiver ran down her spine.

Lately she had been seeking help to overcome both her new and old demons, and had felt she was making real progress. Only this time, the sight of this particular pickup had proven too overwhelming.

Now nightmarish glimpses of Xander, the Ahwatukee massacre, those last days, last hours, flooded her mind. The total darkness beneath the truck's bed cover muzzled and bound, the murderer's house of torture. The RAM had been the psychopath's evil catalyst, it had been her salvation; her means for escaping the monster, for cheating death on Highway 79.

"What happened to one tough cookie?" she scoffed; resolute to start acting like one.

Yet flashes of the dark feed room refused to be quashed.

Xander's silhouette, Michael lying motionless, Mattie's entrance; the gun firing. But mostly the horrifying, the vivid transformation of Xander's smug face into a grotesque contortion. His pompous oration frozen in mid-syllable as he cocked his head trying desperately to comprehend what was happening.

The nausea in her throat watching with macabre fascination as metal tips emerged from the killer's chest cavity. Ripping through flesh, and shirt; much like a science fiction story where the alien explodes out of some poor soul's body. Only this time it was Xander gasping, howling in insurmountable pain. His eyes bugged, staring as engorged crimson circles popped open and blood gushed down the once immaculate shirt. Him, clutching the fabric with one hand, the .22 revolver in the other.

A final attempt to kill her.

The pitchfork's deadly tongs thrust deeper into the monster's body. Hooking Xander like a struggling worm, pitching him out of their harm's way. Denying the psychopath his revenge, vindication; even the identity of the person responsible for turning his icy blue eyes lifeless.

"I'm still here asshole," she had spat defiantly at his slumped body.

Feeling a welcomed relief until the stranger who skewered the monster hurried towards them from the shadows. She, recoiling from the uncertainty of his intentions. Remembering how surprised she was when the older man, a stranger, acknowledged her as he rushed to the fallen Michael Flores.

Immediately placing his index and middle fingers against Michael's windpipe; clearly checking the carotid artery for a pulse. Then Mattie, gesturing to her as she joined the man at Michael's side. Treating the stranger as a friend.

"Mr. Silva… Tell me he's alive," implored Mattie.

"He's got a pulse. It's weak… but it's there… Mattie, grab a towel," Silva directed while speaking conjointly with a 911 operator. "Right. We'll keep him immobile."

"Tante, this is Antonio Silva. I told you about him… in the hospital. Remember? He was helping Michael," she clarified; passing fresh towels to Silva.

She had felt helpless, Esther recalled. Usually being the one who took charge, had the answers. They had an entire medical section filled with supplies, but she had been exhausted, not thinking straight. Also, not wishing to risk harming Michael any further, they all agreed to wait for someone medically trained unless absolutely necessary.

Recalling too, her nervous attempt to thank the stranger.

"Well, Mr. Silva… All I can say is, you sure pick the right times to show up."

His impish grin suppressed as he maintained pressure on Michael Flores' wound. Their collective joy when Michael's eyes fluttered as he groggily regained consciousness.

"Michael… Be still," Mattie had commanded gently.

"Baring," he had tried to say; struggling to raise his head.

"He's dead. Everyone's safe… Ssshhh…Rest," Esther reassured him.

Holding his hand as the distance wailing of sirens grew louder.

Before long flashing lights belonging to responders, including one particular SUV containing Homicide Detective Vernon Rub, sped up the long Palo

Verde tree lined driveway. Pass the adobe house, pass the backyard and its black wrought-iron fence; their thick-treaded tires abruptly braking beside the paddock.

Rushing into the barn with gear in tow, the police and EMTs burst open the bolted doors. Their handheld spotlights blazing the trail as the first paramedics promptly attended Michael Flores while those who followed aided Esther.

The chaos so disruptive it caused a ruckus to break out among the more frightened horses. Mattie, slipping away for a moment to calm the anxious equines before they injured themselves. Returning just in time as two firefighters pushed apart the heavy barn doors, letting sunlight flood the room. Its intensity forcing those who had been light-deprived for hours to shield their eyes.

Meantime, the police had gotten busy securing the area. Some, the same investigators and pathology team from the previous Peter Cavenaugh crime scene; finding their repeat performance especially intriguing.

"So, the initial victim's killed with a utility knife… And this nut job, obviously a pitchfork," commented newly hired Officer Morris Dipp. "Farm tools… how weird is that?"

"And people say city living's dangerous," joked Sergeant Pawlak, signing one of the many forms he would be completing before day's end.

The bright sunlight still smarting Esther and Mattie's eyes when the women heard the well-known voices of Vernon Rub and Kyle Lucas drawing closer.

"You two okay?" voiced Detective Rub; rushing to their side.

"Fine. Vern, how's Michael? she had asked; her spirits lifted. "They won't say."

The paramedic attending her shoving his index finger in front of her face and instructing her to follow it. Instead, she had watched her niece join Vernon

Rub and the stranger, Antonio Silva, exit the room; supposedly to where Michael Flores was being examined.

"How is she?" Kyle asked the paramedic.

Startled, Esther's heart raced until she realized the veterinarian student had been attentively standing behind her the entire time.

"Seems okay... But she really needs rest... And, to see her doc tomorrow," urged the EMT speaking directly to Kyle.

"Do you two not see me sitting here?" she remembered saying; being quite irritated. "Get away from me, the both of you. I may be old, but I'm perfectly capable of taking care of myself."

"Mrs. Hausman's refusing to go to the hospital," said the EMT to Kyle; packing up his gear. "Maybe you can change her mind."

Clearly mistaking Kyle for an immediate family member, the paramedic continued dispensing his medical wisdom to Kyle and not to Esther. Then, after expertly tucking his equipment under both arms and grabbing his last bag, at long last he spoke directly to Esther.

"Mrs. Hausman, I'm going now. Your son has the information. You just need to go to bed now and rest. Okay dear," he had advised her condescendingly.

Then nodding a goodbye to Kyle, he left.

"Why do people assume just because you've got a few years on you, you're automatically muddle-headed and feeble?" Esther scowled.

Hating being treated like an old fool, incapable of understanding information about her own health, and too delicate to handle Michael's condition. She recalled rising too abruptly, and ignoring her lightheadedness.

Catching the wobbly Esther before she fell Kyle gently steadied her; then emphatically stated.

"Yeah I know… An idiot. Let's go."

However before she could protest Antonio Silva approached, politely requesting.

"Mrs. Hausman… Could I trouble you for a cup of coffee before taking off?"

"Absolutely… This way," she had replied; feeling a slight blushing in her cheeks.

Thinking about it now, Esther could not say if changing her mind about going to the house was a successful ploy on his part, her playing hostess to a polite, handsome, stranger about her own age, or simply because he had just saved all their lives.

"Thanks. And, it's Antonio… Or Tony, if you want… Kyle can find out about the detective's condition and tell us before checking the horses. If… that's okay with you," he had proposed.

Too exhausted to suggest anything to the contrary, she simply nodded while saying.

"It's Esther."

Allowing Tony Silva to escort her to her house.

A few minutes later she was relaxing on her living room couch with her feet propped up. Quite surprised when the usually cautious Tashia joined them; comfortably sprawling alongside the older man.

"Why don't I make the coffee," he had offered.

She had not even considered objecting.

Fighting to keep her eyes open, Esther watched the salt and pepper haired gentleman moved about her kitchen without fanfare; yet, with an eerie familiarity.

"Creamer is…" she started saying; leaning on the arm of the couch.

"Second shelf, far left," he had finished; opening the refrigerator. "Hungry? No, don't get up… Rest… I got this."

Remembering she had been drawn to his warm, reassuring voice; much like that of an old friend's. So much so, she had allowed herself to doze; waking almost 45 minutes later to the scrumptious aromas of a masterfully created vegetable omelet and hot, crispy sautéed potatoes.

"A man who knows his way round a kitchen," she had thought.

Admiring Silva's culinary skills as she slowly rose from the couch and ambled to the table; almost drooling at the feast laid out before her.

"Please… Grab yourself coffee and a plate… And, bring the salsa," she insisted.

Brushing aside the twinge of latent guilt feelings she was experiencing enjoying this mystery man's company.

"Not that I'm not grateful… But I have to know…. Who the hell are you? And how come you know my kitchen better than I do?" she asked, a little too bluntly.

Chuckling softly Silva took a sip of coffee; then said.

"Mattie… I was with everyone when you came out of surgery. Afterwards, Mattie ordered Kyle to bring me and another here and feed us. Your niece can be very persuasive… Well, I wasn't going to let the kid wait on us. So…,"

"Ah… Yes she can," Esther had laughed.

Certain he had done more than his fair share preparing that meal too.

Searching his pleasingly-weathered face, she had a million questions; yet, each time she asked one Silva cleverly turned the discussion back to her. Then, she brought up her escape from Xander's house and her rescue from underneath the bridge. Wishing he would open up and tell her the whole story of his involvement.

"Lots of people were looking for you. I was just with the ones who found you," he said modestly. "Anyway... I was happy to help."

Completely side-stepping his history with Peter Cavenaugh, Oliver Baring, and the psychopath's minions.

"This spread's an animal rescue, Right?"

Again changing the subject.

"Yes... My family's dream. My late husband's, Mattie's, mine," she beamed.

Then, after an awkward silence, she blurted.

"Mattie says you know that screwy beer kid from the ballpark... And you work there too. Doing what?" she pried; trying for more than a yes or no answer.

Instead of going into detail about the agent's undercover assignment and him being a suspect in an international theft ring, Silva grabbed the coffee carafe off the table.

"Should I make another pot?" he asked, walking to the sink.

Recognizing his avoidance, she had rephrased the question.

"Funny... For some reason Mattie calls him, Terco. But in the hospital he introduced himself to me as Special FBI agent Aiden Collins... Are you FBI too?"

Quite aware that no amount of coffee was going to keep her drooping eyelids open for much longer.

"Look, I know I owe you my life... And it's none of my business... But Mr. Silva... Tony... What's your involvement in all this? It has to be something. You don't have the poker face you think you have," she had cajoled.

"Let's just say Oliver Baring... uh, Xander... and l had a complicated history and leave it at that for now," he requested respectfully.

Seeing in his dark eyes an old-soul who had experienced far too much pain for any one person's lifetime Esther had pushed no further; but said gently.

"He hurt someone you cared for too."

"I guess it's fair to say Oliver Baring hurt of lot of people... Some more than others," he admitted quietly.

Feeling he had shared too much already, Silva pulled back; silently moving his eggs to one side of his plate as he picked at his golden-brown potatoes.

"Can you at least answer this... And I won't ask anything else... Why'd you come here today? Today of all days. Not that we're all not eternally grateful."

Silva's eyes brightened; tickled by Esther's utter determination.

"I dunno... I had to be in Tucson. Something in my head told me to stop by... See how you all were getting on. You know... Considering."

Still suspecting he was an FBI agent and his reason for coming to town required a security clearance; Esther kept her word, not asking anything further. Nevertheless, Tony Silva peaked her interest; she just could not put her finger on why.

For Silva's part, he had no good reason to withhold he was headed to Tucson Electric Park to work a ballgame that day. Or, for not disclosing he worked simply because baseball brought him great joy; except that would be getting a little too personal. But then, setting the dishes inside the kitchen sink, his back to Esther; he decided to open up and say.

"Did you ever get a really strong, unexplainable voice in your head telling you something terrible was about to happen to someone? I know, crazy... But that's why... When you weren't inside your home, I checked the barn."

"Thank God you did," she said with all sincerity; adding her mutual experience.

"For me, it was a presence. An angel… A loved ones' spirit… The crash on Highway 79 sent the pickup flying pass the memorial towards that damn Tom Mix ravine… I was sure it was the last thing I'd ever see. You saw the truck, upside down… Yet, the entire time it was out of control, it was like invisible hands were lovingly holding my shoulders against the seat, keeping me safe. All I know is someone, something, saved me that day. And today, it was you."

She had acknowledged. Patting his hand while fighting off a huge yawn. Then, rising slightly off-balance, she had allowed Tony Silva to help her into bed. Pretty sure she had again thanked him somewhere between this world and the world of dreams. Yet, vividly remembering Tashia settling into the bed with her as she said to Silva.

"You know, Xander thought himself an invincible demigod to be worshipped. To decree who should live, or die… In the end, no one will shed a tear for him, or say a prayer… Or leave a pebble on his headstone. He became what he feared most… inconsequential… And hopefully, quickly forgotten."

Then she fell asleep, and he was gone.

***

Another obnoxious commercial blasted the airwaves. This time its audio level so loud, startled, Esther gasped; her pounding heart in no hurry to slow to normalcy. And although she categorically resented the hype, it had at least put an end to her unpleasant trip down memory lane of those terrifying months. Choosing instead to focus on life's pleasures; relaxing under her patio ceiling fan, its whirling blades cooling the hot Sonoran summer. The no longer visible, majestic Catalinas; put to bed by the cosmic dark skies. The peaceful sweet smells of warm horse flesh and cut pasture grasses competing with tantalizing whiffs of warm cheesy nachos and cold beer with juicy citrus slices. Tempting her to give in to her hunger.

"Shut up already! I will never buy anything you sell. Ever," she vowed; glaring at TV.

Utterly annoyed by the advertiser's obnoxious tactics, Esther muted the offending dribble and tossed the remote on the table.

Turning her attention to the homestead she and Max envisioned, Esther grinned. Her smile broadening with delight listening to the playful whinnies from demanding Yázhí and their most recent rescue, Scout, emanating from the barn. Her thoughts extending to the people she and Mattie now warmly included in their little family; how they too had found a home there.

"Not too shabby, eh kid?"

Looking to the heavens, lovingly whispering to Max's spirit.

Then, hearing Kyle's voice coming from inside the barn she burst into laughter.

A few weeks earlier she had posted she no longer would be hiring veterinarian students. But instead, Kyle Lucas was now their resident vet for as long as he wished. Free to establish his own practice and put up his shingle onsite if he so chose. To which Kyle had responded with a bear hug and resounding yes.

"You just hold your horses," Kyle was saying sternly. "Dinner's coming."

His hungry charges scolding him with pawing hoofs and incessant nickering.

Unable to hold out any longer herself, Esther grabbed a few chips and dug into the rich multi-layered bean dip, topping it fresh salsa and a heaping of sour cream. The crunchy, savory flavors melding in her mouth; satisfying her Pavlovian urge.

"You too?"

She asked the nuzzling borzoi, offering Tashia a tidbit of seedless watermelon.

The hound delicately taking the sweet, thirst-quenching slice from Esther's fingers; then nudging her human for more. Stealthy repositioning herself inches from the aromatic morsels on the table; watching for Esther to carelessly look the other way.

Lazily stroking the aged Tashia's elegant neck, Esther smiled at her faithful companion with bittersweet joy. Giving the borzoi's long nose a small kiss, she dreaded the day Tashia would no longer be with her; cuddling, stealing treats, chasing rabbits.

"Done!" announced Kyle.

Plopping his exhausted body into a chair next to hers while grabbing a few chips and generously scooping the chunky guac. Shoving them into his mouth with zeal as Esther teasingly protested.

"Hey kid... I waited for you."

Complained Esther, following his lead; attacking the coveted creamy green dip.

"Well, clearly not," he retorted playfully.

Pointing to half-empty Corona bottle as he swallowed a large gulp of the Tecate. After which he changed the television channel to the desired cable program; adjusting the surround-sound speakers until the evening's expert commentors sounded as if he and Esther were actually at the game.

Then, after a few bars of transition music and b-roll loop showing the same Phoenix area and single Saguaro cactus, the viewers were enthusiastically welcomed to this season's MLB All-Star Game in the desert.

"…this year coming to you from beautiful Chase stadium in downtown Phoenix. The roof is open and it's a glorious night…," touted the announcers.

Their presentation leading into the opening ceremonies, including the introduction of baseball Hall of Fame dignitaries. When at last the players took the field, the All-Star game was underway.

Almost immediately Esther and Kyle spiritedly debated about which players were snubbed and which deserved the honor. By the third inning the two, having settled in, became conscious of the cameras zooming in on a specific quarter profile shot every time a new batter readied himself in the box. The upside allowed the viewers to see the players so close-up, so razor-sharp, they could see every thread in a uniform, every grain of wood in a bat, every stubble of beard.

The downside was sometimes the camera lost its focus on the player and would automatically shift behind the batter to unsuspecting fans seated several rows behind the National League team dugout. Clearly giving those who realized they were part of the show their fifteen minutes of fame by performing harmless, yet distracting antics.

It was during the middle of a particularly difficult fifth inning that the camera focus repeatedly jumped from the batter's grip to the aisle seats four and five rows above the dugout.

"Nnnoooo!" shouted Kyle.

"Well I'll be damned," asserted Esther.

Dumbfounded, both Esther and Kyle recognized Mattie dipping a large twisted pretzel into a container of some sort of sauce. Then, watched as she took a large bite while engaging in animated conversation with the very handsome, casually dressed Detective Michael Flores seated beside her.

Him, sipping beer foam and laughing at whatever it was she was saying as a hand from one row behind, positioned between them, shoved an unidentified piece of food into Mattie's dip. The camera angle bouncing slightly up, revealing the hand belonged to Special FBI agent Aiden Collins.

So giddy was Esther at finding her niece in the sold-out stadium that Tashia, quite jostled by her human's excitement, slowly slid off the couch; choosing instead to doze in the backyard's thick, cool grass.

"Guess you're not undercover anymore, Terco," chuckled Esther.

"Hey... How'd they score those choice seats and we're stuck here?" scowled Kyle with a twinge of jealousy.

The two completely distracted from the All-Star game they had waited to see all summer. Laughing hysterically whenever the camera briefly fell back on the threesome. The last time showing Terco reaching between Mattie and the obviously annoyed Michael to hand her a drink.

"Pretty smooth kid," snickered Esther.

Watching the men shamelessly vie for her niece's attention.

"Good luck boys... You're definitely gonna need it."

Suddenly the crowd erupted as the camera quickly switched to a tight closeup of the next ballplayer to enter the batter's box. The broadcaster's announcement of the Los Angeles Dodger outfielder's name drowned out under thundering cheers and applause. Esther and Kyle likewise shouting to the player as if on a first name basis.

A native Arizonan whose father was a retired major leaguer, renowned in his own right. The local fan favorite had been consistently praised for his talent, accomplishments, and community service from the time he played in the Little League World Series all the way into his professional career thus far.

Digging his cleats into the clay surface, the seasoned player calmly readied himself for the first pitch. Currently on a hot hitting streak, almost everyone watching hoped to see one of his signature crushing homeruns.

The collective anticipation rose to a heated frenzy as both the ballpark Megatron and television broadcast split their screens to show the ballplayer at bat on one side, and his family in the stands on the other.

The roar grew deafening.

Adjusting his stance, the All-Star fixed on the pitcher's release; a fastball hurled straight down the middle. Swinging fiercely at the projectile, the Dodger's timing was slightly off. Nevertheless, the ball collided with bat with a resonating loud crack just shy of the sweet spot. Then, sailed high into the air before going foul into the seats.

Expertly tracking the ball's path, the cameraperson captured the exact moment a 9-years-old boy on an aisle step stretched his gloved hand high above his head and made a mindboggling catch. The amazing act brought the house down as fans and players alike celebrated the elated boy's phenomenal feat.

As play momentarily stopped so the boy could bathe in his glory a bit longer, the camera also captured the people standing around him; including a salt and pepper haired older gentleman sporting a red and white ballpark vendor jacket, carrying a heavy steal case strapped against his chest.

Unassumingly standing in the background the older man patiently adjusted his tray; determined not to impede on the boy's spotlight. As the vendor took a couple steps back, that movement caught Esther's full attention.

Bolting upright, Esther stayed glued to the screen as the camera's field widened to include the vendor in the shot standing a row above the boy. With the man's face clearly in focus, Esther's heart leapt; realizing it was the stranger who had argued with the murderous psychopath on the shadowy landing after the ballgame. The same courageous man who had saved them from certain death in her barn.

Antonio Luis Silva.

Sitting in her kitchen, after he had killed Xander, Silva never mentioned the reason he had driven to Tucson that day was to work as a vendor at the charity game she was supposed to have attended. And, whereas he had admitted knowing Xander in the past, he said nothing about his recent encounters. He had only said he was familiar with the monster's propensity for violence, revenge, his self-serving acts. However again, he had not elaborated how.

Now, seeing Silva dressed in his red and white jacket, staring at his face, Esther's curiosity surged into high gear. There was still a hell of a lot she did not know about this mysterious man who had proved to be as modest as he was courageous… Yet.

Eyes wide.

Leaning forward.

Esther Hausman continued watching as Tony Silva adjusted the straps on the food box one last time, centering the equipment against his torso. Never taking her eyes off him as he walked up the stadium steps, almost out of the camera frame. Watching him open his mouth, then shouting loud and clear with an unmistakable gravelly voice that soared above the crowd.

"Rrrrreeeedddssss……. Get your red hots!"

Author's Notes

Death Beneath the Catalinas; the first novel in the Sonoran Desert Thriller series, is a work of entertainment and should be read as nothing more. The names, characters, places, incidents, and depiction of historical facts are the product of the author's imagination or have been used fictitiously. Any semblance to actual persons and peoples living or dead, businesses, companies, events, or locals is entirely coincidental.

This novel takes place over a span of several months during present time with factual and fictitious embellishments about the region, peoples, animals, and flora living in it. Whereas much research has gone into the creation of this novel, the accuracy of the information may have been altered to further the story plot, and should therefore be taken as a fictional tale.

The story is set in the breathtaking Sonoran Desert in the areas of Tucson, Arizona, Phoenix, Arizona, and numerous locals between them. It was written not only as a thriller, but as a celebration of this unique landscape and the many diverse people who have for centuries, and do now, call the Sonoran Desert their home.

Acknowledgements

I am extremely grateful to so many who helped and supported me as I developed and wrote, *Death Beneath the Catalinas*. It is my great fear that in my attempt to bring Esther's story to fruition I omit thanking someone. If I did, I offer you my sincerest apologies; it was not done intentionally.

Above all, I am forever in debt to the love of my life, my husband David, who for decades has been by my side lovingly encouraging and helping me whatever the undertaking. You have earnestly read each draft from its cryptic infancy to final; diligently toiling to catch typos and grammatical errors so I do not look like a fool. For your loving devotion, as well as for not divorcing me every time I fixated on a sentence and became a neurotic mess, I love you forever.

To Ethan Kaplan, amazingly talented cover designer. I am forever indebted to you for capturing the true essence of Esther's story. Ethan Kaplan is a Chicago-born, Los Angeles-based graphic designer and artist. His work can be seen in publications, billboards, books, events, and galleries across the globe. He has worked for clients ranging from startups to non-profits to Fortune 500 companies.

To my editors and readers. My loving husband David and cousin Dr. Linda Kaplan Spitz. Throughout our lives you have been there, helping and supporting me. Words cannot express my gratitude to you both for your many expertise. I am especially grateful to you for your editing knowledge; and for your love and sheer determination to always have my back.

Andrea Sahl, dear friend and reader. Your literary expertise and encouragement was immensely helpful and appreciated.

Sometimes help and kindness come from those you least expect. During the creation this novel I included historical, cultural, and language facts for which accuracy was extremely important to me and also need guidance to navigate the publishing world. To the following selfless individuals who generously gave of their expertise and time I profusely thank you. Alphabetically, they are:

Jocelyn Bresnick, gifted children's author of *Billie's Bubblegum Brain,* Thank you for your time and great advice.

To Karen Brungardt, amazingly talented author of countless sci-fi and fantasy novels including the *Wings of Crystal, Exchanger* and *The Universal Shapeshifter* series; also award-winning watercolor artist. Karen, I have admired your creations for years and so value your both your friendship and expertise. I will be forever grateful to you for your wisdom and countless hours of mentoring. Thank you from the bottom of my heart.

To Ronald Geronimo, M.A. Director, and Frances Benavidez, M.A. Program Director, NSF TEAC (National Science Foundation-Tribal Enterprise Advancement Center), many thanks to you both for your support and expertise in helping me ensure the Tohono O'odham's beautiful words are used, written and pronounced accurately. The Tohono Nation's history plays an important role in my story and I am sincerely grateful to you.

So too goes my gratitude to Jacquelyn Morgan, Senior Office Specialist of the Office of the Speaker of the Navajo Nation Council. Jacquelyn thank you for your invaluable assistance and kindness helping me accurately use and pronounce the Navajo's beautiful words.

To my family…

I wish to thank my children Andrew, Eryn, Jennie who are constant source of love, support, and inspiration. I hope you are always as proud of me as I am of you. I love you to the moon and back.

To my family and friends who have encouraged me; I am so very grateful to you all. A special thanks to my brilliant sisters Cindy and Marcy and to my cousins, who in essence are sisters and brothers. Within our crazy tightknit family, you have always been my biggest supporters.

For some, the strong bond between human and pets cannot be defined. This has always been the case for me, much to my parents' chagrin. Little Markie, collies Pax, Copper, Murphy, Rory and Apollo, borzois Olivia and Gwen, equine Squire, feathered friends Chickie, Pie; you have brought me tremendous joy, taught me patience, and consoled me during loss. Each has left an indelible pawprint, hoof, and claw on my heart in ways no human ever could.

And finally, Rosemary, the desert cottontail who chose to make her/his home in our Tucson rosemary hedge so many years ago. You brought a smile to our faces every morning you graced us with your presence. I hope that when you left us you stayed out of the reach of the coyotes and continued to have a long life. At least that's what I'm going to believe.

Photograph by Jacqueline Cohen: Olivia, The real Tashia

Glossary

A
A KLEYN KIND ZOL NOKH IM HEYSN
Yiddish: (Curse) A child should be named after you soon. In other words; You should drop dead.

AHWATUKEE, ARIZONA
(Pronounced: Ah-**wa**-too-kee) Established in 1935, the annexed community in south Phoenix, Arizona is surrounded by the South Mountain range and the Wild Horse Pass Gila River Indian Community. Supposedly a Crow Nation word, Ahwatukee means House of Dreams.

ANTISOCIAL PERSONALITY DISORDER
ASPD, a personality disorder characterized by impulsive, irresponsible, often criminal behavior. Someone with this antisocial personality disorder is typically manipulative, deceitful and reckless, not caring for other's feelings; act impulsively, recklessly, and sometimes violently.

ARIZONA CACTUS LEAGUE ASSOCIATION
Founded 1947, the League is committed to strengthening and promoting baseball's spring training industry while serving Arizona communities. The League consists of 10 ballparks and hosts 15 Major League Baseball teams.

ARIZONA DIAMONDBACKS
Established March 9, 1995, the Arizona Diamondbacks, or D-backs, began as a 1998 expansion team. One of the newest MLB teams, to date it is the youngest team to win the World Series in 2011. Stadium: Chase Field, Phoenix.

ARIZONA STATE ROUTE 79
Highway 79, also known as the Pinal Pioneer Parkway, a 58.40 milelong U.S. state highway which serves as the main route through the town of Florence, the county seat of Pinal County.

ARIZONA STUPID MOTORIST LAW
Holding person who drives a vehicle on a public street or highway that is temporarily covered by a rise in water level accountable; including costs for emergency responses in flood areas.

ARYTENOID CARTILAGE
Located in the larynx, arytenoid cartilage are paired pyramid-shaped structures of cartilage needed to produce vocal sound.

AUTOPSY
A postmortem examination to discover a cause of death or extent of disease.

AUSCHWITZ-BIRKENAU
Auschwitz, one of the many concentration camps set up by the Nazis in early 1930s. In 1942, it became the largest of the extermination centers where the "Endlösung der Judenfrage" (the final solution to the Jewish question - the Nazi plan to murder European Jews).

B
BANDS (EQUINE)
Separate, small family groups of wild horses within a herd that generally range from three to twelve or more members which are led by a dominant mare.

BORZOI
Russian: (Pronounced: Boar-zoy) Meaning fast, swift. A giant breed of dog. Elegant hunting sighthound of Russian heritage built much like a Greyhound; once known as Russian Wolfhound. Bred to be fast. Tough enough to pursue and pin large quarry like wolves. Borzoi's high prey drive quickly incites them to chase small creatures.

BROWN CLOUD
Atmospheric brown clouds caused by emissions connected to combustion of fossil fuels and biomass, matter from living organisms.

BRUCE SPRINGSTEEN
Dynamic, multi-talented American rock singer, songwriter and guitarist. Nicknamed "the Boss."

BUBBIE, BUBIE
Yiddish: (Pronounced: buhb-ee) Grandmother.

BUPRENORPHINE
A controlled narcotic substance used to treat pain. High risk for addiction and dependence, it can cause respiratory distress and death when taken in high doses or combined with other substances.

BUREAU OF LAND MANAGEMENT
The Bureau of Land Management is an agency within the United States Department of the Interior responsible for administering U.S. federal lands. Headquartered in Washington, D.C., the BLM oversees more than 247.3 million acres of land, or one-eighth of the United States' total landmass.

C

CALIFORNIA UNION CALVARY
The 1st Regiment California Volunteer Cavalry located at Camp Merchant near Oakland, California between August and October 31, 1861.

CALUMET FARM
In 1924, owner of Calumet Baking Powder, William Monroe Wright, established the elite Calumet on a small Lexington, Kentucky farm. Many of its famed thoroughbred racehorses include Triple Crown winners Whirlaway, Citation; Kentucky Derby winner Tim Tam, and champions Alydar, Forward Pass.

CASA GRANDE, ARIZONA
A US Arizona city in Pinal County approximately halfway between Phoenix and Tucson.

CATALINA STATE PARK
Located near Tucson metropolitan area, the park sits at the base of the majestic Santa Catalina Mountains. Haven for desert plants including nearly 5,000 saguaros, wildlife, and over 150 species of birds, the 5,500 acres of foothills, canyons and streams invites camping, picnicking, and bird watching amid its winding equestrian, hiking, and biking trails through the park and into the Coronado National Forest at elevations near 3,000 feet.

CHB EUROPA TRAWLER
A sea-worthy boat which is designed to remain self-sufficient for extended periods at a time.

COLLIE
Scotland and England heritage, one of the most recognizable and beloved large dog breeds. An agile herder, collies comes in rough and short coat. They are intelligent, loyal dogs that make wonderful family pets.

COOLIDGE, ARIZONA
A United States city located in southern Arizona. The 2020 census lists the city's population as 13,218.

COSTA'S HUMMINGBIRD
One of the hummingbird family, Trochilidae. It breeds in the arid region of the southwest United States and northwest Mexico, and winters in western Mexico.

COYOTE (CANIS LATRANS)
A medium-size member of the canine species native to North America, they are closely related the wolf and fox. Omnivores, their diet consists mainly of small rodents, fruit, deer, and rabbit.

CHUTZPAH
Yiddish: (Pronounced: **huts**-puh) Impudence, gall, arrogant self-confidence.

CLAIBORNE FARM
In 1910, Arthur B. Hancock established the elite thoroughbred horse breeding operation near Paris, Kentucky. Claiborne Farm has been associated with famed thoroughbreds such as Bold Ruler and Triple Crown winners Secretariat and Seattle Slew.

CRANIAL BONE
Eight bones make up a cranium, or skull.

D

DARK SKY COMMUNITY
An International Dark Sky Community (IDSC) is town, city, municipality or other political entity that is dedicated to preserving the night sky by carrying out and enforcing quality lighting policies, dark-sky education, and dark skies citizen support.

DEGRAZIA
Ettore "Ted" DeGrazia (June 14, 1909–September 17, 1982). An American painter, sculptor, composer, actor, director, designer, architect, jeweler, and lithographer. Described as the world's most reproduced artist; known for colorful images of American Southwest Native American children and other Western scenes.

DESERT COTTONTAIL
Also called Audubon's cottontail, is a New World cottontail rabbit. A member of the family Leporidae, it is unlike the European rabbit as they do not form social burrow systems, but are extremely tolerant of other individuals in their vicinity.

DEXTROSE
Dextrose a simple sugar, also has medical purposes. When dissolved in solutions that are given intravenously and combined with other drugs, it is used to increase a person's blood sugar.

DON CORLEONE
Vito Corleone a fictional character in Mario Puzo's 1969 novel, "The Godfather."

E

ELECTROSTATIC DISHARGE GLOVES
Gloves that help protect electronic products and employees from the potential dangers of static damage.

E STREET BAND
Bruce Springsteen's primary backup band since 1972; inducted into the Rock and Roll Hall of Fame in 2014.

EXTERNAL EXAMINATION
A detailed examination of the visible marks and injuries found externally on a body.

F
FÊTE DE JOUR
French: (Pronounced: fet day jour) Celebration of the Day.

FERDINAND
Thoroughbred horse. Winner of 1986 Kentucky Derby. It is believed his life ended in a slaughterhouse.

FLORENCE, ARIZONA
Founded in 1866, it's the sixth-oldest non-Native American settlement in the U.S. state of Arizona. The county seat of Pinal County, it is situated in central Arizona, about 45 minutes from both Phoenix and Tucson metropolitan areas. Three major transportation corridors run through Florence: Highway 287, Highway 79 and Hunt Highway.

FORENSIC PATHOLOGIST
A medical doctor who investigates unexpected, suspicious, unnatural and/or violent deaths.

G
GADSDEN PURCHASE OF 1854
The Gadsden Purchase, or Treaty. An agreement between the United States and Mexico where the U.S. paid Mexico $10 million for a 29,670 square mile portion of Mexico that later became part of Arizona and New Mexico.

GARROTE
A handheld weapon usually made of chain, rope, scarf, wire or fishing line, used to strangle a person.

GILA RIVER INDIAN COMMUNITY
Spanish: (Pronounced: hee-la) The Gila River Indian Community is an Indian reservation in the U.S. state of Arizona adjacent to the cities of Chandler and Phoenix. The community is home for members of both the Akimel O'odham (Pima) and the Pee-Posh (Maricopa) tribes.

GILBERT, ARIZONA
Town in U.S. state of Arizona in Maricopa County located southeast of Phoenix metropolitan area.

GLENDALE, ARIZONA
City in U.S. state Arizona within Maricopa County, located about nine miles northwest of Phoenix.

GLOBAL POSITIONING SYSTEMS
Global Positioning System, originally Navistar GPS, is a satellite-based radio navigation system owned by the United States government and operated by the United States Space Force.

GOLDEN HOUR
Time just after sunrise or just before sunset when the light is infused with red and gold tones.

GUTTENYU
Yiddish: (Pronounced: **GOT**-en-yew) Exclamation said with affection, despair, irony.

H
HASENPFEFFER
German: (Pronounced: **hass**-sen-pfe-fer) Rabbit Stew.

HAZARDOUS BIO CLEANUP TEAM
Provides a wide array of professional biohazard cleanup and waste disposal services for crime scenes, businesses, and residents.

HOLOCAUST
The Holocaust (The Shoah in Hebrew) was the attempt by the Nazis and their collaborators to murder all the Jews in Europe. From the time they assumed power in Germany in 1933, the Nazis used propaganda, persecution, and legislation to deny human and civil rights to Jews using centuries of antisemitism (anti-Jewish hatred) as their foundation.

HONEYWELL INTERNATIONAL INC.
An American publicly traded, multinational conglomerate corporation headquartered in Charlotte, North Carolina with facilities in Arizona. It primarily operates in four business areas: aerospace, building automation, performance materials and technologies, and safety and productivity solutions.

HOPI TRIBE
(Pronounced: ho-pee) A sovereign nation of 12 villages on three mesas. Throughout the Hopi reservation, every village is an autonomous government. However, the Hopi Tribal Council makes law for the tribe and sets policy to oversee tribal business. Located in northeastern Arizona, the reservation occupies part of Coconino and Navajo counties, more than 1.5 million acres.

HUHUGAM (HOHOKAM) INDIANS
(Pronounced: who-who-gum & hō-hō-'käm.) A culture in the North American Southwest in what is now part of Arizona, United States, and Sonora, Mexico. It existed between 300 and 1500 CE, with cultural precursors possibly as early as 300 BCE.

I
INTEL®
An American multinational corporation and technology company headquartered in Santa Clara, California with facilities in Arizona. One of the world's largest semiconductor chip manufacturers by revenue.

INTENSIVE CARE UNIT
A special department of a hospital or health care facility that provides intensive care medicine.

INTERNAL AUTOPSY
An in-depth examination of the body cavities and any abnormalities that might exist within them.

J
JEFE
Spanish: (Pronounced: **he**-fe) Boss. Person in charge.

JUAN RODRIGUEZ CABRILLO
First European to explore present-day California. Cabrillo navigated along the California coast on his voyage from New Spain during 1542–1543.

K
KADDISH
Hebrew: (Pronounced: **KAH**-dish) Jewish prayer for the departed.

KETAMIONE
A dissociative anesthetic used medically for induction and maintenance of anesthesia. It is also used as a treatment for depression and pain management.

L
LARYNX
Also the voice box; a cylindrical group of cartilages, muscles and soft tissue containing the vocal cords.

M
MAJOR LEAGUE BASEBALL ALL-STAR GAME
The Major League Baseball All-Star Game, or "Midsummer Classic," is an annual MLB sanctioned professional baseball game between the all-stars from the American League and National League.

MALIGNANT NARCISSISM
An extreme narcissism personality type that causes aggression and sometimes abuse of others. A person may use manipulation or violence to enhance their own sense of wellbeing. Whether Malignant Narcissism is a true diagnosis remains controversial.

MICROSOFT®
An American multinational technology corporation headquartered in Redmond, Washington with facilities in Arizona. Best known for software products including the Windows line of operating systems.

MISHPUCHA
Yiddish: (Pronounced: mish-pookh-uh or mish-paw-khuh) Family. Clan.

MORPHINE
A controlled substance used to treat moderate to severe pain. High risk for addiction and dependence. Can cause respiratory distress and death when taken in high doses or when combined with other substances.

MOTOROLA
American multinational telecommunications company founded 1928 as Galvin Manufacturing Corporation by brothers Paul and Joseph Galvin.

MUSTANG
A free-roaming, wild horse of the Western United States, descended from horses brought to the Americas by the Spanish. Horses evolved in the America around four million years ago, but had mostly disappeared from fossil record about 10,000 years ago. Spanish settlers likely brought horses back to the Americas in 1519, when Hernán Cortés arrived on the continent in Mexico.

N
NARCISSISTIC PERSONALITY DISORDER
A person with NPD has an inflated sense of self-importance. Found more commonly in men, the cause is unknown but likely involves a combination of genetic and environmental factors. Symptoms include an excessive need for admiration, disregard for others' feelings, an inability to handle criticism, and a sense of entitlement.

NAVAJO NATION
A Native American people of the Southwestern United States occupying portions of northeastern Arizona, northwestern New Mexico, and southeastern Utah. As of 2021, the Navajo Nation has more than 399,494 enrolled tribal members; the largest federally recognized tribe in the United States and largest reservation in the country.

O
OCCIPITAL LOBE
The visual processing area of the brain.

OLD PUEBLO

Nickname for the United States city of Tucson, Arizona.

OLD TOWN SCOTTSDALE

Established in late 1880s, nine walkable neighborhoods of unique shops, restaurants, art galleries, nightclubs, contemporary public art installations, world-class museums, and historic sites.

OPERATION DESERT SHEILD/OPERATION DESERT STORM

After Iraqi army invaded Kuwait on August 2, 1990, the United States deployed a major joint force as part of a multination coalition to stop President Saddam Hussein's aggression. The war consisted of two phases: the first Operation Desert Shield (August 2, 1990 – January 17, 1991), the buildup of troops and defense of Saudi Arabia, and the second, Operation Desert Storm (January 17, 1991 – February 28, 1991), was the combat phase.

P
PHANTOM OF THE OPERA

Tragic story by Gaston Leroux about beautiful soprano Christine Daaé, who becomes the obsession of a mysterious, masked musical genius living in a subterranean labyrinth under the Paris Opéra House.

PHOENIX, ARIZONA

Founded in 1868, Phoenix is the capital of the southwestern state of Arizona in the United States. Known for year-round sun and warm to hot temperatures, Phoenix anchors a sprawling, multicity metropolitan area known as the Valley of the Sun.

PHOENIX FIREBIRDS

Baseball team which played 1958, 1959, and 1966 to 1997. Before 1986, it was called the Phoenix Giants, a top San Francisco Giants minor league affiliate. It was forced to leave Phoenix after the 1997 season when expansion team, Arizona Diamondbacks, began play in 1998.

PICACHO PEAK

Spanish: (Pronounced: pi-**ka**-cho) Meaning: peak. An Arizona State Park in Picacho, Arizona. The Peak's summit rises to 3,374 feet above sea level.

PICACHO PEAK CIVIL WAR BATTLE

On April 15, 1862, the westernmost battle of the American Civil War was fought to stop Confederacy westward expansion. It was one of the smallest battles in terms of numbers engaged.

PRESBYOPIA

Gradual loss of eyes' ability to focus on nearby objects.

PRINTED CIRCUIT BOARD

Also PCB, or printed wiring board (PWB), medium to connect or wire components to one another in a circuit.

PRINTED CIRCUIT BOARD ASSEMBLY

Also called PCBA, is a finished printed circuit board after all the components have been soldered and installed on it.

POSTMORTEM

Examination of a corpse to determine cause of death.

PUEBLO INDIANS

Per oral histories. The Pueblo Indians of New Mexico and Arizona share common ancestry descending from ancient Anasazi civilization. The Pueblo people are linguistically diverse, speaking four unrelated language families: 1) The Acoma, Cochiti, Laguna, San Felipe, Santa Ana, Santo Domingo, Zia Pueblos speak Keresan languages; 2) The Isleta, Jemez, Nambe, Picuris, Pojoaque, Sandia, San Ildefonso, San Juan, Santa Clara, Taos, Tesuque, Tiguan/Ysleta del Sur Pueblos speak Kiowa-Tanoan languages; 3) The Zuni language not related to any other; 4) The Hopi, furthest west, speak Uto-Aztecan, distantly related to Nahuatl.

PUERTO PEÑASCO

Founded 1928. Mexican fishing and resort city on the Gulf of California known for dune-backed Sandy Beach and Bahía la Choya's tidal pools. Also called Rocky Point.

Q
QUEEN OF SHEBA

Wealthy queen thought to have lived in either Ethiopia or Yemen. Important to holy texts of Islam, Christianity, and Judaism.

R
RAKKASANS

Japanese: Meaning: falling umbrella. Nickname for 187th Airborne Infantry Regiment of the 101st Airborne Division. The only airborne regiment of the army to have served in all major conflicts and wars (WWII, Korea, Vietnam, Lebanon, Persian Gulf, Afghanistan, Iraq).

RAKKASANS INSIGNIA

Japanese: Rakkasans. Meaning: falling umbrella. Insignia for 187th Airborne Infantry Regiment.

RATTLESNAKE ANTIVENIN CROTALIDAE POLYVALENT

Used to treat poisonous snake bites of pit vipers (crotalids) native to Central, North, South America.

S

SALT RIVER PIMA-MARICOPA INDIAN COMMUNITY

Sovereign tribe established by Executive Order June 14, 1879. The Community operates as a full-service government and oversees departments, programs, projects and facilities. Located Maricopa County, Arizona, the Community is bounded by Fountain Hills, Mesa, Phoenix, Scottsdale, and Tempe; encompassing 52,600 acres which 19,000 acres held as a natural preserve.

SONORAN DESERT

A subtropical desert spanning southwestern United States and northwestern Mexico.

SCHMUCK

Yiddish: (Pronounced: shmuhk) Stupid or foolish person.

SHIMÁ

Navajo: (Pronounced: shee-**ma**) My mother.

SHIVA

Hebrew: (Pronounced: **SHI**-vuh) Seven days of formal mourning for the dead beginning right after the funeral.

SIGHTHOUND

Type of dog that hunts primarily by sight and speed rather than by scent.

SI:S

Tohono O'odham: (Pronounced: sees) Older Sister.

SPANISH, MEXICO TERRITORY

After the Aztec Empire conquest by Spain, 1519 – 1521, Spain called their new lands the Viceroyalty of New Spain, ruling over Mexico for the 300 years. At its greatest extent, the Spanish crown claimed on the mainland of the Americas much of North America south of Canada, all present-day Mexico and Central America except Panama, present-day United States' Florida's, and most of the land west of the Mississippi River.

T
TADAI

Tohono O'odham: (Pronounced: tah-dye) Roadrunner.

TANTE

German: (Pronounced: TAHN-teh) Aunt, Aunty, Auntie.

TÍA LOCA

Spanish: (Pronounced: tee-ah **lo**w-kah) Crazy Aunt.

TERCO

Spanish: (Pronounced: **ter**-ko) Stubborn, obstinate.

THOROUGHBRED

Horse breed developed for horseracing. Sometimes used to refer to any purebred breed of horse; technically refers only to the Thoroughbred breed. Considered "hot-blooded" horses known agility, speed, and spirit.

TOHONO-O'ODHAM NATION

Tohono O'odham: (Tohono pronounced: Thaw-haw-gnaw, O'odham pronounced: Awe Awe Thumb) Meaning; desert people. Federally-recognized tribe of approximately 28,000 members occupying tribal lands in Southwestern Arizona. The Nation is the second largest reservation in Arizona in population and geographical size.

TOM MIX

American Western film actor who starred in 291 films between 1909 and 1935. He was Hollywood's first Western star and helped define the genre in early cinema.

TOM MIX WASH

Tom Mix Wash is a stream (but usually dry riverbed) in Pinal County, Arizona, in the United States. The wash was named for American actor Tom Mix killed in a road accident in 1940 near the spot.

TOYO TIRES

Premium, dependable, long-lasting tires for most trucks, cars, SUVs, and crossovers.

TRIPLE-A BASEBALL

Highest level of play in Minor League Baseball, just below Major League Baseball. Total of 30 affiliated teams compete at this level, with 20 teams in the International League and 10 teams in the Pacific Coast League.

TUCSON, ARIZONA

Founded 1775. Seat of Pima County, Arizona, United States. Second-largest city in Arizona behind Phoenix.

TUCSON ELECTRIC PARK

Big and spacious centerpiece of the 158-acre Kino Sports Complex best known for fantastic views of the Catalina Mountains beyond its outfield. Until 2009, the home spring training ballpark for the Diamondbacks, Colorado Rockies, White Sox and Tucson's Triple-A team.

TURKEY VULTURE

The most widespread of the New World vultures. One of three species in the genus Catharses of the family Cathartidae, the turkey vulture ranges from southern Canada to the southernmost tip of South America.

U, V
VALLEY OF THE SUN

Phoenix is the capital of the southwestern U.S. state of Arizona. Known for its year-round sun and warm temperatures, it anchors a sprawling, multicity metropolitan area known as the Valley of the Sun.

VIPER

A venomous snake with large hinged fangs.

W
WESTERN DIAMONDBACK

A rattlesnake species and member of the viper family found in the southwestern United States and Mexico. Like all rattlesnakes and other vipers, it is venomous.

WIZARD OF OZ

The book, The Wonderful Wizard of Oz, by L. Frank Baum. A classic children's book first published in 1900. Its memorable characters include Dorothy, the Scarecrow, the Tin Woodsman, the Cowardly Lion, and Glinda the Good Witch, The Witch of the West, and Toto, a cairn terrier.

X, Y
YÁZHÍ

Navajo: (Pronounced: yází) Little one.

Z
ZAYDE OR ZEYDE

Yiddish: (Pronounced: zã-dee) Grandfather.

101ST AIRBORN DIVISION

Elite light infantry division of United States Army specializing in air assault operations.

187TH AIRBORNE INFANTRY REGIMENT

Nickname: Rakkasans. Founded 1943. Regiment of the 101st Airborne Division. Originally glider infantry unit in World War II, the 187th Infantry Regiment fought in Korean War part of an airborne regimental combat team, in Vietnam and Persian Gulf Wars. Elements of the 187th fought as helicopter-borne units with the 101st Airborne Division.

About the Author
The Story Behind The Story

Jacqueline Cohen is an award-winning writer who spent most of her career working as a senior writer for Motorola and General Dynamics. She is a recipient of the Telly Award and the Communicator Awards, as well as other honors recognizing her work in various media. She resides in Tucson, Arizona with her amazing husband, David, and mischievous borzoi, Gwen, where she is also a local artist known for her vibrant acrylic paintings.

***

During the period in my life when my father neared the end of his, his hospital admittances became the norm not the exception. Although not his primary caregiver I, like so many with a failing loved-one, lived in a perpetual state of turmoil. Keeping a tattered burgundy overnight bag stuffed with essentials, wedged behind the driver's seat of my ancient 2001 Honda CR-V fast approaching 300,000 miles, I was almost always ready to return to my father's side at a moment's notice. Which in those days usually meant receiving a call as soon as I pulled into my driveway in Tucson after having left my father in stable condition in Scottsdale, about 140 miles away.

Although I can't quite put my finger on exactly day, or time; it was then an anthropomorphic relationship between myself and my trusty Honda began.

Sporting its original boxy design, the dependable old gal and I had an absolute bond till the day she finally said, enough. Never minding her scratches, dents, exterior mounted spare's heat-eaten cover, or 4-cylinder engine performing like the little engine who could. She protected me down to her last nut and bolt. There was simply no other way to explain how I survived those years of driving in a stupor in pitch darkness, or with the desert sun blinding me.

It was then, my mind conceived Esther's tale. Dictating into my phone's Notes as I drove and at the hospital whenever unable to rest while my father slept; I'd embellished my story, develop characters, formulate chapters.

It's safe to say since then the old Arizona State Highways 87 and 79 have changed. The Catholic Church which I thought abandoned and its graves relocated has a newer, greener, burial ground beside what is now truly a gravel parking lot. The Florence bypass near Burger King has new roundabouts leading to Highway 79, and most of the irrigation ditches have been filled in; the land flattened for more pull outs. Too, the highways have been resurfaced; no more jarring potholes. New stoplights support the growing Gila River Indian Community, and trailers and makeshift homes have sprung up in previously undisturbed desert terrain.

I suspect in twenty years this once pristine desert will look nothing like it does now, or did when I first began traveling it. The wildlife, too, sadly will be gone. I tend to look at these encroachments as humanity's scars upon a breathtaking wilderness unlike anywhere else in the world. A place of inspiring vistas, clear open skies, vivid wildflowers and majestic Saguaros. A place where diverse desert creatures roam free on its lands and soar in its skies. On that tragic day I will assuredly mourn the loss of each and every one of them. I will even miss the committee of Turkey vultures eerily gathered in mesquite trees; staring as I drive by them on Arizona's Sonoran Desert backroads.

Did you know? Reader reviews are very important to an Indie Author's success? They validate our work and help others to find our stories. If you enjoyed Death Beneath the Catalina's, please leave a review filled with stars.